32817
6-24-92

Sept

D0982508

Book 1
89

The
Astrologer

The Astrologer

by
John
Cameron

RANDOM HOUSE
New York

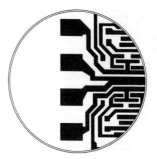

Library of Congress Catalog Card Number: 75–159335
ISBN: 0–394–46426–5
Manufactured in the United States of America by Haddon Craftsmen, Scranton, Pa.
98765432
First Edition

The
Astrologer

1

⊙

After a wide swing through Eastern Europe the jet landed at London International, where Alexei said goodbye to Varnov. After a week in Turin, Palermo and Athens, the tour had taken them to Bucharest, Belgrade and Warsaw, Lvov and back to Bucharest. The trip was a general review of sectional operations and a closer look at certain surveillance problems whose outlines seemed too blurred at a distance. But if it was routine, it did not follow that they hadn't encountered problems. The agency chief at Belgrade had developed a bad case of nerves. At sixty-seven he was among the oldest field officers, and there was nothing to be done except to replace him with a younger man. That had been difficult.

The plane, a chartered Swissair jet, had developed mechanical trouble at Bucharest and there had been a delay while parts were flown in from Lucerne and repairs made, since it would have been even more time-consuming to transfer the complex of computer and other electronic paraphernalia to another plane.

Touchdown at London International had come at 4:00 P.M., with Varnov packed and ready to leave on a commercial flight to Chile. After the steward had connected them with the English telephone exchange and his flight reservation was verified, he joined Alexei for a drink.

"I'm thinking about Warsaw, Alexei. Kermin's solution doesn't sit right with me, somehow. It's not the right kind of manipulation."

"Jail may not be the right direction, either. Do you remember Cubec? He was far more dangerous in jail than out."

"I remember. That was where our problems began. They aren't so far apart, those two, are they?"

"No, they're not. We'd better work on an alternative. I'll tell them to hold. We'll reverse ourselves if necessary."

Varnov nodded in agreement and bolted his drink. He left carrying the soft brown leather suitcase which Alexei knew always contained a supply of bourbon, a drink Varnov had learned to prefer to vodka in the seven years the Russians had authorized him to work for Alexei.

Except for the delay in Bucharest, Alexei would have had an entire day in London, a rare interval he could have spent as he liked—a call on his tailor, perhaps, and a conversation with Wembley, a staff member who had been working in London for several weeks. As it turned out, there was only time for dinner with Wembley. When he returned to the airport in early evening, Alexei was alerted by a voice behind him. "Mr. Abarnel," and he turned to see Harwell, tall and with a youthful look that was only partly contradicted by the spidery lines around his eyes. He wore a rumpled American suit. "Congressman Joe Harwell," he said, as though he weren't sure Alexei would remember him. Alexei did remember him very well, however.

Harwell's hand was outstretched in a manner that seemed peculiar to him, as though he were trying to disguise the burden ·of chronic friendliness, while he explained that he'd missed his flight to New York and that it would be at least another day before he could get on another. Alexei cut him short with an invitation to ride back with him on the

Agency jet, which would be virtually empty on the crossing. Harwell looked momentarily baffled by anyone having a private plane at his disposal, but then gratefully accepted.

As they were making their way through the crowd to collect his baggage, Harwell realized that the surprise of encountering Alexei Abarnel had something to do with finding him in the ordinary surroundings of an airline terminal in a random crowd of returning vacationers who were oblivious to the formidable legends attached to him.

The legends were quite distinct from the official information Harwell had been given. Alexei's name was nearly synonymous with that of Interzod, an agency which functioned as some kind of international advisory body because it had developed computerized astrological formulations reputed to be astonishingly accurate.

Harwell had been told this much because he was asked to vote in committee on appropriation measures. One didn't have to be particularly familiar with congressional manueverings to know that the information presented to him was purposely vague and cryptic. He knew very well that he had been carefully shielded from the full scope of Interzod activities.

The unofficial information—the myriad of Washington rumors and legends—was more intriguing by far. This had it that astrology had been shorn of all its shoddy practices of the past and freed from the taint of charlatanism. It was no longer true that astrology was badly printed nonsense sent in response to mail-order requests or that an astrologer was a wordy visionary found three flights up in a questionable neighborhood. There was a modern astrology, and the modern astrologers were men such as Alexei Abarnel.

He followed Alexei outside the terminal building, where a waiting car skirted the field for perhaps a mile, stopping finally before a plain brick building. A uniformed man came out and Alexei lowered the window and shook hands with him. "Congressman Joe Harwell, Major Alvin Haig." Haig nodded courteously. "He'll be going out with us," Alexei told him.

"Did he enter with you?"

"No."

"Then I'll have to have your passport for a moment."

Harwell handed it over, and Major Haig flipped it open and scribbled his initials without glancing at the name or photo. As he handed it back, he told Alexei, "You have a visitor inside."

"Do you know who it is?"

"I never ask, Mr. Abarnel. It's a young woman."

Alexei nodded, satisfied, and getting out of the car, turned to indicate to Harwell that he wished him to come along. Harwell got out. It hadn't been lost on him that Alexei wasn't expected to produce a passport.

"You can dismiss your driver," Major Haig said. "We'll run you out to your plane. Takeoff is cleared for 9:04 if that's satisfactory; your pilot wasn't sure. It gives you thirty minutes."

Alexei nodded and they entered the building. There was a small office with a desk and a radio crackling with control-tower information. Beyond this was a waiting room with a chair drawn up before a coal fire where a woman was sitting. She turned as they entered, looked directly at Alexei and without changing expression, stood up and leaned forward for her cheek to be kissed. She was beautiful in the striking, unexpected way of Eurasian women that Harwell had always admired. Her dark hair was swept behind her neck, and she wore a gray suit that was a Parisian blend of severity and femininity.

They stood looking at each other for several seconds before she broke the silence. "I am very tired, Alexei," she said simply, with a slight smile as though apologizing for a weakness. Her voice was unexpectedly firm, her accent overlaid with what Harwell thought of as Oxford English, musical but slightly theatrical to his ear.

"Did you find him?"

"Yes, I found him," she said with a note of weariness, turning away to retrieve a rumpled, well-traveled trench coat. She put the coat on slowly and picked up a felt hat. Alexei kept looking at her as though he expected more.

"I saw him, but it wasn't good. I'm going to tell you everything.

Not now, though—I'm coming back with you tonight. You are leaving tonight, aren't you?"

"Yes. But where is he?"

"God, you don't know how much I need a drink. Let's go, please." She took his arm as though she hoped to propel him toward the door, but Alexei didn't budge. She walked on, then stopped and turned at the door.

"Rhav, are you all right?" he asked sympathetically.

"I didn't come through very well, Alexei."

"Where is Alciergas, Rhav?"

"He's dead. What did you expect, I wonder?"

"Are you sure of it?"

"Nobody could be more so. I saw him."

"Who killed him?"

"The hill people. They tried to blame it on Kasjerte's friends, but when they saw it didn't make any difference to us, they gladly took credit for it."

Alexei nodded. Some of the tenseness seemed to leave him and he walked over, put his arm around her shoulders, and kissed her on the cheek affectionately, but in a way that lacked a lover's intent, which Harwell found oddly gratifying. "And Kasjerte?" he asked.

"The troops took him, finally. There was a lot of confusion for a while, but confirmation came a few hours before I left. Porter was on his way to the upper valley again to take charge. I'd have thought you'd have heard by this time."

"No, we've only been getting the confusion until now."

For the first time Rhav took notice of Harwell. "We're being rude," she said. Holding out her hand, she gave him a soul-stirring smile.

"I'm Joseph Harwell," he said to her, surprised that she had moved him to the formal Joseph for the first time in years.

"*Congressman* Harwell," Alexei said.

"I am Madam Rhavangavabia," she said, "but I'm usually called Rhav." With an inquiring glance at Alexei she asked, "Does any of this make any sense to you?"

"Not much, I'm afraid. Except that I'd like a drink every bit as much as you would." She smiled again.

Haig came to the door to tell them that they had only fifteen minutes, and a tan Rover took them to the Interzod jet.

"I want a vacation, Alexei," Rhav said as she mounted the ramp.

"You're getting one."

"I want the entire summer. I deserve it."

They entered a kind of salon similar to a railroad parlor car, and Harwell saw that the interior had been stripped of seats and divided into compartments.

"There are berths in the tail if you care to sleep," Alexei told him.

The plane took off at a steep angle and then made a slow sweep to the north. When they'd leveled off, Rhav took her drink and disappeared toward the tail.

"Are we getting monitor transmission yet?" Alexei asked the steward.

"Since an hour before takeoff," the steward said.

Alexei excused himself, and Harwell was left to stare at lights below that blinked up at him with diminishing frequency as they climbed over northern England, southern Scotland and the Hebrides. Even after the lights of land had disappeared, Harwell continued to stare down at the blackness. Then the rear compartment door opened and he heard Rhav's voice. "I don't care what the monitoring reads, Alexei. Somebody else is going to have to do my share of the caring; I'm too tired." He turned and saw that the room was fitted with all kinds of computing and electronic equipment.

They both came in and sat down. Rhav had changed her suit jacket for a sweater. They remained silent for several minutes.

"I can't see that it was a failure on your part, Rhav," Alexei said finally.

"Death always seems a failure."

"How did you verify that it was actually Alciergas you saw?"

"There's a roll of undeveloped film in my Minox," she said. "It won't help much. He was terribly mutilated. It was horrible. I'd read about primitive mutilation rituals, but I'd never seen the results. But I saw those earlier scars. I'd recognize those scars anywhere, Alexei. I didn't realize it before, but at death scar tissue doesn't seem to alter as quickly as ordinary flesh." For the first time a look of revulsion crossed her face.

"I can't see why you're unhappy about it. He was responsible for a great many murders and an enormous amount of destruction. It was only a matter of time."

Rhav gave him a look of majestic reproach. "You haven't asked about Nganu."

Alexei looked startled. "What about him? He returned safely. Granby talked to him. What are you saying?"

"He's dead, Alexei. Granby talked to him after his first excursion. But he decided to make a second. He had family among the hill people, remember? He thought he'd keep them calm by being there. Kasjerte got him, or his men did, immediately after he arrived."

"That's horrible!"

"I saw what was left of Nganu, too."

"God, I'm sorry. You don't know how sorry I am."

"Yes I do."

She picked up the whiskey bottle from the table to fill Alexei's glass, and in a gesture of sympathy rested her hand against his cheek for a moment. Then she poured Harwell a drink. "This must sound pretty awful," she said to him. "Shoptalk at Interzod sometimes gets grim. Thank God it isn't always that way. It isn't, is it, Alexei?"

"No," he said quietly. "Considering the people we run into I suppose it's remarkable that we've only lost two of our own. Hale was the first. He was before your time."

"Alexei, it was a three-day trip by burro into those hills. I want the summer off."

"You can have it."

"There's someone I'm going to see in New York. I'll be there until August, then in Rangoon."

Alexei nodded.

"While I'm there I'm going to decide if I want any more of this."

"Perhaps you could try liaison for a while."

"Thanks, Alexei. But with a year's practice I could get concert bookings again. Who will ever come to hear me play if everyone's forgotten me?" She laughed lightly, and then she was on her feet again. "I'm going to bed. I've been sleeping in snatches for so many weeks, I won't be able to sleep for long. I'm sorry I've been so rude, Mr. Harwell. I would have enjoyed talking to you."

Harwell rose. "You've nothing to apologize for," he began.

"I'm apologizing for the conversation, which couldn't help but leave you out," she said firmly, taking his hand. "I've heard a good deal about you. I hope very much we'll meet again soon and that you'll let me listen to you."

"Do I understand that she's a musician?" Harwell asked when Rhav had gone.

"Concert pianist. Good promise," Alexei said earnestly. "There are times when I feel it's wrong for her to neglect it for Interzod. Though you wouldn't have guessed it from the conversation, I've urged her to leave many times during the past four years. Twice she took my advice, but she always returned within a month or two. Her threat to leave only means she's very tired."

Harwell wanted very much to ask Alexei about the man they'd called Kasjerte, but he didn't since an explanation hadn't been volunteered. Their conversation made him realize that there was a good deal more to Interzod's international activities than he had suspected, but he knew that it would be out of order to ask about it, or why Rhav had been crawling among strange hill tribes someplace to view the mutilated body of a murdered man. That chilling story was incongruous with everything else about her. But incongruities could be expected from an organization said to be responsible for a resurgence of astrological reckonings, an astrology revitalized by modern notions of the structure of the universe.

This reputation was intimidating; Harwell knew he was not privileged to ask for more information than had been allowed him, just as he had always felt reluctant to mention the first occasion he had met

Alexei. This had taken place in a nearly empty house in the town of Parker's Crossing in Harwell's congressional district, a setting fully as improbable as the circumstances that led up to it, so that for months afterward Harwell could not recall it without wondering if it had actually happened.

The door to the rear compartment was opened by a young man. "Developments have peaked in the 104th sector south," he said in a slight German accent.

"Have we heard anything yet?"

"Nothing directly. The relay from headquarters reads negative at the last signal reporting. That was their final prereading. They did it minus one hour thirty-seven minutes."

"Let me know if they signal."

"Headquarters expects an all-clear." The young man disappeared.

Alexei was silent for several moments, then turned and looked at Harwell thoughtfully, "I meant to get in touch with you again a long time before this. If I hadn't bumped into you, you would have heard from me. I've been wondering if you would care to become more closely associated with us and our operations."

Harwell wasn't certain what was meant. "As a congressman?" he asked.

"Of course, as a congressman. I'm not asking you to give up a congressional career. You're good at it, I understand, which probably means you like it."

Harwell could have replied that one of the things he'd discovered about himself in the past five years was that he didn't have an all-consuming appetite for politics. It distinguished him from most other congressmen.

"It would demand a lot of your time at first," Alexei said. "But after the first few months it would be routine. There are other things to be said against it. All we can pay you is your expenses. And you would be constantly in touch with matters you couldn't mention to anyone else except employees or nonemployees with our Class A clearance."

The same young man reappeared from the rear compartment. "There's a special surveillance session under way."

"Are we picking up anything?"

"All of it. It's full dress."

"Let me know if it gets critical."

"It's that way already. They want something from you. Concurrence, I think."

"Tell them I'll join them in a few minutes," Alexei said.

The young man disappeared again and Alexei returned to their conversation. "You would learn everything there is to know about our operations," he said. "You would see what kind of judgments we have to make and how we perform. You would be privy to everything that goes on. You would not be required to make decisions or join in them or even sanction them, but you would be free to voice objections. You would function as a kind of witness. We're in an unusual position, as you'd come to understand. Our contractual obligations are very complex. It's important to have congressional representation, of course, but it's even more important that whoever it is have a complete picture of what we do."

Alexei paused and swallowed the rest of his drink. "I don't expect you to make up your mind about this now. Just think about it for a while. You'll probably want to discuss it with me before you decide." He stood up. "I'm needed for the next few hours at least. Why don't you bunk down in our dormitory and catch some sleep. There are two more hours before we land."

Harwell agreed. Suddenly he was very tired. He followed his host into the compartment which was so crammed with electronic gear that it left little elbowroom. Alexei pointed to another door at the far end. "We'll have something to eat when we land," he said.

Closing the door behind him, Harwell found himself in a room with three sets of double bunks. By the light of a dim overhead light, he saw Rhav lying wrapped in a blanket. It was hard not to look at her; one shoulder was exposed, as well as an outstretched leg. Her clothes were folded on the bunk. He climbed into an upper bunk, fascinated by her, by the fact that a girl with her elegant good looks slept sprawled face down on the bunk as though she'd been flung there, and that she snored like a state trooper.

Before sleep he had careful thoughts about Alexei's extraordinary career. These, in turn, offered something of a commentary on his own life and on the erratic course that had brought him from a boyhood in a Southwestern town to the privileged comfort of a berth on a private jet over the Atlantic. As worldly accomplishments are judged, Harwell realized that he was more successful than most, but this had always been diminished for him by the fact that he'd done so little to forge the preceding chain of circumstances. He couldn't remember having a strong ambition to become a lawyer. Perhaps someone had suggested it instead of engineering. Finding himself in law school, he knew he could become a lawyer merely by not flunking out. Success had been the culmination of no particular ambition, and sometimes he felt the rest of the world was too gullible.

It seemed highly improbable that Alexei had ever felt the same way about his life. There could be little that was accidental about Alexei Abarnel's; he seemed immune from the element of chance. Harwell had never seen a greater degree of intensity in anyone. Perhaps he was above ambition, or perhaps ambition was a mere exercise of will to be used as a kind of fuel whenever necessary.

When Harwell woke up, he saw that Rhav and even her imprint on the bed had disappeared. The realization that the plane was no longer airborne came second. There were no portholes in the compartment, but he could hear the muffled everyday sounds of trucks and machinery of some sort. He had not bothered to ask Alexei where they were going to land.

Voices erupted beyond the compartment door. One turned out to belong to a man named Granby Courtland whom he'd met at Interzod headquarters. The other man was a thin, elderly Chinese, in blue jeans and a turtleneck sweater, whom Courtland introduced as Pen Li Ko.

"We snatched Alexei away as soon as you landed," Courtland said. "There was a table full of generals and VIPs waiting for his advice. He sends his apologies and asked me to remind you that he'll be in touch with you in a few days. Would you like some supper?"

"Supper? What time is it?"

"Eleven-twenty."

"No, thank you. But can you tell me where we are?"

Pen Li Ko looked at him oddly. "You're at Interzod headquarters near Washington," Courtland said. "Would you like some coffee?"

At the open hatchway of the plane, Harwell sipped from a mug and watched the intermittent takeoffs and landings at the Air Force base adjoining Interzod headquarters. From the proceedings in congressional committee, he knew that if not for its closeness to Interzod headquarters, the base would have been closed down years ago on the grounds that it was small and uneconomical to operate. Its true importance was that it offered helicopter shuttle service from the capital and was a discreet landing place for direct flights from overseas. He doubted that any of the base personnel knew that Interzod existed; if they did, they had little notion of its function. This surmise was immediately followed by the wry thought that *he* wasn't much better informed. Quickly the feeling returned that he was in the presence of men of extraordinary purpose.

"Can I get a ride back to Washington?" he asked.

"We can take you by helicopter," Courtland said.

Harwell had come to dislike helicopters. "Is there a car available?"

"We can manage it."

2

⊙

Alexei put down his napkin and looked across the breakfast table at his wife. "You did *what?*"

She smiled. "I said I went to a spiritual adviser. There's nothing so bad about that, is there? It was the day I was shopping in New York."

He didn't answer for a moment; he wanted to get all the facts first. "No," he said. "It sounds like fun in a way. Who was this person?"

"She calls herself Mother Bogarde. I don't know what her real name is. You can't call yourself Madame O'Brien or Jones and still get people to believe you."

"I suppose not," Alexei said, carefully picking up his napkin and passing his coffee cup. "What happened? Did she tell your fortune?"

"Oh, not really. She said there were great things ahead for me—you know, the usual things people like to hear."

"Did she say what kind of great things were in store for you?"

"Of course not. I tried to get her to tell me but she just kept looking into her crystal ball and smiling at me." She looked anxiously at him. "You're not angry, are you, Alexei? You don't care that I went, do you?"

"No, of course not." He sounded as noncommital as he could, but she caught the false note.

"You *are* angry, aren't you? I can tell." She looked very serious, which was a pleasure, since Kate was a beautiful girl. He made a great effort. "No, no. Why should I be angry? Diana was with you?"

"No. It was all very private."

"Yes, I would think it might be. Did Diana have her fortune told, too?"

"It was something I did by myself. She was shopping, buying things for her family. She's going home for a few days sometime next month. Did I tell you that?"

"No."

"She has three younger brothers and a sister who is to be married. She hasn't seen them for years." Kate's voice wandered off and died, and then she looked at Alexei and smiled.

"Tell me about the fortune teller," he said.

"She didn't call herself a fortune teller. I read someplace that it's against the law. She called herself a spiritual adviser. That makes it legal, I guess."

"To tell the truth I've always wanted to talk to one of those people, but I've never found the nerve to go in there. How do they go about spiritual advising? I mean, do they ask a lot of questions?"

"Oh, you don't *really* want to hear about it, do you Alexei? It's boring . . ."

"I do want to hear about it, Kate," he said evenly. His hands were in his lap, the fingers tightly clenched.

She looked at him and was about to say something but changed her mind. She whispered, "You'll be very angry, Alexei. There's really no reason for you to be, but you know how you are about some things. I can tell you won't like it."

"Nonsense. I promise you I won't be."

Again she smiled a little. Her smiles were quick and expansive. "*Do* you promise?"

"Of course."

"Well, it sounds awful, I know, but there was nothing *wrong* with it. It's just that it was very strange."

"*What* was strange?"

"Well, what was strange was that she asked me to take off all my clothes."

"She what?" His voice rising, Alexei dropped his pretense of patience.

Kate looked alarmed and he tried to smile reassuringly, but he had broken the trust. God knows he didn't want any kind of a scene. She would feel she had to cover up and he'd never know the truth. "Well, that's strange, all right. And what did you say?"

"Say? I don't know what I said. Oh, I told her a lot of things before . . . well, it's strange that you asked me about that. She asked me a lot of questions."

"Such as?"

"Well, it was like the kind of questionnaire you fill out when you're looking for a job."

Alexei winced.

"Oh, Alexei, you promised."

"I'm not angry, Kate. Honestly I'm not. What about the questions?"

"That's what I'm trying to tell you. She wouldn't believe me. She said someone exerted a strong hold over me that prevented me from telling the truth. That's when she made me take off all my clothes. She said it was like stripping away all pretenses, and that I'd be able to tell her the truth."

"*Made* you take off your clothes? Do you mean you actually took them off?"

Her eyes wet with tears, Kate looked at him dumbly and nodded.

Alexei knew that if he gave in to his feelings, truth would be lost to him forever. Anything but those feelings, however, was so beside the point that he couldn't think of a suitable response.

At that moment Kate's gaze shifted to the door behind him and he turned to see Diana coming in to breakfast.

"Eliot's running a little behind schedule. He isn't feeling very well," Diana said, and then suddenly aware of having intruded on an awkward domestic situation, she became silent. During the length of Diana's stay with them, which was now nearly three months, Alexei believed she had not witnessed many such awkward moments—certainly never any real quarrels. Perhaps she supposed that what quarreling they did was decently concealed, but the truth was that there hadn't been any real quarrels. He and Kate had been married for little more than five months and there had been differences that converged, but somehow the convergences had never amounted to a collision. He could not recall any occasion where either of them had lapsed into ordinary anger.

Alexei caught Diana's glance of sympathy for Kate, reminding him of a womanly sympathy between them which in some sense was the basis of their closeness. Diana had been emotionally awash following a traumatic love affair when Kate had suggested that she come to stay with them. Alexei welcomed the arrangement, since he knew that Interzod responsibilities would keep him away from Kate a good deal of the time and he was terrified of her being alone.

"I'm being horrid to Alexei this morning and he doesn't know what to think of me," Kate said, an attempt at relieving Diana's embarrassment, he supposed, but for a moment he was struck by the possibility that there was an exchange of real confidences between the two. No, he decided on reflection; it was extremely unlikely. Admittedly Diana's life consisted of amorous transactions that were endowed with reality only when confided to a third party, but this was not Kate's way; the sharing of confidences would be a one-way street.

"I didn't say you were being horrid, Kate," he said.

"You didn't. But I suppose I have been." She smiled again. "You didn't know that I went to see a spiritual adviser yesterday, did you?" she asked Diana.

"No," Diana said, puzzled. "A spiritualist, really? I wouldn't have thought you went for that."

"I don't. It was my first visit. Alexei thinks it should be my last, too. And it will be. I won't go again, Alexei." She said it lightly to avoid casting him in the role of the tyrannical husband. In the confusion of the moment, he did feel tyrannical, however.

"I just can't imagine what made you want to go," he told her, wishing he could match her light-hearted tone.

"Nothing really bad happened," Kate said. "I just gave way to an impulse. Diana hadn't finished her shopping at Altman's, and there was just a little time before we were to meet Eliot for lunch, so I told her I'd meet her at the restaurant. I started walking—I don't know exactly where because I wasn't paying attention. Then I saw a sign on a second-story window that said SPIRITUAL ADVISER. I thought there would be an old woman who would look at some leaves and tell my fortune."

"But what *was* she like?" Alexei prompted.

"Well, it's hard to describe her. She didn't act like a fake or anything. She was very odd, and I had this feeling about her that she really *did* know something about me. She seemed to know when I was telling her the truth and when I was just making things up. You can see how strange that would be when you aren't expecting it. I began to feel badly about not telling her the truth. How can I say it? I felt badly. That's all."

"Kate, *what* were the things you felt badly about?"

"Well, to begin with, I didn't give my right name. I said I was married to a high school teacher and that I worked part time as a dance instructor. I knew you wouldn't want me to use your name."

"Anything else?"

"Well, she did ask me when I was born and she caught me in a lie."

Alexei turned pale and his face became a mask.

"Darling, don't worry about it so. I didn't tell her anything I shouldn't have."

"What do you mean, she caught you in a lie?"

"I began by saying that I was twenty, and I forgot to subtract a year when I told her the day, the month and the year. She said I had to tell her the truth or she couldn't construct my horoscope."

"Your *what?*" Alexei had risen from his chair. A vein she had never seen before throbbed against his temple.

"Horoscope, Alexei. You know, with all those signs fortune tellers use." Her tears reappeared.

Diana was beginning to feel uncomfortable again. "I'd better leave you two alone together," she said.

"No, stay where you are!" Alexei said.

He poured himself a glass of water and sank back in his chair. "What birth date *did* you give her?"

"Alexei, I promise you I gave her the one you showed me on the birth certificate."

Alexei looked hard at her. She couldn't be lying to him; no woman could look like that when lying. God, but she was beautiful. He felt relieved. "Just tell me one other thing. Why did you take off your clothes?"

Diana looked sharply at Kate, and she blushed. "Oh, I know how it sounds, but I've tried to explain, darling. There were just the two of us in the room. She told me I couldn't tell her the truth because I couldn't see it. I don't know why, but I believed it. It sounded right. Maybe it was the mood of the place, but I felt terribly ashamed of myself for lying. That's all."

"That's all? What happened?"

"She told me to take off my things and put on a robe and stand in front of her. That I would see myself for the first time."

"And you did."

"Yes. It wasn't as though I didn't have anything on. She handed me a long linen robe that went on over my head. It was very old and smelled of perfume or incense, but it was beautiful, with strange figures and funny little things embroidered all over it. I had to go behind a screen in the corner to change. My clothes belonged to my false self, she told me. It sounds ridiculous, now, but then it made sense. Clothes *are* kind of artificial, aren't they? After all, they do disguise the person who wears them, don't they? Did I do anything so awful, darling?" She was almost crying as she looked from Alexei to Diana. "She told me that she wouldn't look at me and that if I saw myself as I really was she would see me in the crystal ball. My spiritual self."

Oh, God, Alexei thought. "Did she say anything while she looked into the crystal ball?"

"No, she just stared into it."

"Then what happened?"

"I got scared, Alexei. I don't know why. I got very frightened. I told her I had to go, and I put my things on and left."

"I think she should be reported to the police," Diana said firmly.

"There's no law against asking someone to take off her clothes," Alexei said.

"There's a law against taking money for charlatanism."

"Oh, she wouldn't take any money. I tried to give her a twenty-dollar bill but she refused it. I didn't understand that."

Suddenly Alexei had a bad headache. They frequently came when he was trying to solve a particularly difficult problem. He stood up and kissed Kate automatically on the forehead and excused himself.

Diana broke the long silence. "Why on earth did you tell him that? No man likes to hear such things."

"I don't know. Maybe I shouldn't have."

"Was it all true?"

"Oh, yes, it was true." She looked up and her expression changed. "But I didn't tell him everything that happened, Diana."

"What do you mean?"

"I couldn't do that. Not *everything!*"

Diana stared at her curiously.

"He couldn't have understood. It would hurt him terribly."

Alexei took three headache tablets, drank a glass of water and looked at himself in the mirror. There were times he felt that the responsibilities of his life were close to being unbearable. These responsibilities he always thought of as being of two kinds—those that were his because of his unique talents and insight into the structure of things most men had no inkling of, and those that he had taken upon himself because there was no one or no institution they could be entrusted to. The latter kind were responsible for the complicated emotional burdens of his life, and particularly for his unending loneliness. Looking out the window over the long sloping lawns and trees, he sometimes allowed himself to wonder what his life would be like if he had chosen a simpler existence, how it would be to look out on an ordinary, pleasant suburban street, to travel daily to and from an office in the company of men whose lives were equally unburdened by matters they did not dare talk about to strangers. Sometimes, looking down the long avenue of trees toward Interzod's laboratory and headquarters building, he wondered what this place had been like in the days when it was a private estate, when you did not see a man walking among the trees every few minutes, a man you knew to be one of scores on distant parts of the estate. They were friendly men, but they were armed, and they never failed to remind him of the burdens of his life, of the terrors of knowing the secrets of a priesthood.

The necessity of manipulating his own life was the source of other regrets, among them the contrived atmosphere of his household arrangements. Diana was essential to Kate, and Eliot, it appeared, had become essential to Diana, at least for the moment.

Kate valued her as a friend and doubtless needed her companionship during Alexei's frequent absences. Eliot had been a member of the household for a much shorter time. He was an archaeologist, papyrologist and a brilliant chronologist, but too erratic and far too fond of drinking to be an Interzod employee. When Alexei found he needed Eliot's unique qualifications for a special historical research project, he had installed him in an office in a small building well away from the main Interzod headquarters and lodged him at his own house. There had been no other way. Eliot had no clearance and so knew nothing of Interzod. Something in his appearance—the heavy face with its long red beard streaked with gray, his inevitable costume of voluminous Irish tweeds—had evidently appealed to Diana.

He had not anticipated that Eliot and Diana would become enmeshed in an affair. But this too did not matter; in fact, the arrangement made for a more balanced household, which was of value to Kate, who was bound to have difficulties when alone. He did not feel comfortable being away, leaving Kate to struggle with her own thoughts and the perplexities of a trying marriage which would not have endured without her qualities of patience and equanimity.

He loved her. He could swear to that without compunction, though he suffered sharp anxieties when he wondered how long she could be made to believe it. On her nineteenth birthday, which came when they had been married only three weeks, she had cried. Perhaps she had cried before and since; he did not know. It had been the only time she had cried openly in front of him, and it had been hard to bear. He hated the restrictions which he knew could not help but erode their marriage but which Kate accepted in a kind of mute loving loyalty. He knew he could not count on that loyalty bearing up under the pressures which multiplied with the passage of time. Time, he knew, was his enemy and Kate's.

Alexei's bedroom had been furnished by the previous owner in dark walnut and leather, with heavy brown curtains at the windows, which he never opened. He examined the monitoring controls which took up most of a large dressing room. There were rows of figures, graphs and dials, all in constant barely discernible movement. He checked these against a tablet of figures on the table, and after a moment's study, picked up one of the telephones.

"This is Alexei. How did the Adlai Factor stack up at midnight? . . . Are you watching it? Have you anything on it? . . . Where? . . . In the Hangchow Province? No time for verification, I suppose. . . . I'll be down in a little while to work on it. It's better than it might have been."

As he hung up there was a light knock on his bedroom door; after locking the monitoring room door, he let his wife in. She didn't come here often, and she looked around carefully as a woman does to see if any changes have been made. Then she walked over to the bed and sat down. "Do you mind, Alexei? Are you busy?"

"Of course I don't mind, darling. I have a little time before they need me." Seeing her here moved him. He knew she wouldn't have come unless there was something she needed to say.

"I don't want you to be angry with me for yesterday. It's just that sometimes I can't help myself."

"I know that, Kate."

"Come sit next to me, Alexei. I need your comfort just now." He hesitated. He knew he couldn't stand another confrontation. There hadn't been one in weeks; they always left him on the brink of almost predictable desperation. But he sat down next to her and took her hand. It was burning hot; it never failed to astonish him. He'd never felt flesh so warm. "Kate, what did you tell the spiritualist when she asked you when you were born?" he asked.

"I told her my *new* birthday," she said. "This time I remembered. But Alexei, why is it so important? Until you found out my parents had made a mistake, I was perfectly happy with the old one. What difference does two days make?"

"Oh, none, I suppose." He had the feeling she didn't believe him because she didn't seem able to look him full in the face. She sat staring at a point somewhere in the middle of his chest, with a kind of self-consciousness that was all her own and of an unendurable intensity. But he couldn't bring himself to break the silence.

"Why, Alexei?" she asked, still not finding his eyes. "I mean, about us?"

It was the question that tormented him more than anything else in the world.

"There has to be an answer. Alexei?"

"There is an answer, Kate. You *must* believe me."

"But an answer for *me*, Alexei. Oh, darling, you don't know how hard I find it not to come up here! Sometimes it's unbearable. There has to be a reason I can understand!"

Alexei felt himself beginning to tremble. "I can't lie to you, Kate. If I gave you a reason it would have to be the real one. There couldn't be any comfort in a lie."

She was crying. "The only comfort I want is you, Alexei. What kind of life is this for me—separate bedrooms; never lying in each other's arms?" Her head fell against his shoulder and her warm arms encircled his neck. Her face came up to his and with surprising strength she pressed his face to hers and they fell sideways on the bed. He felt her tears and hot kisses on his face and neck and hands. She was sobbing quietly and moving against him convulsively. "Love me, Alexei. Be a husband to me. For God's sake, make love to me."

With great difficulty he forced himself to obey his sense of responsibility, and in one motion he rose, gasping and holding her away from him gently but firmly. With a moan she rolled over, buried her face in the pillow and lay still. Alexei caught sight of himself in the mirror and was grateful that she couldn't see his face. The ravages of his turmoil shocked him. He reached over and tenderly rested his hand on her back. Her body stiffened under his touch. "Kate," he said quietly.

She didn't answer. Finally she turned over and looked at him. She'd never looked at him like that before; there had always been tenderness in her own special look of perplexity. Even though she hadn't understood the reason, she'd trusted him. But now, for the first time, she could be hating him.

Alexei was injured to his very core. He felt that no man had gone to such great lengths to make himself miserable. It would have been a relief to know that the complications of his life were due to blundering. But he hadn't blundered; he had worked very hard and intelligently to be where he was. Nor had he miscalculated the strength of the love she would arouse in him; he'd known all along he would be miserable.

Still lying on the bed, Kate looked up at him carefully through the wisps of thick fair hair that had fallen over her face. "Alexei, do you remember what you said when you told me what you wanted things to be like between us?"

He wasn't sure of her mood and so didn't know what she wanted to hear. But there was a precise provocation in her question. "It isn't a question of what I would like," he said.

"You did say it wasn't something you wanted. That's true." She said it softly, by way of apology. "The hardest thing is not knowing how long it will go on like this."

She expected some kind of reply. He couldn't think of a good one.

"I used to think the hardest part was not knowing why. I've tried not to think about that—I mean your reasons. You began by saying that you couldn't tell me, and I accepted that. You said that it might go on for weeks or for months. As of last Friday, it's been five months. Can't you tell me anything, Alexei? Has anything changed? Is anything *going* to change?" She sat up, brushed the hair out of her face and stared at him.

"I don't know, Kate. I'm doing my best to find out. What else can I say?"

"Nothing," she said quietly, and standing up, she glanced at herself in the mirror and left the room.

Alexei remained sitting on the bed, overcome with a despair that had persisted for those five months and colored every thought. He had told her everything he could. He had explained that it did not stem from a physical or emotional disability. And he knew better than anyone that things could not continue as they were now. If only he could find out for certain, for an absolute certainty, he might risk telling her. No, that would be impossible—almost as impossible as not telling her.

In such moments of depression, he felt driven to retrace each step and to review each discovery that had contributed to his dilemma. This nearly involuntary exercise had the effect of helping him maintain the only course he saw open to him, and as well, of stilling the temptations to do or say anything precipitous in the hope of alleviating his and Kate's predicament. This turn of thought would almost invariably come to dwell on Wembley—his special place in Interzod activities and his unique gifts as paleographer and antiquarian. Alexei had a special fondness for the man, and an awesome respect for his scholarship. He often found himself thinking about the evening spent at Wembley's London club shortly after their wedding. As it happened, Wembley had been the first staff member he'd told about the marriage; the first to meet Kate.

Wembley rose to the occasion with an invitation for dinner at his club, the Pythagorean, which was almost the only place that his carefully circumscribed bachelor existence allowed him to dine. It was the sternly masculine province of archaeologists, Egyptologists and the like, where a woman might be asked to dine, but only with advance notice and only then in one of the small private dining rooms. Alexei had been a guest there many times before and knew that to its scholarly members the prestige that was attached to membership was of less account than the fact that the club was within walking distance of the British Museum. He and Kate had been shown through a series of barny common rooms furnished in dark, unyielding furniture, with a clutter of trophies, plaques and obsolete firearms about the massive fireplaces. There Kate looked summery and out of place.

Wembley was seated at a table in the small dining room, a large book spread out in front of him. He was almost hidden by a large bouquet of flowers, meant for Kate, Alexei guessed, in hopes of tempering the grimness of the dark walls and woodwork. All six foot four inches of him rose. "There's beef pie tonight," he said. It was a typical Wembley greeting. Alexei had come to realize this abruptness was his way of controlling a stammer which seemed to be triggered by formal introductions. He was at heart a profoundly shy man who could sit in nearly perfect silence for hours with people he didn't know well. But now, in a burst of courtliness, he had taken Kate's hands in his and given her a bridal kiss and said something that made her smile. It had been the first time Alexei had looked at her through the eyes of someone he knew and liked.

With elaborate courtesy, Wembley had shown Kate the book he'd been reading. "A palimpsest dating from the fourth century," he said. "These are photographic reproductions, of course. Twelve pages of an eighth-century illuminated Bible were found to have been written over an apocyrphal account of the flight of Joseph and Mary into Egypt." Kate glanced over his shoulder. "It's written in Ethiopian," Wembley explained kindly. He ordered whiskey for his guests and sherry for himself and closed the book. Alexei supposed that the matter would end there. It hadn't occurred to him that Wembley would allude to an Interzod project he was working on.

A moment later, however, Wembley leaned forward and in a whisper, forming the words carefully, as though they also might want to lip-read, said, "I believe I have found a new and quite plausible verification of the Madonna typlification." He tapped the volume on the table.

Alexei caught his breath, experiencing a moment of panic. The statement in itself couldn't possibly have had any meaning for Kate but the thought that Wembley might continue in this vein made Alexei acutely uncomfortable. Wembley looked up then and saw the warning in his eye and, with no hesitation whatsoever, proposed a toast which had a rambling and amusing preamble.

The beef pie was served with a bottle of Chambertin. The only thing Alexei could remember about the conversation was that Wembley was unusually talkative, set about entertaining Kate and succeeded very well.

It wasn't until Kate had left them alone for a few minutes that Alexei could explain that she had no Interzod clearance whatsoever and didn't even know of the existence of the organization. Wembley seemed surprised and made a careful apology. "I simply had no idea," he said, shaking his head. Then he returned to the subject of the discovery. "In all probability, a genuine verification," he said.

"Anything specific about her birth?" Alexei asked. He was very much aware of the constraint in his voice.

Wembley didn't notice. "It's only the fragment of a narrative," he continued. "And actually only one of the pages touches on the circumstances of Mary's nativity."

"How did you come by it?"

"The illuminated Bible and text were in the possession of a Bulgarian abbey. It's only a fragment of Genesis and nearly half of Exodus. It was Stancioff who located it and got permission to make the photographic studies which brought out the twelve pages of palimpsest."

"How close is the agreement?"

"A textual agreement?" Wembley asked.

"No, the chronological agreement to the typlification." There was still a discernible edge to his voice, and Wembley noticed that Alexei had downed his own whiskey and had absent-mindedly picked up his wife's glass.

"The maximum latitude is eight days and four hours," Wembley said. "We were dealing with a reckoning based on the Egyptian calendar, which can be complicated to do by hand. I haven't compared my findings with our calendrical computer program, but I will when I get back."

"Will you give me a digest?"

"Yes, but I don't think I'll be wrong by more than thirty-six hours."

Alexei was silent for several moments. "Is there any chance of finding more of the Bulgarian illumination?"

I can't say. Probably not, but Stancioff has some leads he's working on."

Kate had returned then. There had been champagne with dessert and Wembley's car returned them to their hotel.

That evening had always come back to him with special vividness because it was the first time he'd been called upon to exercise what amounted to a deception of Kate in front of a third person. The experience had left him with the feeling he'd been somehow disloyal.

His thoughts drifted beyond London to similar deceptions, to things that had happened before or since, all bearing in some way on Kate, settling on everything that had gone between them this morning, which seemed a kind of cruel culmination.

In a burst of fury, he picked up the object nearest at hand, the coffee cup on his night table, and flung it against the wall. It smashed, leaving rivulets of brown running down the wall. It was not enough. He was reaching for the saucer when the telephone rang.

Alexei didn't want to answer it but it was the special yellow phone that couldn't be ignored. "This is Abarnel," he said.

THE ASTROLOGER

"There's a call from the White House for you, Mr. Abarnel. It's on the scrambler."

"Tell them to go to hell!"

"Oh, Mr. Abarnel! I can't do that."

With a deep sigh, Alexei answered. "Tell him I'll take it in ten minutes."

3

⊙

Traveling by commercial aircraft placed Alexei in a communications blackout for hours. Arriving at midnight at Interzod after a week's absence, he discovered an emergency surveillance session in progress in the monitoring room.

Varnov, standing at the communication booth at the head of the long table, had assumed the chairmanship. Because he hadn't been sure when Alexei would arrive, Beaudine had curtailed a field-service assignment to make up a working quorum of five senior officers: Pen Li Ko, looking grave and inert; Beaudine, his head held between his clenched fists; Granby, tapping out his innermost thoughts with a pencil; and Watubi, very black and looking deceptively morose, sitting next to Rhav, who was wearing her old canvas jump suit and clutching a crumpled bush hat.

They all looked up as he entered. The room was silent except for the soft clicking of the endlessly changing numbers on the main monitoring panel which completely covered one wall. The sense of shared concentration was familiar, but Alexei hadn't expected to encounter it just now and he knew he would not like what he was about to hear.

After a glance at Varnov, Rhav broke it to him. Except for her eyes, with which she commandeered a listener, her facial expressions were compact and subtle. She sometimes gave a false impression of remoteness, which somehow compelled one to listen more carefully.

"Kasjerte and Shoun have organized a large following in the Khesi hills and are moving back to the uplands east of Daflai."

They were all looking at him, knowing the shock he would feel.

"Kasjerte? I thought Porter had him."

"He escaped, Alexei. The government troops never brought him out. They left him in the custody of provincial police in a village near Shillong. They simply didn't know. By the time Porter got to him it was too late. The jailer and his two sons were dead, and most of the village had fled in terror. There's more, of course—there always is with Kasjerte. There's a briefing digest here someplace."

Varnov handed it to him. Alexei knew the background stuff by heart, but the new entries were alarming. "It's worse now than it ever was," he said, knowing that this was something they all realized.

"Shoun," Varnov said.

"Yes, Shoun. Is Porter sure it's Shoun?"

"You can go through his verifications. We went into them pretty carefully. We think they're good. We've been in session four hours and that's about the only thing we're in agreement on."

Alexei suspected that this was an exaggeration. Friction was sometimes staged for his benefit but basic disagreement was rare. "I take it you've agreed this isn't the same level of crisis we faced a month ago."

"It boils down to the question of troops," Granby cut in. His voice was intense, almost curt, a change from his customary well-mannered deliberateness which he usually maintained at surveillance sessions.

"It would be foolish to request government troops again," Watubi said.

"It was successful before," Varnov said. "His escape can't be blamed on the use of troops. The point is they did make the capture."

"You will never take Kasjerte twice in the same way. The use of combat troops to capture one man is, as a rule, foolish," Watubi said.

"We've agreed on that before, I think," Alexei said.

"But Shoun makes it a completely different situation," Rhav said. Her voice was seldom forceful at these sessions, but there was an excitement to it now which Alexei suspected meant that she felt the situation suggested a definite surveillance response. "It is too early to tell about troops. Not now, certainly. We don't know what sort of grouping will form around Kasjerte. If it remains loose, with groups of disciples scattered across a broad area, troops won't do. Granby feels that Shoun's influence will lead to the control of a definite geographic area. Probably Ghevid this time; he's always been strong there. In that case troops could go in. But Watubi is right. Kasjerte has always learned from previous mistakes. However, there's another danger—that Shoun will establish Kasjerte's power on a definite demagogic political base. His popularity might become a political factor, in which case the government might refuse troops."

She slid off her perch on the table. "No matter what happens, he will always be more dangerous and more powerful with Shoun. It is imperative that we separate them before they establish themselves and form a definite plan of action. It must be done at once, Alexei. I want you to send me there."

Alexei had not expected this.

"Porter can't handle him alone," she continued.

"Nobody can handle him alone!" Varnov said.

"You forget. Shoun has been my man once before," Rhav said.

"He wasn't under the auspices of Kasjerte. He didn't have any inkling of his special talents."

"But we had and *I* had."

"This is different; it's far more dangerous," Alexei said. He knew that his response was too weak to shut off debate, but he also knew that she was right. Shoun had to be removed before it became a situation they couldn't handle without more bloodshed. He knew they all agreed on that. Someone would have to go, someone with imagination and as resourceful as Nganu had been. Rhav could do it. Until the situation was clear, she would have to make decisions pretty much on her own. It would be weeks, perhaps longer, before they could give her policy guidelines. Still, he had doubts, and he wasn't ready to admit that they were based on sentiment. He simply did not want to see her exposed to danger —any more than he wished it for anyone else present.

She was being forceful, however, and at heart he knew she was the best qualified officer for the assignment. She had a unique command of the dialects of the area; she had direct experience with Shoun, which might be crucial; she knew Shoun better than he knew himself; she had been there before, blending unseen into the tribal life of lower Bhutan and upper Burma. Moreover, Porter respected her more than anyone else he could send. And lastly, Rhav had a mysterious gift for survival which she would need. She had survived Ablonsky, she had survived Père La Mott, and she had utterly vanquished Tobias Bondel. With good fortune, she would survive Kasjerte.

4

⊙

The young man stopped in front of the poster announcing a folk song festival and studied it for several minutes with flaccid absorption. He had long blond sideburns and longish hair, and his coat and shoes were expensive. While he studied the poster, he in turn was studied by a pair of eyes far more practiced than his own. Mother Bogarde knew her man.

"Sonny," she said in a voice just loud enough for him to hear.

He turned and saw a dark-haired woman in a flowing robe—a housecoat—but the gold sandals and the several strands of long beads gave it something more than a household look.

"Give me a light," she said, holding out an unlit cigarette.

"I'm sorry. I don't smoke," he told her. He was polite, which was a good sign.

"But you have matches. You see? I have the cigarette. Look in your pockets. You find me a match."

It was true that he didn't smoke, but it was also a fact that he had only recently stopped and still had the habit of carrying matches. He found some in his pocket and came toward her.

"You see? I am right," she told him.

He had intended to hand her the matches, but he found himself lighting one. She took his wrist in her hand, brought it to her cigarette and then blew out the match, looking intently into his eyes. His face was blank, unlined and expressionless, pink around the temples like a baby's. If she put him on a spit to roast, the skin would burst long before he was cooked. "You have ten dollars," she said. It clearly wasn't a question and there didn't seem to be any suitable reply, apparently she didn't expect any. She smiled and then, to his surprise, began unbuttoning his coat. She undid the button at the level of his belt, with great good-naturedness as though he came to her every afternoon to get his coat unbuttoned. It was some kind of confidence trick, he realized, and having read of wily gypsy women who induce old ladies to withdraw their life savings from the bank so that the evil spirits can be driven away, he found the resolve to move her hand away.

"You are afraid," she said.

"No, I'm not afraid," he said, hoping to strike a firm but debonair note that would put an end to the business, but already her fingers were back at the next button lower down. Her hand lingered there with just the slightest pressure against his genitals, which raised the question of just what her motives were.

"You are afraid of me," she said again.

"No, no," he said quickly.

"Good. Step inside with me and I will show you something."

"I'm late for an appointment."

"You are afraid I will steal your money."

"I'm *not* afraid you'll steal my money. I'm afraid I'll be late."

"What kind of appointment?"

"It's a dental appointment." This was preposterous, he thought angrily, searching for excuses and inventions so as not to offend a woman whose gall plainly knew no limits.

"How much money do you have?"

"I don't know . . . I don't have any," he said, not only lying and contradicting himself but also stammering.

"Then you have nothing to be afraid of, she said, and still holding his wrist, she drew him toward the open door. He took a few steps out of chivalry or God-knows-what and then resolutely came to a stop. His impulse to run was checked by his desire to make a graceful departure and one that didn't imply that he had indeed been afraid.

"Give me two dollars," she said.

"I told you I don't have any money."

"Then give me one dollar."

"Not even one. Just some change."

She held her hand out.

"No," he said, turning at last to leave.

She was beside him. "Then it will cost you nothing. You have nothing, so it will cost nothing." She was so friendly that once again his flight was checked by his desire to be polite.

"You'll see," she said, and turned and went into the doorway. He followed her, hesitantly, intending to quickly explain once again that he had an important appointment. They went up a flight of stairs to a room on the first landing where she stood with her back to him, getting something from a drawer. The place was lined with curtains, all flowered but in various patterns, some not reaching the floor and revealing a strip of grimy green wall. It seemed smaller than a shop and he supposed that the curtains partitioned a larger room into two. There were two bedroom bureaus, a sofa covered with the same kind of flowered material that sagged wearily in the middle, and two spongy overstuffed chairs. A table stood in the center.

"You sit there," she said, turning and pulling a straight wooden chair out from the table.

"I can't stay," he said, looking at his watch, but nevertheless sitting down. "Show me your palm," she said. "Your right one. You are right-handed."

In obliging her it was necessary to draw the chair to the table. "You have a girl friend?" His distate for personal questions made him hesitate. "Yes," he said.

She shook her head and frowned. "You don't think she is pretty," she said sadly.

"Oh, I think she's pretty," he said, though as a matter of fact it was a subject of concern to him.

Mother Bogarde didn't look satisfied with his answer. "Your other hand," she said. She inspected a particular crevice in his left hand, then asked to see his right one again. "You are very intelligent," she said, but in a way that suggested intelligence wasn't important. "You deceive yourself many times a day."

"What do you mean?"

She paid no attention. "You think your girl friend is unfaithful to you."

This could have been either an assertion or a question. At any rate, he was nettled by it. "Unfaithful?"

"What is her name?" she demanded firmly.

"Karina."

"Karina, yes. Then you are *not* sure that she has been faithful." She pushed his hand away and looked at him fiercely for a moment, then in a gentle voice said, "That will be ten dollars."

"Look here. You said it would be free. I told you I didn't have any money. I explained that."

"Five dollars, then," she said nonchalantly. "You said you didn't have a match. I told you to look for one and you found it. I tell you now to look in your pocket. You will find money."

Lamely he put his hand in his coat pocket where he'd found the matches.

"No, no, in your billfold," she said, tapping the left side of her chest and pointing to him.

This was just where he kept his billfold, and he wondered vaguely if she had seen him remove it on the street to count his money. He knew it contained twenty-three dollars, and he withdrew it now with the intention of covertly looking inside and telling her it was empty. But with catlike precision she reached over and plucked it from his fingers. "Hah," she said, and to his horror she calmly removed all the money, tucking it neatly in her brassière, and handed the billfold back.

"See here," he said, rising to his feet. "You can't do that!"

She gave him a look of disgust. "You tell me you have no money!"

"I did. I admit that. I made a mistake. But that doesn't give you the right to take all of it. You said five dollars, and that's all I intend to give you."

"How much money did you give me?" she asked, her voice becoming conciliatory.

"There was twenty-three dollars in the wallet," he said.

The look of scorn returned. "So you didn't know you had any money and now you know exactly how much. You did not seem the kind to try to lie to a poor woman."

"I didn't try to lie. Just give me my money back. Please take your five dollars so I can get out of here." His anger rose. He didn't know what good it would do because no matter how angry he got he knew he couldn't go diving down the front of her dress. Besides, someone might be lurking in the place. While she had been examining his palm he'd thought he had heard a solid step somewhere behind the curtains. "You've taken everything I have. I don't have a dime."

Scornfully, she reached into her bosom, took out the folded money, and after counting it, handed him a single dollar.

He took it. "The rest of it. All but five. I'll have it now or I'll go to the police."

Mother Bogarde looked grave at the word and immediately peeled off another bill. "The police would laugh at you," she said seriously, as if giving him confidential advice. He took the bill and saw that it was another single. Rage overcame him and he started for the door. "I'll be back with the police in five minutes and you'll see who they'll laugh at."

She was by his side in a second. "It does not pay to be angry. Here," and she pressed another bill into his hand. It was a third single. He crumpled it in his palm. "Twenty dollars is outrageous!"

"We are very poor," she said. "It is not much to you. How much did you pay for your watch?"

"It doesn't matter how much I paid. Twenty dollars is more than you've got coming. Give me back a ten."

"You pay two hundred and fifty dollars," she said.

"I didn't pay anything for it!"

"You steal it?"

"No, I did not steal it. Somebody gave it to me. But that's none of your concern. I want my ten dollars. Please—this is ridiculous."

She looked serious for a moment, then she took his hand and pressed the watch against her ear. To his horror, she began unbuckling the watch strap. He snatched at it, withdrawing his wrist at the same time, and the watch fell off. Grabbing at the air with both hands he managed to snag it before it landed.

"You come back soon," Mother Bogarde said. "No money next time. Free. I will tell you if Karina has been unfaithful. You will bring her. I can read it in her palm."

The door was open and as he went out, he shouted, "I'm going to the police." But he didn't. Within a block, his fury and determination subsided. He was out twenty dollars. What kind of a speech would he make to a police officer about twenty dollars? He would have to appear in court and sign unpleasant papers and state exactly what had transpired. He didn't feel like reliving it for anybody.

However, had he returned immediately with a policeman, he would have found Mother Bogarde standing on the sidewalk with an unlit cigarette cupped in her hand, making demonic appraisals of passers-by to herself, and occasionally turning to exchange desultory insults with old Ede, who stood in the doorway. Ede, a narrow-faced man with thinning black hair and a wide sad mouth who always wore shiny black pants and vest, a red tie, and a khaki shirt with sleeves rolled up to his armpits, had been grumbling for several days, though he knew his complaints would draw no response from Mother Bogarde. After a while she didn't bother to reply, and he shrugged and walked back to the flight of rickety steps in the rear of the building leading to the basement.

There he squatted on his haunches in front of a dozen gallon jugs laid out in the shape of a horseshoe on the basement floor, each with a pretzel-shaped twist of glass tubing stuck through the cork. Carefully he twisted one of the corks free and inserted a length of rubber tubing, and bending low so that his cheek nearly touched the floor, he sucked gently until the syphon took hold and a stream of pink wine poured out into a tin cup. He squeezed the tube closed and took a mouthful of wine, tasting it carefully before he decided it was worth swallowing.

"How is it?" said Gregor's voice behind him. Ede turned; he hadn't known Gregor was watching him. "Not so good," he said. "Not so good as last time."

Gregor was much younger than Ede, and preposterously handsome, with glossy black hair that naturally arranged itself in thick black ringlets, and with very white teeth of which he was vain. Ede fermented his wine in gallon jugs because they were easier to move; in the past year Mother Bogarde had insisted upon moving four times. Neither he nor Gregor had liked making the last move, Ede least of all, since the basement there had been warm and very good for fermentation. Thinking they would remain there for at least six months, he had prepared thirty gallons of wine. But just when the fermentation had begun, Mother Bogarde had told them they were returning to Brooklyn. The Brooklyn cellar was too cold. Ede couldn't figure out why they hadn't stayed where they were, especially since there had been no trouble. Together, he and Gregor had moved the wine, carrying it out two gallons at a time and putting it in Gregor's old blue Cadillac. Gregor had listened to him complain but he hadn't said anything, though he knew why Mother Bogarde wanted to move suddenly. There had been trouble, according to her, though Gregor didn't think it was worth moving for and neither did his brother, Tono. Mother Bogarde had told old Ede that Tommy Boyle of the pickpocket squad had warned her that they would be cracking down on tearooms.

Gregor and Tono knew better; it was the woman. Gregor had never seen Mother Bogarde act like that before. After the woman had left she had been very angry at him and Tono. She was in a fury and cursed them with words Gregor had never heard before. "But *she* didn't mind," he had said in his defense, and he was sure he was right. He couldn't get the lady's deep loving look out of his mind. After all, what did Mother Bogarde expect? Had they done anything really wrong? After all, one of them was always supposed to be in the back room in case of trouble, though it was seldom anything happened that she couldn't take care of herself. Sometimes it was old Ede, but usually he had better things to do. But when the woman had come, it happened that both he and Tono were there playing cards. From the other room, they could hear the voices. Gregor wasn't listening; he seldom did. But Tono heard something that made him get up and go carefully to the crack in the curtain. He stood there for a few seconds before he turned, and putting his fingers to his lips, motioned to Gregor.

The woman was standing in her bare feet behind the screen, unfastening the buttons on her blouse. She was beautiful, with full soft hair. Gregor could hardly believe what he saw. She unbuttoned the blouse and put it on the chair. Then, with no embarrassment, she removed her brassière. Gregor had never seen a woman undress in just that way; in his experience, they saved both items of underwear until last. But he was happy because when she leaned over to step out of her skirt he could see the full shape of her breasts. Tono was very excited; he kept nudging Gregor and turning to see the expression on his face. When she had removed all her clothing she slipped Mother Bogarde's old robe over her head and came out from behind the screen. She stood there quietly while Mother Bogarde looked at her and smiled. Why had she asked the woman to undress? He had never known her to do it before, and so in a way that was the oddest thing about the whole business. But the expression on Mother Bogarde's face also puzzled him. Why was she smiling as she looked up at the woman's face, smiling in a dark ecstatic way as though they shared some serene revelation?

As for what occurred next, Gregor was not sure how it happened. It couldn't be that Tono tripped, because how can a man trip when he is standing stock still? Whatever it was, Tono lurched forward into the curtains, or rather through them, landing on his hands and knees,

Gregor immediately reached into the room to help pull him back, and Mother Bogarde half rose from her chair, looking like a thunder storm. Then Gregor caught sight of the woman's face as she turned to them. Was she frightened? She must have been, in the first instant of discovery that someone had been watching her. Instead of yanking Tono back through the curtains, Gregor found himself staring at her. She accepted his look and returned it, not immodestly, but with a gaze that he could never describe though he'd thought about it many times. A look of surprise, certainly, but there was also a softness and a kind of radiance he'd never seen in a woman and not to be expected in such a circumstance. Certainly there was nothing lewd or shameful in it, like the wives at the encampments who got drunk and whispered how tired they were of their husbands.

Gregor couldn't comprehend everything in that look but he'd understood part of it. In the next moment they were in each other's arms. Had he gone to her or she to him? Tono couldn't tell him because it had happened so fast that he hadn't seen. The probable truth, Gregor thought, was that they had moved together in a shared impulse. She was as lovely to hold as she had been to see, but their lips had barely touched when she twisted her face away from his and pushed him away. Out of the corner of his eye he saw Mother Bogarde staring at them in horror. The lovely woman was breathing deeply. He took a step backward, and then Mother Bogarde began tugging fiercely at his shoulders, digging her nails into his chest and screaming at him. He'd never seen her like that. Her eyes were two black beads, her teeth were bared like a dog's and she was screaming the terrible curses of their language. He and Tono backed into the other room, but before Mother Bogarde in her great rage drew the curtains together, he had his last glimpse of the beautiful woman frantically struggling with her clothes. How could she have done it so quickly? She had already put on her skirt and was reaching for her blouse.

They stood next to the curtain and listened when they could no longer see into the room.

"Take it. Twenty dollars. It's not much, but it's all I have."

"No, no, please. You can't give me anything, child."

Tono turned to him, dumbfounded.

"Take it with you," Mother Bogarde said. "Please. Leave nothing here. And you must never come back. I beg you, never come back here. Tell no one you came."

They heard the woman's heels, then the door and a hurried, choked goodbye, then her footsteps running quickly down the stairs.

Immediately Mother Bogarde bolted the door. This was unheard of at this time of day, when the rich ladies came, often in twos or threes, to hear her read their fortunes from tea leaves. Tono ventured into the front room but came back quickly, his face white.

Gregor had already made up his mind. His decision to follow her was a shapeless, overwhelming impulse. Pulling on a faded blue jacket, he fled down the back stairs and it wasn't until he was on the street that he felt misgivings. The street was crowded and he had no idea of the direction she had taken, but even more discouraging was the abrupt realization that he had nothing to say to her. She had left in embarrassment and confusion and so she wouldn't be glad to see him. The impulse that had driven him down the stairs seemed foolish.

At the end of the block he turned back to the building, and that was when he spotted her. Before she saw him, all his confidence dissolved. He looked away, almost hoping she wouldn't notice him, but when he glanced at her again he saw that she had recognized him. He sensed no antagonism and even some hesitation.

"I was looking for you. I wished to tell you I am sorry." He blurted it out before he'd formed the words in his mind.

She looked at him with curiosity. "It wasn't your fault," she said.

"I don't know how it happened."

"It doesn't matter," she said gently.

"I came to look for you. I hoped I could talk to you. Can I walk with you?"

"Of course."

He understood that she was accepting the offer without intending any encouragement. As they walked east on a crowded side street he noticed, without pride, that people looked at her as they passed. He felt a certain desperation in knowing that eventually they were going to arrive at wherever she was going. "Can't we stop someplace? It's too hard for me to talk here."

She stopped and looked at him as though she could learn everything there was to know about him in a single look. He realized that his plea had been vague. "We could go in here for a cup of coffee." He nodded in the direction of a small restaurant. There were posters in the windows advertising wrestling matches and automobile races. The windows were cloudy and the man standing above the grill by the window looked tired.

She accepted without hesitation. Inside, there were few customers or other claims to prosperity. They sat in a booth where countless carved initials were buried beneath a heavy coat of varnish. Her way of following him in here had been trusting. He was struck not so much by her lack of affinity with this place as with her failure to notice it. He was unused to the quality of guilelessness in a woman. He had always succeeded with them by a practiced artfulness; in fact, he found himself drawn to women who expected it.

"I think you have made me very shy," he said, astonishing himself because it was what he most wished to conceal. "You are very beautiful," he added, a remark which he'd made to many women before but rarely when he meant it.

She did not thank him, for which he was peculiarly grateful, since it had not been his gift. She had evoked it effortlessly and with no contrivance other than the same steady expression.

"I wish I knew you much better," he heard himself say and knew that he was expressing a real regret. "If we knew each other as friends I would be able to tell you that I don't want you to go where it is you're going now."

Her expression was softened by a slight amusement. On another occasion—no, with another woman—he would have taken this as a hopeful sign. With her it didn't matter; it seemed more important to get rid of his own confusion. "If we were friends," he continued excitedly, "I could tell you I love you and you would not think I was lying to you. Do you understand me?"

"I understand you."

"I could tell you I wanted to go someplace with you and make love to you and you would not feel you must be angry with me for telling you or for wanting that. That is true, isn't it?"

Her thoughtful expression returned. "It's true. That's what a friend is for."

"Always when I say that to a woman I am lying," he said. "She is always the wrong woman, so I don't care that we are not friends. I don't care if she knows I am lying."

"Then why do you tell her?"

"Because I want her to pretend I am not lying. I am not," he added with unnecessary candor, "a very good person."

She made no effort to contradict him. Little else was said before she rose to leave. "I don't think I have lied to you," he told her abruptly. "That would be very hard. Maybe I will not have a chance to be your friend, but I could not lie." As she gathered her gloves and pocketbook, he added, "It would be nice to be your husband. Is your husband your friend? Most husbands must lie a great deal, I think."

"We would have to be good friends before I could talk with you about such things," she said, but she smiled at him for the first time as she left. He did not ask if he could come any further with her and when he was alone he began to feel astonished that he had spoken so freely. He knew it must be her doing. He had never met a woman who drew out truths that he'd never even considered before.

He had returned to their building by the back stairs, knowing somehow that the front entrance would still be bolted. Tono, looking scared and runty, sat on the stairs, smoking and whispering to old Ede, who answered him in grunts. Tono wasn't his real brother, and Mother Bogarde wasn't the true mother of either of them. No one knew where old Ede had come from. It was a patchwork family, but it was easier for them to live together than alone.

"Don't go upstairs," Tono said.

Gregor was in no mood to listen. He wanted to be by himself and he didn't want to hear Tono's thin squeaky voice or see his face. He climbed the steps to the little room where they had been playing cards. Mother Bogarde was moving around in the next room, singing to herself. The song was one of her sad ones, sorrowful and low and gutteral, such as those sung for the dead. The words were indistinguishable but her mood was clear.

Moving very carefully, he made his way to the curtain and looked through a tiny hole. At first he couldn't see her because she had closed the blinds and the only light came from two or three little candles on the cupboard where she kept all her private things. There was an old wooden crucifix, a small tarnished brass incense burner and her crystal ball. Gregor did not believe Mother Bogarde was religious. He had never known her to go to church and she never wore a cross, as old Ede did. But there were times when she would light candles by the crucifix. She was sitting at the table, her head in her hands, rocking back and forth, singing to herself and making low moaning sounds, barely mouthing the words in a strange, secret liturgy. She only did this when she was alone, and he knew that it always changed her mood. It was a private thing and there was something terrible about it that he knew she would not share.

He left quietly and was glad to find that Tono was no longer on the stairs. Walking over to a vacant lot near the East River where he kept his old Cadillac, he whiled away the rest of the afternoon puttering with the motor. When he started back, he realized that he'd been thinking about the woman every minute of the time. He had to find her again, he realized. It wasn't because she was rich, although that would be what he would tell Mother Bogarde; it was simply that she haunted him. Didn't it mean something for them to have come together as they had after a single look? He'd never seen eyes like hers. By this evening Mother Bogarde would be in a better mood. Or tomorrow. Then he would tell her that it had not been only *his* fault. He would ask for the woman's last name. How could Mother Bogarde refuse? After all, the woman was rich, and it was understood that he couldn't get along unless he met a rich woman from time to time.

When he got back, however, Ede told him unhappily that they were moving. Already the curtains had been taken down. Ede was angry and said he didn't know why, but Mother Bogarde had found a place for them in Brooklyn—this place—a rickety store front much like the one they'd had in Newark last spring. They had moved that night. The mattresses were piled on top of Gregor's Cadillac and everything except Ede's wine was carried in one trip.

But he had been wrong about Mother Bogarde. She was quiet and morose for days and he couldn't go near her. Finally Tono had managed to change her mood, as could be expected because he had always been her favorite. By degrees she had been less angry with Gregor, until at last he had made the mistake of asking for the woman's name.

"Fool!" she screamed at him. "Do not think of her. Tell no one what happened and forget it yourself."

"She has money, she's rich," Gregor cried.

"Money!" Mother Bogarde screamed. "And you would buy yourself a place in hell!"

That ended the conversation, and Gregor was left with two alternatives. One was Tono; Mother Bogarde *might* tell him if he waited and saw the right chance.

The other was Mother Bogarde's book, very old, with a soft leather cover, and given to her, as she said, by her grandfather who had been brother to a king. Gregor could understand nothing of the old part, a conglomoration of figures and writing in the old script. But Mother Bogarde also used it as a diary, putting in loose pages and sometimes writing down things that interested her. He could read and understand her hand, though sometimes it took a long time to puzzle it out. Of course Mother Bogarde never knew that Tono or Gregor had ever looked at the book. It was precious to her, and she had once threatened to kill Ede, who had put it away by mistake with an armful of papers. It was clear that he hadn't tried to read it. Gregor fully believed that Mother Bogarde would try to kill him if she found him looking at it, but he was willing to take the chance.

5

⊙

Congressman Joe Harwell knew that Alexei would not have broached the prospect of a "closer association" with Interzod unless he was going to broach the matter again. When it did come up it was in the form of a feeler from the White House, which Harwell had not expected, even though his first contact with Alexei had been through White House sponsorship.

On arrival, a harried appointments secretary pleaded that the President was some thirty minutes behind schedule. But Harwell had to wait only fifteen minutes before he was ushered in. The President waited until they were alone before getting down to business.

"Alexei Abarnel has advanced you as candidate for Interzod clearance, Joe. I gather he's spoken to you about it. I don't know what else he told you, but we have a special way of handling the candidates for his operation. The government has veto power and so does he. We usually leave it up to him to advance the name, and then we pass on it. He seemed to think you were undecided. He sounded me out about you several weeks ago, and I told him we thought you'd be really first-rate. I just wanted you to know that you have our support and that I hope you'll accept."

"It's true that I haven't made up my mind completely, but it's only because I'm not sure if I'd have the time, and that I really don't know what I'd be in for." This was a fair way of putting how he felt, except that as matters stood now, he knew it would take far more effort to reject the offer than to accept it.

"Anything you are told about operations must come from Alexei," the President told him. "But he's in a difficult position because he has very stringent security qualifications. He couldn't operate without them. What it means, though, is that he can't tell you very much of how he operates unless he has some assurance of your joining in. He seemed to think you have already seen something more of what kind of things they're involved in than most people who have only Class B clearance."

"Enough to be intrigued, I admit," Harwell said.

"That comes pretty early in the game. Let me stress something: we share the responsibility of maintaining security arrangements. I'm responsible for explaining that it ranks with the highest governmental security classification and that any breach is subject to the same penalties or punishments. However, it's my personal feeling that you would never regret accepting it. I think of it as a great privilege."

Harwell came away feeling that the meeting had been intended to persuade but not to pressure him. He knew that originally he had been given Class B clearance because it was necessary to have congressional support for the passage of the appropriation which supported Interzod. It was a hidden appropriation, of course, but Harwell had judged, from the way it was concealed and from the other congressmen who he surmised also had clearance, that Interzod was not allied with the CIA or any other intelligence outfit or with any armed-forces project.

The conversations with Rhav that Alexei had intentionally allowed Harwell to hear in London went far beyond the limited view of Interzod he'd been given when he had been granted Class B clearance. It had surprised him, as it did most newcomers to Interzod operations, that the participating countries represented the entire spectrum of political ideology. This had been stressed by the Interzod officer who had conducted the briefing for Harwell and other candidates for Class B clearance, who were mainly military men and diplomats. "Controversies that attend the usual political alignments have no place at Interzod," he told them. "It is significant that China—revolutionary Maoist China—has always had one of the best records of participation and cooperation, especially in the matters of nativity reports and in making public records accessible to Interzod teams, which are, as you know, international in character." The officer interlaced a faintly pedantic delivery with a kind of professorial humor. He'd begun with the remark, "I suppose you all know that we do something unusual here." On the previous day the candidates had seen three films. The first was compiled by astronomers at Mount Palomar and Jodrell Bank. It was a simple exposition on the workings of the solar system, somewhat on a college-freshman level of scientific comprehension. The second film was more subtle. It was entitled simply, *How Heavenly Bodies Influence Life on Earth*. Again it was a précis requiring little scientific knowledge. It discussed the earth's dependence on solar energy, lunar influences on tidal variations of the sea, and the possible effects of cosmic radiation on marine ecology. Each showing was prefaced by a lecturer who began with "In the film we are about to see . . ." and fielded any questions at the end.

After the first two documentaries, lunch was served and then they were shown the third film, which claimed to be a historical survey of scientific theories and beliefs concerning the heavens. The first shot was a reconstruction of a Greek gymnasium, showing a bearded instructor and several youthful students examining an early mock-up of the solar system while others were working out geometrical problems drawn in a clay courtyard. A narrator's voice asserted, "In the ancient world, curiosity about the sun and moon and the stars led to the most important scientific and mathematical progress . . ." and followed with a dissertation on the astronomical beliefs of Copernicus, Vico, Galileo, et al.

Then the film shifted and showed a peasant in an ancient but unidentified country standing by an irrigation ditch, his eyes raised toward the sky. "But long before the contributions of Babylon, Greece and Rome," the narrator continued, "even more primitive societies had looked heavenward for spiritual sustenance, as well as for the gifts of sun and rain, and it was natural that . . ."

The short film was simple and direct but explained little, and generally it failed to satisfy the expectations aroused by the extraordinary rumors of the importance of Interzod.

Harwell's *first* contact with Alexei Abarnel had also come about under the auspices of the White House, though then the word Interzod had not been mentioned. He had been asked to come to the office of the President's special assistant, George Partridge, who had been Harwell's friend for several years, and had been told that the President had an odd favor to ask.

Harwell was interested, since a favor is the chief medium of exchange in political life and a Presidential favor, either one rendered or one received, has a somewhat inflated face value.

"It would mean a trip back home for you sometime during the next two weeks. We'd leave the time up to you."

"What would I be doing there?"

"First of all," Partridge said, glancing down at a note on his desk, "it's true, isn't it, that you know a lawyer in Crane county named Archer —William S. Archer?"

"I know him."

"A friend?"

"Old friend."

"Who wouldn't refuse you an ordinary request?"

"I don't think he would," Harwell said. He now found himself pleasantly mystified.

"Now, there's one other thing," Partridge said. "You could not discuss this matter with anyone. Under any circumstances. You would be making a request of Archer, but you could not tell him or do anything that would lead him to suspect that it did not originate with you and, most emphatically, you could not intimate in any way that the President or the government had any connection. Even our conversation has the highest security classification."

This was enough to double Harwell's mystification, but it also aroused suspicions which Partridge was quick to read and quick to allay with assurances that it wasn't any kind of a CIA stunt. "It can't embarrass you, Joe," he said. "Politically or personally. It won't touch your friend Archer, either."

"George, why don't you tell me about it so I can judge for myself?"

"Hell, Joe, I'm not the guy to tell you. I'm just supposed to warm you up. Truthfully, I'm not supposed to know what's behind it and I probably never will."

Was Partridge being serious? Harwell wasn't sure until they entered the President's office and he had left Harwell there alone. At that time Harwell had met the President four or five times, but always with some kind of group or delegation. Alone he was more relaxed and stretched his feet out on his desk. There were a few minutes of political gossip, and then the President brought his feet down off the desk and asked abruptly, "You have a friend named William Archer back in your district, don't you?"

Harwell nodded. "We went to school together."

"What we need from Archer is very small, really," the President said, "the kind of thing that might be refused to a stranger but would be freely given to a friend, especially to another lawyer. It would appear very strange indeed if I were to ask him to do it for me or a member of the government because it would arouse speculation as to why it was important. I'm sorry I can't tell you what its importance is—the truth is that I really don't know."

"Does *anyone* know?" Harwell asked.

The President smiled, but he nodded decisively. "Yes," he said. "Did you happen to know a Cyrus Maitland in Parker's Crossing, or any of the Maitland family? No? They're all dead now, I'm told. Cyrus was the last. He died two days ago in a sanitarium of some kind, where he'd been for more than thirty years. I've been told he was an anthropologist and an expert on Oriental art. He puttered around the Far East for twenty years before the Second World War. His house, or rather the family place in Parker's Crossing, contains a lot of the stuff he collected in the Orient. And," he paused, "there is a library. The house has been boarded up for fifteen years or so, and now that Cyrus is dead the place is going up for auction. So is everything in it. Now, all we want is the opportunity to examine that house before it or anything in it is sold.

"Your friend Archer is handling the liquidation of the estate. You've practiced law down there—you know how such things are handled. If it looks like there's valuable stuff in there, your friend Archer will call in appraisers—experts—isn't that right? He'll have to get some idea of the value of things. He might call in an estate appraiser or else an expert on antiques or paintings or books—whatever they've got in there. I understand it's considered a treasure trove. Anyway, the point is, all we want you to do is to get into that house first."

Harwell knew he looked surprised. The talk had been leading up to this, but somehow he still hadn't expected it.

"We want you to drop in on Archer as soon as possible. Turn the conversation to the Maitland house, tell him you've been collecting books and ask him if you could spend an afternoon browsing to see if there's anything you'd be interested in. Will you do it?"

Harwell said that it sounded possible. He could have said that he wouldn't have to be all that cautious in his approach; he and Archer had been close friends at school and he knew he could get the key without having to give any explanation whatsoever. But he knew there wasn't any point in making a favor to a President sound easy. "But once I've gained entrance what do I do?" he asked.

"We'll give you a phone number so you can let us know when you'll be at this house. You will be in contact with a Mr. Tileo."

Harwell ultimately discovered that this name was used by a man named Eliot, and somehow it seemed demeaning to the office of the Presidency that he had been cajoled into going along with a code name which turned out to be a simple anagram.

Four days later Harwell boarded a plane in Washington that would take him back home. He would not quite admit to himself the excitement that impelled him to make the trip two days earlier than he had planned, by ruthlessly chopping two days from his busy political schedule.

When he entered Archer's office the next day, he was at a loss to understand why he was following the roundabout way of leading up to the subject of the Maitland estate that had been suggested to him rather than making a natural straightforward request for the key. Archer opened the top drawer of his desk and from a massive and untidy bunch of keys selected three which he slid across the desk. "I'll be out of town. You can keep these until Monday," was his only comment.

From a pay phone Harwell called Tileo at the number Partridge had given him. The man said that he knew where the Maitland house was and would meet him there in half an hour. During the interval Harwell drove by the place once. It was a large frame house with a thick growth of uncut shrubbery that nearly obscured a porch running around two sides. The second-story windows were blanked with dirty white shutters. Behind the house there was a ramshackle barn and a scraggly unkempt orchard.

Harwell returned in twenty minutes to find a car parked in the driveway. Two men were waiting for him on the long porch. Tileo had red hair, a red beard, wore glasses and had a careful way of introducing himself. They shook hands and Tileo presented his assistant, skidding over the name so that it sounded like Barnel, the accent falling evenly on both syllables, so that Harwell didn't know if he were being given a first and last name or simply the surname. It was a moment of mild embarrassment, and Joe turned to fumble with an ancient lock without asking for further clarification. The assistant was tall, with prominent eyes and forehead, and his deep, persuasive voice contained the suggestion of an accent.

When they entered the house, Tileo's first act was to try the light switch. The electricity was on. Then they headed for the library, a large room on the first floor which was completely lined with books and filing cabinets. Books were stacked on the floor. There was a large table in the center of the room with chairs, and a desk in the corner.

"We're here to browse and we might as well begin," Tileo said, removing his coat.

Harwell was curious, but some fastidious strain would not allow him to observe them directly. He left the two men alone and began examining the rest of the house. There was a lot to be seen; there were more rooms than seemed possible from the outside. As he had been warned, there were Oriental objects everywhere—vases of every size and description, red lacquer boxes and small china figurines. They were perched everywhere in confusion on stalwart American furniture of dark and gloomy wood. It was not a successful blending of East and West.

Upstairs were half a dozen bedrooms, opulent in a hideous way, with tassled lamp shades, every dark and sagging bed covered with graying dust. Harwell felt depressed and returned to the library, where he found Tileo standing in front of a compact photographic copying machine while his assistant leafed through stacks of papers and old photographs, occasionally handing one to Tileo to be reproduced.

The two men spent a total of six hours in the house. Harwell did not remain the entire time. Though they did not suggest that they be left alone or seem to mind his watching them, he left and visited some old friends in the neighborhood. When he returned two hours later, Tileo was coming down the stairs with an armload of books and papers. "Diaries," he said.

They were nearly finished, they said. On the floor was a shipping crate with Japanese characters on it. "Cyrus Maitland" was stenciled in English on the side. Harwell sat down on the edge of the desk. Apparently they had taken photos of everything in the large crate, and it took them a long time to replace everything and then to nail it shut again and drag it back upstairs to the closet where they'd discovered it.

When the three of them left, the room was in exactly the same state of disorder as when they'd arrived. They shook hands and Tileo said goodbye. "We very much appreciate your help," he said warmly. "I am sure we couldn't have succeeded without you." The assistant, who was carrying the copying machine to their car, only waved goodbye.

It was some three months later that Harwell heard the man's name pronounced again—unmistakably Abarnel—three syllables but accented evenly as one would say ABC. The occasion was Harwell's official introduction to Interzod. He and two other men, an Argentine law professor and a German career diplomat, met at an obscure corner of the old National Airport and were ushered into a helicopter which took them to the headquarters. After they were shown the films, they were introduced to Alexei Abarnel, the director of Interzod. He gave no indication that he and Harwell had ever met. Perhaps he way relying on Harwell's poor memory; perhaps he was counting on Harwell's willingness to put the Parker's Crossing encounter out of his mind. There was nothing to do but follow suit and acknowledge it as a first-time introduction. During the audience, which was not very informative, they were interrupted by a man who whispered a few words to Abarnel and departed. Harwell heard Alexei address him as Eliot, nevertheless he knew very well that this was the man he had met as Tileo.

But it was also clear that during that first trip to Interzod the two men had deliberately reversed the roles of assistant and chief. Harwell had to admit that the idea was a good one. Whenever he'd thought about that afternoon at Parker's Crossing, he'd remembered only Tileo; the assistant had been of secondary importance.

6

⊙

Alexei noticed that Kate was unusually silent at breakfast. They were alone, since Eliot had pleaded illness and Diana was upstairs fussing about the sickroom. "There'll be visitors today," he said.

"I remember," she said, smiling in a way that seemed to him impersonal and absent. "You don't like that very much, do you, darling? Having visitors, I mean."

Alexei didn't, but he couldn't remember ever having told her so. He had noticed that she was very good at judging his moods and reactions to matters of which she had no direct knowledge.

"Who are they?" she asked tentatively. Realizing as soon as she asked it that Alexei would not give her an answer and would be embarrassed and apologetic, she immediately rephrased it so that he could respond gracefully. "I mean, will they be interesting?"

"The usual run, I expect," Alexei said, and then with an openess that was unusual he added, "One is a Russian general and one is a congressman." The trouble with such frankness, they both knew, was that it aroused a curiosity and a natural line of questions which could not be answered. Alexei supposed that his wife minded this, just as she minded the other restrictions on their life together. Sometimes, such as now, when she seemed preoccupied and distant, Alexei wondered if it were around this that her thoughts were collected. Only rarely did she complain, and even then there was seldom any discernible bitterness. Her gentleness had always been constant; it was a quality that marked everything she said or did, with a consistency that resembled the pervasiveness of strong intelligence or incisiveness in men of genius. Alexei wondered how she did it, and it was something he asked himself often during the long hours which, despite himself, he devoted to thinking about her. They were lonely hours, for the most part, and though she never mentioned it, she seemed to sense his loneliness and to sympathize. At the beginning, when he had made clear that the conditions in which they would be able to love one another would be very hard, she had said she wouldn't mind. He'd persisted, believing that if she knew what the limitations were she would reconsider and that they would seem unreasonable—indeed, *were* unreasonable. She replied only that she trusted him. How could she know that he wasn't acting out some insane, tortured notion, some monstrous caprice? But she never questioned that his decisions were for the sake of some unstated higher goodness of which she was allowed no inkling.

The telephone by the breakfast table rang, the yellow one which could not be answered by anyone other than Alexei and, in fact, would cease to function unless the electronic device with which it was equipped was satisfied by highly accurate resonance and pitch sensors that it was Alexei's voice. "There's a call from the Secretary of State," the voice said. "Will you take it or return it, Mr. Abarnel?"

"Hold," Alexei said automatically, and rose and excused himself to talk in the privacy of the monitoring room.

The Secretary came right to the point: could it be arranged for the French ambassador to visit Interzod?

"Of course not," Alexei said. "He doesn't have Interzod clearance." Clearance had been granted to the Third Secretary after the French government assured Alexei it would keep him in Washington—permanently, if Alexei wished. "I could give him Class B clearance, but that only means he'd come here for coffee and a lecture that tells him so little it's fraudulent. I'm afraid the answer is going to be no. I don't see any point to it. The French have six Grade A clearances allotted to them and that's quite enough." The Secretary was unhappy but said he understood, and the conversation ended.

A check with the monitoring board showed that operations were free of any pressing problems. Alexei had three hours before his appointment with Joe Harwell. Unfortunately, Wembley would not arrive until the following day. The three hours would be misspent because he had embarked on a line of thought which raised a spectrum of doubts that he knew would intensify the loneliness of his crushing secret and its complementary burdens. They had bothered him more frequently in the past few days. There were doubts about the knowledge itself; there were also real doubts about his ability to shoulder it alone. He'd known from the start that it would demand an ever-increasing degree of stoicism. He had been able to meet the demands because he had clearly anticipated them in the same way one summons grit for anticipated pain. Whenever possible, he liked to spend these moods in Wembley's company. Wembley did not know; he had never told him or anyone else. If Wembley had somehow guessed—and how could he?—he had avoided making the smallest allusion to it. Still, Alexei found it easier to be with someone who had the understanding and compassion to gauge the pressures that had become the sum and substance of his own existence. If he unburdened himself to anyone, it would be to Wembley.

He knew that some kind of unburdening must take place eventually. Yet, he also knew that it must wait until Eliot had finished his examination of the papers and journals they'd found in the library of Cyrus Maitland. It was a project Alexei could not undertake himself, for it depended on expertise. Eliot was superb in his field. At the age of twenty-three, by a combination of brilliant scholarship and an entirely new scientific methodology which far surpassed the standard carbon-fourteen tests for determining the ages of objects, he had rearranged the chronology hitherto assigned by scholarship to Mittani. Similarly, while working with a commission chartered by the Mexican government, he had greatly refined the accepted dates agreed upon for a vast quantity of pre-Columbian art and artifacts. While in his thirties, he had inspired controversy in the august world of German classical scholarship with a scathing survey of the treasures housed in the Berlin Museum.

Although shy in private life, Eliot was brash in his professional encounters. There was a streak of meanness that drove him to search out and destroy sacred cows. And since he was unorthodox and extremely successful at it, he could not be particularly likeable. His enemies often remarked on his drinking habits. Wembley, however, held him in the highest respect, and it was Wembley's judgment that counted in such matters. Interzod's historical section was Wembley's garden.

Alexei knew that the resolution of his and Kate's happiness depended on such men. The outcome of Eliot's project was fully as important as Wembley's first projects had been—his early published work on Nestorian documents, his discovery of an immense number of papyri bearing on Chaldean astronomers, and the careful work he'd done on the notebooks of Isaac Abrabanel, that wealthy statesman of the early Renaissance, Biblical scholar, astronomer and astrologer, who, if Alexei cared to trust claims of family genealogists, had been his own forebear.

Eliot's project was to attack the same problem from another angle. Of the two, he was more skilled in astronomical correlations and could proceed on his own without reference to Interzod's calendrical computer programs. In fact, he did not know of the program's existence or that Alexei could use it to verify his work. For all Eliot knew, assigning a specific date to an event was nothing more than an astronomical statement. A day or a year are, after all, astronomical events; if Rome was sacked, sailors mutinied in Odessa, or a barn burned in New Caledonia on certain days, these happenings could be of no professional interest to the astronomer. The relationship of astronomical events to human behavior could be no more than coincidental. Astronomy has its own history; its methods enable one to state that on a night in October 1735, Venus lay 15 degrees above the horizon visible in Surrey, England, or that at noon of January 4, in the year 3122, the planets Uranus and Mercury will lie along a line parallel to one formed by an extension of the earth's axis.

The astronomer's history extends forward and backward with equal certainty, extending in the future to a point that can only be finite because of cataclysmic finale. That one event has occurred and another has not is of a little consequence; unlike human history the past and future meet on equal terms.

Because he did not know, Eliot would have to believe that astronomy was a sterile process, with certainties that were dry and mathematical and which could have no bearing on the vastly more complicated process of human history. The latter, Eliot believed, was the result of a kind of layering. The long thoughts of a shepherd in Surrey who paused to look at an ascending Venus in 1735 altered him in some way, no matter how immeasurably or how trivially. He would never be the same man as before, and as a result the total human experience changed, if only by one thought added to the heap. Any point in the human future is everything that has gone before. To try to describe some of this process was the business of the human historian, Eliot believed. When he considers some future point in time, he cannot know what the accumulation of human history will be.

But Eliot could not know that the astrologer as well as the astronomer drew on the relative stability of solar mechanics, or that in fact he did bridge the gap between the human and celestial processes. Neither had he any inkling that Alexei would use the results of his labors as the starting point for specific astrological inquiries.

Alexei knew Eliot's limitations, and he was aware that when the time came, he would probably not include Eliot among those who would share the burden of what he knew. Even though the man's contribution might turn out to be the most important, he would never learn why

THE ASTROLOGER

Alexei found it significant. Alexei was aware that there was a rough edge to Eliot's skepticism, which accounted for much of his success in his field but which left him with a professional distaste for mystery. No, it was stronger than that; it was a genuine *incapacity* for mystery. Eliot would never know.

7

⊙

When Alexei reached headquarters, Varnov was perched on the edge of the long work table in the central monitoring room. Looking up, he smiled and extended his hand. "How was Moscow?" Alexei asked.

"St. Petersburg this trip," Varnov reminded him. "More snow than here. I'll take you with me sometime. At night you find yourself in the early nineteenth century. The old Leningrad is much more evident than the old London or Paris. It makes me feel like an aristocrat. You'll see —it's a good feeling. One understands why they were so tenacious." Glancing at the figures on the large board, he added, "Nativity seems very dull here. I tried to do something about speeding up the reporting in Vzbekistan and Kazakhstan. Hospital births are relatively rare and it doesn't mean very much to a village midwife when she's told that the exact time of birth must be reported on birth records. The sex and name seem much more important. And it's hard to get village and town officials to understand the importance of enforcing the rule. The arts of bureaucracy aren't very advanced in such places. I used to be thankful for it. Oh, well, it should improve."

"I'm going to want your advice later in the day on an analysis problem."

"The one Belgrade passed on to us? The upholsterer in Zadar? I've already seen the report."

"A simple upholsterer no longer. He's chairman of Worker's Guidance Council, or some such thing, which gives him a seat on the municipal board. Also, he has party membership. I hardly call that isolating the man."

"No, Interzod recommendations were ignored, that's clear. It hardly gives him much authority or power but it's the little taste that inflates such people. We've got to make it clear that they can't allow a man like that to take even the first step."

Alexei nodded in agreement. "I'll be free after lunch and we'll decide how to push him back down the first step. There's also a priority appeal from Peking, and a classification request from Athens. Everything else seems routine."

Alexei counted on Varnov heavily for advice on surveillance problems, and he was excellent as their Russian liaison. Only Douglas Gordon was as good in his mastery of the necessary blend of diplomacy and determination.

After a careful study of the monitoring board, which showed a more detailed picture of Interzod operations than the set in his monitoring room, Alexei went to his office, which was central to the computer and research sections. There were several files on a table to the right of his desk. Each was about two inches thick and represented a highly complex problem. Alexei always started the day by reading a digest and recommendation prepared by a member of the senior analytical board, and in the afternoon would generally meet with five members of the board to form a final decision. There were eighteen officers qualified to sit on the board, but since most of them had other duties all over the world, wherever there was an Interzod agency, there were rarely more than five members available. Sometimes Alexei agreed so wholeheartedly with the officer who had prepared the digest and recommendation that he would make the decision himself. But he did this only where a solution was obvious, because it was essential to the continuance of Interzod in its present form that the discipline of making decisions be shared.

Before he'd finished the first report, the telephone rang. "White House," Granby Courtland said. "Scramble code CV142." Alexei picked up the scrambler and dialed the code.

"Alexei? The Security Council has taken an interest in Kasjerte," the President said. "We'd like a review as soon as possible."

"Today?"

"Yes, if that's possible."

"We can manage it."

"I won't be able to make it. Admiral Sherborne will be out right away."

The shape of the day to come had changed. He had hoped to be able to begin orienting Joe Harwell. Harwell would be able to listen in but he would be puzzled by much of it. "I think it would be a good idea if General Dunne sat in with Sherborne," Alexei said. "He needs more exposure."

"We can do that," the President said.

A session with Admiral Sherborne meant tedium. Dunne would relieve it somewhat.

Not all countries subscribing to Interzod chose to have military representation, and though Alexei had no specific policy, he recognized that for some members the military was a more dominant political force than for others. In such cases it was well to have counsel close to the core of political power so that Interzod operations would not be misunderstood. But though representation in the form of a liaison officer on the National Security Council was fitting, Alexei regretted having allowed the same privilege to the American Joint Chiefs of Staff. Their interests were overlapping, and Admiral Sherborne, who had filled this post for six years, was a rigid, unimaginative man who often found himself at odds with Interzod deliberations. At Sherborne's retirement, Alexei had vowed to replace him with a civilian.

THE ASTROLOGER

Six months ago General Powers had been replaced as liaison to the National Security Council. They had all been sorry to see him go. He was a sad-faced kindly man who had been a part of Interzod since its beginnings and had given them support and much good advice during the early organizational stages. Alexei had assumed that the general would select his successor and help train him, but Powers had suddenly been taken seriously ill and the selection of Dunne had been made without his counsel.

Dunne was slim, with steel-rimmed glasses and the serious youthful look of a track star—which, in fact, he had been at West Point. He was also the youngest brigadier general in the army. He had a good theoretical grasp of Interzod operations but not enough experience with specific cases. He needed to have his judgment tested and listen to the kind of talk that was exchanged across the table during case reviews and surveillance sessions.

Joe Harwell arrived in the afternoon while Alexei was taking a call from a young surveillance officer in Mexico City who, Alexei now realized, shouldn't have been given such an important case without having worked more closely with one of his really good men—Lars Peterson or Embotu Tagi. "Of course he's escaped surveillance," Alexei was saying into the scrambler as Harwell entered the office. "He's done it before. But you don't have to consider it a personal failing; he's done it with everyone assigned to him."

The call was badly timed because Alexei wanted to talk with Harwell before Admiral Sherborne and General Dunne arrived. He knew, moreover, that what he was saying to Mexico City must sound strange to his visitor.

"His elusiveness isn't surprising when you consider that his zodiacal potentials demonstrate an astonishing intuitive capability. Both responsive and dominant—very unusual, especially to a high degree both ways. What this means is that he has a highly developed clairvoyance. He's a zodiacal prototype in this respect. Blavatsky had pretty much the same ratings. If you asked him, he could probably tell you the brand of cigarettes you smoked. He could make a living as a mind reader or some such thing. But the highly *responsive* intuitive capability means he senses when someone is watching him. Unfortunately, it means he's extremely imaginative about nearly everything, including means of escaping detection. But keep after him. Put your best men on it. You'll probably find him and lose him again. Remember that he's deeply suspicious and won't feel he can do much damage if he senses he's being followed."

By the time the call was over, Dunne and Sherborne had arrived, and Granby Courtland had made introductions and pulled down a large wall map showing a strip of central Asia from Turkey to Burma.

Sherborne and Dunne insisted on standing up to shake hands with Alexei. The admiral was a stiff man and all his amenities had the cordiality of a salute. Both officers were wearing civilian clothes, which was one of Alexei's rules for the military. They'd chafed at first but knuckled under when Alexei threatened to withdraw Interzod clearance from Sherborne's predecessor. This wasn't a matter of caprice, but rather to make it clear that Interzod wasn't in the business of solving military problems.

Because he was duty officer, the job of review fell to Granby. Alexei had reminded him that Harwell had no experience in this aspect of Interzod operations, and that General Dunne had only slightly more.

"What we are generally concerned with," Granby began, "is the individual's potential for response to an environmental situation. We assign numbers to indicate the strength of the zodiacal potential—or Z P. Specifically, we are concerned with individuals whose zodiacal profile tells us they will have a highly unpleasant response, a response that we know will be dangerous if not subject to careful surveillance. A surveillance review is usually concerned with only one such person at a time, but today our review encompasses the activities of two people. Both have a malignancy rating well above the 360 Z P mark which mandates Interzod intercession.

"I realize that some of you are not yet familiar with our terminology. I will offer, therefore, a few explanatory remarks and definitions which I hope will be sufficient to carry you through this review with some understanding. When we're finished we will have an opportunity to go into any aspect in greater detail.

"I can't emphasize enough the importance of thinking in terms of the individual's potential. We are interested in these two men not for what they have done but for what they are *capable* of doing. They are capable of what we call malignancy because of a severe imbalance in zodiacally determined potentials. It doesn't matter if a man is born with extraordinary personal intensity or a dominant aggressive potential. Kasjerte, who is by far the more dangerous of the two, scores very high in both of these Z P indices. Most of the great accomplishments of this world have been achieved by men and women who were very strong in one or both of these potentials, but the difference is that they had equally strong balancing factors.

"The degree of imbalance is almost always the critical zodiacal aspect of any profile where the determinants are above the 250 Z P range. Now, Kasjerte's imbalance is unique." Granby ran his finger along a chart where a red line had been drawn in the shape of the letter *W*. "The imbalance is astonishing. The first thing we notice is an extremely high dominance factor. You know the sort of man who makes his presence felt in a roomful of people even though he says nothing, and when he speaks conversation stops? We've all encountered such men, but I feel confident in saying that none of us has met anyone who has this quality to Kasjerte's degree.

"Everyone here would feel Kasjerte's presence in a crowd. When he walks through a village in India people turn and stare at him until he disappears, and they never forget him. He does not inspire love or affection but he does induce a kind of awe—I can't find a better word for it. It's a quality that gives him immense power and authority of a very personal kind. This is clear from the zodiacal profile in front of me and, alas, it is all too well documented by events and observers, including Interzod staff officers.

"Such men are unique. There are probably no more than three such men alive at one time. Kasjerte cannot help himself. This factor is so high that it is what we call an imperative. This means he *must* dominate others, and since he must, he very quickly learns how. Incidentally, Napoleon had something of this in him, but not to an imperative degree. In fact, until we established Kasjerte's Z P strength, we called it the Napoleonic factor because his was the highest degree known. Now we'll have to re-name it the Kasjerte factor, I'm afraid.

"To repeat, this man has an enormous imbalance. There are none of the zodiacal determinants which would act as a safeguard—very little of what we refer to as "benevolence potentials." Roughly, these potentials manifest themselves in the ability to be generous—I mean generosity in the larger sense: an extension of one's understanding of others, an ability to love. In its responsive mode, this potential is the capacity for accepting understanding and love. While the malignancy factor usually leads to ostracism, arrest and headlines, a man can have a high benevolence potential, yet still not attract attention. There are of course strong manifestations of the benevolence potential that have attracted a great deal of attention. It is difficult to talk about these without historical examples. It is probably one of the potentials Jesus had to an imperative degree. Lincoln's zodiacal configurations show us that he had it to a marked degree. So you can begin to understand, I think, what a low degree of this benevolent potential would mean in a man like Kasjerte—a man who is compelled to lead, to see his commands obeyed.

"To get a full picture of Interzod contact with Kasjerte, we have to go back three years or so to a man named Alciergas, who was also one of our surveillance subjects. Alciergas was a borderline case. He had a malignancy factor of 120. There was a marked imbalance, and the profile was similar in construction to Kasjerte's, but we were contending with far lower scores. He did not merit as close a surveillance as we give a man such as Kasjerte, and our initial response was only a recommendation that this man not be given a taste of power or authority. This was minimal and routine advice, since Alciergas had little realization what he was capable of. However, he did evade our scrutiny and enroll in a university—a move which we decided to oppose, since a university might present him with a forum, a pulpit, an audience, a base from which he would feel compelled to attract followers. Precipitous action was something to avoid because Alciergas would be almost certain to magnify any resentment and would feel justified in any action he took for revenge.

"Before we could move, however, Alciergas killed two students in a quarrel and went into hiding. At this point, generally, Interzod duties would be over since he was now a subject for local police and courts. But in Alciergas' case, we knew better. Being a fugitive would be bound to give him an identity of a new kind in his own eyes; there would be some intuitive recognition on his part of his powers. His sense of resentment would be strengthened, and every act would be that of a desperate man.

"We sent two men into the field to catch him. Our efforts were not known to the local police, though we were in a position to obtain any information they uncovered in their search. They were not an impressive police force, I'm afraid.

"Alciergas eluded us for six months. In this period he moved on foot along almost the entire expanse of the southern slope of the Himalayan foothills, usually seeking refuge in tiny villages or with shepherds. When he couldn't beg food and shelter, he would slaughter sheep for food. In Nepal he was joined by companions—adherents, followers, disciples—any of these words will do. With several men traveling together it became harder to get shelter or food by asking for it, and the band took to murdering the villagers and shepherds who would not assist them.

"The band grew too strong for any local police force. By the time they moved into Bhutan there were twenty followers, and they had begun to raze and plunder on a larger scale. They developed keen instincts for survival, avoiding large towns, traveling at night, or if by day in twos or threes, taking different routes and making rendezvous at nightfall. They also continued to grow in number. Coming on a village, they would offer some of the men the choice of joining or being killed. Still, this only explains the initial recruiting procedures, not the motivation that kept them together. That motivation, of course, was Alciergas himself, whose zodiacal capabilities indicated strong dominance and persuasion. Our officers could find only two men who left the group during this period.

"Alciergas seems to have made contact with Kasjerte after they'd passed through Bhutan. There they had run into the first determined effort on the part of an organized militia and had responded by scattering, regrouping later in northeastern Assam at the onset of the rainy season. Quite abruptly, the character of Alciergas' activities underwent a dramatic change." Granby pointed to the map. "The group entered the village of Gahor, here in the uplands on the southern slope of the Himalayas. There was some resistance, about a dozen villagers were killed and all of them were subjected to ritual mutilation—the village chief and his sons while they were still alive. But this is where Alciergas settled, making Gahor his base of operations for raids on settlements in the valley.

"These raids followed the same pattern. The men who resisted were mutilated; those who wished to returned to Gahor with the group. I should point out that many of his followers *voluntarily* subjected themselves to mutilation. By this time a religious fervor had permeated all their activities. They now killed not only because their raids met resistance but from some ritual necessity. Alciergas' back, chest and thighs were covered with scars which were shaped to form animals. Other members of the group followed suit, though none of the others had such extensive scars. It seems to have been a privilege.

"Three small villages were raided. Only the older women were left unharmed. The young women and children were invariably led back to Gahor and the women were subjected to great cruelty. One report told of orgiastic revels with public defloration ceremonies, at the end of which the male would be subjected to mutilation. Even so, there was little defection from Gahor and a truly shocking loyalty by the peasants toward their captors. At one period, Porter, the Interzod officer in charge, managed to infiltrate Gahor and live there undetected for nearly a week. It was he who discovered that Alciergas was no longer the true leader of the movement and that Kasjerte was the man we had to reckon with. Kasjerte dominated everything and everyone; Alciergas had become his pawn. The mutilation ceremonies—which were sexual in character, I should add—the religious trappings, the hysteria and the pointless bloody destruction of the villages all stem from Kasjerte. These all served to ensure the fanaticism of the followers.

"I suppose it will be difficult to understand why the Indian government couldn't put an end to this at once. But this is a part of the world where communications, even decent roads, are in very short supply. As you can imagine, the area was in turmoil. Several neighboring villages pooled resources and organized a force of sixty men to try to take Gahor, but they were ambushed and turned back before they came within sight of the place. A week later, a militia of about fifty men who were much better armed tried their hand at it. This effort also failed. A horde of screaming women and children poured out of Gahor, armed with knives and a few firearms, but the militiamen refused to fire and frankly got much the worst of it in hand-to-hand combat.

"The reluctance of the government to act decisively with sufficient troops seems to stem from their refusal to believe the accounts of what had taken place. It is not a peaceable part of the country by any means —there are frequent tribal flare-ups and traditional feuds among various villages—and they interpreted the stories as an effort by one settlement to secure government intervention in such a feud.

"When the government finally did act, they moved in some two hundred troops. Kasjerte sent Alciergas with a group of twenty or so followers across the hills towards Pobha, hoping he would decoy the militia while he made his escape. The plan didn't work. The troops kept on to Gahor, and Kasjerte had to take to the hills himself. They captured him two days later. Alciergas didn't escape either; he ran into some Akas tribesmen who dispatched him in settlement of the grudges they bore him.

"The death of Alciergas and capture of Kasjerte should have been a satisfactory end to all this but I'm afraid it wasn't. Our man Porter, who had slipped out of Gahor seven or eight days before the troops finally took over there, had a strong curiosity about Kasjerte. We hadn't had the man under surveillance previously; we had never heard of him. But Porter was sure that if we could obtain a zodiacal reading on him we would discover a very high malignancy rating."

Alexei intervened at this point. "I think we ought to explain," he said, turning to Harwell, "that we don't often work in reverse order. The normal procedure is to begin with a configuration which we know will be troublesome for natalities in an exact place at an exact time. The next step is to make a survey of natalities which could possibly occur, a procedure which, as you may guess, is especially difficult in both populous and remote areas. The third step is to confirm who was born and to inaugurate suitable surveillance programs for each case.

"Because we have not been in operation for very long, all our surveillance subjects determined at birth are still young. Our next step was to review all configurations resulting in high malignancy profiles for recent years, to do our best to discover who they have affected and to begin surveillance programs for them.

"In a country such as India, we have had great difficulty in discovering the necessary facts for births that have already occurred. But we had extraordinary luck in Kasjerte's case. As it turned out, he was known to the police in Bengali, East Pakistan and Mysore, and from their records we learned that he had been born in a Portuguese hospital at Goa and was the bastard son of a Portuguese army officer. The piece of good fortune was that this enabled us to get the necessary facts of birth, and then it was a matter of routine to learn that Kasjerte was far more dangerous than Alciergas.

"Porter's report on Kasjerte appeared very accurate when compared to his zodiacal profile. He was struck by Kasjerte's utter lack of social responsibility—zodiacally, he could have almost none—and by his immense powers of persuasion and dominance over everyone around him, which we've already discussed. It is the only time an Interzod officer has encountered anyone with a high malignancy factor without knowing anything of his zodiacal make-up beforehand. Frankly, we were somewhat skeptical that Porter's suspicions were verified so neatly.

"Unfortunately we did not have this verification in our hands until the troops had already reached Gahor, or we would have·made certain that the proper precautions had been taken to keep Kasjerte in custody. As Granby has pointed out, there was an element of disbelief on the part of the local government, and this seems to have been shared by the many officers, who took the stories they'd heard about Kasjerte somewhat skeptically.

"Porter started off by helicopter to try to be in on the capture. When he arrived at Gahor the troops had already been there, and finding Kasjerte gone, had spread out in the hills in search. This is rugged country. There are countless tiny villages, and Porter discovered a great reluctance on the part of the tribesmen to discuss anything having to do with Kasjerte. They even disliked telling him whether a column of soldiers had passed through their village.

"The two hundred soldiers had been divided into several columns, and when Porter reached the officer commanding one column he would discover that he had only the vaguest knowledge of the whereabouts of the others. It wasn't until three days had gone by that Interzod in Manipur learned that Kasjerte had been taken. Even then they weren't able to get through to Porter to tell him where Kasjerte was being held.

"What seems to have happened is that the commanding officers turned Kasjerte over to the nearest local official, a district magistrate in a local village. The officer insists that he was following his orders to the letter. Porter didn't reach the place until the following day. Kasjerte had been jailed in a hut whose door stood open so that he could be viewed by the villagers. He was secured only by wooden stocks for his legs and feet. It had failed to hold, as could have been expected. Porter found the settlement deserted except for two or three old women. The bodies of the jailer and his two sons were staked out in the sun; they had been killed by the jailer's wife and two daughters, all of whom had come under Kasjerte's influence and had gone with him as his "brides." The term is slightly euphemistic. One daughter was found dead and mutilated a short distance from the village. The mother and the second daughter were found soon after, wandering across barren hills; both had been terribly mutilated and were unable to tell what had happened because their tongues had been removed. The phenomenon of Kasjerte's 'brides' has since become familiar to us."

There was a file on the table in front of Granby, and he now opened it for the first time. "The information we've given you brings us up to one week from today," he said. "I know it is a complicated account, but I warn you that it has become even more so in the past week. Our next report, still from Porter, cites rumors that Kasjerte has surfaced once again. Evidently he is living in the Khasi hills as a fugitive with half a dozen of his followers. This is an area on the southern side of the wide Brahmaputra valley, a part of the rain forests above the rice and tea plantations on the valley floor. It would be an ideal place for a small group of outlaws to conceal themselves for a while. We can be quite sure that Kasjerte is not alone. It is one of the paradoxes of his lack of social capabilities that he must surround himself with followers who will subject themselves to his will. The term 'zodiacal potential' is misleading in a case such as this; it is *imperative* for Kasjerte not to travel alone.

"Though Kasjerte's whereabouts are now known, Porter has not been able to make actual contact with him, and the next development is open to speculation. There has been a development we find alarming from a surveillance point of view: Kasjerte's followers are promulgating myths and legends that would raise him to a god. He has demonstrated that he has an affinity for the pseudoreligious, and with very little adjustment he could come to think of himself as a god. He would not question it because he knows that it would greatly enhance his powers over anyone who believed it. The man has to find the means for domination. It doesn't matter to him if those he subjugates hate him or love him; neither would he scruple to destroy them.

"I make these observations so that you can appreciate the importance of the most recent rumors. Soon after the troops captured Kasjerte, rumors that he was dead spread over the upper reaches of the Brahmaputra valley from Lakimpur to Pobha. The lie was valuable and pains were taken to dramatize it. A funeral pyre was built at a village not far from Pobha and hundreds of people believed the corpse to be Kasjerte's. There were too many people there for them all to have been Kasjerte's followers. Two women who claimed to be Kasjerte's brides leaped in the flaming pyre, in a form of suttee formerly practiced in the Indian provinces to the south. Two other women were said to have been restrained at the last moment.

"Nothing could be better designed to attract attention and notoriety in India than a revival of the barbarous anachronism of suttee. We know of no other example in modern India, and it is bound to arouse mystical associations with the religious past. Reports of it appeared in Indian newspapers, and a parliamentary commission has been appointed to make an investigation. The effect in the countryside, where news is passed on by word of mouth rather than by newspaper, was even greater. The newspapers, by the way, mentioned only one woman leaping into the pyre, and the first story did not mention Kasjerte's name. The government was on the spot, you see, since officially he had been captured. At the time of the funeral he hadn't yet made his escape.

"At this juncture everything was ready for Kasjerte's reappearance —all that was needed to elevate him to the rank of a god. He first appeared in the riverside villages—still in the Pobha vicinity—in the company of a handful of followers, saying that he was Kasjerte and that he had risen from the dead. We must bear in mind that his presence anywhere is always imposing—electrifying, according to Porter—and if one had heard the story of his death and knew someone who had witnessed the funeral pyre, he might well be left with the conviction that Kasjerte *had* returned from the dead.

"There was no violence at his arrival in any of these villages. There was awe and fear and a strong superstitious awakening. Hundreds of men and women wanted to follow him, but at this point he refused such offers. Porter presumes he did not yet feel confident enough to arouse the authorities. He moved eastward, always avoiding places where there was a constabulary or military barracks, crossed to the southern side of the valley and turned back towards the Khasi hills.

"The rumor reached the government, of course. They didn't consider their sources reliable until Porter was able to verify them. They sent a small detachment of men out from Shillong but were unable to make contact, even though Kasjerte continued to appear in the villages. As of now no one has found him, though he's generally believed to be in the vicinity of the Khasi hills. Information is hard to come by; officials have to contend with rumors and a general feeling of unrest and fear which works to Kasjerte's advantage. He has succeeded in getting the protection of the countryside."

General Dunne had a question. "You say that an Interzod officer was able to verify that Kasjerte was alive at a time when the Indian officials couldn't. How were we able to do this?"

"That's easy: Porter saw him."

"Would it have been possible for him to make an arrest?"

"As a matter of fact, no. Weapons or a great many men would have been necessary. Porter was operating out of Shillong with radio contact to the only other Interzod agent there. He had no way of getting in touch with the police. The village was remote, with no telephone. The local authority was a village chieftain who didn't much care what the government thought; to him Kasjerte was a holy man who deserved respect and protection. Besides, Interzod doesn't function as some kind of international police agency. It is not one of our contractual responsibilities to arrest someone under surveillance because he violated a member government's laws. We can often predict that someone with a high malignancy potential will sooner or later be a lawbreaker, but this isn't always how the malignancy will manifest itself.

"In any event, once a subject is a fugitive from law we will continue our surveillance and, in many cases, give any information to the police we can that will help in his capture. We do not always do this; sometimes the zodiacal prognosis is such that the subject will be less dangerous as a fugitive than he would be if caught and imprisoned. I think something of this kind is true in the next man we have to tell you about. His name is Shoun, a Pakistani who has been under our surveillance for nearly eight years.

"As of now, we know that any surveillance recommendations for Kasjerte must take Shoun into account. General Dunne, when I said that Porter was able to verify that Kasjerte was alive because he saw him, you may have wondered how this came about."

"I did," Dunne said, "but I didn't want to—"

"Porter saw him because he was searching for Shoun, who was known to be in the vicinity. When he found Shoun he also found

Kasjerte. They were together; they have joined forces. As far as we are concerned, this is the most unfortunate thing that could have happened.

"Briefly, I'll tell you why. Shoun has a combination of zodiacal determinants which add up to what we call an extremely high organizational factor. Such a man has no difficulty with mathematics or in solving certain kinds of problems. Put in an army, he would be the best quartermaster the world has ever seen. His organizational capacity is higher than General Eisenhower's and nearly as high as Napoleon's. But Shoun has nothing of their balance; in almost all other respects he is weak, and would appear so to you. He has almost no sense of self, no capacity to yearn to achieve benefits for himself. His organizing capacities are so great that he is compelled to exercise them, but he gets little satisfaction from them because there is little in his make-up that can be satisfied. Do you follow me? The man is a kind of machine.

"Shoun offered very few surveillance problems. It was important that his occupation satisfy these special zodiacally based yearnings, but we knew he could function with very few social rewards. Unlike Kasjerte, he has some education. If a task is put before him he functions with enormous ability, but the problem for us was that he was basically susceptible and had small powers of discretion. We always knew that he would be drawn to anyone dominant or to any movement that was strong—that had simple, emphatic goals of either good or evil.

"Shoun was very successful in a job allocating construction funds and materials for a governmental road building program, but we discovered that he had been embezzling a considerable sum of money. Interzod knew that he could not go through the cycle of detection, arrest and imprisonment without defining himself as a criminal, and we had to prevent the funneling of his capacities in the service of crime. Interzod's response was to fabricate a situation where he could make enough money to cover the deficit. In other words, we footed the bill so that he could retain his self-image of being an honest man.

"We have tried to arrange jobs for him with organizations that are blatantly charitable in character because institutional goals of good or evil must be crude and visible to him. Even then he will be unable to feel any allegiance to them and will be easily able to substitute one set of values for another, because they all appear equally superficial to him. He was once removed from his job as a trade unionist because of his outspoken indifference to the organization's principles and aspirations.

"Now, the dangerous element is Shoun's remarkably low sense of self. What little he has is entirely responsive—or what you might call negative. When the sense of self is in the dominant mode, as in Kasjerte's case, we see it as a capacity for dominating others."

Granby closed the file in front of him and folded his hands on the table. "So, if you were to take the two men and fuse them together, what sort of man do you think you would have? That is what actually has happened. Shoun, weak and incipiently corrupt and susceptible to any domineering factor, has been drawn like a magnet to Kasjerte. And that's our problem: weakness has been drawn to strength. It was inevitable that Shoun would gravitate to a source of strength. The worst possible source was Kasjerte."

"How do you anticipate Shoun will affect the situation?" Dunne asked.

"By himself, Kasjerte was able to reduce part of one province to chaos within a short time. But there was no pervading danger to it because the man had no political base. It was a cult, with only local appeal. But then Shoun arrives on the scene. Having been drawn to Kasjerte and having received some indoctrination in political organization in his days as a trade unionist, he sees that Kasjerte needs to modify his demands so he will have a broader appeal and put his fanaticism on a sound political basis. According to Porter's last report, received today, Kasjerte has devoured the advice, seized control of a village and a marketing town, practiced his ritual murder on the manager of a large tea plantation and has promised to parcel out the land to his followers. Suddenly the government is very apprehensive about dislodging him. They remember the previous effort of government troops to capture him in Gahor, when the entire village came flying to counterattack."

"What is our response going to be?" General Dunne asked.

"The first response is to separate Shoun and Kasjerte," Alexei answered.

"Can this be done?"

"Yes," Alexei said emphatically.

Admiral Sherborne took over at this point. "We should remember, I think, that it is also known that Kasjerte has made contact with Communist guerrillas active in northern Burma."

"This is not Interzod information," Alexei said quickly.

"What difference does it make?" Sherborne said. "If Kasjerte can be used by a pipsqueak like Shoun, I hate to think what the Communists could do with him."

"That isn't an Interzod problem, Sherborne," Alexei said. "Perhaps the CIA considers it their problem and would like to know how we would solve it for them, but I repeat, it is not our problem. We knew of Shoun from the beginning. But Interzod's recommendation, which was to find him a suitable job and make sure that he was always employed, was not followed. We didn't know about Kasjerte until his cult was established. There was nothing we could do; we had no responsibility for Kasjerte. We have done as well as possible in the circumstances. What else can I tell you?"

Sherborne was silent for a moment. "Kasjerte could spread Communist doctrine all across that part of Asia," he said.

Alexei shook his head. "He won't," he said. "Kasjerte won't become a Communist, Admiral. He won't join any group that isn't willing to deify him. He can't be used. He would never share power. Shoun doesn't use Kasjerte—he has no desire for power. Kasjerte has devoured him. The danger is that he will devour all the Communists in northern Burma. This is not an Interzod opinion. It's the opinion Interzod would give if they had a contract with the CIA. But we don't, you see."

"What makes you call it a CIA problem? As I see it, it's a problem of national security," General Dunne said.

"I'm not in that business, General. I have contracts with sixty-seven countries. There would be a conflict of interest if I tried to settle security problems for any of them. Interzod only wants to minimize the effects of Kasjerteism. It has no concern with the flow of Communism. We are only interested in neutralizing people, not movements. That's all we know how to do. If Kasjerte became a Buddhist monk, would you expect me to try to stop the flow of Buddhism?"

Sherborne wasn't happy. Alexei had come up against this kind of problem with him once before and he'd stormed out in a fury because Alexei had called him the CIA's errand boy.

There was a silence which was broken by Varnov entering the room. "Can you take a call from Aberdeen?" he asked. Alexei knew it wasn't important but he nodded because he wanted to break up the meeting. Sherborne was about to freeze over, and whenever he did, further conversation was pointless.

Alexei took the call at the table while Dunne and Sherborne rose to leave. He was familiar with the Aberdeen problem. Surveillance there was worried because one of their cases had announced her intentions of standing for the city council. "Don't bother to discourage her," Alexei advised. "Sooner or later she's going to solve your problem for you. It's a wonder she hasn't gotten herself in a situation before this where her sanity was questioned. The psycopathic indications are very high, remember. The woman will appear testy, argumentative and altogether paranoid. Exposure will be her undoing and we'll be able to write her off. We know of thirty-two zodiacal facsimiles, and all but four are already committed."

He hung up abruptly, shook hands with Dunne and Sherborne and ushered them to the door.

8

⊙

Harwell was slumped in his chair on the far side of the table when Alexei returned. "This isn't the meeting I had planned for us," he said. "These reviews can be very complicated, and if I'd stuck to the usual procedure we would have had several sessions devoted to basic orientation before throwing you into a difficult surveillance discussion. Still, I believe you've heard enough oblique talk to gather something about the scope of our operations."

He might have added that since Harwell had only the knowledge that went with Grade B clearance he could not know of the existence of the modern zodiacal factors. Though he might have had some inkling of the discursive language used in Interzod interpretations, before today he could not have been aware that this language was keyed to precise formulations.

Harwell had heard enough to arouse his curiosity, and as with everyone who was being granted Grade A clearance, Alexei himself conducted the indoctrination, which was always spread over a period of several days to ensure that comprehension was complete at each step. The response was highly individual, the faculty for disbelief varying greatly, with curiosity expanding and demanding fuller explanations at different stages of the indoctrination. By the time the briefing was finished, Alexei always felt he knew his man well. General Dunne went about it like a man learning chess and was courteous enough to stifle what Alexei guessed was an enormous supply of Missouri-style disbelief. In some cases any exposition of the scientific aspects of Interzod was lost on the hearer because of lack of scientific training. Others found the going difficult because they were accustomed to thinking about the areas of Interzod's concerns as psychological, legal or religious.

Alexei's breezy disclaimer that Interzod formulations did not contradict those of other disciplines was not always accepted—with good reason, since it was not always true, and the organization often contradicted accepted habits of thought. But he had no desire to place Interzod notions in the vortex of academic dispute, or even to have their observations emerge as a body of theoretical thought. In this case, however, he anticipated few problems. He had already noticed Harwell's tendency to hold curiosity and judgment in restraint. His questions would be cautious and to the point. "When I've told you everything that's basic to Interzod, you'll be one of the 512 men in the world who know what we do," he began, and then interrupted himself to ask if his listener could join him for dinner.

Flattered and surprised, Harwell accepted. He smiled to himself, thinking of the legendary aura that had become attached to Alexei's name in congressional circles; on Capitol Hill "Abarnel" was pronounced with a tone that gave it a savor of mystery and challenged the man's right to flesh and bone or to such mundane considerations as eating. This stirred a simple personal curiosity which he gave in to.

"How did you get started on this, Alexei?" he asked.

"I've been asked that before," Alexei said cheerfully. "In the beginning, I heard it all the time. Sometimes it came from people who were trying to satisfy themselves that I was a lunatic."

"What did you tell them?"

"If I ever worked up a stock answer, I've forgotten what it was. I remember what an Italian diplomat said. He was also a pretty fair scientist—a biologist, I think—and so his country picked him for a briefing on the project so they could decide whether to be a participating government. When I'd finished he stood up, pointed his finger at me and said, "You have succeeded in bringing astrology into the twentieth century."

"Is that what you've done?"

"That's as apt a description as any, I suppose." Alexei shrugged. "There was a good deal about the old astrology that I *didn't* bring into the twentieth century; it simply wouldn't be worth the effort. At the time, I didn't blame anyone for thinking it was a lunatic plan if they didn't know that we were having some success. Astrology has always attracted a lot of nuts, after all."

"But what made you think it was possible?"

"I didn't know if it was possible or not; I just thought it was worth a try. No, actually, I was very skeptical about it. But I did have the notion that sometimes, if only rarely, astrologists had managed to do what they claimed they could do. Not very regularly, but often enough so that I wondered why they could *ever* do it. I also had in mind that for centuries it was considered as reputable a science—or art, or whatever—as astronomy. In medieval times all the great astronomers were also astrologers. Somehow that never gets mentioned in modern textbooks when Copernicus, Galileo and Kepler are discussed. Even Bacon, the man who was the first to state what scientific method was all about, looked favorably on astrology.

"It's strange that most later astrologers maintained a hopelessly primitive notion of celestial mechanics. They knew, of course, that astronomers had discarded it, but only rarely does it seem to have occurred to them to make astrological computations based on the new developments in astronomical theories. The reason the old astrology remained backward is that it was so rudimentary that there *was* no way it could absorb each new advance in astronomy. It simply didn't matter.

Also, it always had been considered one of the occult sciences; because of its direct appeal to mystical longings, it's easy to see how the spirit of scientific inquiry and innovation would be considered fatal to astrology. Its claim was not to newness, but to esoteric knowledge, a body of lore enhanced by time and with a link to ancient wisdom.

"The Greeks attempted to make astrology keep pace with advances in astronomy, but nobody else has tried very hard. Can you imagine someone in the twentieth century trying to make use of the notion that the earth is the center of the solar system? It's hard to believe that most people continued to believe in that kind of astrology until the eighteenth century. Even in the nineteenth century, men of intelligence and ambition such as Napoleon tried to conceal the time of their birth so that their enemies couldn't get a fix on their destiny. It's no wonder that people thought of it as a form of witchcraft, and that astrologists were considered charlatans. I certainly did. What would you think of the practice of medicine if it hadn't advanced since ancient Greece? Would you believe a doctor who used Galen as his authority, or wouldn't pay any attention when Harvey discovered the circulatory system of the blood?"

Harwell smiled and admitted he wouldn't. "But why didn't you think of trying to bring witchcraft into the twentieth century?"

"Because at bottom, astrology, unlike witchcraft, *was* an attempt at scientific achievement. In that respect it was further advanced than medicine until after the Renaissance. Those old astrologers had the right idea. They were meticulous observers, mind you, and they kept very careful records and statistics which were generally not much encumbered by theory. Medical practitioners, on the other hand, always confused theory with observations. What did their observation amount to if they were convinced the liver contained the soul and moved the blood around? What's more, they didn't have much of any systematic way of sharing or comparing what they did learn. What was known about astrology, on the other hand, was knowledge common to all of Europe.

"Only with its decline has astrology been lumped with witchcraft and sorcery. Medieval astrology was carried on by men of learning and enlightenment. It seems to me unfortunate that it entered into a decline before the period of revolutionary changes in physics and mathematics. If it had maintained a respectable front, it might have come in for the revamping it needed. Medicine has always been in a continual state of revamping and revision because the need for sound medical practice is obvious. This wasn't the case for astrology; it became a neglected art. Its practitioners neglected related sciences, and so the sciences neglected it. Scorned is a better word."

"But hadn't this occurred to anyone else?"

"I don't know; perhaps it had. But did you know that astrology appears in almost identical form in civilizations that could have had no knowledge of one another? It was known to the Incas in much the same form as to the Babylonians and Greeks. Their observations are remarkably alike. That's one of the things I found exciting."

"But a lot of people must have known that and yet still steered clear of it."

"Someone has to be first. Anyway, I remember making a study long before I gave any of this serious consideration," Alexei said. "It was a joke, really. If you know anyone who believes in the old astrology, you'll recall that they have a tendency to make converts. And in trying to convince you that there's really something to it, they talk about the statistical studies done on the incidence of crime and madness during the full moon, or the fact that oysters and various other molluscs open their shells even when placed in an artifical environment, free from the effects of tides and exposed to a constant light. This is presumed to show that heavenly bodies *can* have an effect on life on earth. This argument had always stuck somewhere in the back of my mind.

"Well, about twenty-five years ago I was living in London in an old house with a large barometer on the wall, so that I couldn't help noticing the barometric-pressure readings as I left the house to find a cab to go to my lab. After a while I noticed that on days with a low barometric-pressure reading, the cab drivers were prone to grumble more than days with a high reading. It was an idle time in my life, as you can guess, and I decided to keep a statistical record. I bought a little notebook especially for the purpose and every day I entered the barometer reading and then waited to see if my cab driver was in a foul mood or a good one. The difficulty seemed to be that on a great many days I drew a silent cab driver, and so I decided I would have to improve my methodology and devise a question to ask every morning. It would be a sounder control I figured, if it were always the same question. I knew that it shouldn't be rhetorically weighted to elicit one response or the other. For example, it wouldn't be fair to say, 'Nice morning, isn't it?' or 'It looks like rain, doesn't it?' It had to be perfectly neutral. So after a little experimentation I found one; I'd ask, 'How's the traffic these days?' and nine times out of ten I would get a response that could be classified as grumpy or cheerful.

"At the end of two weeks I began taking a cab back to my house in the evening and entering the barometer reading in my notebook when I came in the front door. When I had fifty entries, I found that forty-two could be classified as relevant responses. Of these forty-two, twelve had been asked during periods of high or rising-to-high barometric pressure, twenty-six were during low or falling-to-low barometric pressure, and the remaining four were on days that couldn't be classified as either. For the twenty-six lows, twenty-two were negative responses, ranging from slightly pessimistic to downright churlish. For the twelve highs, ten responses were positive, and in some cases followed by cheerful anecdotes. Anyway, the score was 84 percent for the highs, 85 percent for the lows. On the basis of early returns, I'd found a definite correlation."

Alexei noticed that Harwell was leaning forward in his chair, fascinated. "But you forgot something," Harwell said eagerly. "High barometric pressure is nearly always a sign of fair weather—sunshine. Everything *looks* more cheerful. Colors are brighter, for one thing. Your optimistic response could be a result of your taxi driver finding himself in more cheerful surroundings."

"You're right, of course," Alexei said. "But I did think of that. As a matter of fact, I realized from the beginning that I would have to impose tighter controls. The daytime survey was only the beginning. I supplemented it with one at night in which I asked the same question.

THE ASTROLOGER

I developed a routine of taking a taxi from my house to the Grovesnor Hotel, having two scotches at the bar and returning home again. I did this for two months. I had started the whole thing as kind of a game, but now I began to be truly interested. By the summer's end I had a substantial nighttime survey and was on a first-name basis with a lot of the regulars at the Grovesnor bar. The night survey was even more exciting because both positive and negative responses were related nearly as closely to the rise and fall of barometric pressures as the daytime. I can't remember the exact figures any longer, but they were within two or three percentage points of the daylight survey, which ruled out what I called the cheerful-light factor."

"What were you left with? Did you consider it a pure correlation between barometric pressure and behavior?"

"No, by no means," Alexei said quickly. "In the first place, as far as I can see, any description of human behavior, statistical or otherwise, can never be considered pure in any sense. When I had finished my survey all I had were the statistics, nothing else. I refused to make any inference as to cause. There was nothing substantive about the relation of barometric pressure and cheerfulness except as they concerned the predictability of my finding a cheerful cab driver in London when the barometric pressure was above 30.5 inches. After all, what other conclusion could I draw?"

"None, I guess," Harwell said. "But it was a temptation, wasn't it? And isn't the point of all this that it led to a serious consideration of astrology and the desire to make it more scientific?"

"There was a temptation, of course, but it was still pretty much of a game. After all, what did the statistics actually tell me that was of any importance? They only verified what any idiot knows: on heavy, oppressive days, people tend to be grumpy. Only a fool would claim that it was a scientific advance to be able to state its probability by a numerical percentage. The world is full of idiots who reduce some aspect of humanity to a number and think this tells them something."

"But don't you use numbers—or mathematics—in your computer program? Don't astrological formulations, as you call them, derive from mathematics or some such thing? I don't know much about computers."

"Of course," Alexei answered. "But the important thing is not to let yourself *settle* for the numbers. The trick is always to keep in mind what they stand for."

"Such as earthquakes or floods, you mean?"

Alexei shook his head. "I really can't predict earthquakes or floods or the change in fortunes of nations or any of those things. Some of the old astrologers claimed to be able to, and I don't say that it can't be done, but I've never tried and I really wouldn't know how to go about it. All we've been able to do is to make predictions about the temperamental equipment an individual is likely to have. You might call it character or personality, but those words have so many associations that we find it easier to avoid using them. Needless to say, this has nothing to do with barometric pressure."

"You *can* figure out how an individual's life will turn out, is that how you'd put it?"

"No, that's not it. Because there are environmental and historical factors that are different for each individual. A man born in the Fiji Islands might have pretty much the same set of potentials as a man born in Liverpool, but obviously their lives are going to be different. Or you might find zodiacal similarities in two people born hundreds of years apart. But their potentials are fed on different worlds. One may live to be eighty-seven and the other might die of diptheria at the age of six. Someone with the potential of a Shakespeare might never have had the opportunity to learn to read and write."

Harwell nodded thoughtfully. "I always thought astrology figured out how long a man would live."

"The old astrology sometimes claimed to be able to do that. Fortunately, they weren't successful at it." Alexei picked up his coat from a chair. "I'd hate to know that about anyone."

For an organization with a high premium on secrecy, the arrangements for physical security at Interzod headquarters had seemed casual to Harwell on his first visit. But this time he noticed that their departure from the building had been noticed by two men in civilian suits, that controls opened and closed the doors, which were operated by someone unseen, and that the narrow vestibule between inner and outer door contained an opaque glass panel. They turned away from the direction of the Air Force base, walking along a path that ran beside a low brick wall. It was unevenly lit by street lamps which appeared among the trees as the path wound up a hill.

A neatly dressed man in a business suit stood at the first lamp. "Good evening, sir," he said.

"Good evening, Mercer. This is Congressman Joseph Harwell. He doesn't have a number yet."

Mercer nodded pleasantly. There was more deference in this exchange than was the Interzod norm. As they passed, he closed a gate across the path, and Harwell wondered if the man was armed. He gathered that the nuances of dress were inverted at Interzod, so that the wearing of suits and ties fell to low-ranking employes.

They climbed a short flight of steps to a landing where the path widened into a terrace, and where one could look down on the headquarter buildings which were two dark windowless shapes. It was the second such terrace they'd come to. Along the path there was holly and rhododendron and deep shadow. Ornamental urns stood along the terrace wall, and in a leafy cul-de-sac was a piece of statuary. The utilitarian gray metal furnishing of Interzod headquarters, the neon lighting and office carpeting had been left behind. The quiet brick and stone, the random pools of lamplight along the path were a composition for someone who wanted a quiet tasteful ramble. A gardener's hand had been at work here.

They came to the top of the hill, and through the trees Harwell saw the lights of a large house. The invitation to supper had conjured up a visit to some kind of mess hall for Interzod officers, perhaps connected in some way with the Air Force base. Now he realized that this was Alexei's home.

The house was large and square, built of heavy fieldstone with tall windows, and it had obviously existed long before Interzod. Alexei led him into the library, which had a dark and vaguely baronial air. "My wife will probably come down. I have one request: there can be no mention of Interzod affairs in front of my wife or anyone here."

Harwell saw that Alexei attached great importance to this, and he expected it to be followed up with some sort of explanation. Instead there was only the offer of a drink, which he accepted. When Alexei disappeared to see about it, he allowed himself to wonder at Alexei's home life. It seemed strange to find that he actually had one. He had never heard of Mrs. Alexei Abarnel, but he couldn't escape the image of a brisk, sensible woman, busy with garden and volunteer hospitals, who recognized that home and marriage were subordinated to her husband's career. The request not to discuss Interzod affairs in front of her might have been a hostess' directive against shoptalk, except that the request had definitely been Alexei's. Was it possible that his own wife knew nothing of Interzod? Could she believe that the center dabbled in cancer research or was a government espionage program?

At that moment Harwell looked up to see a beautiful girl coming toward him—no, not a girl, he saw, but a lovely young woman, clearly not of an age to be Alexei's daughter. She was all of a piece, seemingly surrounded by a diffuse glow that encompassed her eyes, hair and the motion of her arm that rose toward him as she smiled and spoke. "Mr. Harwell? I am Kate Abarnel."

Harwell found her breath-taking. There was a fine, unaffected quality in her voice and movements as she set down a tray of drinks and handed one to him. When Alexei returned and they gathered around the fire, she sat on a low upholstered bench next to her husband, where she could look up at him. Later, Harwell remembered that when he spoke her face took on a great softness. He wondered if she had been aware that he found it hard not to stare at her. While they were together, he had not thought so. His view was of her profile, her elbow resting on her knee and one hand curved around the bulb of her wine glass, and she seemed remarkably unaware of her beauty and utterly lacking the presumption of most beautiful women that they are creating an effect.

Supper was served on a small table in the library: caviar, which, he learned, had its source in Interzod Sevastopol, cold veal and asparagus. Alexei was unusually amiable, and Harwell found himself skillfully drawn out, so that soon he was repeating odd bits of congressional gossip and making them laugh. Still, he had the feeling that such a supper as this should have been a more private occasion and, were it not for him, would have been a more intimate ritual.

Kate Abarnel poured coffee and Alexei offered brandy. She shook her head and put her hand over her glass. "Alexei, I got a letter from Mr. Bell today." She prefaced this with a smile of apology to Harwell for bringing up a subject that excluded him. "He's going to open again this winter. A limited engagement. Three weeks, he thinks."

"And did he ask you if you wanted a part?"

"Yes. He didn't sound very hopeful, since I'd already turned him down when it was to be an unlimited engagement. He said he hoped I'd change my mind if it was only for three weeks. I wrote back saying I wouldn't do it. I really wasn't tempted."

Harwell had the feeling that this was an addendum to a conversation they'd had before. She seemed to be offering reassurance, though apparently it was less important to Alexei than to her.

"Could we go to New York when it opens?" she asked.

"Of course."

She took his brandy from the table, sipped and handed it to him. It was by way of a caress. "It would be fun to go back for three weeks, but I don't think I'd like to go back to the same part or even the same show." She said it not looking at either of them but speaking with the same animation and expressiveness that seemed to infuse everything she said. "Sometimes I think I'm going to get fat and lazy, Alexei." She turned to Harwell. "Don't you think everyone should have something to do?" She smiled gloriously but didn't require an answer. This too seemed to be an echo of a previous conversation. It was not in the nature of a complaint.

Alexei leaned forward then. "I have to go to Switzerland in about three weeks for a few days. You can come and we'll stretch it into a few weeks—or longer, if we can."

Her smile was instantaneous. "Do you mean it? That would be wonderful." Harwell found himself wondering how she managed to achieve such a luminous intensity. Her happiness looked absolute; Alexei had said exactly the right thing.

"We can go by ourselves, can't we?" she asked. Before Alexei answered, the door opened and a large airdale came running over to the fire. A young woman followed him in, carrying a raincoat. "Don't get up, please," she said, and called to the dog. When it refused to come she smiled in exasperation and retrieved it.

Diana acknowledged Kate's introduction while crouching with her hand on the dog's collar. Then a man whom Kate introduced as Eliot entered. But Harwell had already recognized him as Tileo, and once again the incident struck him as absurd. "We've met, I think," he said firmly.

Eliot only nodded and offered his hand as he reached for the airdale's collar with the other.

"He's all right in here, Eliot," Kate said, cupping the dog's muzzle with her hand. "Will you take coffee or brandy?"

When they refused, explaining that the dog needed a walk, Kate stood up unexpectedly. She hadn't been sleeping well, she said, and wanted some fresh air before bed.

Harwell felt that it was time for him to leave, but in the next moment Alexei was explaining that he expected an important phone call in an hour, and Kate bent down and kissed him lightly, said goodbye and left. Harwell couldn't help feeling that Alexei should be going with her and should take his chances with the bedside phone.

When they were alone, however, Alexei didn't seem anxious to return to the indoctrination. After staring into the fire for several minutes, he looked at his watch and then at Harwell. "Some time in the next hour," he said, "a monster will probably be born into the world in the western section of what used to be called Estonia. If we're lucky there will be only one. If we're unlucky, there will be three."

"Can you really predict that?"

"Yes," Alexei said matter-of-factly. "This particular configuration is a relatively rare one. It will be the first occurrence in forty-one years, and because of its brief duration it won't affect many births. The last time it came around, a child would have to have been born in the middle of the Indian Ocean. None were, as it happens. This time, luck is against us. The affected area is highly populated, and prenatal reports indicate that at least three births are scheduled there. It's possible there will be others, but we'll learn about those in time."

"When you say a monster, do you mean that literally?"

"We know that he or she will have a malignancy potential of some 146 points. We begin to worry at 125 points. He will have virtually no sense of responsibility. He will be incapable of assimilating the mores that would mitigate his potential for evil, no matter what society he grows up in."

"You mean he would *have* to behave that way?"

Alexei nodded.

"What will happen to him?"

"I can't say. I can only tell what he's capable of. Once we know the environmental factors we might be able to make a pretty good guess. I'm hoping he'll come into a family with a lot of tough big brothers. Fear of physical punishment might help in this case, but he would have to experience it quite early. At any rate, his progress through life will be observed. There's a good chance he will be murdered before he kills anyone else. He won't be very likeable."

"It could be three births instead of just one?"

"As prenatality reports read now, it's possible, but it's something less than a fifty-fifty chance."

"How do you go about finding out?"

"It varies from country to country. It really depends on the customs and facilities for childbirth. Our prenatal team will move in beforehand and find out what the conditions are. If they find an area with very few doctors and hospitals, they may decide to return in four or five months and literally count and identify the pregnant women. Then, when the time comes, they'll return with a midwife team. These will be native women, nurses or midwives who know the customs and the language.

Usually they have no Interzod clearance, but they can offer help to the women and fill out reports which are turned over to the Interzod officers. From these reports we can figure out exactly which births are likely to be affected by the particular configuration. These women are also on hand to help make an accurate verification of the time of birth.

"I suppose there's something grotesque about all this, but keep in mind that the really dangerous malignancy configurations are rather rare, and so this procedure isn't often necessary. Remember, there are still more places in the world where child delivery takes place at home than in a hospital—and the "home" might be a hut in an isolated village, or even a field. But with certain configurations, it is essential that someone be on hand for the verification. This is where our surveillance process begins. By the time we have the natality verifications, we know what kind of a staff and set-up we will need for the area.

"Of course the job is much easier when there are hospitals, clinics, doctors and orderly systems. One side result of our work has been a large increase in public-health facilities in places that never had them before. Interzod has educated and trained over a thousand midwives and nurses —and also, I might add, supplied them with excellent timepieces. This is a surprisingly large expense; they seem to get lost or stolen very easily."

"Are you able to tell what the potential is for anyone?"

"Yes, anyone at all, really. We had some blind spots in the zodiacal track until about three years ago, but now we're reading all the coefficients very clearly."

"Could you tell me what my potentials are?"

Alexei smiled. "I was wondering when you'd come to that. I could, yes, but I don't think you'd like to know them. I'm not about to relieve anybody's burden of self-discovery. I haven't so far. I've never taken a fix even on my own—at least not since the program began to work accurately. Besides, it wouldn't tell you much. You're pretty well-balanced, anyone can see that. You'll run along pretty well on will power. If there were any imperatives you would have known about them by now."

"Some people are compelled to act in a certain way, if I understand what you mean by imperative?"

"Yes. Imperative. Very rare, you see. In the responsive mode especially. It could be that St. Joan is an example, though we haven't been able to discover the time of her birth to the hour. We do know that a very rare configuration was present approximately at that time. If she was born then, she had a totally compelling destiny."

"I wasn't really thinking of trying to learn my own destiny," Harwell said. "What I hoped was that I could see Interzod's capabilities demonstrated in some way that I could appreciate because I knew the person."

"That's another rule I've kept to. I couldn't do it for anyone living simply for demonstration purposes. That's always seemed like a misuse."

"Someone dead?"

"Certainly. Any time you like. I would have to know when he was born to the hour, preferably to the minute, but only rarely is that absolutely necessary."

The telephone rang and Alexei answered it. "I'll check it from the monitoring set," he said; "alert me for any message at all." He hung up and said, "I'm sorry, but I'll be busy for the rest of the night. I'll have a car for you at the front door that will take you to the helicopter. You'll be in Washington in twenty minutes or so. I hope you don't mind seeing yourself out, but in another two minutes the action will get hectic."

They shook hands. "Remember to learn all you can about your example—your dead one—" Alexei called over his shoulder as he started upstairs to the monitoring room.

Harwell took the liberty of pouring himself a cup of cold coffee from the pot before leaving. The library was at the back of the house. Following a narrow corridor, he reached the large square front entrance hall. Before he reached it the door opened and the airdale bounded in, followed by Mrs. Abarnel, wearing a light raincoat, looking flushed and breathing as though she had been running with the dog. She unfastened a silk kerchief, shook her hair loose and saw him as she looked up. "It's raining," she said. "Can't we lend you a raincoat?"

"Thank you, a car is taking me to the airport." But her offer touched him; she had a simple directness that magnified the value of everything she said or did. As in few other moments of his life, he wished that something more could be said. Then, as Diana and Eliot entered, he saw the car draw up and said his goodbyes.

9

⊙

Few people other than those employed by Interzod ever came to the historical-research section. It was a new steel and concrete building constructed within the weathered wood exterior of the old stable. In appearance it was only one storey high, but a second storey had been made by digging a cavernous basement. The structure was windowless because precise control of temperature and humidity was essential.

By far the largest room was the library, a huge room nearly filled with row upon row of slim twenty-foot-high stacks containing hundreds of thousands of microfilm reels. To the left was a hallway, and at the end a room where two men were standing over a table. Suspended above them was a large flat light, of the kind used in operating rooms, which cast a brilliant purplish glow over the men and the scroll .they were examining. They were engaged in unrolling a scroll of great antiquity, at the rate of less than half an inch per day. At every stage the progress was photographed by a variety of processes because at any moment the resilience that had held it together for over two thousand years might be claimed by time and the scroll would crumble into dust.

"We'll be at it another two weeks," one of the men told Alexei as he came up to them.

"Can it be dated yet?"

"Not yet. But I would say 350 to 400 B.C.—much like the others."

"Where's Dr. Horne?" Alexei asked.

"In the Aramaic section."

There were no doors on this floor. One room led to another by broad arches, each with a table or two, some desks and books. In one, a man stared absorbedly at a slide projection of figures carved on a stone tablet. In another a group of three men, all bearded and one wearing a burnoose, were jabbering over a papyrus they had been examining for weeks. Alexei passed by unnoticed.

Alexei wondered what Admiral Sherborne would have said if he had been brought here. Nothing, probably; Alexei would have had to offer an explanation. That was Sherborne's failing: his inquisitiveness didn't extend to Alexei's world. All Alexei would have to do was wave his hand, mutter something about "historical feedback" and Sherborne would be content.

But if Alexei gauged him right, General Dunne would not pass the first scroll room without demanding, "What the hell goes on here?" and Alexei would happily tell him that this was what Interzod was really all about. History past and recent was examined here, made intelligible and gleaned for vital facts. History that had been buried in the sands of Syria, entombed in scrolls or carved in stone. The recording of history had been accomplished by great labor in previous civilizations, and it was precious. Would anyone today, Alexei sometimes wondered, have anything so valuable to say that he would carve it on a stone tablet?

The international character of Interzod worked both ways. The return was unlimited access to historical information of all kinds. Records of births and deaths and marriages in villages and towns across America, Europe, Africa and Asia had been photographed and stored on microfilm. Most of it was rubbish. But there were treasures to be found, and selected facts were entered into the computer memory banks —a name, a date, the beginning of a life whose accomplishment and character history had reason to record. From monasteries and abbeys came records, long-neglected biographical data, much of it abandoned there by travelers or early Christians and not destroyed, because history and the written word were still considered valuable. Interzod surveillance teams were often composed of people who made unlikely detectives but were highly convincing as scholars. Documents stolen by Crusaders or marauding soldiers inexplicably had found their way to archives in England, Germany and France. Interzod rescued them from their long sleep, photographed them and passed them on. Some participating governments were curious about this, and Alexei, partly to allay their unstated fears, partly to make them understand the contribution history made to Interzod operations, gave them a full explanation. On at least six occasions, heads of state visiting the United States had asked to see the historical-research division. Each of them was impressed; yet the world at large knew little of the undertaking.

Wembley was hunched over his desk. He handed Alexei a sheaf of papers without a word, and Alexei sank into a leather armchair and began reading. He nodded from time to time, then looked up at Wembley, who was watching him carefully.

"You're right; it does rank with other imperative profiles. It's a shame. How did he die?"

"Influenza, apparently."

"The creative imperative is especially rare in writers. We've found how many? Dante, Melville, who else? Oh, yes, Chaucer. We began by calling it the Chaucer imperative, didn't we? Then we discovered Dante. It doesn't seem to say everything for creativity, does it? Or you would have expected to find Shakespeare on the list. Now Josiah Blue, dead at seventeen, Gloucester, Massachusetts, 1744. There wasn't much in American writing in those days. What could you find out about him?"

"What we looked for, of course, was some indication that the imperative had begun to take hold. The last case of this kind of unrealized imperative that we found was born in a Chinese fishing village where there was no opportunity for learning to read and write. She was a woman, and it was believed that she was sold as a bride when a child. This amounts to forcible restraint which *could* counteract the imperative, but we have no record of her life. We can conjecture that the imperative manifested itself in the tradition of oral literature. She may have been a storyteller of the first rank, ordering her world with poetic imagination and leaving her impress to a limited audience, but of course there is almost no hope of verifying it.

"In the case of Josiah Blue we failed to find any evidence that the imperative was realized. We did discover that he had gone through the fifth grade, which would have been enough for him to carry on, but there the record ends. The evidence of his death was a simple notation in a family Bible—no details. If he died in Gloucester we would have expected to find a headstone in the family plot or a record of funeral services in the parish record, which seemed to have been fairly well kept at the time. As it turned out, we did not. I supposed it was going to be one of those cases we'd never learn more about, but now, quite unexpectedly, the rest of the story has come to light. The chances were really rather small, you know.

"A short time ago we came by several hundred old ships' logs from a collector in Portsmouth. Most dated from the eighteenth century and were from American merchantmen. We photographed them for the historical index, and the computer scanner picked up the name Josiah Blue. The log was of the *Margaret Weston*; the entry for August 3rd, 1744. The excerpt is there on the final page."

Alexei read aloud: "Josiah Blue, apprentice to John Waltham, ship's carpenter, departed from this life at the beginning of the third watch. His fever had greatly increased in the past several days and he was unable to take nourishment. At 0700 hours I ordered the ship altered to a northerly course in hopes we could find a wind to take us to Santa Moreno where it was hoped we could replenish our store of medical supplies which have been greatly depleted during the past month. He died in great delirium in the compartment of the forward hatch where he had been removed for fear of general contagion to the crew. The officers and the crew were mustered on the quarter deck where he was buried at sea following Christian burial services in which his soul was commended to almighty God. In compliance with his wishes, as conveyed to me by Mr. Waltham, the great quantity of papers in his sea chest on which he had written with marvelous diligence during those hours allotted to him by Mr. Waltham since joining the ship eighteen months before, were scattered over the seas from the taffrail when we were once again underway. May God in his mercy receive the soul of Josiah Blue."

The discovery of zodiacal formulations indicating an imperative drive were extremely rare, and Wembley never failed to alert Alexei when the computer signaled that one had been located, either in the past or present. An accurate interpretation of how the imperative blossomed was even rarer—impossible in most cases, since the world is so much older than its history, leaving the vast bulk of astrological events with no records. Even when there were records it was usually impossible to place them in an accurate chronology. In relative terms, the year 1744 belonged to the present, to the world of accurate calendars and modern timepieces. Moreover, Gloucester, Massachusetts, was a town with a strong maritime tradition, and since mariners are able to find their precise position in a vast markless ocean only if they possess an accurate timepiece, the habit of recording the time of important events, such as the birth of a son, runs deep. Josiah Blue had presented a comparatively easy problem. Everything important had been fitted into place with only one notable omission: the words he had written on the pages that filled his sea chest. The results of the hours of diligence spent lying in his tossing bunk would never be judged.

In the beginning intensity was the quality that attracted Alexei to Wembley. When he saw that the program's success depended on the excellence of the historical staff, he picked Wembley to head it. At that time he had only known him slightly. Wembley was a scholar with impeccable qualifications. Ancient languages and classical history—Greek, Hebrew, Syriac, Coptic, Egyptian—were his bailiwick, and he was the author of several works of distinction and perception. No one was his match in grasping historical processes. Naturally, his first reaction to Alexei's proposal was point-blank refusal. It took nearly a year of careful cultivation and endless demonstrations to prove to Wembley that the offer was a greater challenge than anything else he might undertake, and since then his astonishing dedication had been transferred to Interzod.

At that time Alexei had known nothing of Wembley's private wartime discoveries; indeed, he had been somewhat surprised to learn that Wembley had been a major in a British tank corps, though when the details were all in place, it seemed eminently plausible. When the war broke out, he was already a scholar with a considerable reputation, but few realized that his reputation extended as far as an unhappy German army supply corporal garrisoned on Crete.

Because Wembley had known Crete well from prolonged stays of as much as two years at a time, he was called in to assist in administration after the German surrender to Cretan guerrilla forces in 1944. It was hard to imagine Wembley in those days because there was nothing of the soldier left in his tall, slightly stooped gray figure. He was assigned to the British occupation forces and installed himself with another officer in a house where he had stayed several times before the war. One afternoon he got a telephone call from a Colonel Bentley, who was in command of the German prisoner-of-war camp, with the message that a German corporal by the name of Karl Haustoffer had asked permission to see him. "Bentley had been sitting on this request for three weeks trying to get Haustoffer to tell him why he wanted to talk to me," Wembley complained in telling the story to Alexei. "Haustoffer would only say that it was a personal matter and refused to detail it in writing, until he saw that Bentley was an idiot; finally he claimed that he had information about my brother. Now it so happens that a brother is something I've never had, so my first thought was that Corporal Haustoffer was making a wild stab in order to get out of the prisoner's compound, possibly to escape. I told Bentley to forget it. About a week later a pretty young woman, a native Cretan, rode up to my house on a bicycle and asked me if I was Professor Wembley. Only the Cretans

I'd known before the war called me that, but then she really made me sit up by saying that Corporal Haustoffer wished to speak to me about a supplement to the Peloponnesian codex. Now only someone with some knowledge of history would know anything about the Peloponnesian codex, which is a seventh-century manuscript. It isn't really a codex at all, just a fragment of one, but it was something I had examined and written about at some length in one of my books. The mention of a supplement suggested that the corporal knew the whereabouts of more of it, which might be a very important find. I thanked the girl and called Colonel Bentley and infuriated him by telling him that I remembered I had a brother after all.

"They brought Haustoffer up to town in a truck with four soldiers, which I thought was overdoing it since he was a thin graying man who didn't look like trouble.

" 'Herr Major Professor' is how he addressed me. Then he told me the suggestion that he knew of a supplement to the Peloponnesian codex was not true. But he did know of some kind of find—a parchment—which he'd discovered in a bomb crater one of our planes had made near an abandoned monastery. He'd heard my name mentioned by another British officer and knew I would know what to do with the thing.

"I asked him how he happened to know of me, and he said he had been a theology major before the war and had hit on my book. He said he believed the explosion had opened some kind of vault or crypt, and as he was on the fringes of a battle when he made the discovery, he'd stuffed it into a soldier's discarded canvas kit bag and covered it up with earth as best as he could before moving on.

"Crete has turned up a lot of Christian apocryphal literature, and I knew that this could be of great interest. Of course it could just as well be rubbish. By this time I had begun to see that the corporal wasn't a bad sort, and I decided to run up to Gortyna to have a look at his monastery. I didn't particularly care to have the four soldiers along, so I told them I'd take custody of the prisoner. Colonel Bentley had given them orders not to let me do precisely that, so this required another telephone hassle. In the end he agreed to let me have Haustoffer for twenty-four hours if I would agree to take along one soldier, named Petrades, as a driver and liaison for any guerrilla troops we might meet.

"It took us a long time to make the thirty miles because nobody had been repairing roads during the past few months and our transport, a German staff car, kept boiling over. Once when he stopped in an orange grove to let it cool off, our driver came up with a bottle of wine and Haustoffer told us something about himself. He said he'd been wounded early in the war and had been put on garrison duty in Crete. When the Germans first began to pull out their combat-line troops a few months before, he'd gone AWOL—took to the countryside by himself—because he'd learned that his supply outfit was to be transferred to the infantry and he knew this would mean duty on the Russian front. He'd lived a precarious existence for a while because either the Germans or the Cretan guerrillas would have shot him, and he figured he'd be in for a rough time no matter who won. After the official German surrender, he'd managed to give himself up safely.

"Petrades asked him what he thought would happen to him; he had some sympathy for Haustoffer, I thought. Haustoffer shrugged and said he knew he'd be sent back to Germany soon but he hoped to return to Crete some day. He was a little shy about it because he sensed that the Cretans might not be hospitable toward a former German soldier. We didn't talk much archaeology, but he did say he'd tried to familiarize himself with the Minoan diggings and had liked to spend his leaves at Knossos and Salmis.

"When we reached Gortyna Haustoffer was a little confused about the location of the monastery, and we drove around the dry hill country for three or four hours before he pointed to a low jumble of masonry. We got out. There were some craters to one side but they were shallow and looked like light-artillery craters. I couldn't see any evidence that the ruins had been a monastery, so I began to be pretty suspicious of his motives. He dug around in several of the craters, but then it began to get dark. None of us felt much like going back to Gortyna that night, so Petrades found us dinner and a place to sleep in a farmhouse close by. I think Haustoffer guessed I was suspicious about the whole business;

at any rate, he made a point of telling me he had no intention of trying to escape and assured me he really had found some kind of early manuscript. Just the same, I was surprised when I found him still there the next morning, wrapped in an old blanket in a corner of the room we all slept in.

"We had breakfast and by daybreak were back rummaging around the craters again. Petrades didn't think much of the expedition but finally when we explained we were looking for a German kit bag he jumped down and helped us and it was actually he who found it. It contained four pieces of vellum and one small papyrus scroll. Both of them were very excited, and were disappointed when I told them the scroll couldn't be opened and read on the spot, for fear of mutilating it. They asked me at least to read the writing on the vellum, which was in Syriac. As I say, the pieces were fragmentary, but they seemed to deal with the Nestorian conflict; the words Ephesus and Patriarch appeared. This would appear to date them from about the fifth century, but the question arose as to why Syriac writing would be found at Gortyna, when presumably any such monastic papers would be written in Greek. We dug further around the crater for quite a while but didn't find any more papers—though I did find a fragment of an enameled object which I quite frankly pocketed."

At this point in his narrative Wembley usually produced the enamel, which he carried as a pocket piece. It was blue over bronze, with a small piece of filigree scrollwork also in bronze. Listeners expected him to continue with an exposition of the contents of the manuscripts after this; instead, he almost invariably returned to Corporal Haustoffer.

"It was late afternoon when we left Gortyna and while we stopped to let our car cool off, Petrades had something to tell me. "It's only an hour out of the way if we take the road to the left." Before I could ask him why we should go an hour out of our way he explained that Haustoffer would like to go that way. "He has a woman in town there," he said simply, and again, before I could register disapproval he confided that it was Haustoffer's wife, quickly amending it to the statement that she had borne him a child and that they were the reason he'd gone

AWOL. "He will not see them again for a long time. Perhaps never."
A Cretan soldier had very little reason to take such a sympathetic attitude toward a German prisoner of war, but such generosity is essentially Greek. To tell the truth the man shamed me, especially since I was personally obliged to Haustoffer for the manuscripts. Petrades didn't take his eyes off me while I made up my mind. I agreed to it, though certainly I wouldn't have if I'd known that we would be on the road again until after nightfall—hardly a good idea, since small bands of German soldiers were still in the hills and the guerrilla troops hunting them down might well blast a German staff car containing a uniformed German soldier.

At the small fishing village, which is typical of that part of Crete, the arrangement with Haustoffer was that he could visit his child and adopted wife under Petrades' escort. Petrades would join me in a little café, where we would try to amuse ourselves for three hours, at which point the Greek would return for him. Haustoffer was very happy about this, as you can imagine. I don't think he'd dreamed he'd have the chance to see them again.

At the café the two of us ordered some wine and a supper of fish. I remember that I was hungry since we'd eaten nothing since breakfast. We were very thirsty but we hadn't gone through much of the bottle of wine before I saw Haustoffer coming across the little square. I didn't recognize him at first because he was wearing a long shepherd's cloak and was carrying his German uniform rolled up in a ball. He came up to us, thanked us profusely for allowing him this privilege and apologized for shedding his uniform, which he'd done in order to walk through the town without being shot. With no other explanation, he got in the car, sat down and stared straight in front of him. Petrades went over and urged him to join us in supper, but Haustoffer refused. Petrades added that Haustoffer appeared to have been crying, and punctuated this with a shrug, as though it was the lot of all of us. Of course it was easy enough to guess what had happened, and a few weeks later when I was leaving Crete for Rome, I saw Petrades again and he said that before they'd reached the P.O.W. camp, Haustoffer had broken down completely and told him he'd found his wife in bed with a Greek soldier. She had restrained the Greek from shooting but ordered him out of the place without giving him a chance to see his child."

Now Wembley would finally get back to the manuscripts, though his reports of their contents might vary somewhat according to his listener. To Alexei he gave a complete and accurate translation. The four fragments of vellum were part of a codex manuscript dealing with the Council of Ephesus, which had been held in the middle of the fifth century. To most listeners he would quickly add that the Ephesian Council had been summoned to deal with Nestorius, a monk with a large following who took an independent view of the significance of the Virgin Birth, objecting, as many Protestants were to do centuries later, to the tendency of the Church to refer to Mary as the "Mother of God."

"Nestorius wasn't a bad fellow," Wembley would explain. "He was highly devout and ascetic, but he was troubled by a metaphysical inconsistency, you see, and thought that the *humanity* of Mary and Jesus deserved the same emphasis as their divinity." After allowing this to sink in, he would sometimes add, "Some people found it pretty tough sledding to worship humanity, especially Cyril of Alexandria, who saw to it that Nestorius would have to back down or be excommunicated. Nestorius wasn't about to back down, so he was excommunicated and banished as well. But we can't forget his followers, who held sway in a good many monasteries in Greece and Syria. They'd written a mass of material supporting Nestorius, all of which was promptly declared heretical, and their position in many cases became quite uncomfortable. For a lot of them, it was a choice of moving on, usually to an obscure monastery someplace where the Nestorian heresy wasn't much of an issue, or else facing up to disagreeable persecution.

"It's my notion, you see, that the fellow who wrote the codex was such a man—a monk, a Syrian, a follower of Nestorius—who came to Crete to find a little peace and quiet and to get rid of some of the smart by quietly writing and thinking in the outlawed Nestorian vein. He goes so far as to refer to Nestorius as a martyr, and he sees the Ephesian Council as a cynical travesty of Christian faith. Interesting, don't you think?"

Whether one thought so or not, the listener *was* anxious to hear what was in the papyrus scroll, having sensed that Wembley had saved it until last for a purpose.

"A good example of early apocryphal church literature," he would say. "Very early example, somewhere in the middle of the first century. It is written in Hebrew, by an early Hebrew Christian. In point of time he could have been an apostle, but neither the style nor the paleography have anything in common with known apostolic manuscripts. The writer appears to have been a priest before his conversion, and parts of the scroll suggest that he had a knowledge of earlier Hebraic apocalyptic literature. Of course, such manuscripts are relatively common, but this one is unique in some respects, the most intriguing of which are references to the birth and life of Mary. The vividness and naturalness of these references give a strength to her humanity. As in other Christian writings, she is depicted as a girl of seventeen at the time of her marriage to Joseph, who was past eighty. A May and December marriage, what?

"As you know, there are two versions of Jesus' conception to be found in the Bible, one having it that Joseph begat him and the other holding out for heavenly begetting." Then, to clarify his position to whoever had listened this far, Wembley would interject, "I don't know your stand on the Virgin Birth notion, but I've always liked it. Without it, Christ has always seemed to me like a kind of superior social worker. I don't say a man shouldn't be critical of any or all of the articles of Christian dogma, but I've always felt that if you can swallow that one, you've come a long way down the road. I, for one, *have* swallowed it . . . But never mind, my point is that our Hebrew papyrus argues quite plainly in favor of the Virgin Birth. In fact, it goes further and makes the highly interesting assertion that Joseph could *not* have been the father. I find a lot of earthly humanity in that, and it in no way detracts from anyone's divinity.

"Of course, there have been other references to Mary's nativity, especially *Nativitae de Maria*, the apocryphal manuscript which, interestingly enough, was written by another Cretan in the seventh century, St. Andrew. The Hebraic papyrus goes further in its detail, however, so that not only are we given the day and year of her birth, but by a homely touch, the hour, specified by the phrase "as the cock crew . . ." Of course, an astronomer can calculate the hour of sunrise on any day past or future, from which we can figure out cock-crowing time."

Before any question could be raised about this, Wembley would say bluntly, "It's perfectly plain to me on the strength of internal evidence that St. Andrew of Crete had access to the papyrus and selected some passages for inclusion in his *Nativitae de Maria*. Of course he was careful to leave out anything that would lead to the accusation that he was reviving the old Nestorian heresy." Yawning, as though he were minimizing the importance of the papyrus and his excellent scholarship, Wembley would then trail off, avoiding any further comment or questions.

10

⊙

Eliot looked up from a magnifier mounted over the map table in the center of his office. He stood perfectly still for several moments, his body so relaxed that he swayed slightly from side to side. It was an unconscious state of concentration familiar to friends and colleagues when he submerged himself in a problem.

Finally he straightened up and turned off the map light. He had done it. Finished! The project known as the Quetor Research Project was complete. It had come to a finale which he would have announced out loud if anyone had been there. Instead he sat down at his desk facing the wall and propped up his feet. The only person who would appreciate this moment was Alexei—in fact, he was the only one who knew anything about it. This didn't bother Eliot; he was used to projects which were of no interest to anyone but himself.

But in this case, Alexei's interest was far stronger than his own. At times it amounted to an enthusiasm which Eliot failed to understand.

In the past few weeks, when Eliot realized that the end was near, Alexei had called him or dropped in at the historical-research center almost every day to find out how he was getting along on "the Quetor business." He was the only person to give his report to, but it would have to wait because Alexei was out of town until tonight or tomorrow. In any case, Eliot would wait until tomorrow because once Alexei knew, he would be sure to drag him back to the office to examine the map for himself. Until then he could finish writing the report; this would be simple because Alexei had assured him he wanted nothing more than an outline of the important points.

Eliot's feeling of satisfaction at this moment was in contrast to the darker thoughts he'd harbored during the past months. Even at the outset he'd had reservations, though the first few weeks had been spent in London, Denmark and Switzerland, which he looked upon as a vacation. But toward the end he'd had to read all the nonsense old Cyrus Maitland had ever written—unpublished manuscripts, monographs, journals, personal diaries and letters. Maitland had been a pretentious old fool with a trashy, fraudulent sensibility, and it had had a highly depressing effect. Then there was the feeling that this work was far beneath his professional skills and capabilities. It was a job for some kind of detective, and it rankled that Alexei treated him as a kind of highbrow sleuth. At times Eliot felt he was valued only for his "expertise." Any clever person could have done this job, and he had said as much, but Alexei had refused to release him from his agreement to see it through to the end. He was adamant even when Eliot had told him that he was being offered a university fellowship for which he had been angling for years—a plea that happened to be true, though it was also true that it would still be available to him in the fall.

Now he would be able to tell Alexei that the legends of St. Quetor were true and that the church still existed. Alexei would immediately want to know where, and Eliot would supply him with the latitude and longitude. He would also have the pleasure of telling him that the natives used the church for drying and storing fish. In the photograph, fish were strung from poles and from the rafters. Why did Alexei give a damn? Not only that he cared a great deal—why did he care at all? Eliot knew he would not ask. Alexei could look very formidable if the subject was broached. Yet his apparently unwarranted enthusiasm—an obsession, it sometimes seemed—had been apparent from the outset. It was in his eyes and voice when he handed Eliot an envelope of papers and said, "Begin by reading this and letting me know if you believe it authentic." The envelope contained photostated copies of an account of inquisitorial proceedings against a Franciscan friar named Alvaro du Fonesca, which were concluded in 1602. The part of the text dealing with the actual proceedings was written in wooden, rickety Latin, and the author's point of view raised questions as to his position at these proceedings. Perhaps in an attempt at objectivity or perhaps because he wished to present it as one might a novel or a romance, he reported the words of each contestant with equal vigor and vehemence, though as might be expected, the inquistors and accuser, a Bishop of Malacca, were allowed to say more than the friar.

The case against Friar Alvaro contained a curious sequel entitled "The Life of Saint Quetor." It was written in a different style and hand. Apparently this account hadn't been heard at the trial and if it had been written by a friend or by the friar himself, its inclusion was a mystery since there were risks in circulating heretical propaganda.

As stated in the part of the text dealing with the trial, Friar Alvaro had been a passenger on a Portuguese ship when it was overtaken by a storm, driving them far out of their course for Malacca. They drifted for several weeks before they were able to put in at an island for supplies. Friar Alvaro was so moved by the islanders' heathen state that he resolved to remain, and to this effect sent a letter to the Bishop of Malacca by way of the captain. He remained on the island for twenty-five years and had extraordinary success in converting the entire island population to Christianity. This success, he claimed, was due entirely to the existence of the legend of a certain St. Quetor, who was given reverence due an important ancestor and was the subject of much of the islanders' traditional oral poetry, which was recited on feast days.

Eliot had to admit that the legend was fascinating in every respect.

Quetor's mother, it went, when a young girl not long past puberty, had a dream in which she was told to go to the other side of the island and live by herself for an entire year. The village elders objected because it was irregular and dangerous, the other side of the island being remote and the dwelling place of evil spirits. But when the girl insisted, they finally relented and she was taken there by canoe.

When the men returned a year later, she walked toward them nursing a newborn baby. The baby was so young that they knew the father must have been one of the spirits. *Tor* is the word for "son of" in the island dialect. Hence the child's name, Que being the local god of practical jokes, minor misfortunes and traditionally accused of siring the island's fatherless children.

When Quetor was old enough so that he no longer ate with the women and was allowed to listen to the men at the council fire, a raiding party from a neighboring island took him, three other young men and two girls captive. At this time, cannibalism was prevalent in that part of the archipelago. Warfare was the principal activity of the men, and the young were always prize captives. There was no agriculture, though women gathered roots in the forest and there was some fishing, so human flesh was highly esteemed and nothing else was eaten on feast days.

It was generally believed that Quetor and his companions would be eaten alive, and the other women of the village came to sit with his mother during the mourning period for the dead. But Quetor's mother refused to mourn and told the women that Quetor would return safely. On the following day he and his companions were returned in a war canoe by six of their captors. Quetor said that he had asked the men not to burn and eat them, and they had not. The men of Quetor's island were amazed, but they seized the six enemies, tied them to stakes and began gathering fire wood.

Quetor was ready to perform his miracle. He came before the council fire and told the elders that they must not burn the six men. To speak at the council fire was presumptuous for a young man; the elders became angry and his request was ignored.

The fires were lit, but when they had burned down to ashes, the six men were still alive and unhurt. As more wood was piled around the victims, Quetor stood up at the council fire again to ask the elders not to eat the victims. Again his advice was ignored, again the fires were lit, and again when they died down the men were still alive. This time many of the elders were frightened and some of them took Quetor's side. But they were voted down and the entire process was repeated once more. After this, all the elders sided with Quetor.

Now Quetor called to the victims and they walked unhurt through the smoldering embers and told the men at the council fire that Quetor had performed the same miracle on their island and told them that if they promised never to eat human flesh again they themselves would not be eaten. (During the proceedings at the inquisitorial trial, Friar Alvaro explained that in the island dialect, to eat flesh and to burn flesh is the same word. "Consume" would be a better English rendering.)

Quetor then told the islanders that if they made the same promise, they too would not be eaten. All the people agreed to this. They also credited Quetor with teaching them how to cultivate yams and taro root, to tame and husband the wild boar and how to preserve fish by smoking. When they had mastered these arts, Quetor set out alone in a canoe, promising to return. According to the legend, he spent the rest of his life visiting other islands, performing his miracle, giving his promise and teaching the arts of agriculture and animal husbandry.

He returned to his own island when he was an old man, using the same canoe he'd set out in. When he died he was buried in it.

The implications of the St. Quetor legend wakened the anthropolgist in Eliot. He was well aware that generally primitive religions did not embody ethical or moral standards; usually they resembled the pagan pantheism of classical Greece, with capricious carefree gods who guarded such practical things as fire, water, fertility and warfare. Primitive gods were never transcendent, were unconcerned with moral precepts and frequently behaved even worse than the run of mortals. The notion of a miraculous birth was common enough in primitive societies, but Quetor's dramatic promise that those who refrained from consuming flesh would not themselves be consumed seemed an uncharacteristic appeal to a higher moral standard, and one which would be expected only in a far more sophisticated religious system.

Among the heretical crimes with which Friar Alvaro du Fonesca was charged were conducting Mass in the native tongue; an incursion on Papal preogatives in canonizing Quetor and having his bones dug up and buried beneath the altar of the church he built on the island; breaking the vows of chastity by taking a native girl as his wife; and allowing the church to be used for smoking fish.

Friar Alvaro had made a tactical mistake in defending himself, rather than admitting all and asking forgiveness, because his defense could not be based on doctrine but only on practicality. It was vain to argue that when he spoke Latin at Mass, the islanders were convulsed with laughter or that they would never accept the authority of a man who was not married and had nothing to do with women. As for St. Quetor, incorporating him into the church did much for the islanders' acceptance of an otherwise alien religion. It was true that Quetor had never been baptized and that therefore the miracles he performed could not be said to have been performed in the name of Christ or Rome, but the alternatives—to disavow him or ignore him—were impossible.

Such a defense was heretical on its face, and the inquisitors would not hear of it. They also ignored Friar Alvaro's zeal in getting the natives to build the church according to his specifications. Constructed of clay and timbers by a method of construction unknown on the island, it resembled a village church in Portugal. The inquisitors were more interested in the fact that once he had caused it to be erected, he had permitted fish to be dried there.

That stirred Eliot to admiration. What a wily friar he was to think of that! If a Christian church was to be superimposed on this heathen pantheistic island, what better way of ensuring acceptance than to sanctify the god of fertility, as well as allowing the church to be a center of his ritual worship?

The inquisitors were less admiring than Eliot; in the year 1602, Friar Alvaro du Fonesca was burned as an unrepentant heretic at Granada.

From a literary standpoint, the authenticity of these documents seemed assured. A fraudulent account would probably be better written, would not consist of two parts and would have a more coherent dramatic structure. However, the Vatican archives yielded no other reference to the trial or to the church mission to the islands, though the bishop was known to have been recalled from Malacca, which might mean that he had stopped off at the island to catch Friar Alvaro in his malfeasance. There was one other reference to the burning of the heretic Friar du Fonesca at Granada in a letter of the same period. This was meager corroboration, but Alexei assured him that technically the documents had been found authentic, meaning that the paper had not been manufactured at a later date.

Eliot answered that he couldn't accept a verification unless he had the chance to examine the documents himself. Two weeks later he had the opportunity, and found their authenticity unquestionable.

Alexei's interest, however, lay elsewhere. Somewhere within nine or ten days sailing time of the Malay straits was St. Quetor's island. The name was unknown; curiously, it was never mentioned in any of the documents. Apparently it was unimportant to the writer. But as Eliot must realize, Alexei said urgently, no matter what had happened to the island in the hundreds of years that intervened, some memory of St. Quetor must still exist there, and perhaps on other islands as well. After all, oral traditions had preserved legends of the past for much longer periods. Eliot's job was to find that island. He had some acquaintance with the area; he knew Malay, did he not? He had published a paper on primitive calendrical systems there, he had worked with a team which had made an exhaustive study of island migrations of a much earlier period. Eliot was offered whatever funds he would need for travel and assistance, and Alexei assured him that he could arrange for unrestricted access to any of the islands or any territory he needed to visit.

Eliot believed that Alexei had in mind a kind of head-on research approach—field trips and so forth. He had some idea of how many islands lay east of Malacca and of the extraordinary variety of linguistic groupings and subgroupings to be found there, and he foresaw endless hard work and probable futility in field trips in search of elderly natives who would talk into a tape recorder. He decided his approach would be scholarly. He knew that for decades all the islands of the Pacific had been in the hands of missionaries, anthropologists and social workers of every stripe. After returning home most of them wrote articles or books, and almost all lectured about their experiences. The anthropologists were his best hope, he believed, because they had an eye for minute details and the habit of putting them into footnotes. Most anthropologists would be delighted to include a footnote or even a chapter proclaiming the discovery of a combination lawgiver and fertility god, or of a society which celebrated their deliverance from cannibalism.

The cross reference he sought might be under a dozen or so words, titles or subjects, and Eliot spent a month in the library of a professional society of anthropologists and in the British Museum. After two weeks of this he had hired a jobless friend to assist him. Next he went to Germany to conduct the same kind of search in the meticulous archives of German scholarship while his assistant continued on at the British Museum. After ten days, Eliot received a letter with a copy of an article that had appeared in an English quarterly in 1944. His assistant had underlined the sentence "The Dutch Commissioner said that Dr. Cyrus Maitland reported the finding of an early Christian church during his annual survey of the archipelago in the Molucca Sea."

Certainly this sentence was promising, beyond anything Eliot had hoped for. He hadn't expected to find such a direct reference to what he was looking for; in fact it had never occurred to him that Friar Alvaro's church would still be standing as late as 1944. With the aim of learning the island's location he went to Holland, where he learned that the Dutch commissioner, L. Vas Dias, had died six years earlier, and that W. H. Hogelund, the author of the article, had been dead for more than two decades. None of Hogelund's other printed works, nor the unpublished letters, notes and journals which Eliot was allowed to examine, contained any further reference to Dr. Maitland or to the church he had discovered.

Eliot called Alexei in the United States and reported on his progress. An hour later, Alexei called back; a Dr. Cyrus Maitland had been an American citizen, born in Oregon, who had spent much of his life in the Orient but was now believed to be dead.

Hogelund and the commissioner having proved duds, Eliot was down to Maitland and this news was disheartening. He returned to the United States, where he learned that Cyrus Maitland was still alive. This was something that most people in the little town in Oregon where Maitland had been born would dispute. The house had been boarded up for twelve years. Many people did not know he'd ever returned from the Orient, but he had, in 1946, and lived there for several years in close seclusion before committing himself to an asylum—where, within a year, he lapsed into the deeper seclusion of madness.

Eliot tried to see the man, though his doctors told him it was useless. Then he applied to the Maitland family lawyer: "Many valuable papers pertaining to anthropological studies conducted in the South Pacific in the years prior to the Second World War were entrusted to your client, Cyrus Maitland, by Professor W. H. Hogelund, at the onset of the war with Japan, and it is known that they are still in his possession . . ."

The Maitland lawyer, William Archer, bluntly refused a request to search for the papers in his client's house. Eliot wrote a longer, more appealing letter and followed it up with a phone call. Archer was firm; he had no authority to allow Eliot to enter his client's house and he had a duty to protect Mr. Maitland. His reply to Eliot's third and last letter was a thundering, angry refusal. Knowing that Archer was in the right, Eliot could not bring himself to write still another begging letter.

Eliot had never met Archer face to face but when, two months later, after Maitland's death, Alexei arranged for the somewhat irregular entrance into the house via Congressman Harwell, it was Eliot who asked not to be introduced by his own name, which Archer would recognize in case the news leaked back to him. Alexei seemed amused by this but agreed to it.

The weeks that followed their incursion were unpleasant for Eliot. Cyrus Maitland had written reams of irritating, mindless nonsense. His journals were cloyingly personal or bombastic, and he was wickedly vain and pretentious. Eliot learned that he had gone to Japan after college; a homosexual passion for a Japanese instructor seemed to have something to do with this. Maitland saved all his letters and copied some of the more felicitous passages in his journal, which at this period were filled with hyperaesthetic and quite mistaken notions about Japanese art and culture. He was viciously anti-Western, with a clumsy inverted chauvinism which permeated his several monographs on various Japanese art forms. Eliot recognized some of them as inept plagiarisms of Japanese scholarship, many of them classics in Japan which had not been translated into English. When he strayed from imitations or outright thievery, and struck out on his own, Maitland was even more insufferable. Still, he had managed to publish two of them, and from other correspondence Eliot realized that he had become an authority on Oriental art and that his advice was solicited by several American and European museums.

There were excursions into China and Korea. These were unpleasant because Maitland had a squeamish and obsessive intolerance, not of poverty, but of the poor, and his comments on Oriental politics showed him to be thoroughly reactionary. Yet Eliot could not give him a cursory reading, could not skim over this early period as he should have; on every page he encountered fresh revulsion, but he could not bring himself to skip a single word, realizing that from this torment he derived some gross, debased pleasure.

But victory over the jumble of documents from the Maitland library was impossible without respite, and at intervals Eliot turned to the large stack of photographs, which were relatively unmarred by the relentless stamp of the man's personality. There were over four thousand of them, many taken in conjunction with Maitland's literary expositions on Oriental art. Eliot began by weeding out all pictures of bronze statues, lacquer boxes and enamel work. His examination of the journals showed that Maitland had not visited the South Pacific island area until 1931. By that time his interest in art seemed to have waned, and his attention had turned to native villages, expanses of beach and children at play. He had ceased being the aesthete and took tourist photographs.

Eliot mentioned this to Alexei one day. "That's because Maitland had different interests altogether when he came to the islands," Alexei said. "He took a great many more pictures than we see here. We only have those which he did not send back to the Japanese government. He took a great many more of gun emplacements and harbor defenses. During this period, Maitland was working as a spy for the Japanese. As an American, he would attract less suspicion."

"A real spy?"

"He lived comfortably in Kyoto during the war. When he saw Japan was going to lose, he asked to be placed in a prisoner-of-war camp and be allowed to escape into Burma. He had good friends in Japan and they obliged. He escaped into Burma in early 1945. After the war, the American government told him that they knew about his spying activities, but since the Japanese had destroyed the record of his intelligence career, they didn't have enough evidence to prosecute him. I don't know how he got all his records back to Oregon."

Alexei did not seem satisfied with his progress and Eliot didn't blame him; he knew he was being slow. On the other hand, Alexei's impatience puzzled him. The matching of an island to an account of seventeenth-century inquistorial proceedings might be fascinating labor, but it hardly seemed a matter of urgency.

Having separated the island photos, Eliot examined them for some signs of the seventeenth-century church Maitland had reported having seen. Failing to find it, he returned to the journals and other papers, but reading them with a difference, knowing now that Maitland was writing with care not to divulge his intelligence work for the Japanese. The journals were couched in a style as if the writer believed they would interest a publisher one day; his anti-Western antipathies were held in check and he no longer dwelt on the philistinism of his own countrymen. However, he made up for this by ill-natured comparisons of the islanders with the Greeks, Romans and Japanese. But the greatest disappointment was that Maitland had deleted from his writings the names of the islands he had visited. Eliot looked in vain for some coded reference or an account of his intinerary. He asked Alexei if the State Department or the intelligence agency that had uncovered his espionage had any information; perhaps the best would be Maitland's American passport. Alexei thought this was a good idea but soon reported back that no such records existed. He also revealed that he had contacted members of the wartime Japanese-intelligence organization. Their records had been destroyed prior to the surrender, but they were asked to draw from their memories. The man who had recruited Maitland was still alive but he had not been Maitland's immediate contact; that man was dead. Japanese intelligence had been interested in almost every island from Australia to Hawaii to Mindanao, a triangle thousands of miles on a side. Maitland's assignments could have covered any number of the thousands of islands it contained.

Eliot was impressed. There were no limits to the information Alexei could muster on short notice.

Alexei was in Eliot's cubicle on the day he returned to the photographs. The reading had produced nothing except a continuous headache, and the pictures might be more promising, Eliot was saying with a random gesture at the hundreds scattered on the work table. Then he looked down and for the first time felt a surge of excitement. It was a shot of a native market, and in the foreground an old man bent over some fish laid out for display on a mat. Beyond was a wide doorway and the interior of a building strung everywhere with fish. But the building was what Eliot was seeing for the first time—a building with thick, heavy walls, apparently stucco. It took an expert eye to look beyond all the fish and see that the walls were different from the spindly native construction in the background of the picture.

Suddenly Eliot remembered seeing other market scenes. Wordlessly he handed the photo to Alexei and began rummaging through the pile. There were others: one from a distance with a small boy gawking up at the camera and beyond him the building, unnoticed when Eliot had first looked at it, but startlingly different from those around it— taller, with a peaked roof and resembling a church because of a construction at one end which looked like a bell tower that had been shorn off or had fallen in.

A third photograph showed a direct view of the front entrance under the truncated tower or steeple. Beneath it, in dead center, was an opening that could originally have been closed off by two large doors, but was now boarded over. There was another market stall at this end, and on the side opposite that used by the fish market were other shorter buildings of makeshift construction. It was the kind of church building one could see in villages all across Europe. It could have been built long before or long after the seventeenth century, for it was the church built wherever materials were limited to sunbaked clay and rough timbers. In this photograph, one saw that the market place occupied a flat space near a harbor where there were a number of native craft. On the land on the other side of the harbor a mountain rose up to several thousand feet.

Instantly Eliot knew their next step. "If this picture was taken in the late 1930s," he said, "the scene can't have changed very much by 1941 when the Air Force took countless aerial photographs of the South Pacific. The British also took a large number before the war. I've had experience with aerial photography; I've used it extensively to locate sites for archaeological diggings. The procedure here is quite simple, really; we look for an island harbor with a mountain on one side and a town with a market on the other. When we find one, we put it on the magnifier and look for the church. It will be a large roof with a squarish tower surrounded by roofs of native buildings. Very distinctive."

Alexei looked at him with respect.

Examining the aerial photographs had gone quickly because it could be seen at a glance whether an island contained the combination of harbor, town and mountain. Eliot had not expected to find their goal in a group as far east as the New Hebrides. The assumption could only be that the document erred in the estimated position of the ship carrying Friar Alvaro when the storm struck. On reflection Eliot thought it was just as likely that Maitland had told the commissioner the church had been in the Moluccas to conceal the fact that he had been spying in the New Hebrides. The structure was perched on the southern side of a native fishing village of five or six hundred dwellings. There were four

THE ASTROLOGER

other substantial buildings of modern construction and two smaller
native communities inland. Eliot was positive that he had found the
right place at last.

There had been surprisingly little personal conversation between
Eliot and Alexei, even though he was sleeping under his roof and eating
at his table. It would be awkward, Eliot realized, to ask him not to
mention to Diana that his project was finished and that he would be
leaving. Of course he could not leave without notice or saying goodbye,
but he would have preferred to. As it was, he was determined to make
the interval between notice and actual departure as brief as possible.
Sentimental passages in Eliot's life were rare. He had almost never given
anyone a birthday present, for instance, because he found it painful to
be thanked. Goodbyes of the kind facing him were a torment.

He liked Diana very much. He had never been the lover of a girl
quite so attractive. He had lived for long periods without women, and
as a rule was drawn to sensible, practical kinds. Students made the best
mistresses, he believed, because the course of an affair was geared to end
after final exams. As Diana's lover, he had been woefully lacking in
whispered endearments. She tried to induce this on his part, but he
couldn't bring himself to comply even when he realized it was something
she needed. In fact, she needed to be *told* she was loved more than she
needed to be loved. She tended to look on everything that passed
between them as either proof or denial of his affection. This was also
responsible for the little demands—the errands, the favors—proofs he
could perform and wanted to because in fact he did like her. He had
never regretted his impulsive though somewhat alcoholic entrance into
her bedroom the second night he was under Alexei's roof. He had first
met her the night before in the library by the fire, and she had seemed
as essential part of the agreeable ambiance of the place. At that point
he hadn't yet sorted out the precise relationships in Alexei's household,
and while he knew Kate was his wife, he thought that perhaps Diana
was her older sister because they were so familiar with each other.

Eliot knew that Diana would want him to suggest that she come
away with him. He didn't believe that she would do so, but she would

want him to ask. The thought of her accepting was appalling; she belonged to this household, or one like it. There was no ambiance in Eliot's life. His only permanent refuge was a furnished farmhouse in Massachusetts which he used largely for storing the mountains of books, pamphlets, papers and crate after crate of artifacts gathered on various archaeological and anthropological expeditions. Once a year he visited it to unearth some lost treasure, but the rats were in such complete possession that he preferred to sleep in a motel down the road. In any case, he preferred motels or furnished rooms to houses, and cheap saloons to drawing rooms. He liked to drink, but not for conviviality. As lovely as Diana was, there was no room for her in his life. He could not imagine her any place but here, any more than he could picture Kate elsewhere.

His first impression of Kate had been of her loveliness, and it was still intact. If anything, she seemed to have become more lovely, and this quality extended to everything she said or did. She was a woman totally lacking in malice or guile, and he sometimes avoided looking at her because there was a temptation not to look away again. Similarly, he never quite trusted himself to mention Kate's name when he and Diana were alone because of the chance that he might strike a too-effusive note which Diana, with her unpredictable temperament, would take as a slight.

But it was just as well that Kate had not become a topic between them. Otherwise he would have been tempted to tell Diana about it when he realized that Kate's encounters with the young man on their shopping days in town were carried on with artful subterfuge. The fact that he kept his thoughts about this discovery to himself made it all the more awkward. Not morally shocking, he told himself, since it must be taken into account that Alexei was a number of years older and that she had to spend long, difficult hours alone while he was away from home. No, it was shocking because he had not expected it—shocking simply because it seemed such a sharp contradiction to the rest of her character.

He did not think that he could be mistaken. On Thursdays, Diana remained behind for her singing lesson, and he drove Kate to town alone. On two occasions she had left to shop by herself, arranging to meet him in an hour, and the first time, quite by accident, he had found her sitting with the young man on the bench by the bus station. Eliot felt that one could go only so far in judging conversations that can't be heard, but in this case he trusted his intuition. There were earnest and sympathetic looks, especially earnest on the young man's part. His intentions were clear; he was pressing. But again by intuition, Eliot would have said that they were not yet lovers.

They did not see him on that occasion, and when he saw them again in the same place two weeks later, Eliot honestly did not feel himself guilty of spying because he'd felt quite sure that they would not be there. He was chagrined at himself for having been wrong; it was something he preferred not to know about. He knew that he was still unobserved, and he wouldn't have continued to look except that the young man made a motion to put his hand on hers, which rested in her lap. It was impossible to turn away from the sequel, Kate's gesture of removing her hands in a graceful yet unmistakable refusal.

The following week Kate did not leave him, but asked if he would come with her to the store. She did not go near the bus station, but on the way home he deliberately drove past it. The young man sat alone; Kate did not look in his direction.

Nothing would have induced Eliot to mention any of this to Alexei or Diana. He believed that he had seen the drama in its last stages, that Kate had decided against any further meetings. He was sure of it the following Thursday when Kate pleaded sick and he went to town alone. Even while recognizing his wickedness, he drove past the bus station once more. The young man sat there as if he'd never left, bent over, his hands dangling between his knees.

On an impulse Eliot parked the car. He intended no melodrama; it seemed perfectly clear that Kate had made up her mind and was trying to stick to it. He would be doing her an anonymous service, one she might even have asked him to do if they had known each other better.

The young man looked up when Eliot stopped squarely in front of him and asked, "Are you waiting for Mrs. Abarnel?"

At first the young man's response was only confusion at hearing the question from someone he'd never seen before. Eliot was glad he hadn't been nasty or supercilious. Then he answered tentatively, "Yes."

"I thought you should know that she won't be here. Do you know that she is married?"

A passer-by turned at this question but didn't pause.

"She told me she was," the young man said. "Are you her husband?"

Eliot tried to answer in his most disarming tone. "No, but I wouldn't like to see anything happen that would make her unhappy."

"Unhappy? I would not like that," the young man said firmly, straightening up suddenly.

Eliot tried to place the accent; there was something about the way the fellow wore his clothes and a quality of studied sincerity in his voice and manner that he could not identify.

"I will not make trouble for her. I promise you." He smiled, his teeth very white. It wasn't an objectionable smile and Eliot was thrown off pace. He didn't think he disliked the young man, but since he could think of nothing more to say he turned and left.

11

⊙

The car used to take guests from the airport to the house was parked on the apron runway at the Interzod gate. Eliot leaned against the fender, nodding and listening to Diana inside the car. Takeoff had been delayed for half an hour. The jet stood close by, its generators humming, looking like an ocean liner with light blazing from all the portholes and open doors.

Harwell had been late because arrangements to include him on the trip had begun only that morning. A jeep had taken his luggage to the plane, and he had disappeared inside. When he came out he started toward the car in search of Alexei, but stopped and returned to the plane when he saw him with Kate some distance from the car. They were walking slowly, Alexei's arm around her shoulder, Kate hugging herself to keep warm. Then the pilot came down the gangway and waved, and the two of them turned toward the plane, Alexei still talking. At the bottom of the gangway they kissed, and then Kate stepped back, smiling and waving, shifting from one foot to the other and shivering. As Diana and Eliot waved, Alexei climbed the gangway, the door closed, the stairs were removed and the jet began taxiing to the head of the strip.

"This trip we'll have a larger crew to handle the routine monitoring," Alexei told Harwell. "I've told Varnov he won't be hearing from me unless he has a real emergency. Except for any news from Shillong or Calcutta." He made himself a drink and settled in his chair. "We'll probably pick up Pen Li Ko at Singapore," he said.

He seemed preoccupied and not anxious for talk. Harwell had come aboard with only a sketchy idea of their itinerary. Alexei had called him at ten A.M. to tell him that he was going "east" for two weeks or so, and would he like to come along? Since Harwell's office phone was not secure by Interzod standards, Alexei had alluded to the trip's purpose by saying that he had to "check on the matter we discussed with Admiral Sherborne and General Dunne in my office."

This meant Kasjerte and Shoun, and east meant the Far East, reached via San Diego, Hawaii, Manila and Singapore. Harwell had spent a harried day canceling appointments and arranging to shirk scheduled congressional business until he had cleared a two-week hole in his calendar.

Alexei felt that he was being impelled toward a crisis whose realities had the maddening inexactitude of dreams. As in a bad dream, he was oblivious to the right course of action; he would bicycle over the cliff because, for reasons dreams don't explain, he was powerless to steer away, or he would be rooted to the beach watching the tidal wave that he knew would engulf everything. Everything around him seemed to have a velocity all its own. Saying goodbye at the airfield had put him in a foul temper. Tender moments, or moments which ought to be tender, gave him a whiff of self-consciousness—self-contempt, really. What *could* he say to Kate without hearing the fool talking? He believed he'd been much smoother at first. He supposed that forging ahead without asking himself why had a lot to do with it. Curiosity, overwhelming curiosity, had brought him to the theater that night, and it had been the first fatal step. Arriving late in the middle of the second act, he had immediately guessed which of the six actresses on stage she was. It was a dreadful play, but she was electric. Little stage movement, but expression and a fine voice. Only four lines to deliver in that act but he still remembered each of them.

In the next four hectic days he tried to do the conventional things with her. He had proposed without forethought. He actually felt sorry that she didn't find something fishy about it. None of the things they did came off conventionally. She liked to tell him things but talked little about herself. Father dead, mother in a nursing home near Philadelphia —they'd gone together to see her on the third day and he'd bought her the airdale at a kennel on the drive back. She said little about her childhood. No wonder; at eighteen it wasn't over yet. He believed he would be the closing episode.

What had he expected to find? He couldn't remember. But there had been surprises. She was light-hearted, for instance. She was simply and unaffectedly kind—but that wasn't unexpected. She was oblivious to politics and her education was minimal; he was grateful for that, he remembered.

Whenever they'd kissed, he wondered what he might have felt if he had allowed himself feeling. He began by asking her if she thought she would like to be married. He meant it as a general question—had she ever thought of marriage—and that's how she understood it.

She didn't answer quickly, but began talking carefully about all the ways she'd thought about marriage. He interrupted her; she could be very touching at such moments and he risked being deterred if he listened. "I'd like to marry you," he told her. "I'd like that very much."

He had never figured out whether she expected this. He hadn't framed it as a question because he was afraid of what an impulsive answer might be. She looked at him carefully and gravely for several moments. "Would you?" she asked at last. It was a very straightforward question; she genuinely wanted assurance. Had he mentioned love? He couldn't remember, but if the word had seemed necessary at the time he would have used it. It was a time for eloquence, and he hadn't yet begun to rebuke himself for his calculated intervention in this girl's life.

He felt that she would accept him, and a day later when he put it as a simple question she answered that she would. He remembered her willing but rather awkward kisses of the first two days—awkward on his part too because there was more to be said. He hadn't thought of how he would put it but he had known that he must proceed very carefully and that it couldn't wait. Any delay would imply he was having second thoughts. "There *are* complications, Kate," he began earnestly. "If you hear me out you may not want to go ahead with it." Then he had to go into the absurd conditions under which they would have to live— those preposterous denials of fulfillment. Urging abstinence on a beautiful girl of eighteen called for appeals to a higher value. Yet proposing a mutual martyrdom for this sake seemed sappy and unconscionable. For how long? He couldn't tell. She must believe him that it was loathsome to him, but he could not tell her the reason. It was very complicated and he didn't know if he fully understood it himself. It was something that couldn't be changed by them, but in time it would change of itself.

He could have made the proposition simpler for her if he had lied to her—pleading a physical disability, for instance—a simple fact for her to grasp and relieving him of the problems of imposing on her something which could not be explained. But he had no stomach for lying. She listened carefully to everything he said, but her perplexity aroused such tenderness in him that he was impelled to a greater degree of honesty than he'd planned on, pleading with her to trust him but at the same time pointing out that such a marriage would be preposterous.

More eloquence. He played devil's advocate to his arguments; he spoke as her lawyer and his, even as a hypothetical marriage counselor to make her laugh.

Had he mentioned love? If love had come into the conversation, Alexei realized that he had meant it.

Finally she put a stop to his arguments. "Don't say any more about it, Alexei." She smiled. "If I'm going to marry you, I'm going to trust you. We'll take everything as it comes. We'll have plenty of time for everything."

They were married in Boston the following weekend during a

surveillance lull. Immediately thereafter, Interzod affairs became hectic again and he was needed in London. Kate went along but the trip was a failure, for Alexei could not get free and she was lonely. It was only when they were ready to leave that she had run into Diana again, befriended her and invited her to stay with them for a while.

Sitting in the jet with Harwell beside him, remembering that bleak London autumn, returning to their rented house and finding Kate alone every night, Alexei recalled with a jolt that he had promised to take her to Europe this time. He had not forgotten; that part of the trip had been canceled when the Calcutta review achieved priority. But he had not told her, and as far as she knew, he was still going to Switzerland and had not remembered his promise. From the expression on her face the night he had suggested it to her, he knew that she had been looking forward to it, but though it had never been mentioned again she had made no reproach.

Once again he was overwhelmed by the dark feeling that he was an intruder on her happiness. He reproached himself not only for neglecting her but for not giving the difficulties of their relationship enough thought in the first place. He had done the only thing he could, but he hadn't thought of all the consequences or tensions. He had warned her, but not himself. Of course he had forseen difficulties, but he had not realized that in order to survive he would have to become harder. He had glimpsed it in himself at times and supposed it was a kind of involuntary protective shield. He remembered a doctor friend of his who could not prevent himself from being outspokenly rude to those patients whose suffering he couldn't alleviate; once, quite involuntarily, he had slapped a dying man.

Alexei was beginning to understand the effects of helplessness. Nothing in their marriage had resolved itself as he had predicted. It was true that he'd believed he would have more definite knowledge by this time so that he could make up his mind what to do. But he'd had to depend on people like Eliot, and Eliot had been damn slow.

*   *   *

Harwell turned in shortly after takeoff and didn't reappear until several hours out of San Diego. During the service and refueling stop at Honolulu, they drove out to the local Interzod headquarters, a large house east of the city overlooking Kaiwi Channel, and had a drink on the verandah with two of the staff members. "We're closing this place down," Alexei said. "There are no surveillance activities on the islands at present and no chance of any indigenous activity for the next three years. We'll leave one person here for communication purposes and to keep an eye on any of our transients who might stray into the area."

After takeoff again Alexei spent a half-hour in the communications room. When he rejoined Harwell, he returned to the conversation they'd had in their long session at Interzod headquarters. "Do you remember our discussion of the old astrology? It has almost nothing to do with the modern Interzod programs, except that it was a place to begin. The first program didn't veer from traditional astrological practices that had been in existence for centuries."

"What could the old astrology do? Anything?"

"From what I've discovered, it wasn't consistently good at anything. Occasionally, but only occasionally, it was remarkably good, and that's why it endured. But I was curious to find out if the successes of the old astrologers were only a matter of luck. There were many kinds of astrology. For instance, there were branches that claimed to be able to foretell the fortunes of nations or natural calamities. But I was interested in judicial astrology; my motive was curiosity. I had no notion of attempting to rehabilitate it as a science or art. As you probably know, the basic premise was that a person's destiny could be determined if the configuration of the planets at the time of his birth was known. That premise still stands, though destiny isn't the right word."

Alexei paused. "Except in some cases," he added. "And they didn't know enough about the planets. More important, they didn't use the knowledge that they *did* have. When the great strides were made in astronomy, the gap between it and astrology became greater. At that point it still retained the character and reputation of some form of divination like necromancy, palmistry and physiognomy. Even so, their predictions were based on a detailed horoscope that was complex and took months to prepare because of the intricacies of all the necessary mathematical computation. Obviously the computer can do these very quickly, and so my first step was to construct a program for the computer that was modeled on old astrological theories and practices. It was complicated because there were so many variations in method; the one I eventually used was something of a composite."

"Had anyone ever combined astrology with a computer before?"

"Not that I know of. Computers were new. But I wasn't interested in being first. I don't think I would have done it unless I'd had a computer at my disposal—and of course I didn't have any idea that it would work."

"You didn't believe in astrology at this stage?"

"Of course not. No sane man who knows anything about science would believe that destiny was written in the heavens, would he? What I did believe was that there was a distinct possibility that astrology had been shunted out of the scientific mainstream for one reason or another and had not developed as other sciences had, and that therefore it was impossible to judge its true potential. I kept discovering that over the centuries it had been respected by men of intellectual distinction. As a general rule, astronomers were sympathetic to it. The astronomers of thirteenth-century Spain, as well as Tycho Brahe, Kepler, Huygens and Gassendi, were all astrologists. Like Bacon and Sir Thomas Browne they did not always approve of the astrological practices of their times, but they didn't waver in their belief that eventually astrology would come into its own.

"But while these men of scientific acumen gave some credence to astrology—at least to some improved future form—opposition often came from poets and humanists such as Cicero, Juvenal, Savonarola, Pico della Mirandola, La Fontaine and of course Swift. Modern sceptics, and that would include you and me, are put off, I'm convinced, because of its association with charlatanism. We cannot accept the idea of a magical causality, but we do accept the magical association. After all, this goes back to Babylonian and Chaldean notions, and they might very well have ascribed a religious or magical explanation to any modern scientific notion—electricity, for example.

"I decided I wouldn't get anywhere if I didn't rid myself of the prejudices of astrology's critics. Modern science is more concerned with observing and describing how things behave and how they work than with looking for explanations of all the phenomena it observes. Why is no longer *the* essential scientific question. Einstein could compute tables for gravitational fields that have proved more accurate than Newton's gravitational equations, but he didn't suppose he knew anything more about the true nature of gravity than Newton did. So I decided that if I put astrology on a strict empirical footing, scrapping all the old mystical associations, I would be taking the approach it had deserved for centuries. No, that's wrong—I didn't know whether it deserved it or not; that was yet to come. I was fortunate, I suppose, in having a varied academic background—physics, history and mathematics—and I also knew something about evaluating statistical evidence. My next step was to gather this evidence to test the astrological method. I compiled a hundred detailed histories of individuals for whom I knew the exact date and time of birth. In some cases I used standard biographical data about well-known people. For some—a very few—I used information about people I knew personally, and for the remainder I selected records of prison inmates and pyschiatric patients whose lives and personalities had been described in detail.

"Then I ran off these one hundred horoscopes on the computer and compared them against what really happened to them. I can't say that I was disappointed in the results because my expectations were so low. But of those hundred cases, four were very accurate indeed. Thirty-five were accurate in about forty percent of their analyses, and in the rest the horoscope had little discernible relation to what had actually happened. Of course, a lot of predictions were too vague or too general to be interpreted with any accuracy. Something like a fortune teller saying that something unusual will happen to you in the near future, which can be fulfilled by being run over by a car, unexpectedly meeting an old friend, or almost anything. Anyway, the upshot was that I saw that I would have to make changes in what I wanted astrology to predict.

"I'll come back to that in a moment. But I also decided to revamp astrological theories to take into account what science had learned about astronomy. This was by far the most important decision. In the first place, astrologers have always been hampered by a geocentric theory of the heavens, even though Aristarchus of Samos knew in 300 B.C. that the earth and planets revolved around the sun. Furthermore, their calculations were supposedly based on the positioning of the planets and sun and moon in relation to the individual at his birth, but they made no allowances for relative distances or the planet's mass, and only the most sophisticated systems took into account the precise location of the individual's birth.

"My first test came by calculating the supposed solar influence to the degree that corresponded with the sun's distance at time of birth. Then I ran my hundred cases through the computer again, and this time I was dumbfounded at the results. The overall accuracy had improved by some 30 percent, *none* of the horoscopes were completely lacking in relevance, and six more cases were predicted with remarkable accuracy.

"Of course it was still preposterously inaccurate for any useful purposes, but the important thing was that I had improved it by improving on methods which were basically astrological.

"Next, I began to change the astronomical base of astrology. As it stood, it was very crude indeed. I removed from the program the supposed influences of constellations and stars so that my astrological 'influences' conformed to modern astronomers' knowledge of solar physics, with equations for concepts of force, known values for mass, the known variations and perturbations of the planetary systems, and so forth. The astrologers' greatest error in this respect had been that they didn't think of the solar system in terms of a constant pushing and pulling by each solar unit on every other; instead, long after they knew better astronomically, they saw it as a fixed picture with the planets moving across it on the same plane. With this innovation the results were so altered that it was clear I was on the right track, and I decided to devote all my energies to perfecting the system.

"Now, the other aspect of the old astrology that I knew needed changing was the kind of things that one could hope to learn from it. So after I had changed the formula, I began to examine what it was that astrologers had hoped to find. By examining the output of the modern formula, I discovered that accuracy had improved in some respects much better than in others. An example was the question of longevity. When they did a complete study on a man, the old astrologers would come up with an estimate of how long he would live. I not only discovered that they were usually wrong, I discovered that the new method wasn't any better at it. At the same time I discovered that the old astrology was most successful in predicting character. They were often wrong, mind you; because their formulae were so crude and inaccurate, they couldn't have been right more than 13 percent of the time. But the old concepts of character qualities such as Saturnine or Ariel were the ones I was able to predict with an accuracy that improved with each modification. What I discovered was that longevity, like all the rest of the astrological failures was a product of properly environmental situations. Do you follow me? A thing such as happiness, which they'd also thought they could predict, depends on environmental circumstances as much as it does on astrological factors.

"Of course, I couldn't continue very long with just my original hundred dossiers; I needed thousands of case histories in order to work out refinements. In Germany, I obtained records kept by the War Crimes Commission and by the German army itself, from which I could make studies of ethical judgments made by men under various kinds of environmental stress. I obtained army court-martial records from several countries—not always by means they would approve of, I might add. I also obtained records of civilian criminal proceedings and case histories from pyschiatric institutions.

"All of this took many years, but most of it was done in a five-year span in Switzerland and Cambridge, Massachusetts. After a long period of examination and evaluation of this immense amount of statistical information, I discovered that what I could do with a fair degree of accuracy was predict the capacity or the potential of an individual to act a certain way in a specific environmental situation. A man born today in Paris may have had a potential better suited to life in fourth-century Rome or nineteenth-century Polynesia. Taken in concert, the environment and potential provide an almost unique situation each time.

"As we have assumed for years, the individual feeds on the environment, taking from it what it will or can give, according to his potential. Astrology can tell us something about that potential. But the important thing to remember is that it isn't a science. It's always been suspect because even when it worked there didn't seem to be any *reason* for its working."

"You've put together a body of information that tells you something," Harwell said. "Doesn't that make it a science?"

"I've always been leery of calling it a science. I think of it as a collection of statistics that can be used as a tool. After all, it really doesn't reveal anything about a person that his close friends couldn't tell us. It only enables us to know it in advance, or without ever having known him or his friends."

Harwell smiled to himself; Alexei seemed determined to give his program a modest billing. "How many people knew of your project?"

"No one—no one at all. I had several assistants, primarily to gather and correlate data, but they believed it was for quite another project. I had a decoy—another computer-based study in the behavioral sciences; it wasn't known that I fed the data into more than one project. A computer memory bank is generally a very good place to keep information that you wish to remain confidential. The output is in codes and numbers which are unintelligible unless you know what they stand for."

"You felt this was necessary because of men like Admiral Sherborne?"

"Yes. Not specifically Sherborne, but every country I deal with has a handful of men like him. They're not only members of the military, of course, but they take a narrow view of Interzod and always would like to convert its operations to their own exclusive national interests."

"I can understand the problem. How do you get around them?"

"I kept the project quiet until I had refined it to a high degree of accuracy. It took seven years. My first move was to put a check on the project's possible misuse by any one country by making certain that it would be conducted on an international basis. I negotiated contracts with five governments simultaneously when it was still regarded as no more than an interesting and rather entertaining project and before they quite realized its astonishing accuracy. I knew that eventually I would have to secure the confidence of scores of governments—at this moment there are sixty-seven of them—each with its own national interests and almost all of them at odds with one another in varying degrees. I knew that there would be tremendous pressure to tackle military and intelligence problems, and it was clear to me that Interzod would be very good at this."

12

⊙

In one of those urgent last-minute changes of plans that seemed to Harwell to afflict Interzod at every turn, their transpacific flight terminated at Brisbane. Alexei was vague about the reason. "Shillong came in last night," he said. "Rhav is safe, so we can delay our arrival there by a day."

Harwell hadn't known she had been missing. When he wanted to know more, Alexei said only, "She's been in the hills for more than a week and made no contact with Shillong until a few hours ago. Now we know we'll get her firsthand report on Kasjerte when we get there."

Because Alexei hadn't mentioned it to him before, Harwell was left with the feeling that even a Class A security clearance hadn't admitted him to the inner circle of surveillance officers who worried together about the dangers to which they were exposed.

"If you don't know Australia, you might want to stay here for a day and take a look around," Alexei said. "Or you can join me if you like.

I'm switching to a smaller plane for a run to the New Hebrides. If all goes as planned I'll be back within twenty-four hours and we'll fly on to Shillong."

Harwell had once spent a week in Melbourne, but since he had never seen any of the smaller outer islands, he decided to ride with Alexei. The plane was a small four-seater with amphibian landing gear and a long cruising range especially adapted to island use. They took off and flew at an altitude of only a few hundred feet over turbulent reef-strewn water, then climbed through heavy rain, passing over New Caledonia, overhung with dark clouds and invisible except for an occasional brown rock mountain, its base wreathed in dank vegetation. After an hour their pilot shifted to a more northerly course and a little later they began to lose altitude. There were many smaller islands in view now, and pointing out one to their left, Alexei leaned forward, looked closely at an aerial photograph and nodded. They passed directly overhead, then came down in a tight circle, skimming over beach and long rollers and heading directly toward a small harbor where the plane came down in a jolting spray. They taxied up to a flimsy wooden pier, where they were met by a man in a white suit with a bandanna knotted around his throat, wearing sandals and carrying a cheap dispatch case.

"Mr. Abarnel?" he asked. "I'm Scholz."

Alexei nodded and introduced Harwell and the pilot. Scholz turned and walked back down the pier, Alexei and Harwell following in precarious single file. A group of swimming children had already formed around the pontoons, and the pilot decided to stay with the plane.

Small native fishing craft were drawn everywhere along the water's edge, and here and there nets were hung to dry over poles. Beyond a fringe of palm trees they came to a square which seemed an amalgamation of European and native enterprise. At the far end stood two white stucco European buildings. Anyone looking to pay his taxes or to make inquiries about visa regulations would tend toward that end. It had a lonely look, with patchy uncut grass and a splayed white fence.

At the other end were numerous makeshift buildings, stalls and desultory native crafts practiced in the open air. Alexei and Scholz walked ahead in this direction, carrying on a conversation from which Harwell excluded himself, since Alexei had not volunteered to tell him the reason for their trip. They stopped in front of a large brown stucco building that dominated that end of the square, and then walked over to a plump middle-aged Chinese standing by a fish market laid out on the ground in front of the building. The conversation quickly became earnest, and Harwell turned away to make an inspection on his own.

Native dress predominated, but with a sprinkling of European shirts and trousers among the men. At the stalls there were bolts of machine-made cloth in bright colors, but none which looked like native manufacture. At a display of jewelry, an old man sat before a table assembling tiny pieces of coral and polished stone, but most of the wares for sale displayed cardboard with HONG KONG printed on them. Intermittent with the native dialect was an occasional word of English or French. Harwell was regarded with only mild curiosity, and nobody undertook to ask him to buy anything. Further on there were magnificent displays of fruit and vegetables, most of which were strange to him. Beyond that, a wide unpaved street with dense foliage growing on both sides extended up a gentle slope. Harwell turned into it, and after walking two dozen yards found himself in a completely changed atmosphere. The thick growth shut out the sight and noise of the market square. The real island began here, he decided. He walked a little further until he came to a grove of palm trees which gave him a view of the hillside above, where he saw two or three new-looking European residences.

Since he hadn't asked how long they would be here, he decided to return to the square again. Alexei was standing outside the large building, his hands in his pockets, as Scholz came out of it, followed by a native boy with a spade. After Scholz gave him instructions, measuring an unseen hole with his hands, the boy disappeared into the building again.

"We've been invited to have a Chinese lunch, but Scholz warns me it will be impossible to get away in less than two hours," Alexei said as Harwell came up. "He's going to find us some good native food instead."

They followed Scholz into a shanty in a narrow alley which had a little room with two tables. The proprietor, a large native woman, brought them three bottles of native beer, which was bitter and very strong, and platters of fried cubed pork, heavily flavored with juice of an unknown fruit and highly seasoned with pepper. This was accompanied by something resembling a taco, fish, identically flavored, and a dish of something like squash, flavored with nuts. A bowl of fruit and coffee served with what might have been pure grain alcohol came last. Making no effort to identify any of the ingredients, Scholz gestured to the woman to put the liquor bottle on the table and downed three more shots in quick succession.

In half an hour they returned to the building, and this time Harwell went inside. It was obviously used as a drying shed for fish, and the proprietor was evidently the Chinese. An area at the rear had been cleared of boxes and drying fish and he stood beside a freshly dug trench, the native youth stood quietly to one side, while Scholz and the Chinaman talked rapidly in Chinese and occasionally German. When the negotiations were completed, Scholz counted out a sum in French bank notes and they returned to the narrow pier. It wasn't until they reached the plane that Harwell noticed Scholz was carrying a large covered basket of woven bamboo. As this was stored carefully on board, Alexei turned to Scholz and counted out a sum of money in American currency.

There was little talk on the return flight to Brisbane, and as soon as they had transferred to the jet for the last leg of the flight to Shillong, Alexei pleaded exhaustion and went to bed. But Harwell knew that he didn't sleep well. He woke up during the night and saw the glow of a cigarette from the other bunk, and when he got up several hours later, Alexei was sitting in the main salon with an empty glass beside him.

Harwell realized that Shillong could be expected to be a tense and demanding situation. Rhav might be responsible for Alexei's anxieties, but Harwell sensed that it was something of a more personal nature.

"Assam is one of the wild places," Alexei remarked in a transparent attempt to be sociable. "Superficially it's primitive, but it has a strong cultural entity and clings tenaciously to ancient tribal usages."

"How does Kasjerte fit in?"

"He was driven there. He needed someplace that was out of the way and relatively inaccessible."

Harwell had expected a different answer. "You remarked yesterday that you looked upon a zodiacal potential in relation to its environment. Aside from its remoteness, what is there in Assam for Kasjerte?"

"That observation doesn't apply to Kasjerte. It is true in most cases, but it differs according to the strength of the potential. Loosely stated, the stronger the zodiacal urges, the less important the environment. Kasjerte is an extreme case; his potential is imperative. It's not a matter of accommodating himself or adjusting to an environmental situation. If he doesn't find one that will allow him free expression, he will create one. He must."

Suddenly Alexei took up a brief case. "I've brought the profile for your friend in Bennington," he said. When Alexei had proposed that he join the flight, Harwell had reminded him of his agreement to make a zodiacal analysis of a dead person. Alexei had told him that for the purposes of the demonstration they would work with only the minimal zodiacal coordinates—a date, hour and place of birth, which would be translated into latitude and longitude. Harwell had given him the statistics on the figure he had chosen—born at 1:30 A.M. on March 18, 1837 in Bennington, Vermont—and before boarding the plane, Alexei had gone to the computer room and given them to the attendant on duty.

"Do you want a historical analysis, Mr. Abarnel?"

"No, I only need zodiacal determinants and potential formulations." The young man nodded, went into the computer key-punch booth, and returned in a few minutes with a long roll of printed forms which Alexei carried with him on the plane. Historical analysis was what he intended to work out with Harwell as they went along.

"I hope you know a lot about this man. It's far more interesting if you have a feeling for him and know the circumstances of his life and how he responded to them."

"I know the broad details, and a lot of the minor personal facts as well."

Alexei spread the long forms out. "These," he said, "are the zodiacal determinants. We actually don't need them; they are simply the background material for the formulation, which is what we work with. I brought them along in case you're interested in the technical aspects. If you'll notice, there are fourteen entries in the left hand column. They are the determinants—the coefficients, if you like. The equations that follow concern their relative effect on each other and the effect on natality at this particular latitude and longitude. As in navigation, it is necessary to know both time and place on the earth's surface to know what configuration values apply. Let's see what we can know about your Bennington friend."

Alexei studied the other forms for a few moments. "He has the potential of being an extraordinary man," he said finally. "But he could live his life peacefully and quietly and nobody, not even he himself, would be expected to know there was anything exceptional about him unless he was confronted by an extraordinary situation. He would not, for instance, set out to find the Northwest Passage, nor would he be likely to be an actor or, saving your presence, a politician. In most situations he would be shy, very slow to anger. These sound like negative potentials, and in a sense they are, because the Beta factor"—he pointed to a jumble of figures—"is very strong, but is almost entirely in the responsive mode. He would not seek out ways to demonstrate his remarkable qualities. He would not, for instance, be a deeply suspicious man, because the factors add up to a strong sense of self. However, if he saw that there was a true injustice, he would go to any lengths to rectify it. He would not be likely to choose soldiering for a profession —though it's possible, because soldiering was traditionally a respectable profession. But if called upon, he would be a first-rate officer. Let's see, he would be of soldiering age at the time of the Civil War, so if he were in the war and literate he would probably distinguish himself. Let's get down to choices; it's the only relevant thing in someone with almost all responsive factors."

"So far you've described him very well."

"But only in generalities. That's how they sound when I translate

the factors into words. I'm guessing that he was literate; after all, education was a strong environmental standard in New England. But with his
determinants he would succeed in attaining literacy if he were rich or
not—unless, of course, he were blind or had some equally strong accidental roadblock."

"He was literate."

"Was he wealthy?"

"By local standards, yes. His father owned two farms and rented
both on a share basis."

"The family lived in town, then."

"Yes."

"Then quite possibly he had a higher education. It would be his
strong inclination to go on to college or a professional school, though
it was rare in those days. The year we're talking about now would be
around 1855. It's quite clear that if he went to college, he would be
attracted to some profession. But even if not, he would become educated
one way or another. If not college, self-education. Which was it?"

"A seminary."

"Aha! It all depends where."

"Virginia."

Alexei raised his eyebrows. "Why Virginia? New England had
seminaries of its own."

Harwell smiled. "Because he lived there. You didn't catch that."

"No. Only newspaper astrologers seem to know when someone is
about to take a long trip. At what age did he move there?"

"He was eleven or twelve years old."

"That gives us a real conflict to work on. From free state to slave
at a period when his moral judgment had already been formed. In his
case, it had to be; the capacity is enormous. The conflict in ethical
standards of the time was too clear-cut for him to have missed it. Even
if he saw a relatively benevolent side of slavery he would have been
deeply affected by it."

"You're quite right, Alexei."

"Still, he could not be a crusader in the flamboyant sense. Instead of organizing antislavery groups he would suffer inwardly, and since he doesn't have the capacity for moral deceit, he would not conceal his opinions, which may have caused him some rough times outwardly as well."

"You're doing very well."

"But it's not fair. It's too easy. The man has no contradictions. If he has a choice to make, he'll make the reasoned, morally good choice every time. Look—" pointing to the paper again—"all these potentials are perfectly balanced. Why go on with it? I've seen this man before in other prototypes. If you put him on a farm, he'll have the cows fat and the barns painted all his life. If you put him in charge of a ship, the crew will never be known to grumble. But just one thing more about your friend. He's in an interesting situation. His perfect balance has been met by an unbalanced environmental situation. He's an abolitionist at heart, but even at the age of eighteen he is quite incapable of being brash. By twenty he'll be old enough to make himself heard. As a youngster, he's bound to consider the proprieties, even the proprieties of a social system he finds unjust. He'll change. However, his response will be in keeping with the proprieties. He can join the army, where he has a cause on his side. Or he might go back to New England where he could air his lungs. There were too many ways for him to express his choice for me to be specific. Which did he do?"

"Neither of those you suggested, but it was on the same order. I'm sure you'll go on pegging him. As a matter of history, he went to Delaware and worked as a courier on the Underground Railroad. He didn't survive very long, however. Nobody knows what the circumstances were, but he was shot in a farmhouse outside Alexandria, Virginia. He came back to Washington with gangrene and died ten days later."

"The potential formulations wouldn't have predicted that, as you know. His prototype often lives through a lot."

"He was my grandfather's uncle on my mother's side," Harwell said. "My family has a journal he kept from the time he was twelve years old and some attempts at writing poetry that I've read. The journal was very honest, and by the time I'd finished it I felt I'd come to know him pretty well."

"Washington was a man with a very similar formulation," Alexei said, "perfectly balanced, without a chance of airing his exceptional talents barring an exceptional opportunity.

"But given your ancestor's character, a good social anthropologist would sketch him pretty much the way I just did. Social anthropology errs in supposing people are equally gifted in accepting or rejecting social pressures. Certain people are capable of acting as though social pressures didn't exist. They are the truly gifted or the truly damned. They are grateful to the world they are born into only to the extent that they can swallow it whole. They can crush it, or remake it into something very much better. Was Europe the same after Napoleon fed on it? Can we explain Genghis Khan by surmising that he was aping his neighbors? Of course some environments are capable of more resistance than others. You understand that we use environment to mean everything that meets a man from the time he opens his eyes on earth until they are closed for him. Rocks and trees, other people, customs, government, weather, history—everything that can change him or he can change."

There, quite unaccountably, and Harwell wasn't at all certain that it was the product of their conversation, Alexei stood up and began walking agitatedly back and forth across the aisle. "You understand," he said, never looking up from the carpeting, "that I dislike the word destiny. It's what they expected us to be able to tell them, especially the scoffers who were certain at first that Interzod was so much witchery. They actually blamed us for bringing astrology out of the Dark Ages, but once we had done it they blamed us for not doing more." He threw up his hands in a gesture of impatience. "We didn't *try* to do more," he said with irritation. "They wanted us to prove their God to them. They're uneasy about that, you know. Every last one of them, would you believe it—God-starved, every one of them!" He paced back and forth in increasing nervousness.

Harwell hadn't allowed himself to consider the pressures under which Alexei and everyone connected with the program must be working. "What's wrong with destiny?" he asked suddenly. "Isn't that what you've shown them? Is it because they refuse to believe destiny is a matter of circumstance?" He realized that he was using "they" as Alexei had, but that he wasn't at all sure to whom it referred. Alexei was privileged, of course, lumping together everyone in contact with Interzod, having seen that doctrinaire preconceptions had dissolved in its withering glare. Every head of state in Europe and South America had finally come to realize that Interzod could do exactly what it promised. Alexei had pointed out that doctrinarians had become the first supporters of Interzod, while the Swedes and the Swiss still hung back. His explanation had seemed more than adequate: countries that were worried about their governing institutions were the first to recognize that they would be less able to withstand the machinations of the truly malignant. The Swedes had nearly had a governmental crisis before an appointed consulting committee could come to an agreement that there was such a factor as personal malignancy. They never did make up their minds to be a participating country because, Alexei suspected, they didn't want to undertake the expense; however, they did allow him the same unquestioned entry and exit privileges as the participating countries.

"But that's what you've managed to do, isn't it?" Harwell repeated. "Destiny. You've given them destiny, haven't you?"

"Absolutely not!" Alexei snapped, stopping abruptly and looking Harwell full in the face. "I've given them all the destiny they deserve," he said, and then, as though he realized his listener couldn't understand his meaning, he began pacing again. "Destiny is a very rare thing, Joe. You and I don't have true destinies. Your relative from Vermont didn't have a true destiny. He was like us, a creature of circumstance. Only once in every two or three hundred years is someone born with a configuration so powerful that it adds up to what can truly be called a destiny."

He stopped in his tracks—later Harwell remembered it very well —and pointed a finger at an imaginary audience. "Only the truly great are above it all. The imperative factor is what it should be called. They expect everyone to have a destiny. It just doesn't happen that way. Our only destiny is to become bogged down in our neighbor's mud. Only the zodiacally privileged few are above it. Oh, there are such people, and they remake the world. History has given us the prototypes. Their zodiacal configurations are truly astonishing—I'll show you sometime. The Buddha configuration, the Napoleonic, the great messiahs—really remarkable. We are prisoners of our environment, you and I and almost everyone around us. Our only destiny is to fight the clay that clings to our feet. Some are truly great, others are uncompromisingly evil, but the great imperatives are above the mud. They are prisoners only of themselves. Do you follow me? *Only of themselves.* Quite truly, they can't help themselves. God help the man who would stand in the way of someone truly destined!"

Harwell felt embarrassed at the passion in Alexei's voice. Though he didn't understand why, something told him that the man needed nothing so much as sympathy. To his surprise, he found himself rising to his feet and involuntarily putting his arm around Alexei's shoulder in a gesture of compassion.

13

⊙

From the administration building of the ruined tea plantation where Interzod field headquarters had been established, Gavin Porter gestured toward the heavily forested hills that rose in the east. "What we weren't prepared for was that he would succeed in disorganizing tribal structure so completely."

For two days Porter had paced up and down the wide latticed verandah that protected them from the incessant rainfall, reporting on the devastation that Kasjerte had worked. Porter was awkwardly tall, in his late thirties, and he never called Kasjerte anything but "he," avoiding pronouncing the name as though from distaste. Looking up at the hills or gesturing toward them had become habitual. Somewhere in that green forest vastness, Kasjerte was an established presence.

"The day after Rhav left," he told them, "we heard of the bodies coming down the river. We feared the worst—and Avanganhi went to look at them. Eleven bodies in three days. Except for one old woman, they were girls and young women. Some were Assamese—they're among the most beautiful women in the world, I'm convinced—and some were apparently Nagi women. All except the old woman had been tethered together in twos or threes by means of a thin plaited leather cord run through holes piercing the heel of the right foot. Avanganhi has had medical training, and he says that the holes were made at least two months ago. Most of the women had been mutilated—blinded, usually. All the streams coming out of the hills are very fast, so they hadn't been in the water more than twenty-four hours. All had died from drowning. I wouldn't have let Rhav go in there alone if they'd been discovered before she left."

"She's not easy to stop," Alexei said.

"No, but that's when Avanganhi decided to go after her. His scouts had told him that most of the lower villages had been abandoned and the population had followed Kasjerte to a place called Nagao. That was where she'd have to go." He looked at his watch occasionally, then at the road that circled the cluster of three buildings, cut across the half-mile width of the plantation set in a flat basin in the hills, and then disappeared into the heavy tropical forest beyond. The glance at the watch was pointless except as an unconscious demonstration of anxiety. Rhav had been expected since the day before, and Alexei knew that soon they would openly be discussing what to do if she hadn't arrived by sundown. Porter and Avanganhi must each have worked out contingencies.

Food was brought from the cook shed and Harwell, Porter and Alexei were settling down to a meal for which none of them had an appetite, when a shrill whistle sounded from outside. A man wearing short white trousers and a tall cone-shaped straw hat came running across the tea fields, and one of the Indian soldiers walked out to meet him. They talked for a few moments, then the soldier ran back toward them and shouted something to Porter, who looked immensely relieved. "That was one of Avanganhi's scouts. Rhav and Avanganhi arrive before dark."

An hour later they appeared in a battered Rover, Avanganhi driving. He was young and slightly built, with long black hair, a precise way of speaking and smiling.

"We're tired and hungry. Food is in short supply in Nagao," Rhav said, climbing down. "Avanganhi says you fretted about me," she added to Porter.

"He wasn't the only one," Alexei said.

"It was really quite safe. I avoided Kasjerte. I went in as you see me, in European dress, as a foreigner, my theory being that Kasjerte would ignore me because I was alien to the structure of power and authority. Porter, you stayed alive in a village with Kasjerte by posing as a district government official. A bureaucrat in such a place isn't a symbol of authority because he has no immediate hold on the villagers. I knew that Kasjerte would ignore me for the same reason. He'd sooner turn his attention to his jailer or a village chief or a local seer."

All this came out in a cheerful babble, but when she stopped talking she looked exhausted. They'd both been without sleep for two days, but that could wait. They would like something to eat and then they would talk.

After supper they dragged the crumbling rattan furniture into a circle.

"Unquestionably, Kasjerte is the most impressive person I've ever encountered," Avanganhi began.

Rhav agreed with a shudder.

"Did you talk with him?" Alexei asked her.

"No, neither of us did. I didn't care to risk that. He lives in a house at one end of the village. The place has an atmosphere all its own. People avoided it, or if they entered it their expressions changed, their voices had a different quality, they walked differently, their postures altered.

"Shoun sleeps in a house nearby but he takes his meals with Kasjerte. They talk at great length. It's hard to conceive of what their conversation is like. Kasjerte appears only rarely, and when he does, it's always an occasion—the entire populace seems to sense it. There's no doubt that they believe he really died on the funeral pyre and returned to life again after his body was consumed. Undoubtedly Shoun engineered that drama, but whether or not he recalls that he did so, or whether or not he believes it actually took place isn't clear.

"They see him appear in the doorway to his house and everything becomes quiet. Oh God, I swear even the village dogs stop barking. In the morning and again at evening, he walks to the stream to bathe. Everyone watches as he takes off his robe and folds it on the bank and then immerses himself. He stands on the bank for a few moments to dry himself, then gets dressed and returns to his house. Occasionally he will stop and speak to someone in the village. His voice is very soft and he speaks quietly with little gesture or facial expression. Sometimes he walks beyond the village into the jungle for an hour. On these occasions only one or two men will go with him, but the place seems deserted until his return.

"He is never openly cruel in these public appearances. It would be a mistake to believe that he rules by fear. Fear is a part of the process of control but he doesn't make himself the focal point. It's difficult to understand his process of transmitting or projecting his authority. He doesn't appear to be giving orders—or even to be responsible for what goes on about him. Things happen as he wants or needs them to, without his appearing to be responsible in any way. I don't believe I ever saw him deliver an order."

"What about the bodies? The eleven drowned women? You knew about that?"

"Yes, from Avanganhi after he'd found me at Nagao. I heard no talk about it in the village, but—" Rhav's thought died uncompleted. She stood up, walked over to the piano and sat down on the bench, then turned her back to the keyboard and faced Alexei. "It's so hard to describe what happens between Kasjerte and those people. Nothing ever seems to be said. Everything seems to be beyond words—beyond rationality. One knows the zodiacal prognosis shows that he is the initiator, the aggressor in every relationship, but that's not what one *sees*. It's the utter resignation on all sides, the abject passivity! The weakness is the most horrible thing up there!

"I don't think Kasjerte drowned those women himself, or even that he ordered it done. It's more likely that they committed suicide or that someone else did it. His presence arouses either self-destruction or a frantic total self-subjugation. The desire to do the unthinkable, to perform an act so repugnant that one's self is destroyed, is overwhelming. It becomes their way to seal the compact. Obeisance to old ethical strictures is overthrown through murder or other forms of deliberate cruelty. In that way the psychic destruction is completed, so that there can be no turning back from Kasjerte's embrace.

"But there's more to it than individual destruction. Destruction of any kind takes place as a matter of course whenever it's advantageous. In every village over which he holds sway, social and political structures have been obliterated. In three of the four Rengama villages I passed through, the clan chieftains had been murdered. In one, the body hung from the charred rafters of his house—a profound violation of religious feeling. Before Kasjerte, it would have been unthinkable. Yet no one seems to mind, or even to notice. The passions generated by his presence cut across all traditional bonds of language, religion and caste. Shoun said to me, 'He will unite all India.' And I think that perhaps he could, in some dreadful way."

Rhav stopped, looked at Alexei and smiled bleakly. Then she rose and walked to the window which overlooked the ruined tea fields. All at once it was raining again, the steady relentless downpour that never varied in intensity or diminished until it closed as abruptly as it had begun. When looking at it from inside, Harwell found that he tended to turn away.

"You'll have to hear about my conversations with Shoun," Rhav began again. "They began very soon after I arrived. I initiated them. I wasn't sure of how safe I would be, and it seemed wisest to try to establish some kind of rapport with him as quickly as possible. I'd never talked directly with him before, you know; in Calcutta I'd always worked on him through intermediaries. Still, I'd observed him at close hand and had developed a definite impression. I'd say he has changed a great deal."

"He's susceptible to change—more so than almost anyone we'll ever encounter," Alexei remarked.

"He has a new confidence. I know it must be chimerical or an imitation of something he sees in Kasjerte; nevertheless, it made him easier to deal with."

Alexei nodded. "Bear in mind that he'll lapse back into his former weakness once he's out of Kasjerte's orbit."

Rhav looked thoughtful. "But as it stands now, he's more aggressive, more willing to take risks. While it lasts, we might be able to work this to our advantage. Do you know what I told him when he said Kasjerte would unite all India? I said, 'Yes, he will, and you're the man who will help him.' He agreed with me, which suggests a new sense of self, even if it's synthetic and temporary. Prior to this we could never manipulate him by flattery; there was nothing there to flatter. The point is, Shoun has plans for Kasjerte, as we knew he would have. He won't take pride in achieving them, but he's openly dedicated to carrying them out. The fact is, I've proposed making a contribution to those plans— and it's going to mean getting governmental intercessions to cover for me. I know that governmental intercession is one thing you like to avoid, but in this case it will work out. Moreover, it's necessary."

"Let me hear it," Alexei said.

"It involves a direct payoff to Indian army officers—money from Kasjerte to a certain Major Bahnaptu."

Harwell expected questions at this point, but Rhav was allowed to continue without interruption.

"Pen Li took me aside just before I left and said he was worried about me. I was touched." Rhav smiled. "He also said, 'We have talked of Kasjerte's great strength, but we have not talked about his weaknesses. He can control those in his presence, but he knows that he cannot exert his influence at a distance. He will fear what he cannot see or touch and therefore cannot control. This fear will be very strong because he senses it represents his downfall.' "

"Alexei, you once said that Pen Li's greatest strength is in not being afraid of stating the obvious or giving it careful thought. Pen Li gave me something to look for, and I think I've found it. What Kasjerte knows he cannot control is a body of troops. When we talked about using troops against him again, I think we were right in saying it would be futile; Kasjerte would surely flee before the troops reached the village. This time the hill people support him and in any case government troops have never been successful in any operations up there. The British never tried to extend their influence or their jurisdiction beyond this point.

"But even if the troops can't be used to capture him they can be used as a threat. One of the first things Shoun asked me was if I had seen the government troops at Manipur. I told him that I had come directly from there because I wanted to draw him out. He wanted to know how many there were and what they were doing. He especially wanted to know if they had been sent to rout out Kasjerte, like the first time.

"I decided I had to make myself interesting to him, so I told him that Major Bahnaptu was very concerned about the bodies of the girls that had washed down the river. I'd just heard about that. I made up Bahnaptu, by the way. It was clear that the presence of the troops worried Shoun, and so I decided to take advantage of this. I told him that I thought it was possible to manage the major. I would be the intermediary, I told him, but he would have to make it worth the major's time. Have I made it clear so far?"

Alexei nodded.

"You've accomplished more than I thought you would be able to, Rhav," Porter said, getting to his feet. "It's the first time we can do something besides counterpunching."

Alexei agreed. "This *does* give us some options. We can do the initiating and proscribe their choices for the first time. Hopefully we can maneuver ourselves into a position of even more complete control."

"I want to see a change in the surveillance strategy we worked out at Headquarters," Rhav said. "We started with the assumption that the combination of Kasjerte and Shoun was volatile, dangerous and nearly unmanageable. But on the basis of what I have seen, I would like to discard our immediate objective of isolating them from each other. Our only contact with Kasjerte is through Shoun, and our only hope of manipulating Kasjerte is by manipulating Shoun. It would be wrong to separate them before Kasjerte is committed to some course of action that will deliver him into our hands."

"The key being their fear of a military force," Alexei said.

Rhav nodded. "They haven't forgotten his arrest and capture. Kasjerte had faced local police action many times before, but he's always been confronted by men in small groups, never by men trained to ignore the elements of personality and following orders from some higher-up at a distance. I don't think we can be sure that Kasjerte might not prevail against even well disciplined troops if given time, but evidently he does not yet fully realize how powerful he is. It's a classic case of an artificially thwarted imperative, and as such we know that he must strive to overcome it. Eventually he would force himself to try once again."

"At any rate, we don't have to risk it. We use his fear of the troops, not the troops themselves," Alexei said. "Very good."

"But Shoun will be led to believe that he has control of the situation. He must be made to believe that he has successfully bribed an army major and will be free to operate without interference, so we must give him token proof that he is right. When he feels that it is safe to come down from the hills, we will be in a much better position. Our goal will be to have him return safely and convince Kasjerte that it is safe for him too."

"Shoun wouldn't say, 'He will unite all India,' unless he meant it," Alexei said. "We know that the union with Kasjerte would stir him to designs far more grandiose than any he's had before. The scope of his activities depends purely on Kasjerte's dimensions. He will want to bribe other government officials, and he will quickly organize to obtain the money to do this. We can fake it up to a point, but we'll have to stay close and keep someone in his confidence at all times. We'll need someone else up there besides Rhav and Avanganhi."

"I need sleep, Alexei, but first I have to know what you think of specific proposals Avanganhi and I have worked out. The most important thing is to get Kasjerte out of the hills and back down into the valley."

Rhav's voice was tinged with impatience and this drew Alexei's complete attention.

"Nothing can be done as long as Kasjerte is up in those hills," she continued. "Our strategy *has* to be to work toward bringing him out."

"If I were Kasjerte, I'd feel safer in the hill village than anyplace else," Porter said.

"Yes, but we know that Kasjerte can never accept a static situation," Alexei said. "He is gripped by the compulsion to continually exercise his zodiacal predilections. We could not expect him to remain forever in the hill villages. He has been unsuccessful in the Brahmaputra valley, and the choices open to him are to move west into the Khasi hills, move toward the northern part of Burma, or move east of the great bend in the Brahmaputra into Tibet or southern China. In doing any of these, he will be in the same kind of countryside as he is now. He could move from one small village to another in comparative safety and we would have a difficult time dislodging him."

"How far will he be compelled to extend his power?" Porter asked.

"That's a complex question," Alexei said. "Kasjerte himself is not interested in extending his influence over any great geographical area. His need is for *direct* personal domination. Power over a village forty miles away means nothing to him because such domination is not tangible. But Shoun is a different matter. While Kasjerte is illiterate and has little notion of geography, Shoun's capabilities are greatest when dealing with abstractions. Shoun will want domination over the greatest number of people, and he will continually concoct strategies toward this end."

"It is Shoun who will bring them out of the hills and into the valley," Rhav said. "But we will need cooperation from the Indian government in order to fool him. He must convince Kasjerte that the valley is attainable after all."

Alexei went to the window, after a moment's thought turned back to Rhav. "It can be done," he said. "I'll have to go to Shillong to make the necessary contacts."

"Thank you," she said. "I'll get some sleep while you're gone."

Harwell was impressed at how quickly Alexei moved once the

decision was made. Within an hour he and Porter were on their way to Shillong, leaving the large house suddenly quiet. Avanganhi and Rhav had gone to bed immediately after the conference.

Harwell had a drink alone on the verandah and then he too went to sleep. His room was dark, and he had no idea what time it was when the piano roused him from a deep sleep. Getting up and going into the main room, he found Rhav playing.

It wasn't until he saw her seated at the piano that he remembered hearing about her interrupted career as a concert pianist.

A light flickered at the far end of the room, and when he came closer he saw that it was a candle on the piano. Because Harwell's knowledge of music was uncertain, he didn't know what she was playing, but he sensed that she played very well. He stood to one side, where he had a view of her face. It was unguarded, lacking animation, very much as though he had come on another person altogether—a woman not so pretty. At close proximity, the music seemed unpleasantly disordered and he started to tiptoe away to find a place to listen at a distance, but without looking at him or changing her expression Rhav said, "Stay."

He remained by the paino until she had finished, lifting her hands from the keyboard and dropping them to her lap in a kind of concert hall flourish. Only then did she look at him and allow her face to regain its customary softness.

"Sit down," she said, giving him room on the piano bench. "I'm glad you're awake; I had no one to talk to. I came to your room but didn't have the heart to wake you. You seemed as tired as I was. Has anything been heard from Alexei?"

"I don't know. Avanganhi is sleeping in the radio room."

"Avanganhi found this piano in a storage shed, wrapped in burlap to protect it from the damp," she said. "He spent the entire first day getting it in tune. It's not a bad instrument, considering that probably no one has played it for years." She ran her finger across the keys. "After such a long time the ear becomes just as rusty as the hands. If I play any more now I'll begin to listen carefully again and will hear how really bad I've become." She smiled vaguely to herself and turned her head away briefly. "Are you hungry?" she asked.

"No."

"But you'd like some coffee, wouldn't you? Come on. We can make some in the cook shed." She stood up and took him by the hand. Outside, they walked across the small compound at the rear of the house. It was cooler in the night air, and there was a moon and deep shadows on the foliage. Suddenly a figure emerged from a grove of trees ahead, as though to check their approach. Rhav spoke in a calm voice as they came closer, and Harwell saw that he was a very tall soldier carrying an automatic rifle. Rhav exchanged a few words with him, then sniffed the air and turned in the direction of the hills. "He says they're burning again. Can you smell it?" she asked Harwell.

For the first time he noticed a slight scent of burnt wood on the night air. A look of mournful disgust crossed her face as they walked on. On the other side of the compound, a dim light glowed in the doorway of a low building. They entered a room dominated by a large old-fashioned hearth, with an iron stove and shelves and cupboards lining the wall. At one side was a modern refrigerator, empty and unused, its door standing open.

"When Kasjerte's people passed through this place," Rhav said, "they tore out the power lines and wrecked the spare generator. They left us an oil stove. I'm surprised they didn't burn everything. The guard said they'd fired one of the Ai villages about three miles from here. It was nearly deserted, but it means that everyone too old or sick to follow Kasjerte is homeless. I passed through another village they'd burned. It's horrible to see. Those villages can be very beautiful. The houses are built on stilts five or six feet off the ground, with walls of woven rushes and steep, thatched domed roofs. The workmanship is wonderful, and they're always placed at a comfortable distance from each other among the trees around a large commons that has been partially cleared, giving the impression of a cool airy grove. All the houses were burned down to the supporting stilts. I asked Shoun about it. I learned that I could ask him almost anything and that it was better not to let him think that anything had escaped my notice."

"What did he say?"

"He shrugged, that's all. He has a single shrug for all questions he doesn't care to answer. He would not trust me if I registered disapproval of this or anything else I saw. Sometimes it was very hard to conceal my feelings. Rightness or wrongness is totally irrelevant to him; he is only interested if I point out that some things will arouse the authorities. He sees that as a possible hindrance and a potential danger to Kasjerte's success. When I speak of the authorities I always say 'troops,' 'soldiers' or 'army.' At this stage it is very important to him if the 'army' disapproves of burning villages. That's why I have to go back; I'm the only person who has his trust and can remind him of it."

She put two mugs of hot coffee on a long wooden table and they sat down. "You probably think it's very crude and primitive up here," she said as she sipped, "but to me it's an elegant outpost of civilization. I don't mind living in primitive places. Lord knows I've done enough of it, and usually I like it. But the horror of everything I've seen up there is overwhelming. For nearly ten days I crouched on the floor of a hut, talking to a madman. Everyone I saw had been mesmerized into a horrible madness; I was the only person trying to reason out what was happening. I wasn't the only frightened one, though; they're all horrified at what has happened but they know they've become a part of it. There's mass confusion mingled with mass horror, and the spontaneous acts of terrorism seem to offer a kind of relief.

"I wasn't afraid of them, but I began to be afraid of what it was doing to me. To force oneself to remain in such a place requires some sort of tolerance. It's a kind of psychic trick that one plays on oneself in order not to scream, or run away, or go mad.

"From the doorway of the house I could see Kasjerte's brides huddled in a field on the other side of the stream. There must have been fifty or sixty of them, of all ages but mostly young. They've all become ragged and unwashed—some of them are naked. They sleep on the open ground at night; when it rains they crawl to the edge of the forest, where the trees give them some protection. They behave as though they're under the influence of some drugs, but I don't know for sure whether they are. Shoun won't discuss this with me; he tells me they are happy and that this is how it should be. I didn't dare pursue it. Happy! It's the most miserable lot of humanity I've ever seen! They become 'brides' of Kasjerte after submitting to various mutilations. Perhaps they *have* acquiesced to whatever is done to them, and there may be some kind of sexual act involved in the ritual. I know I've heard terrified screams coming from Kasjerte's house, but there's no way of finding out what's happening.

"The brides live apart from the rest, seldom crossing the stream and entering the village proper. When they do, they come in groups of six or eight, moving in a slow listless walk they've all adopted. Their eyes are listless too. They don't speak to anyone and no one talks to them, either; everyone finds something else to look at. Their quietness is one of the most terrifying things about them. Some of them are bound together by lengths of cord drawn through the heel like those that were drowned. Others have fresh knife scars or wounds on their thighs and buttocks—as though someone had tried to carve a design. They don't seem to be in pain or bothered by anything. They work in the fields and are put to all the hard physical labor, but everything is done in a slow trancelike reverie. The only sound that comes from their field is a kind of singing—low-pitched, vague and indistinct."

Rhav had hardly touched her coffee and Harwell marked a trembling in her voice.

"Others have died!" she went on relentlessly. "Not just the girls they found in the river. They're *all* dying. No one can live that way very long. There were two girls lying dead on the other side of the riverbank. No one paid any attention until they'd been there for several hours. Then some of the others came and dragged them back into the field and buried them. Nobody thought anything about it or wondered how they'd died or seemed to care at all. You're the only person I've told this to. I didn't tell Alexei and Porter. I couldn't bring myself to talk about it. Neither could Avanganhi. We've hardly mentioned it to each other because we know there's nothing we can do about it. I felt like a coward because I found myself trying not to look across the stream at those bodies. I would have given almost anything to speak to someone who wasn't infected by that madness. If Avanganhi hadn't come . . ."

THE ASTROLOGER

There was the sound of voices, and two soldiers entered the cook shed followed by a young man with a dark, round, earnest face. One soldier talked earnestly to Rhav, pointing in the direction of the hills and nodding in the direction of the young man, who was trying to make himself heard. When Rhav spoke to him, he came forward, talking rapidly and making emphatic gestures. The two soldiers listened intently, and when he was done they looked expectantly at Rhav.

She seemed worried but said nothing for several moments and then turned to Harwell. "This is one of Avanganhi's scouts," she explained. "Two hours ago he saw Kasjerte's followers set fire to a village. It was a small place but it's not far away. There are about thirty of them. Their leader wants to return and fire other villages that have been abandoned by Kasjerte's followers—it's typical of the kind of fanaticism he inspires. They're also talking about coming here and firing this place. He wants me to wake Avanganhi, but I told him he must wait. He's badly frightened."

"I can't say I blame him."

"No. But Avanganhi needs sleep and I depend on him. Besides, this band isn't armed, and there are eight soldiers here with automatic weapons. I don't think we have to worry on that score."

Harwell could not find it in himself to be equally confident and Rhav sensed this. "What really worries me is that things are getting out of hand in Kasjerte's village. He seems to derive some nourishment from anarchy and mayhem. I've been counting on Shoun to keep it in check, you know. Right now everything depends on that."

When they returned to the house, Harwell did not see her again for several hours. She was going to try to contact Alexei at Shillong, she said, and there was other work to be done.

He did not remember falling asleep again, but when he awoke, Rhav was sitting beside him, moving his shoulder gently and talking to him, urging him to take the cup of tea she held. "There isn't much time," she was saying. "Please wake up. I need you to come with me."

She watched while he splashed water on his face, from a canvas bucket hung from a nail on the wall, and then, they left the house and started off down a road that crossed the plantation toward the hills.

"Alexei will return in a few hours," Rhav said. "Porter, too. Pen Li will arrive tomorrow or the day after. You won't have much company until then." The sleep had left him dull and it didn't occur to him to question the implications of this. "The guards are nervous after last night. Another scout told Avanganhi that there are groups of men within three miles of us. It's possible there may be some attempt against us, but they'll back off when they realize the guard is here. The sergeant in command is the tall one with the mustache, and he's very competent."

The road was deeply rutted from the daily rains and cart wheels, and they walked single file, picking their way around puddles of brownish water. When they reached the line of taller trees on the far side, the road curved upward, becoming narrower and dryer. They reached the point where the road entered the forest. The place was green, damp and overripe, with queer acoustics that inspired silence. After a quarter of a mile they came on Avanganhi standing by the Land Rover.

"I made you come to see us off," Rhav said.

Harwell hadn't understood that she was leaving, but now he realized that the two of them were returning to Nagao. He suspected that they had made the decision on their own.

"It has to be done this way," Rhav said, as if reading his thoughts. "The situation is getting out of hand. I'm worried. We simply can't afford any gap in trying to influence Shoun."

"Isn't it more dangerous if the followers are in a burning and pillaging mood?" Harwell asked.

"Who knows? In any event, we'll lose all the control we've worked for if we don't get back at once. In two hours we'll come to the place where we have to leave the Rover. I'll make radio contact with Alexei then. Your only contact with him until he returns will be through the

Indian guards. The sergeant's name is Manghi. He's good, but keep in mind that he doesn't have clearance. Good luck."

As she climbed in the front seat of the Rover, she self-consciously inclined her face toward him. He kissed her and then returned to the plantation alone.

14

$\odot$

Sometime in the hours before dawn, Harwell was shaken awake by a hand thrust through the mosquito netting around his cot. "You dress and put on boots quick. We must leave now. Hurry." The voice was unfamiliar and the message was repeated over and over monotonously.

Harwell fumbled for his flashlight. "No light by window," the voice said, and a flashlight was turned on behind a blooded palm. The guarded light revealed the dark, bearded face of one of the Indian soldiers. Harwell did not know the soldier's name, though in the two days since Rhav and Avanganhi had departed he had come to know them all by sight. This was the only one besides Manghi who spoke English. He had spent several hours drinking beer and playing bridge with them, Manghi serving as his partner and translator. On the field phone he had twice spoken to Alexei, who was apologetic about having left him alone. The business was more complicated than expected; he'd had to go to Delhi to negotiate the assistance they would need.

THE ASTROLOGER

"You come? You hurry?" the man asked, stepping back from the bed. He was holding Harwell's boots in his hand, and in spite of his urgency he seemed determined to be polite. As Harwell sat up, the soldier placed the boots on the floor and disappeared. As he laced them up in the dark and pocketed his few belongings, a voice called from someplace in the house below, "Hurry, Harwell!"

He nearly collided with Sergeant Manghi standing in the darkness at the bottom of the stairs. "You have everything? We are leaving. Now. Alexei tells us to go to the rear station at Pahil. You too. The Nagi will come down from the hills very soon. Who knows. Maybe they will want to burn this place too. If we stay we must shoot them, but Alexei tells us to leave." Groping for Harwell's hand, he thrust a canvas bag at him and a wide-brimmed Aussie campaign hat.

Outside there was enough starlight to see a few yards. At the cook shed, the other soldiers were loading a truck, working quickly with little talk. When two more soldiers appeared out of the forest and spoke to Manghi, he rapidly whispered orders to the men loading the truck and their pace quickened. One of them ran off toward the house as the truck was started. When he returned, the soldiers began walking the road in single file, automatic rifles slung at their backs. Manghi motioned Harwell into the front seat and got in beside him as the driver put the truck in low and started off, leaning out to find the road in the darkness.

The truck lurched and bounced heavily in deep ruts, and oozed through sheets of stagnant muddy water. They moved no faster than the pace of the soldiers on foot just ahead. After a short way there seemed to be even less light, and Harwell judged they had entered a forest. A little distance further one of the soldiers outside said something to the driver. They came to a stop while the soldiers continued on ahead. Manghi and the driver stared ahead into the darkness until finally the driver grunted and they got back into the truck. "The signal. The road is clear ahead," Manghi said. Harwell had seen nothing. They shifted into a higher gear and moved ahead more quickly for another hour.

"We have left the others behind," Manghi said. "They will go by road through the forest. It is shorter but the truck cannot go there. We will meet them later."

Daylight broke abruptly above the top of the forest and they were able to drive more quickly now, but the jostling increased and conversation was impossible.

They endured it for six hours, stopping only twice for tea. At one of these breaks Manghi told him that Alexei and Porter would be at the rear station when they arrived. When he asked Manghi how long before they arrived there, he was shocked by the reply: "Tomorrow or the day after."

Late in the afternoon they met up with the other soldiers who had taken the trail over the hills. They made camp in a clearing and spent the night in army sleeping bags. When Harwell woke up in the morning, the soldiers were already gone and only the driver and Manghi remained. Looking up from a map spread on the ground, Manghi told Harwell that the tea plantation had been overrun during the night; a huge fire had been sighted, and presumably the place had been burned down. He had already contacted the rear station where Porter and Alexei had arrived. According to the latest information, a section of the road up ahead had been overrun by Nagi tribesmen. Alexei advised them to remain where they were; a helicopter would be sent to pick them up.

The helicopter didn't arrive until dusk. All the gear and equipment from the truck was loaded aboard and they took off, breaking with the direction of the road, swinging out over the trackless rain forest, following a line of hills, and finally descending at a clearing streaked with the light from automobile head lamps.

Interzod installations at the rear station consisted of just two trucks, one housing communications equipment and the other food and gear. The only people on hand were Alexei, Porter and the youthful communications man who had served on the transpacific flight.

Again Alexei was apologetic. He was sorry that Harwell had had to rough it, but it had been necessary to evacuate the plantation in order to lure Kasjerte's followers into the area. "To bring in a helicopter to shift you out of there would have made the Nagi shy away. The idea is to encourage them to spread themselves thin and lure as many as possible away from Shoun and Kasjerte up at Nagao." He seemed satisfied at the way things were shaping up. "It took Rhav and Avanganhi six hours to reach the village. I believe they've got everything in hand. So far, the Indian authorities have done a good job; troops and local militiamen have been moved out of all the barracks on the south bank of the Brahmaputra at the eastern end of Assam and a big show was made of their departure. Shoun believes it's because he bribed Major Bahnaptu. But the timetable for the whole operation has had to be shortened drastically. We have to get it over with by the day after tomorrow. Rhav will have to play some of it by ear, but she's confident that by then Kasjerte and Shoun will be taking over the town of Pohinal.

"The situation changed when Kasjerte's followers at Nagao began marauding the countryside. This indicated that too many followers had collected at the village and that Kasjerte and Shoun had allowed the situation to become static. Both of them will feel a need to counter this —Kasjerte especially will want to keep things fluid and dynamic. They're also having trouble feeding everybody. The marauding raids are partly to scour around for food. The time to draw them to Pohinal is now, while so many of the menfolk are in the vicinity of the plantation and before Kasjerte gets it into his head to move further east into even more desolate hill country. We're not sure what all our moves will be, but we think we know what kind of situation we'll face in forty-eight hours.

"The way Rhav presented it, Shoun saw that the key to the situation was money, and he was made to think he'd discovered a way to find it. The more involved the transaction, the more satisfactory to Shoun. Rhav told him that for the sum of three hundred and fifty thousand rupees Major Bahnaptu would withdraw his troops for six months. She said that she was unable to bargain him any lower, but that she could borrow a hundred and seventy-five thousand rupees for three months on her own property. This made Shoun believe anything was possible. There was an actual meeting between Shoun and the supposed Major Bahnaptu, who is actually a young Indian army lieutenant acting on his government's instructions. He was instructed to allow Shoun to bargain him down to two hundred and fifty thousand rupees. He also put Shoun in contact with another officer, in civilian dress, who told Shoun that he would advance him a hundred thousand rupees if his opium-smuggling activities based at Pohinal were not interfered with when the soldiers left. Rhav and the spurious opium smuggler advanced him the money, and he has already paid off Major Bahnaptu. As you see, it's been arranged so that he has twenty-five thousand rupees left over for his own pocket—which will contribute to his desire to move on to someplace it can be spent.

"Of course, all the money that changed hands was provided by us. During the twenty-four-hour period it was in Shoun's hands he counted it very carefully. To a certain extent Shoun can be expected to measure achievement by money—Kasjerte, never. It is the first time his movement has been affected by money.

"So Shoun now believes he will be in control of Pohinal, where there is no longer any army, and he will urge Kasjerte to leave his followers and cross the river into Pohinal. It's a market town, not nearly so primitive as the Nagi hill villages. We know what will happen because we have several firsthand reports, including Porter's, of past entrances. Kasjerte will be accompanied by no more than a dozen followers, perhaps less. He will move slowly through the streets—Porter described it as "majestically." People will look at him and move out of his way. No one has to tell him where to go. He will see where the crowds are and he will know who are the most susceptible. A certain number will begin to follow him. An Indian village is accustomed to the arrival of holy men, but this will be different from anything people there have ever seen. He will seat himself somewhere and the crowd will stare at him. By this time, fully a fourth of those present in the village will have sensed Kasjerte's arrival and been affected by it. Others will sense it in time, but it will take days before the entire village, including the least susceptible, is affected by him.

"It's at this moment that he must be taken. We've thought of every conceivable way of handling it. In some respects it would be better to prevent him from penetrating so far, but an ambush is out of the question and it would be a mistake to underestimate the fanaticism of those dozen men who are closest to him. The troops who captured Kasjerte last time found that out. They will not be cowed by the sight of a weapon, and their lives mean nothing to them. It would be an even greater mistake to try to hustle him out of the crowd. Crowds are Kasjerte's best defense because people feel compelled to come to his aid. Drugging him will arouse the least trouble and will render him incapable of promoting assistance from the mob."

A man came up and motioned to him, and Alexei clambered into the back of the truck. After a few minutes he returned and said, "That was Avanganhi's relay from Shillong. Shoun moved into Pohinal ahead of schedule. He didn't like the building we had picked out for him. Smart fellow. Rhav thinks he can be persuaded to move into a house next to the administration building, which would put him near the market, if not in full view."

"And Kasjerte?" Porter asked.

"He's about three kilometers out of Nagao. His followers are leaving too but they're straggling behind by a kilometer."

"That gives us about twenty-four hours. I'd better be moving out," Porter said.

Alexei nodded. "Your backup is Antonin Cracek. He'll get there before you. He's experienced and as resourceful as anyone we could get, and he has some medical training under his belt."

"I remember him at Cairo. He's fine. What about the out transport?"

"Two trucks. One in the village, one at a rendezvous point outside. Also some sort of native produce cart if you need it. Just remember to give us a full appraisal before you swing into it."

Porter put a kit bag over his shoulder just as a dusty ancient Mercedes drove up. "I think I've been through all this before," he said, holding out his hand to Alexei.

They watched until the car disappeared at the first bend down the hill.

"Our policy has always been to plan as closely as we can," Alexei told Harwell. "But we can never anticipate all the options. This time everyone out there is going to have a chance to make some decisions."

"The plan is to drug Kasjerte?"

Alexei nodded. "By far the best when deception is called for. Muscle is out of the question. We're outnumbered—there's only four of our people in there. Firearms would be preposterous. Anyone with a gun would be sure to trigger a reaction from the crowd."

"How will you give it to him?"

"It comes in two doses. The first Avanganhi will take care of—a soporific in Kasjerte's drinking water. The man's behavior is highly ritualistic, which also makes things easier for us. When he puts himself on display, he's even more predictable. One of the first things he will do in Pohinal is eat and drink something. As in the ceremony of bathing in the stream at Nagao, he will make a public ceremony out of a simple everyday act. He will not drink from the town well, but from his own goatskin which one of the followers always carries for him. Avanganhi will have doctored that water by a hypodermic needle through the goatskin. In fifteen minutes Kasjerte will become sick; in half an hour he will be unconscious.

"This is where Shoun comes in. We can't get him out of the way just yet because he must be on hand to take charge, to call a doctor and find a place where Kasjerte can rest. Prior to this, Rhav will have seen to it that Shoun knows there's a doctor in the town, and he will be called in to look at Kasjerte. It will be Porter, who will administer a second drug, a shot that will keep Kasjerte zeroed for the next twenty-four hours."

"Wouldn't it have been possible to slip him some kind of drug before this?"

Alexei shook his head. "It would be pointless unless he was in a place we could control, and we couldn't control anything while he was in that village. At Pohinal, however, he will be among new followers who regard him with great awe but haven't yet recognized him as their leader."

"What about the band following him from the village?"

"They won't have arrived yet. Look here." Alexei quickly sketched a map in the dust on the side of the truck. "The hills are on the right, the valley on the left. Most of his supporters who would ordinarily give us trouble are in the hills where they are strung out all the way down to the tea plantation. The important thing is that they are still on the right-hand side of the road, while Kasjerte is in Pohinal on the left-hand side. The bands can be contained because we will have two companies of Indian troops along that road, but they can't be in evidence anywhere until Kasjerte makes his entrance. He's stopped for the night ten kilometers south of the town, will move on again at sunup and will arrive an hour later."

That night they slept in the rear of the equipment truck. Harwell awoke in the morning when a jeep with three Indian soldiers pulled up. Alexei came out to talk with them, carrying a map which became the center of discussion.

When the soldiers left, Alexei returned to the truck. "Kasjerte's arrived on time," he said.

"At Pohinal?" Harwell asked, and Alexei nodded.

"How long will it take the soldiers to get there?"

"They won't enter the town, you know. They only perform the blocking assignment. Any uniforms in the town would spoil everything."

"Even after you've drugged him?"

"Especially then." Alexei looked at his watch and glanced at the young man handling communications. "That's the critical moment— and it should be taking place just about now, by the way. It comes down to Rhav's steering Shoun through it. Kasjerte must be attended by the European 'doctor,' who will say that he has to be taken to a neighboring town where there's a better infirmary. If Shoun doesn't agree, Porter will simply give Kasjerte another dose of the drug, pack him into a truck and make off with him."

"Doesn't that leave Rhav at Shoun's mercy?"

"There'll be no reason for him to suspect her complicity."

That was the beginning of the long wait. Alexei warned that there would be no word from beginning to end unless something went wrong, but he spent the next hour glancing at his watch and then at a chart, which Harwell saw was a kind of rough timetable.

"If there's no military report in five minutes, try Avanganhi again and see where he stands," Alexei finally told the operator. "There's no report of the troop deployment being completed," he said, turning to Harwell. "They're twenty minutes behind schedule. We allowed them a thirty-minute leeway."

"Here it is," the operator interrupted. "It's from Shillong. 'Troops deployed on time per orders. Sightings but no contacts at intersection.' "

"That's better," Alexei said. "That would be a relay from Avanganhi's scouts and can be trusted. What about Avanganhi?"

"No response to signals. I've been sending continuously."

Alexei looked at his watch again. "They should be at work now," he said.

For the first time, Harwell detected traces of anxiety in Alexei's voice and manner. "Keep sending," he told the operator. Then he climbed down from the truck, walked over to the canvas ice chest, took out a bottle of brandy and poured drinks for both of them.

A moment later the operator yelled something from the truck and Alexei ran to join him. The period of waiting was at an end, but what took its place had the appearance of chaos. The operator began shouting a cluster of foreign words over and over into the microphone while Alexei tried to work an old field telephone. A truck containing three soldiers roared down the road and shrieked to a halt in front of them. The operator ripped off his earphones, shouted something at them and waved them on. Alexei gave up trying to operate the phone and sat down at the radio desk, usurping the earphones. The operator looked on nervously for a moment, then came over to Harwell. "They managed it," he said, trying to contain his excitement. "Kasjerte's out of there and in the custody of Porter and Cracek. The town's in an uproar. Kasjerte's handful of companions got wind of it and stormed the place. They've pinned the blame on Shoun and are after his head for turning him over to the doctor. Avanganhi was sending just now, before he was cut off."

"What about Rhav?"

"He didn't know anything about her or Shoun."

Alexei turned the radio back to the operator and began pacing. He looked as worried as Harwell had ever seen him. "Avanganhi was cut off in the middle of sending. There was a lot of noise in the background —some kind of riot. It's impossible to guess what's happening—except that we've got Kasjerte." He poured himself another drink. "I've got Shillong trying to contact Avanganhi's scouts. There are two of them in the hills just a few kilometers from the town. They're going in there to report back as soon as we can contact those troops to tell them to let them through. There's a pass-word, but God knows if those soldiers will remember it."

"And you won't know what's happened to Rhav till then?" Harwell asked. It seemed to him that he was stating the all-too-obvious.

Alexei's answer wasn't what he expected. "I'm not worried about her, Joe. I know you think I should be, but I've seen her in places like that before. She's very good. If there's trouble she'll have anticipated it and will be able to protect herself."

"How can she protect herself against a riot?"

Alexei smiled carefully. "If I didn't have people like Rhav, I wouldn't be able to operate with a handful of people in places like Pohinal. I'd need an army or an air force, and we wouldn't be nearly so successful."

An hour passed before Avanganhi signaled again from Pohinal. There had been a riot, the nucleus of it formed by Kasjerte's dozen fanatical companions. The building to which he had been taken had been stormed and set afire. There had been a hue and cry for Shoun, but Avanganhi did not know if they had found him or what had happened to Rhav; when last seen, she had been with Shoun in the ransacked building. Avanganhi himself was in no danger and would remain and continue to report in at fifteen-minute intervals. It would not be necessary to send the scouts in unless he stopped sending.

At the second fifteen-minute interval, Avanganhi reported increased rioting; dozens had been injured but none were dead, as far as he knew. So far, it had been impossible for him to reach the vicinity of the gutted building because it remained the center of the street fighting.

Ten minutes later Alexei received a report from Porter. Kasjerte was out cold, and they were about twenty kilometers clear of the town.

Neither he nor Cracek knew anything about Rhav's whereabouts. They had decided not to turn Kasjerte over to the Indian authorities before reaching Shillong and, as planned, would continue to maintain surveillance indefinitely after the government took charge.

At the fifth Interzod report, Avanganhi reported decreased fighting in the town but also conveyed a rumor that Shoun had been killed. There was not even a rumor about Rhav.

Alexei had become silent. The good news of Kasjerte's successful abduction was more than offset by Rhav's disappearance, and Harwell was beginning to feel the oncoming of shock as it dawned on him that the chances of her emerging safely were diminishing with every moment. Alexei sat in a self-enveloping silence by the radio desk and Harwell felt a strong wave of pity for him.

Nearly four hours had passed when a car appeared at the top of the hill, coming to a hesitant stop on the far side of the road fifty yards from the truck. There were two figures in the front seat, but it wasn't until the driver had got out and was halfway to the truck that Harwell realized it was Rhav. He took a running step in her direction and was about to shout when he saw by her expression that he should remain quiet. She said nothing until she was a few yards away. "Don't show that you know me. I'm supposedly stopping here to ask directions. Are there soldiers nearby?" she asked, then quickly cautioned Alexei as he appeared at the rear of the truck. "Shoun is in the car." She was jubilant.

"How did you manage that?" Alexei asked in astonishment.

"It wasn't hard. When Kasjerte disappeared, Shoun was inconsolable, so I promised we would look for him. Instead, I've brought him here." She took a deep breath and smiled.

"You're not armed?" Alexei asked.

"It isn't necessary. Without Kasjerte, he's helpless. He's quiet and easy to manage. He's become absolutely dependent on me. For four hours I've been filling his head with plans to take over all of Assam and Northern Burma. Right now he's busy calculating the cost of raising and feeding the army he'll need."

Alexei suppressed the impulse to throw his arms around her. Instead, he said, "You've really done it, Rhav!"

"Yes, this time I think we really have."

"But how did you escape the riot?"

"I'm afraid I started that riot," Rhav said. "It was the only way to get him to agree to leave. It took fifty men pounding on the door and calling for his head to make him realize he had to get out of there. We picked that building because it had hidden access to the street where the Rover was parked. Now I want to get rid of him. Don't you have soldiers here?"

"The soldiers who were with us at the plantation are bivouacked just beyond the bend straight ahead. I'll take over," Alexei said.

"Wait, there's no point in letting him know I've turned him in. Can you contact the soldiers?"

"By field telephone."

"Ask them to stop the car at gunpoint, take him into custody and march me back here alone. That way he'll still think of me as his friend. Who knows? Maybe we'll need that some day."

As Alexei made the call, Rhav returned to the car and drove by slowly. Shoun was a small, narrow-faced man, utterly ineffectual in appearance, a man who would never, one would suppose, have to be reckoned with.

15

⊙

Eliot backed the station wagon out of the garage and drove around to the front door, where Kate was waiting for him. It was part of his Thursday routine whereby he relieved Diana of her daily drive to town with Kate. He had never understood why his performance of this and other little husbandly duties pleased Diana, since he was so convinced of his ineligibility that he assumed others took it equally for granted. He supposed, rather, that she needed signal reassurances of his affection. He good-naturedly obliged her, paying her off, as he saw it, in the feckless currency of lighted cigarettes, refurbished drinks and garments retrieved from the dry cleaner. Of all these small burdens, he least minded the Thursday trip to town with Kate. At times he felt a constraint in her presence, but there was none on these occasions, perhaps because there was a legitimate purpose in their being together.

As Eliot drove past the gate with a wave to the security guard who would, he knew, jot down their departure time, and turned down the narrow unpaved country road toward the town, he realized with a pang that this would be their last such excursion. By Monday he would be gone. That he had remained this long surprised him, especially since five weeks had elapsed since he'd pinpointed St. Quetor's island. Having fulfilled his agreement with Alexei, he believed that all that remained was the drafting of some kind of report. Alexei had made it clear that he didn't expect much, that the end product was the information itself. All along it had been an irritant not to be told the reasons the information was wanted, and it certainly had never occurred to him that Alexei actually intended to go to the island. And then he had begged Eliot to stay on; indeed, implored would be more accurate. "A month, six weeks at most," he had said. All the urgency Eliot had detected in him had come to a head; embarrassed, Eliot had cut the conversation short by agreeing to remain.

Alexei made it clear that he didn't expect Eliot to stay on in the house if he did not wish to, and that he could come and go as he pleased. But he must return when Alexei needed him, and then it would take no longer than a few days—a week at the most. There would be full salary, of course; there would even be a bonus—this as evidence of gratitude after Eliot had agreed.

When Alexei reappeared, looking tanned and fit, he arrived at Eliot's studio at Historical Research with a package heavily wrapped in moisture-proof plastic, placed it on the table and perched himself next to it, resting his arm on the top. "This contains several items recovered from diggings beneath the church which you discovered in the New Hebrides. Do you recall the accounts of the heresy proceedings against Friar Alvaro and the manuscript dealing with the legend of St. Quetor?"

It was highly improbable that Eliot would have forgotten them, since they had been the cause of so much drudgery. "It was one of the counts against him that he had caused the bones of a native god-hero to be dug up and placed beneath the church altar, transforming him into an ex-post-facto saint," Alexei said, and patted the top of the plastic bundle. "There's a good chance that we have those bones," he added, trying to speak matter-of-factly.

Eliot's interest soared. Bones were the very core of his precocity. He had a way with bones; bones had made his reputation.

"How can you tell? Was the altar still there?"

It was a question that Alexei seemed pleased to answer. "The place is very much as it was in the photographs. One wall at the front under what may have been a bell tower or perhaps some kind of spire is badly damaged and probably will collapse within a few years. The interior is as we thought: there are fish everywhere. Wherever you look there is nothing to remind you that it was once a church. But at the point where one might suppose an altar would be placed there is a large worktable. At first glance it appears to be supported by four logs standing on end, but if some of the clutter is removed it can be seen that the logs are only balancing supports; the central support is a pile of stones. They are fit neatly together; it was obviously the work of a craftsman. Taking this to be the remains of the altar, we dug a trench behind it and in front of it. Underneath we found a flat stone, beneath it a layer of smaller stones and beneath that the remains of a slab of long-rotted wood. Then we came on the bones. They were just jumbled together, as might be expected if they had been dug up, after a long burial had reduced them to a skeleton, and then reburied beneath the altar. There are also remnants of something resembling leather and a small cross carved from whalebone. I have taken great pains not to break or injure any of this. The bones are very dry. This bundle is very light."

Alexei paused for emphasis. "What I need from you, Eliot, is a date for everything in here. I need to know how old everything is, as close as they possibly can be measured."

Alexei had rarely called Eliot by his first name. His guard was down; again there came an imploring look. Eliot felt no animosity toward Alexei, but his task had kindled a certain amount of exasperation and it prompted him to take advantage of this momentary defenselessness. "I can put a date on anything in that bag, Alexei, but I think I'd have to know what the hell it's all about."

As he was saying it he was sorry that he had spoken so curtly. Whenever word drifted back to him about his reputation for churlishness, it stung; he tried not to give any justification for it. To his relief, Alexei smiled, then looked carefully at Eliot. "After all, these may be the relics of a very important saint," he said. He was still smiling, but Eliot did not think he was being facetious. "He *was* quite a man, don't you agree?"

"Yes, of course."

"Think of his legend. For his people, he underwent ridicule and great pain so that they would not suffer. In that part of the world, he was a great man."

No, there was no facetiousness. But Alexei may have thought his listener would think so, and with hitherto unknown warmth he put his arm around Eliot's shoulder. "I really can't say," he said with great seriousness. "I really don't know, Eliot. I'm not a scholar, as you know. Certain aspects of esoteric knowledge fascinate me. No, that's not it; they puzzle me. I want to know everything I can about it."

It wasn't the answer Eliot had hoped for, but Alexei's mood was too imponderable to protest. He felt he was being intimidated by kindness. "Maybe we can discover a use for it," Alexei suggested, turning as he reached the door.

"Such as?" Eliot ventured.

"With relics like this, you and I could start a pretty sound religion."

Eliot had gone about the task of dating and identifying the bones and other items with meticulous care, though the scientific procedures were familiar to him and presented no unusual problems. From the history of Quetor's original burial as the legendary tribal god-hero and the reburial in the church after the enterprising friar had made him a saint, it was theoretically possible that they would find the complete skeleton of a man. Eliot had too much experience, however, to count on this. Of the lower portion of the body, only the pelvis and left tibia remained. There were six vertebrae, eight ribs, the breastbone, both femurs, fragments of the collarbone and left hand, the skull and jawbone. Except for two ribs still adhering to the breastbone, none of the bones were attached to one another. Out of habit, Eliot had positioned them on his worktable according to their true skeletal relationship, but this told him little except that the size of the tibia and femurs suggested that Quetor had been a smallish man. The first tests showed that he had been between sixty and sixty-five at death.

Eliot had been just as meticulous in fixing the date of death, subjecting each bone to three different tests. Two were refinements on standard tests; one was his own, which was fast superseding the others as standard procedure. All the tests were limited to organic materials, but the older ones only narrowed the dates down to one-hundred-year delineations and were more useful to a paleontologist or anyone content with broad historical delineations. With ideal specimens no more than five hundred years old, Eliot believed he could narrow dates down to within six or seven years.

That Quetor had remained in his tribal place one hundred and eighty years before reburial as a saint could be established by applying tests to the wood found on top of the bones. It was a tropical hardwood, and evidence that it had been placed there at the time of the reinter-ment came from Eliot's discovery of the letters *SA* faintly marked on the surface of one of the pieces. The imprint was negligible, not visible to the eye and discovered only by photographic tests.

A definite *S*, a negligible *A* and then abandonment of the project. Speculation suggested that the word Sanctus had been intended. The wood had been dry at the time of carving, and was then at least a year old. From the day it was cut, one hundred eighty years, give or take six or seven, had passed since the death of Quetor, the god-hero who had brought his people moral, ethical and economic enlightenment. There-fore Quetor's death had occurred in the period between 1491 and 1498 and his reburial from 1671 to 1678. By subtracting the estimate of his age of sixty to sixty-five, it appeared that the man had been born somewhere between 1426 and 1438.

In moments of exasperation with Alexei, Eliot had toyed with the idea of giving him a date false by one hundred and fifty years, wondering if Alexei would catch it and if he did, whether he could be goaded into revealing how he knew, so that Eliot could learn what was really behind all this. But when it came to drafting the report, and on the evening he and Alexei sat in the library and discussed it, his exasperation had vanished and there was no malice left, even though he learned nothing more of substance.

It had taken Eliot six days to conduct the tests. Another day was spent in writing the report, and the next evening—last night—they had sat in the library until midnight. When Alexei left, Eliot lingered on for another fifteen minutes, congratulating himself that his sojourn was over at last and thinking how fitting it was that it had ended by the fire in the library where it had begun. Now he had only to mark time until Monday.

When they arrived in town he and Kate arranged to meet back at the car in one hour. Eliot had possessions scattered around town which had to be retrieved as part of the surreptitious preparations for his Monday departure—a watch at the jeweler's, a restrung tennis racket at the hardware store. When he had finished, he sat down on a bench in the square. Still basking in Alexei's warmth of the night before, he was prepared to look back on the past few months as a more agreeable experience. He told himself that Alexei's geniality had been there all along; it had only needed tapping, and he had been equally at fault in not finding out how to go about it. He saw too that he himself had been rigid, and from the point of view of the Abarnels, no great shakes as a houseguest. He had certainly been stupidly constrained around Kate, and suddenly he felt very sorry to be leaving her with the impression that he was dull-witted and socially inept. After all, they'd come on a dozen afternoon excursions to town, and he hadn't once asked her to so much as join him in a cup of coffee. Perhaps he could ask her to join him in a drink that afternoon. The bar at the hotel looked passably respectable.

With this in mind, Eliot returned to the car fifteen minutes early. Kate was already there, but she was not alone. The person in the driver's seat was the same young man she'd met at the bus station. Eliot knew that they had met at least twice, probably oftener and he felt an intruder, a violator of lovers' right to privacy. Stopping abruptly, he tried to sidle into the pedestrian traffic, but he realized that Kate had seen him. With one hand she beckoned to him, and with the other she reached over and tapped lightly on the car horn to get his attention. He responded, recalling with keen guilt his meeting with the young man, who was now speaking to Kate. He could be saying, *There* is the man who spies on us. He knows our old meeting place. He warned me about meeting you. Justice would be on their side.

Kate rolled down the car window. "Eliot, this is Gregor," she said.

Gregor leaned across to shake hands, his easy smile genial and puppylike. He gave no hint that he even remembered their meeting.

Eliot became aware that Kate was trying to say something to him silently, forming words with her lips, something not intended for Gregor. Eliot could not catch it, and she gave up, reached behind her and unlocked the rear door. Since it seemed to be what was expected of him, he got in. "Gregor says there is a gypsy encampment nearby and that we can all go," she said, turning around, her eyes pleading with him.

Eliot did not understand.

"A large gathering of gypsies. They've come from all over," Kate explained.

"It is like a very large picnic," Gregor explained, "only it goes on for many days."

Eliot felt uncertain and uncomfortable. He realized that he had been included on artificial grounds, but it wasn't clear whether Kate's silent message was meant for him to accept or refuse. It would be safer to begin by refusing, or to suggest that they both refuse, since she had made him her partner. If this was not what she wanted, he could always change his mind—though he was not at all sure that it was a good idea for them to go. "I think we're expected back," he said tentatively.

"We could go for a few hours," she countered.

Eliot was thinking of Alexei, and of the kindness he had discovered in the man. Diana's allusions to the contrary, he believed that Alexei was very much in love with his wife. Of course, if he hadn't known of her meetings with this young man, he would have sworn that Kate returned his feelings with equal intensity.

She was smiling at him. "We won't be missed," she said. "Alexei left this morning and won't be home until tomorrow. Besides, he wouldn't mind as long as you're with me."

Eliot still did not like the prospect, and his face made it evident.

"I couldn't go unless you came with me," she said.

Eliot realized he was being used, but since it had been put to him so forthrightly, he could not take offense. If anything, he felt flattered and it was this feeling that she had made him her accomplice that weighed strongly against his urge to protect Alexei and divert Kate from her own impulsiveness. The idea of being her partner in a harmless escapade *was* appealing, and without quite realizing it he became anxious to believe that nobody could find fault in their going.

"How far is it?" he asked.

"Not very far," Gregor answered.

"How long would it take to get there?"

"Not very long," Gregor said with great sincerity.

"Would it take as long as an hour?"

"An hour? I think a little less than an hour, or a little more . . ." This answer died with a shrug. Then he looked at Kate and smiled, not only with fondness there but also with great respect. Eliot found some reassurance in this; it seemed obvious that Gregor would do anything that Kate asked him to do.

"Shall I drive?" he asked Eliot. "It will be easier. I know the way." At the same time he was already starting the car. The debate was over, though later it revived from time to time in Eliot's head.

Gregor was not an easy driver. He drove fast and skillfully, but with an absorbtion so complete that it bordered on a trance; he seemed impregnable to anything said to him under a shout. He drove for perhaps twenty minutes before slowing down and peering carefully at a stretch of woods, finally stopping at a narrow two-rut trail. He sounded the horn several times, then got out and walked up the trail a few yards, whistling shrilly. There was an answering whistle, and a moment later another young man came down the path, wearing what appeared to be an old army blanket. They stood talking for several minutes before Gregor returned to the car, grinning, while the other disappeared into the woods again.

After a few miles they turned onto a heavily trafficked four-lane highway. "We take this for a way," Gregor said. There was little conversation. Gregor was too absorbed in his driving, and at high speeds the luggage rack on top of the station wagon made unrhythmic clacking noises which discouraged talk.

Kate sat sideways on the front seat, near the door, her face, half-turned to the traffic ahead, looking happy and expectant. Eliot's thoughts returned to Alexei. He was a complicated man, and one who could be ruthlessly matter-of-fact. This was probably mistaken for coldness, but Eliot had seen that on occasion he could show great warmth. He allowed people to see the changes in his mood but not the reasons for them. It occurred to Eliot that at times he seemed to want to give the impression that at heart he was a man of few emotions.

Eliot dozed and woke in a stupor. They were still on a heavily traveled turnpike, and from the light slanting across the fields it seemed to be early evening. His newly repaired watch had stopped, still showing the same time as when he'd last looked at it. Kate was facing the road ahead, her head tilted back, her hair falling in sunstruck diffusion over the back of the seat. Eliot was sorry that he wasn't privileged to reach out and touch it. "What time is it?" he asked.

Gregor glanced at him in the rear-view mirror and shrugged. Kate didn't move; evidently she had fallen asleep too.

Gregor leaned back in his seat. "We are not far."

Eliot saw that there were New Jersey highway signs on the road, and though he had no idea of the distance they'd traveled, this made him anxious. A few minutes later they left the turnpike for an unmarked two-lane road. Eliot found himself trying to believe that it was none of his concern if Kate was wrong about Alexei's not minding her going on this expedition, but he couldn't help realizing that it would be at least midnight before they got back. He tried to reason that anxiety was pointless; anxiety persisted nevertheless.

Coming to a crossroads with a gas station and a grocery store, Gregor pulled to the side of the road and turned off the engine. "I must wait a few minutes for Tono," he said. "He is the one you saw. He is driving my car here and he doesn't know the way. Only a few minutes."

He addressed these remarks to Kate, turning toward her and smiling apologetically. Eliot felt that Gregor had been far from truthful in his estimate of the distance and was about to reproach him when Gregor forestalled him with an apology. "I didn't realize it would take so long," he said gravely. The little grocery store had closed for the night and a truck coming toward them had its headlights on. Three hours, perhaps four, had elapsed since they'd started off. But any protest was up to Kate, Eliot reminded himself.

The other car appeared, slowing at the crossroads. It was a scarred camper whose front door had been replaced by one of a different color. Boxes and bundles were roped to the top, and the windows were crammed with faces. Suddenly Gregor pushed the horn, rolling down the window and waving violently. The men in the camper waved and pulled to the side of the road, and Gregor whooped impulsively and climbed out. "They are my friends," he called back to Kate and went running down the road. The camper emptied itself of half a dozen men, who met Gregor with arms outstretched.

Kate was smiling. Eliot had observed that she treated Gregor with amusement. It also seemed to him that she did not allow the young man the claims of a special friendship, or even offer him hope for the future. No, he did not believe they were lovers. Gregor would treat her differently if they were; his style would be broader, less tentative. Instead he was not fully at ease and always slightly off balance. Kate handled him with gentleness and kindness, and Eliot saw that she was clearly in control.

16

⊙

Alexei's projected two-day conference with six South American surveillance teams had been cut short, and so he was able to return to Washington in time to attend a White House reception. His visits there had been
rare since he had come to the realization that maintenance of a truly
international organization precluded the obligations one ordinarily as-
sumes toward the Presidency. He shied away from being there in an
official capacity, and had deputized Granby Courtland, an Australian by
birth and not an American citizen, to be Interzod's liaison with the
United States government. This had stemmed from a White House
meeting in the days when the organization's importance was first being
recognized. It was a time when United States participation was undergo-
ing a kind of unofficial ratification by the twelve men in the various parts
of the government who were to have knowledge of Interzod activities,
and after listening carefully to Alexei's description of what Interzod
would do to fulfill its contract with the government, a ranking CIA

official had stood up, and in a windy, ingratiating speech, said that he would appreciate it if a report could be prepared as soon as possible, detailing the technical aspects of Interzod's computer program and the ways in which CIA participation would be most effective. The request had taken Alexei's breath away because he thought he had made it clear that the organization was to be independent of the operations of any one government.

"No, I'm sorry," Alexei said, immediately regretting the last two words.

"I can't see how we can be expected to make an intelligent appraisal without it," the CIA man said, quickly getting to his feet.

Alexei heard himself become unnecessarily nasty. "Under what circumstances you could make an intelligent appraisal of anything is not Interzod's concern. Any appraisal is unlawful under the terms of our contract, and any information you or anyone else obtain from Interzod can be shared with Interzod only. As for CIA participation, I don't anticipate there will be any."

The CIA man kept his feet. "Any problem affecting national security is a CIA problem," he asserted. "You are a newcomer to problems of surveillance and related problems with which we have had a great deal of experience."

The man's density was impressive. "We are not an agency of this government or any other government. Our operation depends on the kind of international cooperation which we would lose if the CIA had anything to do with it."

"Mr. Abarnel, who would know about CIA participation?"

"I would," Alexei said. "So would the men who work for Interzod. May I point out that every participating country has a certain number of men working for us, all of whom have full knowledge of our operations in every country? Surely you know that Russia, China, Cuba and all the Communist Balkan countries are participants and have contributed to our staff?"

The CIA man was ready for this. "Are you aware, Mr. Abarnel, that your Russian staff member, a man by the name of Varnov, is a colonel in Russian intelligence?"

"Yes," Alexei said. "And so is everyone in this room. Did *you* know that Pen Li Ko, who is our ranking member from Communist China, is also an officer in their intelligence setup? And that the same can be said for every member from Communist countries except one, and that it's also true of Egypt, Brazil and several others?"

"But how do you justify participation from their intelligence services and not our own?"

"There is no participation by their intelligence services as far as I know. It makes no difference to our operations what these men were in their home countries. I have had to make allowances for the differences in dealing with countries with a closed society. You and I know very well that Red China wouldn't allow anyone whose patriotism and loyalty wasn't proven to participate in any international organization. A Chinese couldn't attend even a Bulgarian Baptist conference unless he had open or covert connections with their intelligence establishment.

"I think your objections to this are pretty much those any intelligence agency would have. You vastly overrate what one man can do. He can steal secrets from you, true. But that's your lookout. I'll fire any member of my staff if I learn that he does so. But they can't pass on Interzod secrets because there are no secrets. Information from every country, including ours, is as open to them as it is to you. The one exception is what you call the technical aspects; presumably you mean the computer programs which enable us to carry on our work. They are the property of the Interzod Agency. No one else knows their contents."

Everyone knew that Alexei owned Interzod lock, stock and barrel, that therefore he was defending personal property, and that presumably only he knew exactly how Interzod programs were designed. "Varnov may take information back to his service, for all I know; so may the others. I also know that it couldn't amount to anything because Interzod is completely uninvolved with security problems of this country or any other. You can argue that one of our surveillance cases might be a threat to our national security, and that could very well happen. But he could just as well be a threat to the security of another country. In any case, this country and all participating countries will know what the man is doing. That is our contractual agreement, as you know.

"Moreover, did you know that Pen Li Ko doesn't report to his government about Interzod activities in Communist China? That is carried out by Niels Tonder, a Dane, and they afford him full cooperation. Did you know that Varnov, the Russian, is our liaison to Britain and that Douglas Gorden is liaison for Egypt *and* Israel?"

The CIA man knew none of this and dropped his arguments. But to dramatize the point, the next time there was a White House request for a briefing on Interzod activities within the borders of the United States, Alexei sent Pen Li Ko, who, as it happened, was more familiar than anyone else with the activities of Interzod New Orleans, Interzod Milwaukee and Interzod San Francisco. The reaction from the White House was slow in coming, but when it came it was clear that Alexei had made his point. Pen Li Ko had made an impressive presentation, according to a White House aide.

For a period of time thereafter, Alexei had declined most White House and governmental invitations which came to him in the capacity of an Interzod official, substituting anyone on his staff who was familiar with whatever was to be discussed, without regard for nationality. However, whenever there was an invitation of an unofficial sort, such as the one to the reception this evening, he made it a point to accept. If an Interzod question was raised, of course he would answer because he would have done the same at casual receptions at Number Ten Downing Street, the Palais Elysées or the Kremlin. To refuse under these circumstances what he had granted other heads of state would have been unfair. Once the essential rules were understood, relations had changed for the better and been particularly easy with later administrations who had inherited the unusual and even eccentric compact with Interzod without having had to undergo its somewhat acrimonious evolvement.

Still later, when Interzod formulations had generated an extraordinary interest and curiosity in surveillance procedures, liaison obligations to the White House resulted in long, drawn-out sessions, frequently ending in impromptu lunch or supper invitations. Alexei had succeeded in carving a place for himself in the structure of governmental authority where none had been before. He had little appetite for such encounters but a show of contention had been necessary. He thought of it a year or so later when he was immersed in learning all he could about the life of his ancestor, Isaac Abrabanel, who had been a diplomat and king's minister, and whose life had been spent in struggles waged at the foot of the throne. Isaac Abrabanel had a feeling for political infighting and presumably would have felt at home with the late buffet meals eaten while lounging on leather furniture in the presidential map room with generals, diplomats, Cabinet members and frequently the President himself.

Isaac Abrabanel had lived five hundred years ago but Alexei had closed the distance by establishing parallels between the two of them. The Abarnels had been a powerful and aristocratic family who bore the resplendent claim of direct descent from the house of David. The claim of Alexei's descent from Isaac Abrabanel was real enough. The name had lost a syllable only a hundred years after Isaac's death, the Abrabanels having been driven from Portugal and Spain long since and settled and resettled in wanderings across the map of Europe, their name being frequently whittled down or otherwise transformed to meet some exigency or for convenience. In his search, Alexei had encountered Brabanels and Barbanels by the dozens. In France he had found Barnels, in Italy Barbanellas and Barbarossas. In Greece he had met a lawyer, Babaras, in Kiev an Abravenov and in Odessa, a poor rabbi, Barbanov.

His fascination for the man didn't stem from family pride. It was ridiculous to entertain family feeling for a forebear of five centuries before, and in any case, Alexei had come to be cautious of historical allegiances. It was a mistake to shoulder the passions of one's ancestors: too much heat over ancient wrongs had generated the crucible effect in Jewish history. This was understandable, but tainted with tribal demagogery. The intellectual past might be shared equally by all. The act of will was paramount in the acceptance of cultural legacies. You did not have to depend on those available to your grandfather or great-grandfather; birth could neither include or exclude; a universal electicism was available.

Isaac Abrabanel was Portugese, Milanese, Spanish and Venetian;

he was a Jew, a diplomat, a nobleman, an exile, a Biblical scholar, a financial wizard, an astrologer and a courtier. You could choose your own Isaac Abrabanel. He was all those things, but he was different at different times of his life. His genius had the breadth of the Renaissance. Alexei was spellbound by the vitality revealed by the man's pursuit of simultaneous careers which, taken singly, would content most men as the accomplishment of a lifetime. But Isaac's devotion to astrology, a thread running through his entire career, was of paramount interest to Alexei because it paralleled his own so closely and obviously, even to the startling discovery that the two of them had been tormented by some of the identical astrological problems. The search for the astronomical identity and hence the astrological certainties of the Star of the Magi, and the discovery of the clue, by astrological means, of the fulfillment of the prophecy of the Messiah had been a lasting torment to Abrabanel.

It was not simply this that had precipitated Alexei's minute examination of Isaac Abrabanel's life, but also the discovery that this ancestor had come near to being right in the year—4 A.D. His further refinements of dates were, alas, far too broad. This was to be expected, but the puzzle was that it did not appear that he'd had enough knowledge of astronomy at his disposal for such accuracy. Nearly one hundred and fifty years later, Kepler, working on the same problem, had come up with a nearly identical date, but by that time, astronomical knowledge and mathematical skills had been greatly advanced. It was easy to follow Kepler's reckonings, but not Isaac's. The question lingered whether or not he'd had a direct source for his date, rather than astronomical knowledge. To Alexei, the question was fascinating and a source of anguish.

But Isaac Abrabanel's political life was equally fascinating. The fates of nations were identical to the fortunes of the kings and queens he served. Alphonso the Fifth of Portugal reached for the throne of Castile but stretched too far, losing to Ferdinand and Isabella, and returning embittered to the monastery at Cintru to die of melancholy. With him died the Portuguese expectations of Isaac, along with those of the rest of Alphonso's ministers, who were expelled following the confiscation of their wealth and lands. He next surfaced in Spain, where he became minister of state to Alphonso's enemies, Ferdinand and Isabella. Not surprising; it was a day of fragmented loyalties. A king chose his minister for his skill in statecraft with the same cold reckoning that went into the selection of a general or a mistress.

Expelled from Spain with the forced exodus of Moors and Jews by the Inquisitors, Isaac next found employment with the king of Naples and lastly with the Venetian aristocracy. During this period he maintained a close connection with the great communities of Jewish intellectuals in Sicily and Venice, where they had been driven from Cordova, Granada and Lisbon to pursue their knowledge of philosophy, medicine, philology and science. These communities had been touched frequently by messianic hopes and had felt the shudders caused by the announcement from time to time that the King of Kings had appeared to restore the Jews to greatness.

From the notebooks, there was evidence that Isaac Abrabanel had remained cool to the notion of the Jewish millenium for the greater part of his life. But the idea was contagious, and at the end of his career, in Venice, he made his famous astrological prediction that a Messiah would arrive on earth in the year 1503. The prediction was based on an astrological duplication of the Star of the Magi, and it was widely circulated, for by then Isaac was famous and respected on many scores.

The later notebooks, those that contained the historical basis and the astrological reckonings for his predictions, were not discovered at the time of Isaac's death; indeed, there was little reason to suppose they existed. It wasn't until Alexei took up the search for every scrap of information bearing on the subject that he deduced that there was a missing notebook compiled in the later years of Isaac's life. There were, in fact, two such notebooks, and Alexei traced them as far as Odessa. These Varnov recovered from a poverty-stricken rabbi named Abarbanov, who parted with them reluctantly, even though he had no stomach for their astrological nonsense or the elegant Latin in which they were written.

When brought to light, those old researches of Abrabanel's had given Alexei a long-sought historical insight. It had been an important victory, the second of its kind. The first had been Wembley's discoveries, based on the Nestorians' recovery of documentation that they hoped would prove their doctrinal position of a Mary and a Jesus who were undisputably flesh and blood. The third victory, was the discovery of the approximate date of birth of St. Quetor. But for Alexei, there was a terrible ambiguity in each of these victories. His increasing certainty meant greater restrictions on his life and added to the burden of his love for Kate.

Entering the White House by the 15th Street entrance, Alexei was ushered down the long, heavily carpeted underpass and then up a broad flight of stairs to the small room where the reception was being held. Entering, he thought of Kate because he saw that it was one of those small affairs, partly government, partly diplomatic with no more than twenty or thirty people. There were ladies present, and he wondered if the invitation had included wives, but before he had a chance to look around, a White House aide was at his elbow. "Telephone call for you, Mr. Abarnel. A Mr. Granby Courtland has been trying to reach you. If you want privacy, you can take it in the Vice-President's office. Follow me."

The glimpse of Mme. Forsueil, a diplomat's wife, a pretty woman and intelligent, although a little aggressive by Alexei's standards, gave rise to thoughts of Kate. He followed the aide through backstage corridors to an office with a scrambler attachment. He had brought her to other White House functions and was well aware of the comment her looks and presence caused, taking particular pride in her because he knew she was unaware she was the despair of such women as Mme. Forsueil.

These thoughts assumed a particular poignancy when he began reviewing his life with Kate—which he was to do constantly from the instant he spoke to Courtland a few minutes later. He followed the aide through backstage corridors to an office with a scrambler attachment. Granby's unscrambled voice had far more reserve and hesitancy than ordinarily. "Alexei, I'm not exactly sure what's happened. I think Diana Talbot here should be the one to tell you. It's about your wife, but she isn't very clear about it."

"Kate? What's wrong?"

"Miss Talbot is worried about her and thinks it's something you'd want to know about."

"Is Kate at home, Granby?"

"No. That's just it, you see. She was driven to town by someone she calls Eliot. Do you know who he is?"

"Yes. He's on special assignment at historical research."

Granby hesitated again. "The thing is, they haven't returned. Miss Talbot said they left at about ten-thirty this morning."

Looking at his watch, Alexei saw that nine hours had elapsed. He found himself searching for a plausible explanation but could come up with nothing. "Doesn't Diana have any idea where they are? Has anyone gone to town to look for them?"

As these questions formed themselves, he had the suspicion that Granby was trying to protect him from something. With this thought he felt himself turning to stone.

"She's not being very coherent about it, Alexei," Granby said, "but one of the guards *did* go to the village to look for the car. A gray station wagon, wasn't it? He didn't find it."

"Let me talk to Diana, Granby."

"I'll put her on, Alexei, but she's not in good shape."

"Good shape? Granby, for God's sake tell me what's going on."

"Well, I'm trying to find out. Here she is."

"Alexei?" Diana's voice was quavering. "Alexei?" she repeated.

"Diana, will you please tell me what's happened?"

There was no response, and he heard the telephone receiver strike something as though it had been dropped.

The next voice was Granby's. "Alexei, I think she's a little sotted. Does she have a problem that way?"

"Not that I'm aware of. Didn't she say anything else?"

"Nothing I'd pay any attention to. She's very rattled, Alexei. Tell me, does she have some kind of attachment for this fellow Eliot?"

"I believe she may have. What difference does that make?"

"It seemed to me that she was as much concerned for his safety as for your wife's. And tell me, does he know any gypsies?"

"Gypsies?"

"She kept saying that he's gone off with gypsies. It doesn't make sense, as you see."

Alexei's heart began to pound. "Granby, you're sure?"

"Yes."

"What exactly did she say about gypsies?"

"I can't ask her now. She's passed out, Alexei."

"Listen, Granby, how did you come in on all this?"

"She called me. I'm at your house now."

Mesmerized by the introduction of the word gypsy, Alexei asked again, "Exactly what did she say, Granby? Can't you remember?"

"When I first got here it was something like, 'Kate has gone with Eliot to the gypsies and I don't know whether or not Alexei would want me to call the police.' When I asked her what she meant and she started to laugh, I caught on that she'd been at the bottle. But she did seem very concerned about calling the police and didn't know what you'd want her to do."

"Eight hours later she wonders about it?"

"That's right. I thought I'd check on her story. The security guard at the gate said they left together in the car at ten thirty-two A.M."

"Granby, listen to me. Call the local police. Describe the car. Security has the license number. Tell them to go all out in finding the car. Make it absolutely clear that this can't reach the newspapers. Underline that. Tell them to find out what else should be done and then call you back. I'll be there in twenty minutes. Is Wembley in yet? No? No matter. When you've gone that far, get someone to sober up Diana."

When he hung up, Alexei realized that he was breathing heavily. Interzod thrived in a state of constant emergency and he was used to it, but he knew that this was going to be a different kind of agony. If he didn't locate Kate quickly he wouldn't be able to stop thinking about their marriage or the restrictions which were an outgrowth of his knowledge about her. Once again he would be drawn into questioning whether or not he had been right. He had known for some time that he had become the prisoner of his own knowledge; he also knew that he might be destroyed by it. Having taken the responsibility of protecting her, it seemed unfair that he should also be taxed with suffering for it. Still, a loving protector was preferable to other choices. He couldn't have permitted any other kind of surveillance arrangements. The thought was monstrous.

He got up slowly, trying to find the resolve to put these thoughts out of his mind. Following the corridor, he found his way to the lower level that housed the President's offices. The President, he was told, had left his office and was at the reception. "I believe you're expected, Mr. Abarnel," an aide told him.

"Please tell him I must speak to him right away," Alexei said. "I'm afraid it can't wait." The effort of trying to suspend his emotions gave his voice a constricted quality, and from the way the aide looked at him it was apparently written in his expression.

"Excuse me, Mr. Abarnel. Are you ill?"

Alexei shook his head impatiently. The aide reached for the phone, and when the President was on the line, handed it to Alexei.

"Is anything wrong?" he asked Alexei.

"Yes. A surveillance problem. I may need special assistance. The special squad at Quantico on stand-by alert. Five additional helicopters for an indefinite period of time—probably no more than a few days if I'm lucky—with pilots and radio air-control facilities for the east on a nonmilitary wavelength."

"Done. But can you give us a briefing before you take the special squad any further than alert?"

"Of course."

"What case are we dealing with?"

"There is no assigned number," Alexei said.

"How serious is it, Alexei? Does it affect national security? It's a legitimate question since you've requested military equipment."

Alexei agreed. It was a condition of the contract. "It's possible it does affect national security; I don't know yet. I won't know how serious it is until I get back to headquarters."

17

⊙

When the helicopter touched down at the Air Force base, Granby was waiting behind the wheel of the jeep, unshaven and wearing an old sweat-shirt and khaki shorts, the kind of outfit that the Interzod staff recognized as his problem-solving clothes. The degree of informality was the key to Granby's current mental exertion. Often Alexei had seen him worry a particularly knotty problem through several sleepless days and nights, and the solution never seemed to come until Granby was down to shorts and sockless tennis shoes.

They shook hands; speech was pointless against the roar of an Air Force trainer warming up nearby. Granby pulled to a stop inside the guarded barrier fence separating the airfield from Interzod grounds where it was suddenly quiet.

"You look awful," Granby said, and reached under the seat for a bottle of cognac, unscrewed the top and handed it to him. "Alexei," he asked hesitantly, "does your wife know anyone in New Jersey?"

"New Jersey? How does New Jersey fit in?"

"It's a very tenuous connection. Nothing very reliable seems to come from Diana Talbot. I really hesitate to bring it up at all, except that it does seem to have some confirmation from the guards at the gate."

"What has confirmation?"

"Not confirmation, surely. I've used the wrong word. A connection would be a better one, perhaps."

"A connection to *what?*"

"To what Diana had to say. After I talked to you she revived temporarily. I'm not at all sure she wasn't faking when she went into her faint, but she did go on in a thoroughly scurrilous way."

"Get to the point."

"I *am* getting to the point, Alexei. From her conversation it seems she goes with your wife on errands here and there quite a bit, isn't that right? According to her, there were occasions when she saw your wife speaking to a young man, and she insists on characterizing it as some kind of flirtation."

Alexei said nothing.

"She was quite adamant about this, I'm afraid. There's a coarseness in that woman that gets under my skin."

"She's not so bad, Granby. What exactly did she say about it?"

"Just that she had seen them talking together—little else, really."

"Except that she considered this a flirtation . . ."

"Yes, that. And she kept referring to him as "her gypsy.""

"Kate's gypsy?"

"Yes. But there's more to it, or else I wouldn't have paid any attention. It seems that she's heard from them. This fellow Eliot phoned her at about four P.M., as near as I can make out, to say that they were attending some kind of gypsy function and would probably be late. This seemed to me to show some responsibility on his part, but apparently she doesn't think so. It's what infuriated her, I think."

"Eliot called? What do you mean, a gypsy function?"

"A sort of get-together. She claims he didn't tell her where it was or when they would be returning. It strikes me that she's making an unnecessary amount of trouble."

"I think I'd better talk to her, Granby."

"She's still not in very good shape. I'd wait a bit if I were you. Rhav is with her. I hope you don't mind my ringing Rhav in. I know it's a personal matter, but Diana wasn't cooperating much with me, and I thought a woman might do better."

The cognac was having a restorative effect. Alexei took another swallow. "I think I'd better give it a try, anyway."

Granby seemed reluctant. He started the engine but then turned it off. "As far as I'm concerned," he said, "her story is very silly. I wouldn't have placed any stock in it at all except that the gate guards produced photographs which she recognized."

"Photographs?"

"They tell me it's standard security to take the license numbers of any car going past, which is something I didn't know. They do it with some sort of automatic roadside camera. Apparently an old blue car has been seen driving past on several occasions. Security says this same car drove by the front of the house four times between six-thirty and eight-thirty A.M. today. One of the guards was there when Diana was talking. There wasn't anything I could do to prevent him from hearing. Sorry. But he brought in the pictures taken by their camera arrangement, and she recognized the driver as the young man she says waits for your wife in town."

"Waits for her?"

"That's how Diana put it. But remember, she was raving. Everything she said had a vicious edge to it. What good is the word of a woman who would wait eight hours before reporting something of this kind if she thought it so serious?"

"What was she doing for those eight hours, do you know?"

"Doing about twelve hours worth of drinking, by the looks of it. Alexei, you have to realize that the woman's impressions are not to be trusted."

By now Alexei was convinced that Granby was withholding something. "Damn it, Granby, which impressions don't I know about?"

"Well, she seems certain that they've 'run off together.' That was the way she put it."

"Run off together?"

Granby nodded unhappily. "Alexei, it would be a mistake to put any stock in what she says." He reached for the starter button but paused for a moment. "I think I can appreciate how tough this is for you," he said, looking straight ahead. "Pretty easy to let yourself think all sorts of things. But as far as I can see, it might very well turn out to be nothing at all." As he pressed the button Alexei's question as to whether Wembley had arrived yet got lost.

When they pulled up at the headquarters building, Granby climbed down briskly. "Maybe we've got something new. I've been handling the communications myself. The police have been alerted and are looking for your car, as well as the blue car, which has a New Jersey registration. There's an all-state alarm out—unspecified federal charges —which they tell me means that if they're picked up by any local police we'll have to be ready to move in ourselves because they can't hold them for long without charges. I've also set up our own highway-surveillance network. All we can manage is the turnpikes and superhighways. I haven't used your name so far; I didn't think you'd want that."

Alexei moved behind the wheel. "Call me at the house if you find out anything," he said and roared off down the road, aware that Granby had expected him to come into headquarters. Security was very much in evidence at the house. Morrison, who headed the gate and grounds detail, stood with three officers at the rear entrance and nodded curtly as Alexei brushed past. Marshall, the West Indian who headed the house-guard detail, was standing at the door of the library talking to Rhav, who had settled herself on a window seat.

"Where's Diana?" Alexei asked her.

"She won't be talking to anybody for a while."

"Sleeping?"

"Yes. I gave her an injection."

Alexei raised his eyebrows.

"She wanted to leave. Her bags were all packed. She was pretty wild," Rhav said shortly.

Marshall disappeared and Alexei perched himself on the arm of a chair. "Granby couldn't make it clear what happened."

"It's hard to separate Talbot's convictions from the facts."

"I see."

"There's been no word, Alexei?"

"No."

"I'll stay here until she wakes up. She should be over her hysteria by then and I'll talk to her."

"Call me immediately."

"Of course," Rhav said, but it seemed to him that she looked dubious.

Feeling uncomfortable about it, Alexei went upstairs and entered Kate's bedroom, which was long and L-shaped, built with French windows that opened onto a little balcony. He'd always felt ill at ease here and realized that he'd never been here alone. To his surprise he found that she was one of those women whose presence is somehow secreted in her possessions. Though he'd tried to look at her in her unguarded moments, he had never tried to experience her here in her absence. He had come to believe that her moments were all unguarded, and had believed this to be part of her directness and simplicity—qualities that were present everywhere in the room, even in the arrangement of a bed in one part, a desk in the other, even to the few books on the night table and the cheerful disorder of her desk.

He knew very well what was expected of a husband whose wife is missing; he must go through every scrap of paper in the room for names and addresses, a procedure that might promise some husbands a distinct if perverse pleasure. Instead, he found himself intensely curious about the kind of attachment, if any, she felt for these personal objects which reflected so much of her. He looked at the desk. There were scraps of paper in her handwriting on the top of a big folder that bulged with letters; he hadn't known she'd carried on such a large correspondence. Could he bring himself to search for a fragment of a letter complaining about her life, a confidence that implied an unknown intimacy or even something that could be construed as an endearment? They would be painful to read, of course, but this wasn't what deterred him from coming even within a few feet of her desk. Rather, it was the barrier of his doubt, of his *right* to know these things. Not for a moment had he doubted the quality of the feelings he and Kate had for each other, and certainly not the strength, but the strength was drawn from a sense of shared pain, of the poignancy of trying to balance his responsibility with her trust. Still, this didn't give him the right, even less the will, to smooth out crumpled scraps from the wastebasket—or even the right to be jealous. Looking up, he caught sight of himself in her mirror, and the tight rigidity of his face shocked him. It seemed that his life was suddenly opened wide, like a split sausage, for examination. He didn't have the right to question Kate's faith in him, but without that right, what *did* he have? In foreswearing that, had he spoiled everything? Had he really hoped to learn anything from such a marriage?

It was a tempting time for self-pity, but Alexei knew that he could not pity himself for the outcome of his own measured choice. It was Kate who deserved pity. He could only ponder whether or not he had been right and whether his loss was irretrievable.

He needed a drink more than he wanted one. Leaving the desk untouched, he walked out of the room. There would be questions from some FBI expert. Suggestions, rather; they would know they couldn't take over the investigation. He would tell them he had searched her room carefully for letters, that he had even found an address book, but that they revealed nothing. He couldn't pry, couldn't do what he had no right to do, or feel what he had no right to feel. In his bedroom he took a drink standing up, staring at the ridiculous electronic paraphernalia in the monitoring room. Then he picked up the phone and called headquarters.

Granby sounded out of breath. "Alexei, this is going to sound like a damn silly question. But—Wait a minute. When was it?" He seemed to be carrying on two conversations at once. "Alexei, are you with me? Interzod New York—Carlton and Abramovsky, you know—got on the

car angle. The FBI traced it to a fellow named Gregornyi Prdzatorgnyi"
—he spelled it out and made a mush out of pronouncing it—"with an
address in Newark. They checked the address, found it was a vacant
boarded-up store, assumed it was a phony address and came to the
conclusion that the name must be false too. But in digging around the
neighborhood, they found out that the store had been occupied seven
months ago by a group of gypsies."

Alexei felt his throat contract. "What's the number?" Granby
asked, apparently returning to his other conversation.

"Go on. Get on with it, for God's sake," Alexei croaked.

"Oh, yes. Gypsies. A palm reader or something like that. The local
police remembered them. They didn't stay long, a few months. Three
complaints during that time, one for defrauding someone of three hundred dollars which ended up in a complaint against a Pala Bogarde, who
skipped town before it came to court. No effort was made to track her
down, but apparently there were several gypsies living at that address
and this Gregornyi person was one of them. Do you know anything
about them? Anything I can send back to Interzod New York?"

"Just a minute," Alexei managed to say. He put down the receiver
and bolted down another whiskey from the bottle, wiping his face with
his sleeve. Then he took four deep breaths and picked up the receiver
again. "Granby," he said carefully, "didn't Hartford Interzod have deal-
ings with an old gypsy last year?"

"Savanelli handled it."

"He became something of an expert, as I remember. Get on to him
immediately and ask him how to proceed. Now, about this Bogarde
woman. All I know is that she runs a palm-reading shop in New York,
someplace within ten or fifteen minutes' walk from Altman's. Maybe the
New York police can give Carlton and Abramovsky a lead."

"Are you coming down here?"

"Immediately. Is Wembley there?"

"Message says that he arrives in New York shortly."

"Arrange a jet charter to get him down here as soon as he lands."

"I will. Congressman Harwell is here."

"Do you know why?"

"No. Just looking pleasant and asking for you."

Alexei knew very well that Harwell had been deputized to be the ears and eyes of the White House. He couldn't blame anybody; they'd been alerted that something was in the wind and they were uneasy. "Is he asking questions?"

"He looks as if he wants to."

"If he does, go ahead and give him the answers."

"Everything?" Granby asked, as though he thought it was improper.

"Anything you want to tell him," Alexei said, seeing that at this moment Granby's powers of discretion were functioning better than his own. "And you might as well brief the rest of the staff on it. You can't go on running it by yourself. They might come up with some good ideas."

Alexei hung up and stared at the phone. Just beyond it was the whiskey. He rejected it. The crisis had come at last and he would meet it with a clear head.

18

⊙

Alexei entered the central monitoring room in the middle of Granby's briefing, and at a glance he saw that Varnov, Mendes-Menares, Beaudine, Pen Li Ko and Sakaphus were there, as well as others. Harwell, the only nonstaffer, was standing a little apart, looking uneasy and bewildered.

"No. Emphatically no," Granby was saying in response to someone's question, and then paused at Alexei's entrance.

"Go on," Alexei said.

"We are cooperating with the various police agencies, but not in the ordinary sense. They've been asked to do legwork because that's the kind of thing they can do better than we can. But they're working blind; they haven't been given any background. I want to emphasize that. As it stands, police agencies at all levels in thirteen states have been asked to search for the car and hold the occupants while the FBI is notified. Any notification we get will come from the FBI. But no one in this chain has been given Mrs. Abarnel's name, and this is important for you to remember if you are working the message desk. The police have orders to halt the gray station wagon. They've been given Eliot's name and that of the owner of the old blue car seen driving past the house—this Gregornyi What's-his-name. The orders state that either or both may be in the company of an unidentified woman and that any of the three is to be held until the FBI is notified."

There was a brief silence while Granby looked in Alexei's direction for approval.

"Has the FBI entered the case yet?" The question came from Beaudine, who doubled as chief of Interzod Palermo and Interzod Marseilles.

"No," Granby answered. "The FBI is an investigative agency only. They wouldn't be much help unless we gave them the full background of the case, which will not be done unless we have to. We have always had access to their files, as you know, and in this case we've used their facilities to issue the thirteen-state alarm and relay messages. But that's all. We'll maintain control. They haven't been given any reason for our requests, and they don't know we are looking for Mrs. Abarnel."

Alexei looked at the clock on the board. Fourteen hours had elapsed since Kate and Eliot left the house.

Granby slid off his perch on the edge of the desk and a wave of his hand signified that the briefing was over. As he motioned for Alexei to join him in his office, he remembered another detail and turned to the group. "As I have said, there is no evidence that gives a clue to the motive of Mrs. Abarnel's disappearance. Therefore whoever is on message detail must be on the alert for any attempt to contact us. Ransom kidnaping has not been ruled out. Neither has the possibility of blackmail in order to get information about Interzod operations. Until further notice all incoming phone calls must be taken on equipment with recording and tracing devices."

Closing the door to his office behind them, Granby perched on the edge of the desk, which was a familiar symptom. When he was concentrating on a problem, desks were for sitting, chairs for sleeping. "Wembley is landing now," he said.

"Good."

"About the briefing. I thought you ought to know that I gave them only the necessary details."

"Has anything come in yet from the local police on either of the cars?"

"Nothing."

"Not surprising. They had a ten-hour jump. Were there any proposals from the staff?"

"Several good ones on gypsies. Both Pen Li Ko and Mendes-Menares have some knowledge there, it turns out. Pen Li Ko has taken over strategy and operations. I'll be backup on strategy, keep on the message desk for a while and handle liaison with the FBI and whoever else needs it. Including you, I guess. You don't look so good."

"I don't suppose I do. Somehow I have the feeling that you haven't told me everything that Diana mentioned. I appreciate your wanting to make things easy for me, Granby, but it would be better to know everything than not."

"Nothing of any consequence, Alexei."

"Then there's no reason why I shouldn't hear it."

Granby looked offended. "The woman is simply demented," he said as a kind of refuge. "She said nothing that bears repeating," he continued, in the kind of desperate confusion common to people who are incapable of lying.

"Repeat it anyway."

"It was just a lot of hysterical things about separate bedrooms, and that . . . well . . . that you were inattentive as a husband—" Granby's embarrassment seemed genuine. To his undisguised relief, he was rescued by the arrival of Wembley. Varnov had his arm around Wembley's shoulder and was in earnest conversation with him as they entered the office. Looking as craggy as a Roman ruin, Wembley listened with mouth open, nodding at what Varnov was saying, until he looked up and saw Alexei.

"What's this fellow telling me? Your wife, Alexei? Is it possible?"

Alexei nodded but did not speak until Varnov and Granby had given Wembley the rest of the details. Retelling what happened meant thinking through every detail and he didn't have the stomach for that. In the next room he saw Pen Li Ko and Beaudine huddled at one end of the table. For a moment the tableau had all the force of a premonition, and he was struck by a strong sense of unreality. As if somehow he'd known all along that these men would be bending their heads together to try to gather up the fragments of his all-but-incomprehensible marriage to Kate. He'd seen them like this hundreds of times before in an atmosphere of crisis, restlessness and expectancy, each in his familiar attitude, when they came together to plot out the Interzod response to an intricate surveillance problem. This was how it had been when Interzod pursued Bayard Krim across the face of Europe from Helsinki to Angola, when Cartour plotted and nearly brought off the mutiny of a Brazilian armored cruiser and when, by hectic maneuvers on the Geneva stock exchange, they had forced Lambert et Cie into bankruptcy, thus pulling out the props from Mustafa Koylan's career in heroin distribution. During these times Pen Li Ko took to breathing through clenched teeth, Beaudine kept a lighted Gitane in every ashtray, and Varnov drank tea and gradually took on the stolidity and assurance of a judge. Alexei had seen them in action and knew they were good. They would go on and on for days until they had won. Only when they had found a solution would they sing, sleep, get drunk or play the piano —each to his own. He supposed that all along he had known that if he failed they would be there to improvise.

But now he sensed a new element. Granby's briefing had been more formal than was usual, and the staff response, from what little he'd heard, had seemed far more guarded. This was to be expected, perhaps, since they had been invited to eavesdrop on a family matter. There had always been a marked restraint among them in discussing their personal lives. Most of them were married and many had children, but only a few had taken the option of bringing their families to live in the United States. There had been three divorces that Alexei knew of; others had probably gone unannounced. It was a measure of the claim Interzod activities made on them and the tendency in nearly all of them toward total absorption, so that family and other aspects of the day-to-day world went by the board. Occasionally there was a nearly complete transformation of interest, ending in a kind of monastic dedication. Rhav had stopped being a concert pianist, and everyone close to her knew that she would never elect to return. Mendes-Menares had stopped being a doctor, except when a medical opinion was needed for an Interzod evaluation. Only Alexei, it was thought, had been able to maintain some kind of normal family life—nobody knew, of course, that his privilege was his sacrifice. Only one or two knew Kate; most of them had not even met her.

There was sudden activity at the message desk, which was separated from the monitoring room by a plate-glass partition and had direct connection with a larger, more elaborate message division where routine information was culled and separated from the critical. The alert light flashed, and Granby and Varnov both headed for it, leaving Wembley alone and looking perplexed.

Taking him by the arm, Alexei began walking him to the far side of the room. "See here," he said, speaking rapidly because out of the corner of his eye he saw that most of the staff were now gathered around the message desk. "All hell is going to break loose here in a short time. I've got to explain myself and I'm going to need your help." They had reached the large double doors; still grasping Wembley by the elbow, Alexei pushed them open.

"Alexei!" Granby's voice boomed from the message desk.

"Action?" he called back.

There was a pause while Granby considered his answer. "No. Information," he finally said punctiliously.

"In five minutes," Alexei called, then ushered Wembley down the corridor to the central computer room, passing behind the clerk at the desk with a nod and closing the sliding doors.

Wembley said nothing but stared at Alexei in a state of curiosity that he had suspended until his friend had his say.

Hurriedly, Alexei punched out the information that was always in the forefront of his memory. The year, the month and the day—the same year, month and day that Alexei had shamelessly brow-beaten Kate into exchanging for a purely spurious birth date of his own contriving, in the fear that someone would stumble on the in-credible truth—were duly punched out, along with the hour, the minute, the date, the latitude and longitude of the drab Pennsyl-vania town where Kate's mother had been allowed to linger just long enough to bring Kate into the world before being hurried on to other towns much like it in dreariness and insignificance, always in the wake of a gloomy husband's search for better work. Then he punched the button that set the program in motion.

"What on earth are you going to tell me, Alexei?" Wembley asked.

Alexei went over to the table where the output printer spewed out paper.

"Does this have anything to do with your wife?"

Alexei nodded, but said nothing until the printer had finished and he had gathered up the papers in an untidy roll and handed them to Wembley. "Take this someplace where you have privacy. Examine it and tell me what you think. That's what I need, Wemb-ley. They're going to want to question me, and you'll be able to tell them what they have to know."

"But what is this? What am I to look for? What kind of ques-tions?"

Alexei couldn't blame Wembley for his confusion, but he couldn't bring himself to offer the kind of careful explanation his friend would like. "You'll know what kind of questions they'll ask," he said shortly.

The five minutes he'd given himself had passed. The clerk was rapping on the plate-glass partition to get his attention and pointing to the telephone receiver. He started to leave.

"Alexei," Wembley said urgently, and he stopped at the door but didn't turn around. "Is this your wife's zodiacal material?"

"Yes," he said, surprised that he hadn't made at least this clear.

"But how in the world am I to do anything with it? I know nothing at all about the environmental patterns—only what I know about you. Don't you think you're the person to make an analysis?"

"The environmental data isn't necessary," Alexei said abruptly, and then, seeing that Wembley's face had taken on an expression of intense curiosity, he turned away and hurried back to the monitoring room.

Granby handed him a sheaf of papers. "Data on Gregornyi Prdzatorgnyi from our own sources. Just beginning to come in."

"Can't you give me a brief? Whose reading?"

"So far, background only," Varnov answered. "Don't see anything relevant. Arrest record trivial—one count petty larceny dismissed in Chicago. Nothing shows predisposition to violence. No occupational patterns whatsoever. Petty chiseling and confidence games. Bilking rich women of money if they come his way, carried out with minimum initiative."

He was cut short by Pen Li Ko, who emerged with more material. Granby glanced at the papers, handing them to Alexei one at a time. The first read:

SOURCE: ISRAELI INTELLIGENCE. AOP INT. CONSTANT. 18629. KRD. GREGORNYI PRDZATORGNYI. BORN HUNGARY 1943 IN SPELMA, GERMAN CONCENTRATION CAMP. MOTHER, TILLA PRDZATORGNYI. FATHER UNKNOWN. IMMIGRATED GREECE JUNE 1946 WITH TILLA. NO FURTHER CONTACT.

The second:

SOURCE: MEXICAN BORDER POLICE. ZAMPINO. CONFID. GUADALAJARA. AUGUST 1953. GREGORNYI PRDZATORGNYI, TRAVELING ON BRAZILIAN PASSPORT OF TILLA PRDZATORG-NYI, MOTHER, MARRIED TO U.S. CITZEN RONALD BRONDIZO, OCCUPATION OIL RIGGER. ENTERED GALVESTON, TEXAS.

The third:

> SOURCE: FREDIN. CONFID. RE: BRAZIL IMMIGRATION, 82936 ARL
> INCRET. NO ENTRY VISA TILLA PRDZATORGNYI. NO BRAZILIAN
> PASSPORT ISSUED TILLA PRDZATORGNYI.

The fourth:

> SOURCE: FREDIN. CONFID. SUPPLEMENT BRAZIL IMMIGRATION
> RE: RIO DE JANIERO DEPT. OF POLICE. TILLA PRDZATORGNYI
> ARRESTED RIO DE JANIERO SOLICITING. DECEMBER 1951. DIS-
> POS. UNKNOWN. FORGED ALTERED PASSPORT BEARING HER
> NAME AMENDED TO INCLUDE MINOR CHILD GREGORNYI AND
> PHOTO RETRIEVED NEW YORK ARGENTINE LEGATION 1955. EN-
> TRY VISAS RECORDED PANAMA, MEXICO, U.S. GALVESTON. PRIV.
> PASSPORT DEALER BELIEVED MEANS OF RETRIEVAL. NO CON-
> TACT BY LEGATION WITH SUBJ.

Alexei frowned and handed the reports on to Varnov. "Is the contact with Israeli intelligence any good?" he asked Granby.

"Quite good."

"Israeli intelligence has all the Nazi camp records. They'll have vital statistics for Spelma. The Germans were methodical in 1943. I want a zodiacal fix on Gregornyi," Alexei said.

"I thought you would. Contact is already working on it. It might take a day or two."

"Can't we do better than that?"

"I don't see how. I know the setup. If we put more than one contact on it, it's bound to slow things down," Varnov said.

"I'll see if I can't put a gun to his head," Granby said, heading for the main message room.

Joe Harwell loomed behind Varnov, looking grave and slightly embarrassed. "Can you account for it yet, Alexei?" he asked anxiously.

"No," he answered abruptly.

"Have you been in contact with the President?"

"No," Alexei said, not entirely surprised at the question.

"I just learned from his staff that he was on his way here," Harwell said.

"Here? Are you sure?"

"I talked to his appointment secretary. I thought you would have heard."

Alexei had anticipated some official static following the request for men and equipment, but he hadn't expected it so quickly—and he certainly hadn't expected the President to appear in person at this stage. Later, after Wembley had been heard and the zodiacal configuration had been explained, there would be a clamoring for information from all quarters—not only from the President but from a great many other heads of state. This was something he had foreseen and was prepared for. There would be demands for explanation, documentation, an endless round of conferences and perhaps even a reconvening of the International Zodiacal Seminar. In the early days when Alexei was still experimenting with procedures and hadn't yet assembled a confident, experienced staff, some of the tracking and communications had been handled through diplomatic and intelligence organizations, though rarely with their full knowledge, and the seminar had met regularly to review and coordinate operations. Now he had a strong premonition that a suggestion to bring the seminar back into existence would come from one quarter or another. If the pressure was strong enough there would be little he could do to prevent it, especially since the member countries could reconvene without Interzod sanction if they wished. Besides, they were entitled to full information.

But this was not the moment. There were obligations he could not fulfill while struggling with the blackness of his disappointment and the damnation of his failure, yet maintaining vigilance over the chaotic information and responses that, pieced together, might result in Kate's safety.

Confirmation of the President's imminent arrival came a short time later from Air Force Security. By longstanding prearrangement, their signal sent most of the Interzod guard force on a swift, sweeping search of the grounds. Alexei began to feel that he was being crowded.

On the arrival of the presidential party none of the usual courtesies were extended. But there was no help for this lack of hospitality; his good intentions were aborted by Granby's battle cry of "Action!" just as Alexei was on his way out to the portico in front of the building where the limousines from the airport had drawn up. At once he checked himself and delegated Douglas Gordon to take his place, which not only meant deputizing the usual handshaking and customary cordiality, but also answering the President's inquiries about the crisis.

At the message desk, Varnov was holding a bulletin on orange paper, which meant that it was about to be printed on the monitoring board. The President and Admiral Sherborne were coming across the monitoring room floor and Joe Harwell was making his way over to them. All eyes turned to the board as the letters began to form:

N.Y. INTERZOD MON RB3 BELLMAN 47 INTRI 7 7 RE: FBI INFOR-
MATION RE: GREGOR PRDZATORGNYI OBTAINED SPECIAL AGENTS
DUNN AND DULANY INTERVIEW ESTRA BOGARDE—SUBJECT'S
MOTHER—TERMED COOPERATIVE INFORMATIVE. TOLD AGENTS
SUBJECT LEFT N.Y. FOUR DAYS AGO—TUESDAY—VISIT FRIEND
IDENTITY UNKNOWN—LANCASTER. SUBJECT TELEPHONED
MOTHER FROM LANCASTER 9:00 A.M. TODAY DUNN-DULANY
CHECKED LONG-DISTANCE PHONE RECORDS. CONFIRM E. BO-
GARDE RECEIVED CALL FROM LANCASTER 9:00 A.M. NO VERIFI-
CATION SUBJECT WAS CALLER. AGENTS DUNN-DULANY GIVE
GOOD CREDIBILITY BOGARDE STORY. HOLD. MORE.

Varnov made a sound of disgust. "This is crap!" he said.

Alexei nodded in agreement. "What the hell is New York Interzod doing besides listening in on what the FBI is up to? Why did the FBI beat our staff to an interview with this Bogarde woman?"

"I don't know. We instructed them. Bellman was on communications up there. Carlton and Abramovsky were going to tackle Bogarde."

"Find out what's holding them up," Alexei said, noticing for the first time that the President, Harwell and Sherborne were standing just behind him and were party to the conversation. As he turned, the President immediately grasped his hand. "You should have told me all this, Alexei," he said with grave concern. "We can all appreciate how you feel, but it's a situation which demands action on the part of all governmental agencies. Joe tells me that the FBI hasn't been fully briefed on it. I think this is a mistake. I want you to let me have the FBI go all out. There wouldn't be any break in Interzod security."

Alexei looked dubious.

"But we can do more than that, Alexei," the President continued. "We have a stand-by plan for just such a contingency. It was set up in case of the sudden disappearance of anyone with top security clearance, or of any members of their families where there is a risk of blackmail. The CIA goes to work on it as well as every other intelligence service we have. It takes top priority . . ."

Alexei shook his head. "Let's wait a bit," he said.

Sherborne wore a look of angry impatience. "But Alexei," he said, with a wave toward the messages on the big board, his voice just barely in check, "it doesn't seem certain that you're even looking for the right man. He was in Lancaster, Pennsylvania, at 9:00 A.M. He couldn't very well have been the man who drove your wife from town a short time later."

Varnov saved Alexei the necessity of an answer. "But our man did *not* make a phone call from Lancaster this morning. We have photographs of him driving past our security gate several times just before 9:00 A.M. Also, the woman who talked to the FBI agents is not his mother as she claimed."

Harwell looked impressed. "How do you know?"

"His real mother is Tilla Prdzatorgnyi, who entered this country illegally in 1953. The woman the FBI agents spoke to is not Estra Bogarde, but Pala Bogarde, a gypsy tearoom fortune teller who's been in this country since at least 1943. That's when she first had a brush with the law."

Harwell was about to interject a question but Varnov kept the floor. "I'm not blaming the FBI agents who interviewed her; they probably didn't have the background material that would tell them she was lying. In any case, she's very experienced in confidence games, and being a convincing liar is one of the arts of her profession. She wasn't interested in bilking the FBI agents out of their savings. She was lying about the phone call because she wanted the FBI to shift their search to Lancaster, rather than to where he really is. Claiming to be the mother was to make her story more convincing. I don't know anything about these particular FBI agents, of course, but in my experience FBI agents give the impression of being too respectable—ah, too clean-cut, I believe the phrase is. This produces a curious reaction in someone such as this Pala Bogarde, who would not have been tempted to tell such an elaborate lie to one of our men. The elaborate lies are always more revealing. In this case, the lie tells us that she has strong reasons for protecting Gregor Prdzatorgnyi, and that she probably knows where he is."

Only Varnov was at ease with the name Prdzatorgnyi, rolling it into three faultless syllables without hesitation. Most of the staff had moved closer to hear his explanation, but Alexei had caught sight of Wembley at the far end of the room and slipped away without comment. Clutching the roll of zodiacal information, Wembley had pushed his way through the double doors, and after looking over at the message desk, sank into a chair at the far end of the briefing table. As Alexei came up to him he seemed a stranger to anything but his own thoughts, staring at nothing, his mouth slightly open like an old man dozing on a train.

At that instant Alexei was struck by the special qualities of Wembley's friendship. It was a unique relationship because Wembley alone could stand as his judge. In his own ruminations on his marriage, Alexei had often found himself carrying on lengthy mental dialogues with Wembley, trying to anticipate his responses, trying to decide whether his friend would see it as ludicrous—as indeed he himself often saw it —or whether he would grant him sympathy in his dilemma. Now he turned to him as he would to an old friend. Wembley would have the authority of the necessary knowledge; and for the same reason, only his censure could have any sting, though Alexei was prepared for censure from all quarters.

Wembley was so fixed in contemplation that Alexei actually had to touch him on the shoulder. He sat up then and asked simply, "Is she safe?"

Safe? Alexei couldn't bring himself to guess, even though with Wembley he was free to point the zodiacal indicators that suggested she could confront wickedness and malignancy and not be touched by it. She would not even censure it; she would recognize it with equanimity and compassion. Alexei knew her equanimity, knew the smile that came from a goodness more alluring than mere charm. But what did he know of the malignancy and wickedness she was facing now? Was she safe? "I don't know," he said.

Wembley let it pass. "Does she know, Alexei? Have you told her anything?"

"How could I?"

"Does she sense anything about herself?"

"I don't know," Alexei said truthfully. "I doubt it."

Wembley fell silent. He looked around the room, at the printer for a few uncomprehending moments, at the group at the message desk, then back at Alexei. "Does anyone else know?"

"No, you are the only person I've told."

"You've always kept it to yourself? It's hard to see how you've managed, Alexei . . ."

"I thought about telling you, Wembley. Perhaps I should have."

Wembley's mouth twitched. "No," he said. "I don't know if I would have been any help. I just don't know . . ." His voice died. "But now you've decided not to keep it a secret any longer—is that right?"

"Yes. I'm afraid it's the only thing to do now."

Wembley didn't answer.

"Do you see anything else for me to do?" Alexei asked anxiously.

"No," Wembley said. "You must tell them, Alexei. You may lose something by it—you will certainly lose something, and so will she. But you must."

"I want *you* to tell them, Wembley."

"Yes." He understood without questioning that Alexei couldn't give an objective briefing. "I'll do anything I can."

Their conversation ended abruptly, for the alert bell sounded, the printer on the board started again and a moment later Alexei was surrounded by his staff and the President.

INTERZOD N.Y. H.Q. SOURCE BELLMAN. CONTACT LOST WITH PALA BOGARDE. REPORT—REPEAT REPORT—ABRAMOVSKY AND CARLTON ARRESTED BY NEW YORK CITY POLICE. CHARGE UNKNOWN. PRECINCT UNKNOWN. NO DETAILS. WILL SUPPLY, HOLD.

A groan went up from Granby, who hurried to the message desk to confer with Pen Li Ko.

"Who are Abramovsky and Carlton?" the President asked.

"They're surveillance officers with New York Interzod," Varnov said.

"Does this have a connection with Mrs. Abarnel's disappearance?" Sherborne asked.

"Yes. They were working on it," Alexei answered. "We don't know if getting themselves arrested has anything to do with it."

The alert bell sounded again and Pen Li Ko ducked behind the glass partition. Alexei followed, and he waited while Pen Li Ko muttered a few unhappy monosyllables into the telephone receiver and hung up.

"Do you know what in hell Abramovsky and Carlton are up to?" Alexei asked.

Pen Li Ko blinked. "Abramovsky is very good," he offered.

Alexei didn't want such assurances.

"But this has come in now," Pen Li Ko said, handing him a decoded message.

SOURCE: ABSTRACT FROM SELMA CAMP RECORDS. MICROFILM TEXT. ISRAELI INTELLIGENCE ARCHIVES TEL AVIV. GREGORNYI

THE ASTROLOGER

MALE CHILD BORN ALIVE TO TILLA PRDZATORGNYI JAN. 7, 1944,
12:05 A.M. FATHER NOT KNOWN, MOTHER UNWED, ATTENDING
MIDWIFE HELDWIG BADENHAUSER.

"Did you dig up a location for Spelma?" Alexei asked.

"Yes, everything has gone to the computer. They will give us the configuration in a moment."

Alexei waited nervously, feeling peeved at himself because Diana Talbot's remarks about his marriage had begun to intrude. He had seen the photographs of Gregor taken at the security gate that morning, gray and grainy and enlarged by the lab. One brawny arm hung over the car door, and the window framed a head of full glossy hair and a face that struck him as insipid, but which was the kind of face that might be seen on television programs or on the covers of popular record albums—the kind of face he'd always found both weak and insolent, the expression only a twitch away from a sneer.

There was nothing complicated about Gregornyi Prdzatorgnyi's zodiacal formulation. Mildness could be said to be the most pervading characteristic. In a strenuous or rigorously organized society he would be at odds, though this would not manifest itself as either ambition or protest, but rather as a kind of passive sluggishness. He would be thought of as a laggard. This conflict would be covered up with ease and with no resulting inclination to eccentricity. These low-keyed, fairly well-balanced factors extended to the range of personal responses except for one curious malformation, a slight imbalance which probably resulted in a degree of vanity rather than of self-esteem. It would also result in a shyness or reserve in the company of men he did not know well and a tendency to curry favor with women.

"What do you think?" Varnov asked.

They had all crowded around now. Granby took it upon himself to answer, which was proper, since he had taken the dominant role in strategy so far. "I think it's very reassuring." he said. "Better than we had reason to hope for. I don't see much strength there." He gestured toward the zodiacal chart. "I don't believe we'd find much viciousness here. Just on a zodiacal basis, I can't see that he could be the instigator of any serious trouble. I doubt if he's capable of physically harming her. There's nothing here that even approaches the uncompromising kind of malignancy we're accustomed to dealing with."

Granby's analysis was conventional and perfectly correct, but there was something about his optimistic interpretation that Alexei found highly irritating. True, Gregor wasn't a man to draw and quarter anyone, but what did that have to do with it? Granby was blind to the nature of the threat that was implicit in the insipidly handsome face.

"Maybe *you* feel reassured, but I sure as hell don't," Alexei said with more choler than he meant to display. Suddenly it was clear to him that zodiacal analysis, no matter how intricate and accurate, couldn't allay his innermost fears. Had he ever pretended that the zodiacal analysis could forecast passion accurately? Admittedly Kate's zodiacal indicators were so overwhelmingly allied to the benign that she was immune to almost any evil or malignancy, but who was he to say that a passionate alliance with this vagrant Adonis constituted a form of evil? The confusion of physical love with wickedness had dogged the early Church fathers and comprised the arrogance of ascetics in all the botched corners of history. Had he unwittingly fallen in step with those brown-clad monks and crabbed cave-dwelling holy men who for centuries had clung to a stingy self-denial as a kind of smug talisman? Had he not always considered himself heir to a humanistic tradition? Had he not held the view that uncompromising continence was a self-serving mark of an all-consuming vanity? And who the hell was he to say that, given his neglect—it was pointless to employ a softer word—Kate had not found a dignified love? Was it not possible that this gypsy clod had qualities of kindness and gentleness that were not at all counterfeit, to which she in her own gentleness could not refrain from responding?

They were still looking to him for comment, but Alexei couldn't bring himself to make any. Overcome by something he did not care to define to himself, he broke away to the message desk and punched out the word BRIEFING on the printer keyboard. "This briefing," he announced carefully, "is to acquaint you with my wife's zodiacal potential." Clearly this was not what the staff had expected to hear. "Mr. Wembley is to give the briefing," he added, which also took them by surprise, since Wembley, although an occasional onlooker at special surveillance sessions, took no active part in strategy and had never conducted a staff briefing. But knowing very well that there would be questions enough for him to handle when Wembley had had his say, Alexei was determined not to take an active part. Oddly enough, when they had gathered around Wembley in the informal way that characterized all briefing sessions, he experienced a feeling of imminent relief and freedom, the feeling that the burden of his life was about to be unbuckled and allowed to drop around his feet.

Wembley's voice seemed curiously constrained. "I would like each of you to examine this," he said, carefully spreading the zodiacal data on the long table. They crowded around. Most of them had very little experience with zodiacal configurations of the kind that implied historical significance, and Alexei sensed that they were waiting for Wembley to elaborate.

"Is this complete?" someone asked.

Wembley nodded.

"I've never seen a configuration pattern anything like this," Varnov said with a frankness that seemed to speak for the others as well. The President and his party gave the chart no more than a cursory glance, realizing that it was a matter beyond their expertise, and then sat down at the table and exchanged a few words before Harwell got up and came over to Alexei.

"There's a logjam on the President's schedule, Alexei, and his appointment secretary is raising hell. Is any of this going to demand his personal attention? Sherborne and I can draw up a report for him and he'll see it as soon as this is over."

"Ask him to stay, Joe," Alexei said. "He'll want to hear what Wembley has to say, believe me. I know about presidential priorities, but as you've probably guessed, this isn't just a matter of my wife's disappearance. It's something that's going to run to top-level deliberations, and his response is important."

"In a zodiacal configuration such as this," Wembley was saying, "the problems of content are almost invariably very difficult ones."

Harwell turned to look at Wembley. "I'll urge him to stay, Alexei," he said, rejoining the President and whispering a few hurried words.

"As you see," Wembley continued, pointing with his pipestem to the columns running along the right side of the chart, "in these important delineations, we find extraordinary strength, a strength that is unparalleled in my experience." He tapped the chart in quiet emphasis. "And as you know, these delineations comprise the coefficients critical to the benevolent factor, as we have termed it. But lacking opposing coefficients in strength of any relevance whatsoever, we cannot make a prediction in terms of ordinary zodiacal conflicts and oppositions, which is the usual formula for predictive procedures." Wembley paused, but his audience was so emphatically with him that none of them appeared to breathe in the interval. However, just as he seemed to have readied his next thought, Douglas Gordon interjected a standard question. "Has this been coded against an environmental synopsis?" he asked.

Wembley shook his head. "In this case, and in cases like it, the environmental factors count for very little," he explained.

"Then how can it be analyzed?" This question from Beaudine and was a natural one from someone whose chief preoccupation was with surveillance problems.

"Only by historical patterning," Wembley said quickly, and just as quickly he realized that the phrase would have little meaning to Beaudine and most of the others. "By examination of historical replicas," he began again, but stopped short, feeling an obligation to make a fuller explanation, since his work in historical analysis was not generally understood.

"As you know," Wembley said carefully, "these environmental factors figure much more strongly in some cases than in others. Where the combined strength of all the zodiacal factors is weak, the subject is apt to be more a creature of his surroundings. I know that these ratios figure in your surveillance judgments, and that badly balanced sets of determinants aren't of much interest to you unless they also have a combined strength. Of course, we're not interested in surveillance problems in historical analysis, but we've discovered that it's unlikely anyone could make his influence extend very far without a level of combined strength of at least 100 ZP. Anyone with a combined strength lower than 50 ZP is not likely to extend his influence beyond the family group, and by the same token he will be basically unaware and uninterested. Whatever cultural endowment he lives by will have been painfully learned, and he would assume that his was no different than anyone else's. Even a marked imbalance at this level would be noticed only by those with whom he was in daily contact.

"But, of course, I don't need to explain all this to you gentlemen." Wembley removed his glasses and polished them with an enormous handkerchief. "You know better than anyone that he would be submerged in his environment, incapable of moving it in any direction. Historically this seems to account for the fact that kings were often not as important as their ministers, though anyone seeking to extend his own influence in a well-established kingdom had to take into account the office of kingship, either working through it or opposing it. But history gives us many instances of a monarch who could have little notion of the strength of his actions other than through displeased courtiers or ministers. Although what they did might have far-reaching effect, they were nevertheless environmental kings, so to speak.

"But a zodiacal configuration such as this is an entirely different matter. It is at the other end of the scale." Wembley gestured toward the array of paper on the table. "An extraordinary configuration. Such a person would be very little affected by the world around him. Of course there would be the natural assimilation of the environment—the language, customs and so on—but no matter what the environmental contributions, the destiny of such a person would be unaltered by them."

At the word destiny, the silence at the table seemed to grow more profound.

"As you can see, it is a transcendent destiny. There is an entire cluster of potentials whose strength ensures imperative resolution—a zodiacally ordained destiny. This is a duplication of what we've discovered by historical pattern researches to be the Messianic Prototype."

Alexei had been only half-listening to Wembley's words, for he had known what they would be. But his attention was caught at the use of "messianic." It was the first time the word had been used, and it wasn't clear whether anyone grasped the meaning.

However, Wembley was still rambling on without pause. "And it follows that this duplication, as well as all other duplications of the prototype, have an imperative destiny."

"What did you call this imperative destiny?" Sherborne asked abruptly.

"Messianic," Wembley replied.

"Can you explain?"

Wembley was accustomed to talking in his own mild and professional way. An inattentive listener might think he was rambling in irrelevant byways, but he stubbornly refused to hold up the kernel of his thought without showing everything that went before it—the husk, the tree, the changing seasons. Sherborne's impatience seemed to put him off balance. "I'm afraid," he said at last, "that none of us fully understand." He paused again. "Ordinarily, an understanding of any duplication comes through our familiarity with the prototype, which is nothing more than an arbitrary designation we give to the best-known replica."

Once again he came to a full stop. "In this sense," he went on carefully, "it is really a mistake, a misnomer, to refer to this configuration as the Messianic Prototype, since none of the known replicas was an actual Messiah. It is so named because each of the replicas as far as our scanty, very imperfect information tells us, has given birth to a true Messiah. What *is* imperative is that a Messiah will be born to her. Interzod has reason to believe that it has much more information about the Messiah, you see, than has heretofore been available to scholars. Not from zodiacal investigation, understand; it so happens that we have no accurate or precise information about the hour and date of any true messianic birth. On the contrary, our information about a Messiah always comes from historical sources. Messiahs invariably make an impact on history, you see, even if our knowledge is only fragmentary or reaches us through story or legend."

"By Messiah do you mean *Jesus?*" Granby blurted out, discarding all of his customary reserve.

"Jesus, yes. But let me caution you that there have been others . . ."

Wembley's attempt at caution was punctured by Beaudine. "Are you telling us that this woman is a Virgin Mary?"

Wembley looked shattered. He closed his eyes for a moment before answering. "No, no. It is true, Mr. Beaudine, that Mary, the mother of Jesus, is the best known duplication of the prototype, and in a sense we could call it the Mary Prototype. But I'm certain that this would lead to many unnecessary confusions. After all, what do we actually know about Mary or her life? Of Jesus, on the other hand, we know a great deal. We know, for instance, that like other Messiahs, he cared nothing for political alignments or national aspirations. He was the instigator of a vast moral rejuvenation by appealing to the best and noblest in every man—an appeal, I must remind you, that is understood to be universal, rather than narrow or chauvinistic. The result is generally some form of moral upheaval, a cataclysmic realignment of values, by which established authority is severely judged and usually condemned or overthrown."

"Are you suggesting that this is what's in store for us?" Mendes-Menares asked.

"All he's saying is that this is what we know of messianic activities we're familiar with," Varnov explained, and Wembley nodded in agreement.

"Moral upheaval . . ." Douglas Gordon began.

"I can't help but feel that *all* heads of state of participating governments are entitled to the same information we have heard here," Varnov said, obviously referring to the President's presence.

The President felt compelled to reply to this. "I agree. I think it's something we should discuss thoroughly. But I recommend that we postpone it until we're more familiar with the case." He looked around for confirmation and nobody had any objection. "Quite frankly," he added, "I find this bewildering."

From the expressions around the table it was clear that he was not alone. Alexei couldn't blame them.

"Please," Sherborne said in a loud voice to Wembley, unconsciously, raising his hand, schoolboy fashion, for attention. "Please, can we review what's been said here about Mary? Is that who's missing?" It was a throwback to his earlier outburst, and realizing that his impetuosity had led him into error again he tried to correct it by adding, "Or someone just like her?"

"With the same *imperative*, Admiral Sherborne," Wembley said patiently. "Just like her in some respects, taking into consideration the two thousand years that have intervened. But it doesn't leave us with much, because as I've said, we know so little about Mary in the first place."

"The *Virgin* Mary?" Beaudine asked suddenly.

"Virginity isn't part of the issue before us," Wembley replied. "Of course," he added, "for many of us it is not easy to discard or at least discount notions of the Mary Prototype that have a theological basis. But it should be recognized that the persona of Mary is clouded by legend and religious doctrine which has been constantly changing in shape and emphasis for nearly two thousand years and on which there has never been unanimity. In any event, it is nearly impossible for us to separate fact from doctrinal claims."

Alexei felt grateful to Wembley, but he'd had enough of the briefing. If he remained, he might be prompted to remind them all that his wife meant something more to him than a zodiacal oddity. It would have been awkward to leave, but he was rescued by a signal from the message desk that new information was pending. Pen Li Ko had remained alone at the control panel, which had a switch that would allow conversation at the table to be heard on the other side of the glass partition. Joining him there, Alexei could still hear clearly.

". . . you say that there are indications of a virgin birth in duplications besides that of Mary?" He did not recognize the voice.

"There are just ten replicas known to us," Wembley answered. "It is a very rare zodiacal configuration. Its effect is of very short duration, so there are few natalities. We have been able to learn very little about any of those ten—indeed, nothing at all about seven of them. There *are*, admittedly, legends about some form of miraculous birth connected with the remaining three. But you must understand that stories of miraculous births, even virgin births, frequently occur in mythology and folk legends in all eras and among people of all stages of civilization. These have no apparent basis in fact, and it is not unheard of for such legends to attach themselves to the birth of any person of extraordinary power or influence."

There was a moment's silence; then there was another voice. "I understand what you mean, but I should think that everyone concerned is going to want to know if there has been any issue in this particular case. Do the Abarnels have any children?"

Alexei could have seen who was asking this question simply by turning his head; instead, he impatiently switched off the sound and began leafing through the messages Pen Li Ko had handed him. By his odd expression, he realized that Pen must have been listening to the briefing while the messages were accumulating.

The first bulletin was businesslike and altogether satisfactory:

NEW YORK INTERZOD BELLMAN TO INTERZOD H.Q. HSTR. 8 SOLU. 42 RINT. SURVEILLANCE RESUMED PALA BOGARDE 4:40 P.M. INTERNAL RESIDENCE AUDIO MONITORING. EXTERNAL RESIDENCE VISUAL. ITEM IRM CONVERS. FOREIGN LANGUAGE. BELIEVED ROMANY. TAPING PLUS TRANSMITTING DIRECT INTERZOD H.Q. FOR IMMED. TRANSLAT. SUBSTANCE UNKNOWN HERE; PLEASE ADVISE IMMED. HOLD.

"Is someone on translation?" Alexei asked.

"Central Coding. I've been monitoring. The tapes are unclosed. Very little talk so far. Nothing interesting."

By "unclosed" tapes Pen meant that they were unedited, so that everything that transpired in the interior of Pala Bogarde's establishment—silence, footfalls, running water—was recorded, and that Central Coding would monitor and alert him to anything interesting.

The second message was preposterous:

NEW YORK INTERZOD BELLMAN TO INTERZOD H.Q. LSMR MONTI
56 RINT. ABRAMOVSKY CARLTON ARRAIGNED BROOKLYN CRIMI-
NAL COURT. CHARGE THEFT OF LADY'S WRIST WATCH, DIAMOND
RING, TOPAZ BROOCH, TWO IVORY FIGURINES. RELEASED ON
BAIL $500 EACH. HOLD. MORE.

"Don't we pay them enough?" Alexei asked in exasperation.

Pen Li Ko didn't answer. Alexei looked up and saw that he was standing at the door of the glass enclosure, looking at the group around Wembley and listening attentively.

"What's all this about?" Alexei asked, waving the bulletin.

"There is more." Pen Li Ko pointed toward the desk, not taking his eyes off Wembley.

There were three more bulletins, one an explanation from Carter:

ABRAMOVSKY CARLTON ARRESTED AT STOREFRONT PALM READ-
ING PARLOR PALA BOGARDE FOLLOWING INTERVIEW RE: SUB-
JECT GREGORNYI PRDZATORGNYI. INTERVIEW RESULTS NEGA-
TIVE. BOGARDE UNCOOPERATIVE HOSTILE CONTRADICTORY.
INTERV. TERMINATED BY ARRIVAL OF POLICE WHO SEARCHED
ABRAMOVSKY CARLTON ON BOGARDE COMPLAINT AND RECOV-
ERED ARTICLES SHE IDENTIFIED AS STOLEN. BOGARDE VERY IM-
PRESSIVE VERY STRONG.

"Strong" was Interzod shorthand for a clever and resourceful opponent. The word also appeared in the next bulletin:

NEW LONDON INTERZOD FABINI INTERZOD H.Q. ALLEN KO. CON-
TACT MADE ARLO. SAYS HE KNOWS NOTHING OF P. BOGARDE;

PRESSURE AS PER YOUR INSTRUCT. UNAVAILING. ARLO BAD BUT
OBSTINATE LIAR. OTHER SOURCE COOPERATIVE BUT NO KNOWL-
EDGE. SAYS BOGARDE VERY REPEAT VERY STRONG. AWAIT IN-
STRUCT.

"Who the hell is Arlo?" Alexei asked.

Absorbed, Pen Li Ko didn't hear, and Alexei repeated the question.

"Arlo?" Pen Li Ko blinked. "He's a very important gypsy. He knows everyone and everything, but he's afraid to say anything about Pala Bogarde."

The last bulletin was the most interesting:

NEW YORK INTERZOD TO INTERZOD H.Q. BELLMAN SURVEIL-
LANCE EXTERNAL VISUAL REPORTS PALA BOGARDE LEFT PREM-
ISES 5:02 AND CONTINUING. CARRYING ONE SMALL PIECE BLACK
LUGGAGE. WEARING BLACK HOODED CAPE. ENTERED TAXI N.Y.
REG. OL 5987 TO BROOKLYN BRIDGE 5:10. HOLD. NORTH ON
WEST SIDE DRIVE 5:14. HOLD. SURVEILLANCE CONTINUING.
VISUAL ONLY. HOLD. MORE.

"Did you reply to this?" Alexei asked.

"Just to tell them to proceed with full priority."

"Tell Bellman to make sure he's got at least three vehicles on that car, and that they shift around so that the tail isn't always the same one. Bellman isn't as experienced as Abramovsky; he needs coaching. Arrange for joint helicopter tracking. If that taxi moves out of the city, make sure that the copter has infrared tracking, and once communication is established between air and ground, make sure that we get the frequency and code so that we can monitor from here and keep them on their toes."

Such instructions were far more elaborate than customary, since H.Q. usually left such tracking decisions to the field agents. These precautions seemed to puzzle Pen Li Ko, and after he had instructed Bellman he turned to Alexei. A man of few questions, he invariably was a dozen chess moves ahead of any opponent, and his greatest value in strategy sessions was that he always grasped the full significance of any question or development. But now he seemed at sea. "Why the attention to Pala Bogarde?" he asked.

Alexei didn't care to answer fully, but it was hard to conceal anything from Pen. "She has clairvoyant powers," he said. "Probably genuine ones. That's the problem . . ."

"Yes?" Pen Li Ko was prompting.

"We have to conjecture that she may have some clairvoyant insight into what we know about Kate."

Pen Li Ko mulled this over. "There has been contact between them," Alexei added. "My wife had her fortune told by Bogarde."

Pen Li Ko raised his nearly nonexistent eyebrows.

"Bogarde is the unknown factor so far in all this," Alexei continued.

"If she *did* have some such insight, we must speculate on what she would be moved to do about it."

"You are afraid that she dreams of a gypsy Messiah?" Only Pen could ask such a direct question, and Alexei winced.

"Is it possible that your wife could have told her? It frequently happens that gypsy fortune tellers are adapt at extracting information in order to give it."

"Tell her what, for God's sake?"

"Of her destiny, of the zodiacal—"

"She doesn't know anything about it."

"You did not tell her?" Pen seemed surprised.

"What could I tell her? What do *I* really know about it?"

"Then you do not believe it yourself?"

The questions were coming too close to the core that Alexei had kept secret for so long. "Can't you see that it's impossible for me to believe one way or the other?"

Pen Li Ko said nothing for some time, and the two of them stood in silence. "Ah!" he said finally, smiling to himself, but that was all for nearly another minute.

"Ah!" he said again. "Your dilemma, if I may say so, is part of the ancient dilemma of the Jews. There has always been a longing among the Jews for the perfect king—the Messiah to deliver them from national anguish—has there not? In Isaiah there is the hope for a Messiah to help them repel the Assyrian invasion. In Jeremiah the Messiah will return them from the Babylonian exile. In Daniel he will conquer the Greek kings. Is this not true, Alexei? There has always been the longing for the Messiah who will be Israel's salvation, from the yearning of the great Judaic prophets for the rise of a great Davidic king, a yearning continued long after the coming of Jesus, always nurturing the hope of salvation. It is a cry heard at every national crisis. Always the Messiah will be a king. But was this not a mistake? Always the sins and evil he will do away with are the sins which the enemy invader has inflicted on Israel, and it is toward the invading oppressor that the terrible judgment is to be directed."

Concealing a growing amusement, Alexei listened carefully nevertheless, since Pen Li Ko generally kept his thoughts to himself. If it weren't for this rare outburst of talk, he would never have glimpsed one of Pen Li Ko's secret selves, the Biblical scholar. How many other selves remained hidden?

"But in the light of later history," Pen Li Ko continued, "it has always seemed to me that the Jews made a mistake in not accepting Christ as the Messiah they'd been looking for. It is easy enough to see why they didn't, of course. They were looking for a king, for national deliverance. Christ came as a poor man, which is always a bad credential. He could only promise personal deliverance, so naturally he would not be received as a hero.

"The Jews were defeated by politics and Roman armies, and even then Josephus hoped for a Messiah. But he never came. Still, Christianity wasn't defeated by the Roman army. In a sense the opposite was true; the Roman army learned to march under the cross. Ironic, is it not? Don't you find it so?

"All those early Christians were Jews. What did they do? They shared with the Greeks, the Romans, the Egyptians what Christ gave them. But the other Jews refused the gift. Was it because the old prophets misled them, do you think? Is it possible, Alexei, that you are afraid of making the old mistake again? Is this why you cannot either believe or disbelieve now?"

Alexei felt very tired. The vexations of ancient Judea interested him less than those at hand. More than anything, he wanted someone to tell him that Kate was safe and sound. "The world is full of ironies," he told Pen Li Ko. Then, turning to leave the glass booth, he added, "But you're right. The Jews have always been busy finding that out. And I suppose I do risk being accused of making their same old mistake, once again."

19

⊙

Eliot decided that he ought to take matters in hand. They had now been gone three to four hours, or perhaps even longer. This meant that even if they only spent a couple of hours at the gypsy encampment they would not be able to get back before two or three A.M., and even though Alexei would be away for the next twenty-four hours, there was Diana to consider. It would make matters far less complicated in the long run if he notified her now. The sight of an outdoor telephone booth by the grocery store where Gregor had parked gave him the opportunity.

Eliot had never known a possessive woman before. He had not recognized this neurotic emphasis in Diana until too late, but he still was not accustomed to it, and so he was quite unprepared for her reaction when he told her that he and Kate wouldn't be home until late. Eliot thought he was being considerate. He did not mention Gregor, but in reply to her questions he told her that they were at a gypsy camp meeting. When the phone went dead he supposed that it was a faulty connection; he did not realize that she had slammed the receiver down and did not think it necessary to call her back since his message had been delivered. Besides, Gregor and his four friends were starting back to their cars and he didn't want to delay them.

Gregor returned carrying a bottle. "This is very good if you'd care to try it. Bella makes it," he said, adding, "He is the old man," which somehow seemed a benign recommendation. Under the impression that it was some kind of beer, Eliot leaned his head back to allow himself a large swallow, and a slightly caramel flavor exploded in his throat and nasal passages. Eyes streaming, he inhaled great gulps of air to rid himself of the violent nausea the drink induced.

They were following the camper of Gregor's friends and after a few miles it pulled to the side of the road so that Gregor could lead the way. In a few minutes he slowed down and turned onto a narrow unpaved road running through pine woods with a great deal of uncut brush, which gave them a dense unkempt look. After the road dipped and mounted a little rise, the trees became taller and the ground clearer. Soon the road diminished and then vanished, and Gregor was steering his way between white rags attached to trees.

Abruptly they were there. Ahead was a clearing where hundreds of cars, trailers and trucks were parked. There were small bonfires everywhere, each the center of a group. Someone stepped in front of the car and waved them to a parking place, but Gregor ignored him and drove straight ahead, jamming on the brake every few yards to aviod running down an obstinate dog or a darting child. Cooking pots, chairs, tables and domestic articles of all kinds were scattered in clearings, and under one tree stood an iron bedstead with mattress and pillows.

Eliot realized that his anticipation of what they would see had fallen short. "How long do these things last?" he asked Gregor.

"It is different each time," Gregor told him. "Sometimes a week, sometimes longer. Some people stay only one or two days."

The din of children and barking dogs and music was intense by the time they came to a stop. Just ahead was a large moving van; in front of its open doors a group of men were seated along a trestle table, and beyond it a woman in a long flowered dress was singing to the accompaniment of an accordion.

Gregor got out of the car and went over to the table. These were the old ones, the most important men Gregor knew. Several of them turned to shake hands with him, and Bella, who was always kind to him, rose and embraced him. Gregor was thankful that Bella did not ask about Mother Bogarde. Each of them had a name far more important than Mother Bogarde, yet Gregor knew that they were all afraid of her —even Bella, who had once been her lover.

Gregor decided against introducing his guests to the table. It would have been courteous to do so, but he was unsettled in his mind about them and apprehensive about their remembering Kate's name and mentioning it to Mother Bogarde. Besides, he wasn't sure how to behave toward Eliot. To introduce him at the table would have been good because it would be a mark in his favor to bring a substantial and educated person to the gathering. But he didn't feel comfortable about it because he was sure that Eliot couldn't have a very good opinion of him. On the other hand, he felt grateful that Eliot had agreed to come, because he knew that Kate would not have come alone.

However, Gregor had not foreseen that Bella would link arms with him and return to the car with him, expecting to be introduced to Kate and Eliot, who stood watching the Bodesian sisters dance while two nearly naked children wrestled in the dust at their feet. With a wave of his arm, Bella brought them all back to the table where he poured them a glass from the wine bottle. Gregor noticed that all the men were watching Kate, who seemed to rouse them from their customary staid dignity.

When the accordionist was joined by an old man with a violin, Bella gave a little gallant bow and asked Kate to dance. He held her carefully by her waist at arm's length. It was a dance Gregor did not know. Bella was tall and massive and his heavy shock of black hair, tinged with gray at the edges, kept tumbling onto his forehead. To Gregor, it seemed that they moved beautifully together. Others had begun to dance, which was proper when an important man such as Bella had initiated it, but soon they stopped to watch Kate.

By now Gregor realized that Mother Bogarde would find out that he had brought her, but he felt proud and decided that being proud was more important than being afraid of what she would do. During the last few weeks he had come to believe that Mother Bogarde had been both wrong and unfair to him. By waiting for her in the little town where he'd discovered she sometimes came, he had managed to see Kate seven times. The first time he had been worried that she would not recognize him, or that she would be angry or not pay any attention to him. Camping alone in the woods near town, he had lain for hours listening to the frogs and distant barking of farm dogs, trying to think of what he would say to her. But when she did turn up unexpectedly on the street, he had forgotten what he'd planned to say, and had told her simply, "I wanted very much to see you again."

"That's very nice of you," she had said, and she had stopped for a few minutes to talk with him. He felt comfortable talking with her, but when she had to leave she would not agree to meet him again the next day. That was how it had continued. She would always stop and talk with him if she saw him when she was alone, but when he wanted her to agree to a time and place for another meeting she always smiled and shook her head.

Frequently he and Tono had spent months camping together, spending very little money, foraging in farmers' fields for vegetables, sometimes picking up an afternoon's work repairing cars when they needed money for gas and oil. Sometimes Tono had driven him to town when he went to see Kate, but he had always refused to stay and would return to the campsite. But yesterday they had quarreled because Gregor had said that he was going to ask her to come to the encampment. Tono had said that she wouldn't go, which Gregor suspected was true, but it was a taunt that reminded him of Mother Bogarde because she had said the same thing when he'd tried to learn Kate's name; she had made it clear that it was Kate she was protecting, that she was too good for Gregor. He could not understand her saying that about a woman who was not of their people. Tono had suggested that there would be plenty of women for him at the encampment, a suggestion Gregor found revolting; the single girls were all too young, and after thinking so much about Kate, he knew he could not be interested in the wives who were tired of their husbands.

Suddenly the music stopped and Gregor saw that another of the old men had risen to dance with Kate. He hurried over; in this respect the old men were not entitled to special courtesies.

It had grown dark, and above the table two lanterns burned with a hard white light casting the dancers' shadows on the grass. Eliot had been watching Kate dance, but when the music started up again she had disappeared. A great many more people were dancing now; they were younger for the most part, the music was faster, and some of the young men danced in their bare feet. These young ones all seemed to have a look of practiced insolence, a muscular kind of vanity that was in direct contrast to the older men, who seemed grave, slow-speaking and sedentary.

Among the women, age seemed to have the opposite effect. The young ones were not much in evidence, except for a few standing together on the far side of the dance area. It did not seem right to call them demure, but they were not as vivacious as the older ones, who seemed to have become bolder and unabashedly forward. Eliot was in the habit of grouping people in categories, as on an anthropological field trip. Observing it as a tribal ritual, he saw that the older women frequently initiated the dancing, boisterously seizing partners from among the younger men, but he wasn't inclined to pursue his studies further. He felt very tired and he wanted another drink, so he refilled his glass from the brown bottle on the table. With Kate's disappearance, he had lost his only contact, but he did not feel up to searching for her. The best thing to do, he reasoned, would be to get in the back seat of the car and take a few moments' nap.

The car was parked far enough from the noise for some relief, but when he closed his eyes he knew that he was not going to lapse into sleep easily. He lay there for a long time, it seemed to him, trying not to hear the music and shouting before finally deciding to give up any attempt to rest.

The car was unbearably stuffy and he didn't feel very well. When he opened the window the air was cooler and the din had died down; there was only the sound of a guitar and a man singing quietly. Emerging into the night air, Eliot realized that he must have slept after all, but he had no idea for how long. Most of the bonfires were burned down to embers. The lanterns on the long table were extinguished and had been replaced by a single candle near which two men sat talking and playing cards. The guitar player sat at the far end, almost hidden in the darkness.

As Eliot came up, one of them asked expansively, "So how do you feel, my friend?" It was Bella. "Your friends were looking for you. You do not feel well. You like something to eat." All three comments were statements, but Eliot took the last to be an invitation and said he would like some food. Bella climbed into the rear of the moving van and brought out a plate on which there were figs and what seemed to be some kind of white cheese that had been rolled in seeds and spices. He also produced a tin cup of very strong tea. Eliot ate everything but the tea seemed to revive his nausea and he asked if he might have a drink instead.

Everyone had gone "below," Bella explained; Eliot wished to find Gregor, he would lead the way. Once on the other side of the van, Eliot was surprised to see the flickering of more campfires, as well as more cars and trucks. Until now he had supposed that he had seen most of the encampment. Just ahead there was a haze of orange in the sky, and when they came to the crest of a gradual hill, suddenly they were looking down on an enormous bonfire in a broad clearing. There were hundreds of people in the area to the left. The noise came up in a tremendous roar from the fire, which was in a shallow circular pit, piled high with logs. Through the din could be heard shouts and singing voices and fragments of wild instrumental music. "You will find them there," Bella said, pointing.

Somehow the scene was shocking to Eliot. Not only was it unexpected, it was also forbidding because he didn't feel up to anything so Dionysian. He stood there transfixed by the flames and noise, wondering just how much responsibility he had for Kate. After all, Alexei could not hold him accountable for what his wife had chosen to do, and he was in no way an accomplice; on the other hand, in view of his fondness for them both, to do nothing seemed somehow immoral.

When he turned, he found that Bella was gone. He wished he could return to the car and sleep—the gypsy drink seemed to have the effect of a soporific on him—but he found himself starting down the hill, occasionally stumbling over people sleeping near the path, or startling couples who giggled and rolled out of his way. The noise increased steadily and the smell of food was everywhere. Occasionally someone would beckon to him to join them in a drink. At one of the fires, two men seemed to be roasting a small animal, basting it with a liquid that smoked and crackled in the embers. Every few yards there was some kind of music, most of which was drowned in the general din. He passed within a few feet of a man playing an accordion without hearing a note, but above the laughter, singing and shouting, he could occasionally hear snatches of a trumpet or a violin.

Near the fire the crowd became so thick that it seemed futile to find anyone. The crowd was drunk and exhilarated, and frequently his path was blocked by someone with a bottle urging him to have a drink. Once the crowd shoved him against a pretty woman who smilingly raised a cup of wine to his mouth, and a minute later a heavyset woman startled him by throwing her arms around him and kissing him ardently.

Near the fire, the heat was almost unbearable and every face was streaked with sweat. Eliot took off his jacket and threw it over his shoulders. When he had struggled partway around the fire's perimeter he found himself wedged among a group of people standing in a cleared space where there were dancers and a group of five musicians.

Many of the dancers were men, who did a kind of high-leaping dance which at times seemed like a track event. The music was very fast and the men would twirl with their arms crossed over their chests and then leap straight up, kicking their heels together.

When the musicians shifted into a slower tempo, most of the men quit or took female partners. Eliot caught a glimpse of Kate among them on the far side of the clearing and began to work his way toward her.

As he came closer, he saw that she was happy and excited. She was smiling, and the fire behind her made her hair glow. She had discarded her shoes and had fashioned a costume from a long black sash tied loosely around her hips, pinning up her skirt at the side to give her legs more freedom. As he watched, he had the impression that she had drawn everyone's attention. When the dancing stopped an old woman reached out and took her hand, turning her around carefully, removing a long string of dark beads she wore and placed them around Kate's neck. In response, Kate lightly kissed her on both cheeks. To Eliot this illustrated a special quality of Kate's. There was kindness and generosity in everything she did, as well as laughter and incomparable gracefulness. It seemed natural that she moved strangers to some impulsive generosity.

The five musicians switched again to a faster tempo, and Gregor took Kate's hand and swirled her out of sight. Eliot couldn't remain any longer. His queasiness had returned and the heat and noise were insufferable. Pushing his way to the rear of the crowd, he found a place to sit down by himself, feeling tired and light-headed. It was clear that the dancing would continue for hours. He would return to the car, he decided, and wait there for Gregor and Kate; there seemed nothing else to do. Home was four hours away, which meant that they would arrive no earlier than breakfast.

But as he started in the direction of the car, he discovered that he didn't know where to look for the path he'd taken down the hill. From below, the hills all looked alike. He wandered around for a long time, always keeping the fire behind him, and then sat down to rest.

He awoke stretched out on the ground, his coat bundled under his head. A few feet away lay a figure in a sleeping bag. There was enough early gray light to see that he had stumbled in among a family of five who lay in a circle with their feet pointed toward a smoldering fire.

There was a light breeze and Eliot felt cold. He put on his coat and headed back toward the big fire which still was burning fiercely. There was nobody at the dance ground, but here and there people were sitting at smaller campfires. Someone was playing a transistor radio and he could smell coffee. He stood close to the big fire to warm himself, then started off to find the coffee across the slope covered with bodies in sleeping bags and tents.

Suddenly it occurred to Eliot that Kate and Gregor might have left without him. This thought, followed by the realization that they might actually be glad to be rid of him, gave him pause. Perhaps they saw it as a godsend, as the fortuitous chance they couldn't have arranged themselves but which they both desired.

Off to the right he saw the figure of a woman bending over a fire. Stepping around sleeping forms, he made his way toward her. When he was a few yards away she looked up and nodded vigorously to him. Just beyond her his eye caught a swatch of dark golden hair. He took a deep breath before looking again, despising himself for his suspicion. A lock of blond was protruding from the top of a blanket, mingled with a shock of glossy black. Of course it could be a fair-haired child sleeping on the ground; he'd noticed a few during the evening. But he had not seen an adult with that hair.

He felt a strange desire to put off finding out the truth as long as he could, and so he asked the woman for a cup of coffee and sat near her fire to drink it. Three small children and a large dog slept at his feet and there was no attempt at conversation. After returning the cup and thanking the woman, he approached the sleeping couple, walking quietly up the hill and flanking them so as not to disturb them. More than anything he did not want to be found looking at them.

Gregor and Kate lay together on a worn canvas ground cover under a single blanket. Her feet lay outside the blanket, and both of them were covered with the fine light dust from the dance ground. She was doubled up on her side, her face nearly buried in Gregor's chest, her head pillowed on Gregor's forearm. Instantly he was sorry that he had found them, and he moved quietly away. The thought of discovery, of their embarrassment, or even worse, of some kind of disclaimer, sickened him. He would give them all that was due in the way of tolerance and understanding, but it saddened him to know that what he had seen would in some way color his friendship for Alexei.

When he'd gone a little way up the hill in search of the car, he heard the dull heavy whirring of a helicopter. There was nothing over-head, but he knew it must be close by, probably flying low beyond the ridge of the hill. He worked his way past more sleepers and reached the top, not far from the clearing where the cars were parked, which he found by following the noise of an engine in the woods.

Here there was great activity, in contrast to the somnolence below. He could hear excited voices, and when he came in view of the long trestle table by the moving van he saw a group of people who appeared to be holding an urgent conference. Then a man in a bathrobe saw him and said something to the others, pointing a finger at him. The talk stopped, and as they all turned to look at him Bella broke out of the group. "You must come quickly," he said, putting his arm firmly around Eliot's shoulder.

Eliot stiffened, then allowed himself to be led to the table. He could not abide commands, but he liked Bella. "Please, you must leave at once," the gypsy said. "You must take the girl and leave."

They were all looking at him. "Leave?" Eliot asked in surprise.

"Yes. We will show you the path," a woman said. Eliot hadn't seen her before. She had fierce eyes and wore a dark cape with a hood within which her long black hair was coiled. The men were looking at her with respect and seemed to defer to her. The word "path" suggested they wanted him to walk, and for the first time Eliot saw that the car was not there. The woman anticipated his question. "It's here," she said; "Come with me. I will show you." Then she gripped his arm fiercely. "If you don't leave now, there will be great trouble for us. You know where she lives. Take her away with you now." She began dragging him in the direction of the woods.

Eliot had questions, but he didn't ask them. After all, the host had the right to ask a guest to leave. He felt that he must go without question even if some misunderstanding was back of it all. A warm, friendly touch on the shoulder from Bella added to his confusion.

At the woods, the woman charged straight ahead, gathering her cape up to avoid the underbrush, stepping over dead saplings with determination, never relaxing her grip on his forearm. They came to a narrow clearing where the station wagon was parked in foot-high weeds.

"We must wait. She is coming," she told Eliot as they stood by the car. "Listen to me," she said fiercely. "There is danger here. There are soldiers. Do you understand?"

"Soldiers?"

"Yes."

Eliot thought she probably meant police officers, but he didn't pursue it.

"You must be careful. They must not find her here. There is danger for everyone. For you too."

In other circumstances he might have pointed out that he had done nothing wrong, but whatever her madness, they would be departing more quickly than he could have hoped for.

"They must not see you," she said, grabbing his arm.

Suddenly Kate, in the company of two men he had never seen before, was beside the car. As she got in, one of the men wrapped a blanket around her shoulder and handed her her shoes. Eliot supposed that she must be as confused as he was about what was happening.

The woman in the cape got into the back seat. "Go ahead!" she said, pointing her finger past his ear. As Eliot started the engine, Gregor came running through the underbrush. The woman shouted something in a language Eliot supposed to be some variety of Romany and the two men lunged for Gregor and held him by the arms.

"I am coming!" Gregor said, plunging in their hold like a young bull.

"You have made enough trouble," the woman yelled.

Kate turned around and the woman put a hand on her shoulder. Eliot looked away, not wanting to read the expression on her face.

Suddenly Gregor broke loose, but the woman pointed her finger at him and said a single Romany word that brought him to a full stop.

"Fool, I warned you!" she said in English. "I told you not to look for her. I told you not to take her away from her people. Gregor, you did not listen. You have brought disgrace on all of us. You have made trouble that you cannot understand. She is not for you. It is forbidden!

Go!" she said, tapping Eliot sharply so that he knew the command was for him as well as for Gregor.

As they moved through the woods, Kate looked back once and then turned away. After a quarter of a mile, the woman told Eliot to stop, and she got out and walked a little way ahead, peering among the trees. Then she motioned him forward again, and when he came abreast he saw that they were skirting a large field. Behind the shelter of trees, in the center of the field, were two helicopters, the blade of one moving slowly. Several men were standing there. Eliot looked carefully, and to his astonishment saw that they were soldiers, just as the woman had said. Several men in civilian dress were beside a jeep, and just before they were lost from view, Eliot saw a second jeep coming across the field.

The woman returned to the car and they followed a vague road for a quarter of a mile further before she told him to turn off the path. Pointing out the way over ground of flat rock strewn with pine needles, she directed him without hesitation between clumps of shrubbery until they came to another road. This wound slowly downhill until they came to a man standing beside a car pulled off the road.

Here they stopped, and the woman said, "Follow this road. I will leave you now. There are no turnings until you reach the highway."

She got out, then reached in, took one of Kate's hands and held it to her lips, closing her eyes and murmuring something to herself. Then, bending close, she whispered something in Kate's ear and kissed her on the forehead. Kate was moved; she took the woman's hand in hers and held it. There were tears in the woman's eyes, and tears streamed down Kate's face. She raised the woman's hand to kiss it, but the gypsy snatched it away. "I am but a *sinustra*," she said humbly. "You must go." She joined the man at the car, and Eliot started down the road.

20

⊙

At midnight Joe Harwell was pouring himself a drink when the phone rang. It was Alexei. "Can you go to Brussels right away?"

"Brussels?"

"Yes." There was an uncomfortable pause. "It would be a favor, Joe. The European partners are getting irritable. No, not just the Europeans—all of them, actually. They have questions, and they've convened another seminar. It isn't any of their business, really, but I've decided to tell them everything they want to know. I can't see there's any other way. Granby will be in overall charge, but Wembley will be going too; he'll handle the briefing. But I can't burden them with all of it. I thought that someone who wasn't an Interzod employee should be there as an observer to pick up reactions. I don't expect it will last more than a few hours. You'll be comfortable," he added irrelevantly, a remark which made Harwell aware of the nakedness of the appeal.

"I'd gladly go, but I don't know if I'm qualified to be of much help."

Alexei cut him short. "Don't worry about that. I'll fill you in. You'll be our diplomatic representative; Wembley will be answering all the technical stuff."

There was no possibility that Harwell would refuse. He packed hurriedly, and thirty minutes later, a car picked him up at his house. Within an hour a helicopter had deposited him at the Air Force base where, looking tired and preoccupied, Alexei was waiting for him on board a jet. Harwell had called Interzod twice earlier in the day to find out if there was any word about Kate's whereabouts, but there had been no news, and he sensed now that Alexei didn't want to discuss it.

"I can't tell you what you can expect to find at Brussels," Alexei said. "Granby's already there. He's our expert on arrangements. He tells me that there are pretty strong ground tremors about this affair. Apparently the idea for the seminar came from the French. They wanted it held in Paris, but Granby thought we would have more privacy and better control in Brussels. For the most part it will be a cross section of people with Interzod clearance, but fewer from the military and more from governmental and academic fields. No top-level government people that I've heard of, but their questions will all be top echelon in origin. They'll be curious, and from what Granby tells me, some of them are upset and pretty demanding.

"My plan is to keep everything cool, tell them everything they want to know, and keep it from becoming any more of an international event than it already is. Do you follow me?"

"So far."

"Do you know what an international conference looks and sounds like?"

Harwell knew. Someone in the Department of Agriculture had assumed that since he came from an agricultural state, international conferences on livestock and grain production would interest him. After two such affairs he had concluded that spying was the only efficient way for governments to exchange information, and that by classifying agricultural data, conferences could be abolished.

"There hasn't been an International Zodiacal Seminar since Interzod's early days. They served a useful purpose then; we knew what could be done, but we didn't know how to go about doing it. I didn't know what would be acceptable to various countries and until we did, we tried out our ideas in the seminars. When we had a staff trained in surveillance techniques and knew where we stood, we set up representatives to every country, and the seminar was disbanded.

"It's nasty business taking power away from anyone. It's easier not to give it away in the first place. Therefore during all that time we were careful not to allow them actual power. We kept it absolutely informal. They were listeners—no voting on resolutions, no electing presiding officers, not even the semblance of parliamentary procedures.

"As I'm sure you know, institutions like to grow. Instead of individual delegates, soon I'd have been dealing with delegations, and eventually we'd have created an international bureaucracy. We knew we couldn't operate that way, so our plan was to keep the seminar stunted.

"So much for what's gone before," Alexei said with a shrug. "Now for what you have to know. In the first place, there's the question about how this all came about. Granby tells me there's speculation that I stumbled on it because I happened to take a reading of my wife's zodiacal potential. I don't think anyone will be comfortable believing in that kind of coincidence. Besides, it isn't true. Discovery of the configuration involved years of brilliant research by Wembley. But you won't have to worry about that part; Wembley will be there to defend his own work if necessary. But it was from his work that we were able to work out the other times and places the configuration occurred. Hers was only the most recent, and the likelihood of a natality was very small. When I learned there *had* been one, I tracked her down. No one else knew anything about it."

Alexei paused and shifted restlessly in his chair. "Now," he said, "for the next thing. There is bound to be speculation about my private life. I imagine you've thought about it yourself, and everyone there will have asked himself the same questions. I can't blame them. Traditional doctrinal ideas about Mary do provoke certain rather coarse speculations. Naturally I would prefer that they didn't become a subject for open debate in the seminar, but if they do, there's nothing that can be done about it. It can't help but be recognized that it was an *unusual* kind of marriage.

"Now for the third thing. I believe I made it clear the other day that Kate knows nothing whatsoever about her zodiacal potential. As far as I know, she doesn't even have a notion of what one is. What I wish you to make perfectly clear is that this information about her is and must remain classified Interzod information. As you will see, Granby will enforce the rule that there is to be no note-taking at the seminar. Nor will Interzod issue any reports; all displays that Wembley will offer are microfilmed and will be shown to members by slide. As you may or may not know, most Interzod communications are oral. Our branch offices and field groups keep only minimal temporary records at any time. Granby will emphasize that any written references to the seminar or its subject matter will be a breach of Interzod security regulations.

"What I should like you to remind the seminar is that not only is Kate ignorant of everything about her own zodiacal potential, but that she's also completely in the dark about Interzod. She doesn't have any idea of the business I'm in. That may sound strange to you, but she agreed to this before our marriage. She wasn't to ask, but she had my word for it that what I do is not in any way dishonest. I suspect she believes that the H.Q. buildings are part of the Air Force base and that I'm connected with a secret project of some kind. It would be the easiest inference for her to draw. She does know that I travel a great deal from the base."

"Wouldn't it have been easier to tell her you *were* working on a secret Air Force project?"

"Perhaps. But you see, that wouldn't explain everything."

Harwell was sorry he'd asked the question because he saw that it was leading the conversation into matters that made them both uncomfortable.

Alexei looked at his watch. "Just one more thing," he said. "Don't let yourself be drawn into a discussion about theology, religion or whatever. Perhaps this is the course the discussion will take, though I hope not. But since you'll be answering for me about personal matters, I don't particularly want it thought that there's been a religious impulse behind all this."

"I understand."

"I recall from the research our staff did on you that you're not Catholic and are an indifferent churchgoer—Protestant of some sort? Whatever, it didn't seem to me that you'd have any strong doctrinal feelings about Mary."

"If there was any doctrine about it, I wasn't paying attention," Harwell said, thinking of the Fundamentalist pine-pewed church of his youth. "She was simply called the Mother of Jesus."

Alexei appeared to have finished his formal briefing, and his next question seemed to stem from simple curiosity. "Not *Holy* Mother, or Blessed Virgin, or some such phrase?"

"Not that I remember," Harwell said. It seemed natural for him to ask a question on the same order. "But won't everyone at the seminar suppose that you were brought up in the Jewish religion? Would they expect you to have a strong opinion on Mary?"

"No. Faith can have it any way it wants. I've been concerned with facts. The facts of this replication are simple. In the five thousand-year span in which there is the remotest chance of there being a replication recorded, there have been 138 fifteen-second intervals in which a Mary replica could be born. Of these 138, we have definite evidence of only two natalities. But there are also three other natalities for this configuration for which there is Grade B proof. This means that it is incomplete and fragmentary, with the precise time of birth missing, but that each can be tracked back to approximately coincide with a time and place in which we know the configuration to have occurred. In all three cases there are strong legends of messianic activity. More to the point, in all three there are also legends or reports of a miraculous birth. There isn't time to go into these replications in detail. They won't be discussed at the seminar, and I mention them only because they are a partial answer to your question. My dilemma wasn't a religious one; it just turned out that all the historical digging brought me to the same kind of uncertainty."

*   *   *

To Harwell, the word seminar had always conjured up a picture of a long table surrounded by people with a lot on their minds. The International Zodiacal Seminar was never going to be gathered around a single table because the hundred or so participants—all of whom did seem to have a great deal on their minds and to be bent on serious talk —couldn't even have been jammed into a single room of the house where the meeting had been convened. It was a large mansion on a country estate several hours drive from the Brussels airport, with one enormous room, numerous medium-sized ones and a long verandah with a stone balustrade. The big room, with a fireplace large enough to stable a horse, which possibly could have accommodated all the delegates at once, was at all hours the scene of a lavish buffet. A true seminar was not possible because there was no other adequate space, and a seminar with only half of the people present was unthinkable. Anyone urging his opinion had to contend with the possibility that someone was urging an opposing one on those gathered in another room. A consensus of delegates was not possible; neither was much disagreement on any one point.

The dispersal of people bothered Harwell at first. Granby seemed to have taken over the duties of host, meeting delegates at the door, ushering them over to the long buffet table, then making a few cursory introductions and leaving them on their own, rather like the country squire at a large house party. Harwell moved from one room to another, introducing himself to strangers, who were milling around and chatting as if at a large cocktail party. Several hours elapsed before he gave way to his unfulfilled expectations and stopped Granby in flight from the large hall to the verandah outside. "When are things going to get started?" he asked.

"They've already started," Granby told him briskly. "Wembley's hard at work filling them in. All that's necessary is that you get in there and answer any question you know the answer to. Alexei told me that between you, Wembley and you know everything. Answer whatever questions they ask; they deserve it."

Granby looked confident and relaxed. Harwell had always sensed that Alexei had an extremely high opinion of Granby, but he had never known what his particular strength was. Granby was a man who knew how to be in charge. In American politics his counterpart was a congressional whip.

"It's going very well, don't you think?" he asked in a guarded tone.

Harwell was puzzled by the question. He had heard a great deal of talk about moral rejuvenation. The notion had been phrased in many ways, such as "ethical reorientation," and someone had questioned him about the effects of "a strong divisive morality on political stability." The phrase sounded rehearsed; whatever it meant. Harwell had no idea whether the seminar was going well or not.

"From what I've heard, there is a general feeling that this marks the beginning of something rather than its end," Granby said. "No one seems to think there's any more to it now than we've told them, but they do know there's more to come, and they don't want to go away thinking they won't hear any more about it. I've heard several people say they think that before the seminar is adjourned, a committee should be formed to keep abreast of everything that happens."

"I can't say as I blame them," Harwell said.

Granby looked at him shrewdly. "Do you really think so?" he asked.

"If they want a committee, give them one. It will be less trouble than a seminar," Harwell said.

Granby nodded. "But whoever heard of a seminar electing a committee? That makes it *more* than a seminar, you see."

"Appoint one yourself, then. Beat them to it."

Granby's eyes narrowed, and without another word he gave Harwell a friendly clap on the shoulder and disappeared.

Shortly after this, Harwell wandered into the library of the house, where he found Wembley in one corner with a group of men. There were introductions, but Harwell focused on only two people, a professor from the University of Dresden and a young Chinese who wore a Mao tunic.

Wembley was explaining the difference between astrological duplications and historical parallels. The German professor considered himself an expert at what he called "messianic parallels" and pronounced the names Marduk and Krishna with a special emphasis. "From everything we know of Marduk," he pontificated, "his messianic message was very similar to Christ's. His appeal was to a personal religiosity each man could find in himself. It must have been astonishing for a slave to learn that in the sight of God he was the equal to his master, even to the king."

Wembley, however, answered the man seriously and with a patience that suggested he'd made the reply several times before. "Of course," he said, "the historical similarities are remarkable, and it may well be that there are astrological similarities or even astrological duplications. But there is no way for us to tell. There is no way for us to discover the astrological make-up of Marduk or Krishna. And," he added with even more revealing patience, "we are concerned only with a duplication of *Mary's* astrological make-up. Theology, which is an imperfect kind of history, tells us only that she was the mother of Christ, but *astrologically* we know that she was remarkable."

The professor didn't budge from his theme. "I believe you said you knew of *other* duplications?" he asked.

"Well, that's not quite correct," Wembley said. "I know of three others which are primitive legends roughly coinciding with the time and place such a duplication *could* have occurred. But it doesn't amount to precise knowledge, and I can't see that we can learn much from them."

"Legends? What kind of legends?" the professor asked.

"Very sketchy for the most part," Wembley said evasively.

"But certainly something enabled you to identify them with what is known of Mary."

"Yes. Each of the three legends has to do with a miraculous birth of some sort."

The professor nodded with self-satisfaction. The young Chinese hadn't moved a muscle. "And do any of them deal with messianic activity?"

"Two of them do," Wembley said rather unhappily, as though realizing that now it would be rude not to proceed further. "In the

Southern Melanesian archipelago, there is a legend of a miraculous birth for the mother of St. Quetor. She is said to have retired alone to a remote part of the island of Pamosan at the age of fifteen and returned a year later with an infant. There are only a few relics of the legend extant, the most detailed being the records of the sixteenth-century Inquisitional proceedings against a friar who found he could gain converts among the islanders by absorbing those elements of their own pagan religion that more or less corresponded to Christian doctrine."

Wembley coughed slightly and continued. "The claim for Quetor's messianic activity rests on a series of miracles by which he succeeded in changing the prevailing cannibalistic customs. In pre-Quetorian times, the natives were said to have regularly raided the neighboring islands for prisoners. The miracle Quetor performed as a young man was to lead the victims unharmed from the fire in which they had been roasting and to enjoin his own islanders from eating human flesh or from warring on their neighbors. He taught them how to make nets for fishing, as well as the elements of animal husbandry. Then he set off by himself in a small boat to other islands in the archipelego where he repeated the miracle. On many of the islands the legend was that he himself was the intended victim, emerging from the fire unscathed to preach abstinence from human flesh. The friar, who took it upon himself to canonize Quetor, shrewdly rendered these events into the eleventh Mosaic commandment: "Thou shalt not consume thine enemy or thine neighbor.""

Again Wembley hesitated, but when confronted by silence he continued to the end. "Somehow, word of the friar's activities reached his bishop and he was recalled to Spain, where he was charged, as I recall, with heresy for having usurped the papal prerogative of canonization. He refused to recant and was burned at the stake at Toledo.

"The question arises, how is it possible to assign a date for the origin of a legend such as this? Well, years later, an Arab trader found that the natives of one of the larger islands had dated a crude calendar from the time of the friar's mission there. Maritime peoples always had the best primitive calendars, you know. This trader made careful notations for a period of years, which gave us a good idea of its disparity with our modern-day calendar. The only thing we don't know is Quetor's precise age when their calendar was established. If he was thirty-two years old, which is not unreasonable, we know he could be the product of a Mary duplication. But more convincing proof comes from our dating of certain relics—skeletal remains—believed to be those of St. Quetor."

With this, Wembley excused himself abruptly and walked out of the library.

Continuing his wandering, Harwell learned that "apocalyptic" was another word rapidly gaining in popularity, along with "moral resurgence," "regeneration" and "rejuvenation." Apocalypse was a word whose exact meaning wasn't clear to him until he looked it up. He also received several startled looks when he happened to mention that he had met Mrs. Abarnel. Of those present, he later learned, Granby and Wembley were the only others who had.

The exchange of information among the delegates was surprisingly accurate. Harwell dutifully expounded on the points Alexei had briefed him on and only once did he hear his remarks repeated in garbled form. He held forth to groups of a dozen or more, avoiding his subject in smaller gatherings whenever he could because it seemed to provoke questions which penetrated too uncomfortably into Alexei's private life. On the whole, he preferred to listen. The place was overrun with experts, and everyone seemed to have primed himself with esoteric knowledge and difficult questions. Most of these were directed at Wembley, who should have been exhausted. He was indefatigable and remained very much in command, only allowing his impatience to flare up when confronted by a pest.

"Pest" was Wembley's word. He applied it to a very thin, hawkish Spaniard who seemed to know everything about medieval astrologers. "Do you know that to discover the Star of the Magi was the dream of astrology for hundreds of years?" Wembley said he had known that. "Do you know that Kepler pinpointed it to a conjunction of Saturn and Jupiter that occurred in 7 B.C.? Are you aware that Isaac Abrabanel, an accomplished fifteenth-century statesman and a truly great astrologer, came to the same conclusion?" Wembley knew this too, but stiffening under the man's insufferable tone, he pointed out that both had found three such conjunctions during 7 B.C., that they were of no value to a scientific astrologer, and turned away.

The other pest was a woman who asked Wembley if he had examined the astrological credentials—a phrase new to Harwell—of the mother of James Ford Light, who, it developed, had been a missionary doctor working in the Gold Coast at the turn of the century.

"No, but astrologically there was no possible Mary duplication anywhere during the nineteenth century," Wembley said. As the woman persisted in enumerating Dr. Light's similarities to Jesus Christ, a very black man groaned under his breath and walked away.

"I'm sure Mr. Light was a good and selfless man," Wembley said gently and then added, more firmly, "Someone is forever telling us that Jesus was in Dublin in Easter, 1916, or was leading a strike in Liverpool during the Industrial Revolution. There are a lot more of these paper Christs than there are true historical parallels. They're intriguing, but I don't know of any who are also astrological parallels."

Still, for the most part Wembley was heard with silent respect. It was necessary for him to repeat his story continually because delegates were constantly departing and arriving; many of them seemed to be interested only in what Wembley had to say and remained for no more than a few hours. Harwell observed that those whose interest seemed more political were reluctant to depart.

There was general interest in how Wembley had come by the time and place of a birth that had occurred two thousand years before. "Most facts about the past can't be dug up because they've never been buried in the first place," Wembley would answer. "They are facts nobody thought important enough to record. Some facts are important enough to be destroyed; some are deliberately falsified. In this case there are two sources who thought they were important enough to record. One was a Samaritan astrologer called Simon Magus, whose reason for searching out Mary's time and place of birth and recording it was much like our own. His task was comparatively simple because he was only a few years younger than Mary. It may be that he also searched for the data of Jesus' birth, but we will probably never know if he was successful. Nobody claims that he was.

"The second source interested in this material came along much later. They were not astrologers but theologians, such as the Arians and Nestorians, to whom proof of the actual humanity of Mary and Jesus was a burning issue. Acting from deeply religious motives, they searched for every scrap of evidence about the birth of Jesus and Mary and zealously preserved it. Among their scraps of written evidence, some of it disguised to prevent its being destroyed by rival theologians, was the material gathered by Simon Magus and his successor, one Meander. We have found supporting evidence from other sources—not so important, perhaps, but gratifying because it confirms this data."

Wembley spoke in an entirely different vein to the men he considered his peers in knowledge. Harwell especially remembered two small, restless men who followed a shattering exchange of historical expertise with a technical discussion about rectifying calendrical errors. "Mere calendar reform is not enough," Wembley agreed. "All history must be remeasured, the days and hours made to correspond with modern astrological standards. An astrologer must work with absolutely true hours, true days, true years." Although he understood almost nothing of the discussion, the remark stuck with Harwell.

Often, when someone showed a keen interest in a particular part of his presentation, Wembley would willingly allow himself to be drawn out. "Nestorius? We owe everything to him and to his followers. I've always felt a kind of sympathy for the man and for his outlook—wanting to find the true man in Jesus and the real woman in Mary, willing to stand up to fellows like Cyril of Alexandria and all the rest who emphasized only the mystical side of religion. There must have been something down to earth and likeable about a fellow who couldn't see anything wrong with thinking about Jesus as a man instead of as a kind of super ghost.

"Nestorius simply could not bring himself to believe wholeheartedly in the virgin birth of Jesus, to say nothing of the immaculate conception of Mary. He wasn't a small-time heretic. His point of view grew from the sentiments and teaching that flourished at Antiochus, which by the third century ranked in importance with Constantinople, Rome or Alexandria in the Christian world. You know, just as soon as they became reconciled to the probability that Jesus wasn't coming back to establish the Kingdom of Heaven on earth, the early Christians got down to the job of trying to decide what they were supposed to do, what Christ really *had* said and what his words meant.

"Much of the early Christian theology was shaped by Greek metaphysical habits. All the notions about the relationship of Jesus, God and Mary had to fit exactly, and it was considered bad metaphysics to say that a perfect God could have anything less than a perfect son. Therefore Jesus was held to be God's equal—in fact *was* God, just as much as the Father. This is quite a step up from the rank of God's messenger or ambassador. Similarly, Mary was elevated to a state of perfection and perpetual virginity, which was proper and metaphysically becoming to the Mother of God." To Harwell it seemed that the woman who on this occasion had asked to know more about Nestorius was looking bewildered. But he had seen enough of Wembley to know that though he occasionally indulged in circumlocution, he invariably returned to the question at hand and that the answer always was better for the detour.

"In the fifth century, the time of Nestorius, the Trinity was still being defined. The relationship of God, Jesus and Mary was established so as to be harmonious with philosophical principles. As *logoi*, as philosophical principles, they were a nearly perfect fit, but there is no denying that as a result the humanity of Jesus and Mary was dimmed. Making Mary immaculate from her conception to ascension, has caused her to become unbelievable. We cannot imagine such purity in the act of singing, crying, eating, laughing. The humanity is gone. Some of the worst apocryphal literature—blatantly apocryphal—has passages of conversation in which we are told that Mary laughs. Naturally, the reader does not believe it; she has no human voice.

"When I think of Nestorius, I picture him as an honest fellow who understood the verities of humanity better than those of theology. Of course his viewpoint was doomed to failure. Cyril of Alexandria arrived at the Council of Ephesus in 431 with a denunciation of heresy against him. Also, he was traveling with one hundred twenty armed bishops, and Nestorius could muster only sixty. Theological disagreements were serious matters in those days. Against such odds, there was little point in Nestorius' presenting his point of view for debate. The populace of Ephesus was hostile, there were nasty riots, and he fled back to Constantinople. In his absence he was condemned for heresy and eventually was banished to a monastery on the upper reaches of the Nile. The Nestorian monasteries were closed, the Nestorians themselves were subjected to ruthless persecution, and they dispersed. The issue of Nestorianism provoked countless riots in many Christian cities, and since Christianity at that time ringed the Mediterranean, only a few dared linger anywhere within the reach of the furious bishops of Alexandria and Rome. A few did dare to take refuge on the island of Crete, and this turned out to be an important exception to the general direction of dispersal, because at the close of the war a captured German soldier presented me with a number of early papyri he had discovered among the ruins of a fourth-century church. The papyri were Nestorian and gave us the clue to other Nestorian documents which described the birth of Mary. It remained for us to try to find them.

"At the time of their great dispersal, most Nestorians fled to the East, taking with them documents pertaining to their beliefs. These were precious to their creed and would certainly have been seized and destroyed. Their heresy was considered very serious. The Church was committed to its mysteries and to a mystical interpretation of the Scriptures. But to the Nestorians, who cared little for allegory, the apple was still an apple and the serpent a real serpent, just as Jesus was a strong, good man and Mary was a fruitful woman.

"In any event, they traveled through Asia Minor with great missionary zeal, gaining converts and building churches. Some of them settled in Iran, northern Turkey and southern Russia; others went south into Arabia or east into India. By the sixth century, they were established in Malabar and Ceylon, and by the seventh—636, I believe it was—one pair had reached the Chinese Middle Kingdom. As a matter of fact, the remains of the earliest Nestorian church are to be seen at the Chang 'an district of Hei en-fu in Shenoi province.

"In following the Nestorian migration and the amazing success of their missionary efforts, I've often speculated on the possibility that they could have converted China, and perhaps all of Asia, to Nestorian Christianity, making the fundamental religious difference between East and West one of a literal humanitarian Christianity as opposed to a mystical, transcendental Christianity."

At this moment Granby loomed up next to Harwell and drew him from the group with a firm hand.

"I'm bowing to pressure. I'm telling three people that they will be apprised of all future details so that they will be able to keep the seminar informed. They'll be shown every courtesy by Interzod and they'll be meeting in New York tomorrow." Granby paused. "You'd better get packed because you're one of them."

Harwell hadn't expected it. "Me? Why me?"

"You seem like a good bet. You're not an Interzod regular and Alexei has been willing to confide in you."

"Was it *his* idea?"

"He agreed to the principle and left the choice of people up to me."

"Why New York?"

"Because that's where something seems to be happening—just what, I don't know. Pen Li Ko will fill you in when you get there."

21

⊙

Alexei had been told what he could expect to find. The interior of the room had been described—its flowered curtains, its shabbiness and pretentiousness, the mixture of sacred and profane, symbolized by a crystal ball nestled on a shelf of gaudy icons, the Christ slumping from a chipped cross, dejected and sorrowing beneath layers of laminated gold. They had described Mother Bogarde too, but not so well that he was prepared for her. When he entered the shop, she was sitting at a round table playing solitaire. The blue light of a television screen flickered in the back room.

"Are you Mother Bogarde?" he asked.

She looked at him carefully. "I don't know you," she said. "Are you the precinct? You are not on the squad. I know the squad."

"I am not from the squad or the precinct. I am not a police officer."

She seemed to believe him but still appeared puzzled.

"My name is Alexei Abarnel."

Mother Bogarde gave no indication that she recognized the name. "What do you want here?" she asked coldly.

"I would like to talk to you." When she made no response, he sat down in the chair opposite her. "You know my wife. I would like to know what was said when she came to see you. It's something I'm ready to pay you for."

Mother Bogarde continued to play cards. Without looking up, she asked, "Why do you want to know that?"

"I have very good reasons."

"It cannot be done."

"I know it can be done," Alexei said. "It would be for her good."

Laying down the final card, Mother Bogarde looked him full in the face. Her eyes were the brightest black he'd ever seen. "What are you to her?" she asked. "You are the husband. What is that to her that I should tell you anything?"

"The husband, yes," Alexei said. "But I'm more than that, more than she knows about. I am protecting her for what I know her to be."

"Know?" Mother Bogarde asked. "Did she tell you? She could not tell you."

"She didn't tell me, and it's true that she couldn't, because she doesn't know. But *I* know." His special emphasis on the pronoun seemed to interest her.

"You know," she repeated quietly. Then, lowering her voice almost to a whisper, "Do you have the gift?"

"No."

She looked scornful.

"But I know," Alexei said. "It wasn't a gift. I had to earn what I know."

Mother Bogarde seemed interested again. "How?" she asked softly.

"I am an astrologer."

She looked at him even more carefully then, examining his shoes, his shirt, his tie, his suit. Then she studied his face, which appeared to her, he supposed, too bland. "You do not look to me like an astrologer," she said at last. "You do not have the eyes or the hands of an astrologer.

Not the voice, either," she added, shaking her head but continuing to examine him carefully.

"I don't suppose I do," Alexei said, "but I don't see that it should matter very much to you."

Mother Bogarde considered his answer for a moment. "How do I know I can trust you?" she asked.

"If you have the gift, you will know that I am an astrologer and that I am not a policeman."

She snorted. "If a man comes to see me for advice he will always walk by the door before he comes in. He comes by and looks at me and goes on. Once, sometimes twice, sometimes many times. But only a policeman comes in without walking by first. You did not walk by."

Alexei attested to the truth of this with a small nod. "Sometimes he comes to arrest you. Is it true that you've been arrested many times?"

"Arrested!" Mother Bogarde said with contempt. "I have been in many prisons. What does it matter? I don't *always* have the gift, but I must earn money every day. When the gift is not there I still must eat."

It was clear that Alexei's remark had nettled her. If she believed that it came from an astrologer, it was a slur from a professional peer.

"Listen to me," she said, leaning over the table. "In Drobuja when I was a little girl, my aunt held séances, sometimes three times a week. They arrested her many times. The police would come in disguise and trick her. Sometimes students from the university would come to make fun of her. In those days I did not know I had the gift. I was very young. I thought she was a fake, like the police and the students said. When they arrested her, I would be ashamed of her. But one night when we were all alone I heard voices, and I crept into her room and saw her lying on the little cot where she slept, staring at a white light above the table. She looked at it and spoke, and a voice in the light answered her. That was no fake! Spirits *did* look kindly on her sometimes and would talk to her. But not always. Sometimes not when the people came for the séances. To earn money she had to pretend. But that night I learned she had the gift.

"I don't always have it either, and spirits do not talk to me. But sometimes I *see*, Mr. Astrologer. Sometimes I see things in people that are part of them, and I understand what they are better than they do!"

Alexei nodded, and after a long silence asked, "What did you see when she came to you?"

"It is not for me to say. But I had the gift that day."

"Why that day? Do you believe in God?"

Mother Bogarde glared defiantly at her shelf of icons. "Don't trifle with me! I tell you I have seen and understood. I had the gift the day she came to see me. I hadn't had it in nearly a year. I had it that day as soon as she came into the room. Do you know what it is like? It is to be suddenly blinded by what you know. There is nothing else at all except the knowing. When I saw her, I understood that I had known her forever—even in the years when she and I were not alive. Do you understand me? I had known her for more years than I have lived."

Again Alexei was silent a moment before replying. "What did you tell her?" her asked finally.

"Tell her? I told her *nothing!*"

"Does *she* know?" Alexei asked quietly.

"She knows *nothing!* What do any of us know about ourselves? Does anyone have the gift for that?"

"And what do *you* know about her?"

"What do I know?" Mother Bogarde said. "You ask and ask. What I know doesn't come in words. Sometimes I do not even *understand* what I know. It is always hard to find words for what I have seen."

"Do you know *when?*" Alexei asked. "I mean the child," he added in desperation.

Mother Bogarde leaned back in her chair and looked at him searchingly. "So you *do* know. You *do* know," she said in amazement. She leaned forward, her eyes intent on him but her mind concentrated on some idea of her own. "Your stars tell you this, but they do not tell you everything. They do not tell you *when.*" She leaned closer to him then, her voice dropping to the register she used for confidences. "Tell me something. Why do you care about *when?* Why do you want to know such a thing?"

"My own reasons," he replied, but her question puzzled him.

"I cannot tell you that," Mother Bogarde said. "I do not know the answer. What I know does not have words or dates. It is not like a book. Do you understand? It is not like a dream. I know everything because I see it all at once. But there are some things I cannot answer. It was three years, maybe, or maybe four or five years ago. But that is not important."

Alexei turned pale. *"Ago?* Did you say four or five years *ago?"*

She saw his consternation and glared triumphantly. "You did not know this," she said accusingly, and then gave him a surprisingly kind smile. "Mr. Astrologer," she said, getting to her feet and leaning over him, one hand on her hip, "your stars did not tell you the child has already been delivered?"

"You're wrong. You must be wrong," Alexei said, his voice shaking.

"I am wrong? Oh, no, I am not wrong. I *know* the child is born!" she said triumphantly. "There were nuns with her. She was happy. I know this! There were nuns. It was not a holy place, but it was a good place. This I know too. She was happy and there was rejoicing, but no one there knew why they were rejoicing. You do not understand this, but I have seen it in her. She was happy because she was innocent and beautiful. Have you not seen this in her? Doesn't your astrology tell you anything, Mr. Astrologer?" she asked scornfully. *"When!* It does not matter *when!* Do you want only to write a book about her?"

22

⊙

In the Convent of St. Agnes Harwell felt strange and an alien. It was an unsettling experience, peculiarly like the stray moment during a campaign for reelection when he found himself shaking hands in the kitchen of a Chinese restaurant, or sitting down to ham and mustard greens in the basement of a black Baptist church.

Unquestionably the day had not turned out to anyone's satisfaction. The other members of the committee obviously had anticipated cooperation from Mother Superior Catherine, who represented all that was official about the place. The only bright spot had been the unexpected meeting with Rhav.

The convent rested at the edge of a little Maryland town and consisted of a cluster of buildings resembling old red-brick schoolhouses around a patchy grass compound. One of the townspeople to whom they applied for directions had referred to it as the Home for Wayward Girls. But this was censorious parlance belonging to an older morality; by now it had become a refuge for any girl who found herself pregnant but unwed. No one asked questions; no one thought it necessary to discover if it was a matter of waywardness. There was a near-total absence of inquisitiveness. A girl found a quiet, sympathetic place to wait out her term, medical care for the delivery of her child, and advice only if she wanted it. If it could be believed, it was here that Kate had come for the birth of her child four years before. She had been fifteen years old when she discovered she was pregnant.

Harwell thought it could be believed. Just before boarding the jet at Brussels, Granby had confided to him and the other two members who made up the committee that a child had already been born to Kate. The scores of people still at the seminar had not yet been informed, but would be within the hour. Granby could give them no other details, but he assured them that it was true; the source was Alexei himself.

When they landed, Varnov was on hand to meet them. Further information was now available. The baby had been delivered at the Maryland convent, but so far nothing had been learned about it. It was the practice at the convent to put such children up for adoption when the mother gave her consent, but it had not yet been verified whether it had been done in this case. In fact, it had not even been possible to discover if the child had been born alive.

When they were alone, Varnov confided to Harwell that some of the information about the convent had come from Kate's mother, with whom Alexei had been in touch after Kate's disappearance. At the moment, Alexei was out of contact with everyone, Kate and the child were no longer discussed at headquarters, and a tactful silence seemed to prevail. If Harwell and the committee were going to learn anything, Varnov said, they would probably have to do it on their own.

The committee had seen no other choice than to turn to the convent, which, it developed, also served as an adoption agency. Women who had fulfilled every domestic role except childbearing took the unwanted issue of the girls the convent had befriended. Both services were free, though the adopting parents were expected to make a contribution to help the convent carry on its work. There might be as many as fifty girls in residence at any one time. Most of them were from neighboring parishes, but many, as though their circumstance carried with it an impulse to flee, came from distant parts of the country. Most of them were young—"very young," Mother Catherine had emphasized —"though I think many of them don't care to give us their true age for fear we will get in touch with their parents or the authorities of their home town. We never do, you know. For the same reason, many of them don't give their true names. We never do call or write anyone, unless the police bring it to our attention that a girl has been charged with a crime. Then we see that she has proper legal advice."

The actual interview with Mother Catherine had lasted less than an hour. Van Kooy and Bareth, the other committee members, had emerged looking baffled and out of sorts. They had said little, but their looks suggested deep suspicion. Since Harwell had a greater familiarity with American adoption procedures, he had not found Mother Catherine's answers surprising. The creation of a "legal" mother who was assigned the rights and privileges of the natural mother was such a frail legal fiction that the real mother could be allowed to entertain the hope that one day she could reverse her decision, seek out the adopting parents and claim her child. The law allows almost any practice that ensures that adoption may not be reversed or revoked. Therefore it was a cardinal rule at the convent that an adopting parent and natural mother never meet, never learned each other's identity and never, in Mother Catherine's prim phrase, be told "anything of the other's circumstances."

All the diligence at Mother Catherine's command was concentrated on not discussing with three strangers, or anyone else, what she knew about the disposition of a child born four years before to a frightened girl of fifteen named Kate Grandjean. "I could not make an exception," she said. "Children are very important—too important for exceptions."

If Harwell had been the only one asking the questions, he would not have persisted with the request that she make an exception once she had explained the rule and the great care with which it was observed.

It wasn't surprising that she had looked offended at their persistence, since this was tantamount to implying that her policy was without value.

What had been surprising was Mother Catherine herself, a large, efficient woman who looked like a complacent penguin and who did not once rise from behind her desk. On the desk was a calendar notebook, a small clock mounted in a leather frame and a photograph which faced her. These were the trappings of bureaucracy everywhere; Harwell had not expected to find them in a convent. Such accessories disappointed him; they seemed to indicate that life in a convent lacked the transcendency he expected. Of course he knew that all the complex undertakings of the convent demanded a shepherdess with executive talents, and divorced from her habit, Mother Catherine *was* the model of a corporation president, even to the calm, gestureless speech, the refusal to be flustered, even to the desk kept nearly bare of papers by her secretary. This was Sister Theresa, a slender and unsmiling young nun who spoke to Mother Catherine in discreet undertones, and took no notice of the visitors.

As flat and unevasive as Mother Catherine's answers had been, she had taken pains to extend an apologetic note. "I'm sorry I am unable to help you. We are able to help most people who come to us." This left the committee feeling awkward, since they were unable to state the case for the seriousness of their request. Harwell had realized immediately that three disinterested strangers would have no success and had hastily represented himself as Mr. and Mrs. Abarnel's attorney. In the Mother Superior's eyes, this still did not give his plea legitimacy, and he lamely amended it by adding that he was also a "close personal friend." Later he discovered that she would have given the same answer if he had claimed to be representing the President himself. Indeed, she gave no sign of recognition at the mention of the name Abarnel, which he marveled at the next day when he learned that she had received two calls from the White House and one from Alexei in the past twenty-four hours.

Negotiations having stalled at the very outset, Harwell saw that there was little room for maneuvering. Since he was unable to claim more impressive credentials for their demands, he shifted tactics and tried softening them. He understood her policies perfectly, he assured her, and he agreed that to expect her to be able to trace the child was essentially unfair. However, could she not at least verify that Mrs. Abarnel had been delivered of a child at the convent, quite apart from its disposition?

Her smile seemed frail for so large a woman. "There is no way I can help you," she answered.

"I don't see how this would jeopardize anyone or betray any confidence," Harwell countered.

"It's not a matter of persuading me to do it, Mr. Harwell," she replied evenly. "The information doesn't *exist*. There are no records of any kind, you see." Clearly she was saying something far more discouraging.

"What would be the point of maintaining records when it would be improper to put them to use?" she went on. "You understand that regret is a natural thing for these girls. We warn them that someday they will know what it is to want their child back. But we also warn them that when that time comes we won't be able to help them. It's very hard to watch them struggling to make up their minds. We encourage them to keep the child if it is at all possible, and many of them are able to make arrangements to have it brought up by a relative or friend until the mother can care for it herself. Of course, sometimes this isn't advisable."

Mother Catherine went on to relate, with great compassion, stories of girls who had returned to claim their children, girls prompted by the memories of birth pangs or the sudden refreshening of moral responsibility. There had been tearful scenes, threats of suicide, letters from psychiatrists claiming psychic degeneration, even lawsuits. Harwell's was not the first intervention by a congressman. All attempts had foundered, as the sisters had told each girl they would, on the fact that records were not maintained.

It was the final impasse; to persist in the face of it was to invite the stigma of lunacy. As they rose to leave, Bareth asked, "Is it possible that you keep no records of the parents who adopt the children?"

"The only records not destroyed on completion of the adoption are turned over to the adopting parents. The name of the natural mother does not appear on any of them. The birth certificate records that the child was born to its legal mother, not to its natural mother, who never sees her child."

It was raining and the car that was to take them back to Washington was delayed. They returned to the small waiting room to which they'd been ushered on arrival. On a table stood a lamp with a ceramic base and pink lampshade that was reminiscent of a baby bonnet. A price tag was still attached to its cord, and it was hopelessly ugly. Again Harwell felt a pang of disappointment: life in a nunnery was indeed not as elevated as he had supposed. The thought would be more apt to occur to a non-Catholic, he realized. In spite of the passion of Holy Orders, the renunciations, and marriage to Christ, vulgarity had somehow intruded here. Immunity from venality might be inviolate here; nevertheless, whatever was transcendent in her life had in no way armed some sister against the crass temptation of pink organdy and green ceramic.

The committee would have to make decisions about how to continue, Harwell reflected, and what to say in their so-called progress report. Unquestionably it would be read with suspicion in Brussels. But the room was inimical to talk or to making decisions; even opposed their looking each other in the eye. He got up and waited outside alone.

In front of the convent a woman emerged from a car, turned and hurried inside. As she opened the door, Harwell recognized Rhav. The Convent of St. Agnes wasn't a place he expected to meet someone he knew. She emerged a moment later with a nun who seemed to be giving her directions, and, as it happened, she pointed directly beyond Harwell. From the lack of surprise in her manner, he gathered that Rhav had known he would be here, and from that moment, the tone of the day improved.

"Have you already spoken to the Mother Superior?" she asked.

"Yes," he answered, though it occurred to him that Bareth, who had a bureaucratic sense of propriety and a basic distrust of almost everybody, would probably object to his discussing matters with anyone before their report was filed with Brussels.

"What did you think?" Rhav asked.

"To tell the truth," he said, "I haven't made up my mind."

"None of us know what to think at this point. There may be more to come." She smiled swiftly. He was aware that she was looking at him with immense concentration, weighing everything he said and watching his reaction.

"I'm going to talk to Father Cyril. It's Alexei's idea—he's made me a kind of personal envoy. I don't know what I'm up against, really. All I know about Father Cyril is that he's said to be slightly eccentric, but that could mean anything." Then, as though it had just occurred to her, she added, "Why don't you come with me? It won't take more than an hour and then I can drive you back. Alexei thinks he's the only hope as far as information here goes."

Harwell hesitated.

"I don't mean the others. Four would be too cumbersome. From what we know of him, he's the kind of man who might freeze up at some kind of a delegation. It's going to be delicate."

Harwell agreed to come with her. At the rear of the convent was the large open commons, with a church and three buildings on one side. The complex was more extensive than Harwell had thought, though he had realized that there must be dormitories and a hospital. The commons had an agreeable rural look to it, with large elms and unkempt grass.

At the far end of the commons the grass gave way to a plain field, and at its end was a row of trees, through which Harwell could see patches of water. Rhav stopped. "Father Cyril's down at the bay. Crabbing is rumored to be his chief indulgence," she said. "I suppose it would be better if I talked to him alone first. I'll bring him along up here in a few minutes."

Father Cyril was a priest at the rectory in town who said Mass at the Convent chapel and, according to Mother Catherine, devoted much of his time to interviewing the couples who came in hopes of adopting children. As it turned out, Rhav was much longer than a few minutes, and when the two of them finally appeared, Father Cyril was chatting amiably about matters of policy. He was a large man who wore an old sweat-shirt with a rent in the sleeve, through which a tattoo could be seen on his arm. His blue jeans and boots were caked with mud, and there was no trace of priestly cloth on him.

"It doesn't make any difference to me if they're rich or not. They have to earn a living wage and they've got to give me the feeling they'll keep it up. Usually they seem to think that they have to own their own house, but I always put them straight on that. I'm glad if they do but it's not as important as they think.

"The truth is, I don't like too stiff a man. Sometimes I have to work to get a man to level with me. I've met almost every one of the adopting couples in the past five years. What counts most is whether they truly want the child. I don't care much for women who have to make a science out of being a mother, but I don't let that count against them if they want a child. I can't be too critical. God doesn't pass on people before he lets them bring children into the world, and it wouldn't look good for me to be stricter than He, would it?"

When they reached the convent a few moments later, Father Cyril left them abruptly.

Rhav and Harwell broke up the drive back to Interzod at a bar on a crumbling quay in Annapolis filled with yachtsmen, fishermen and a contingent of construction workers. Harwell wondered whether Rhav was aware how exotic she appeared in a place like this, and for a moment he found himself looking at her with the eyes of a lobster fisherman. He still wasn't accustomed to being with her. American girls did not have her kind of composure, and Oriental girls were not brought up to drink whiskey in a men's bar. But it was impossible to imagine a place where she would not be altogether at home, or a setting in which she would not be exotic, incurring curious glances as she did here, but oblivious to them because of some inner pride, her hands at rest on the dirty table while she talked to him.

During the ride she obviously had been thinking carefully about what they had learned at the convent. "It doesn't come to enough for you to make a report that will be accepted at Brussels," she said.

"I'm sure they'll want to know more," Harwell said, "but they can't expect us to give them something we don't have."

"Do you believe that Mother Catherine has no way of finding out?" she asked.

"I feel certain of it."

Rhav smiled. "That's only because you've met and heard her; she's very convincing. But there will be a large doubt at Brussels—and from what Granby tells me, a very dramatic one. There's been a great stir in the past two days, an undercurrent of suspicion that in the last analysis they will not be kept informed about everything."

"Granby told you this?"

"Anybody can spot it in the WF transcripts," Rhav answered.

Until then Harwell had been innocent of WF, or more fully, WFMS, which stood for Wide Field Monitoring System. "It transcribes the total sound of everything that takes place in a given area," Rhav explained. "Everything goes into a single highly sensitive tape, which sounds like a crowd scene before the computer sorts it all out. It prints everything that anyone says, and it classifies each voice the first time it's heard. It can pick up distinctions in voices that the human ear can't detect; it's also very accurate in identifying the speaker. Didn't Alexei tell you it would be in operation?"

When he shook his head, she shrugged. "An oversight. Everyone else probably knew. We used it in Khartoum and in Sidney. It's a basic surveillance tool used to isolate a single voice in a crowd. Remember Fantana? At the end, when he became suspicious, he took to meeting all his contacts in a noisy theater lobby."

"That was before my time," Harwell reminded her.

"I forgot. Yes, it would be." She smiled. "Using it to document the seminar proceedings was Granby's idea. He's the only one who has immunity. The computer is programmed not to print out what he says. He claims that with so many people on stage there needs to be at least one producer."

From habit, Harwell was sidetracked by an ethical consideration. "Does the seminar have access to the tape?"

Rhav nodded and said, so concisely as to be conspiratorial, "But it isn't every easy. Alexei won't allow copies of it to be made, though anyone with clearance may see it by coming to Interzod headquarters. There's no other way, really." She was not apologizing. "Alexei couldn't allow the seminar to document itself."

He lost the thread of what she was saying at this point. Whenever she touched on anything that was familiar to him, his attention involuntarily wandered from the subject to Rhav herself, centering on her voice or expression. Since he was familiar with Alexei's mildly Machiavellian maneuverings with the seminar, he watched as her eyes narrowed and widened, a pastime that was the more charming and absorbing for her total lack of awareness of the habit.

"Would you like to know what I said to Father Cyril this afternoon?" she asked. "It's not something for the Brussels seminar; you couldn't include it in your report."

It seemed a tacit invitation to some kind of conspiracy, as well as an acknowledgement that everything she'd said so far had been a preamble. There was no question of his response; his duty to the seminar did not imply anything more than a perfunctory kind of loyalty.

"Alexei looks on the problem of getting the information you want as a simple surveillance exercise. It's hard not to think that way after you've been doing it for a while. But it's often necessary to extract information from an unwilling secondary source. You approached Mother Catherine directly and, as you said yourself, you had almost no hope of success. On the one hand, you were told that the information is not available; on the other you now realize that if it *were* available, it would not be freely given because they cannot establish the precedent of giving out this information. Not to divulge information about the adopted children or the adopting parents is a point of conscience for the Mother Superior—what Pen Li likes to call a "primary scruple." You could not hope to be successful. No experienced surveillance analyst would expect much from a direct confrontation of a primary scruple. It is simply not true that everyone has a price. Everyone is stringently principled—by which Pen Li means a strong principle on which his existence is dependent. It may take the form of familiar, culturally ordained loyalties to ethnic grouping, country, or it may involve more sophisticated abstractions—political or religious convictions, say—that the individual cannot betray without destroying himself in his own eyes.

"At bottom, really, it's a very selfish principle, and you have to go on the assumption that people are generally unwilling to destroy themselves. I suppose you think that this is a very complicated way of saying something quite simple which most people would probably grasp instinctively. But in surveillance sessions it is often revealing to state simple problems with all the complexities we can bring to bear. Maneuvering people can be a highly delicate business. Pen Li is very good at it, and so is Granby. Alexei is the best, of course, but he often acts as a kind of coordinator instead of intervening directly. He sees it as necessary to develop surveillance teams that can perform accurately and independently.

"In this case, Alexei was by himself. None of the others were in on it; and I don't think any of them even know about it. It's comparatively simple, as you'll see. The central issue is that any request for the information confronts a primary scruple, and that if we press, the resistance will become even greater. In such a situation, we often proceed by circumvention. In this case, Father Cyril would probably feel that there was no dishonor attached to telling us what we want to know if he were directed to by a higher authority. Undoubtedly this is what the seminar will do, and a request will go to the Vatican. But the Vatican response is not altogether predictable. If they agreed with Father Cyril and Mother Catherine that the information should not be divulged, it's quite possible that for reasons of tact or politics they would maintain that the information was simply not available and we would still be faced with the same dilemma, but with the additional complication that it came from a higher source. Though this might satisfy the seminar—and I think probably it would, in which case the pressure on you would be ended—we would still not have learned what we want to know.

"In addition, by this time the scruple against letting us have the information would have grown to insurmountable proportions. For this reason it is absolutely necessary to discover if there *is* any possibility that we can find out what we want to know before there is any intervention by the Vatican. And that was the point of my conversation with Father Cyril. Of course it wasn't the substance." She paused and finished her drink, then added, "Frankly, I offered the man a bribe."

"Somehow, that wasn't what I expected you to say," Harwell said.

"Of course not," she answered, smiling. "But there's more to it than that."

"Truly a bribe?"

"That's what it amounts to. It was an offer to construct a new hospital at the convent if they could possibly discover if the child was in good hands. I don't think he would have listened to me if I had asked him to tell me where it was. I told him that the mother's husband was very wealthy, and that if they would locate the child and assure him it was being properly cared for, he would be happy to donate a hospital. A small hospital runs about a quarter of a million dollars these days, so that's the amount of the bribe."

"I don't think he could agree even if he could find out," Harwell said after a pause. "After all, they're on record as swearing under oath in court, in previous cases, that it can't be done."

"I agree," Rhav said. "I'd be very surprised if they accepted the offer. But that's not the point, you see. Alexei's strategy is designed to stimulate conversation about the *possibility* of accepting it. What is almost certain to happen is that Father Cyril will discuss the offer with Mother Catherine. The prospect of a new hospital will generate a conversation about whether they should make an exception, and, of course, about whether or not they *can* do it. If it is true that they have kept no records, they will see whether they can remember Mrs. Abarnel's case, or whether they can find out who the adopting parents are by other means."

Harwell was perplexed. "I guess I've missed something," he said finally.

"I'm going to explain everything," Rhav answered. "Alexei may even tell you himself; he has great confidence in you. But it has to be explained carefully because it's quite exacting. Alexei put together most of what I've told you so far by a secular analysis. That's Interzod jargon for any analysis without reference to astrological data. It's basically nothing more than common sense, though admittedly it can be a highly complex exercise of common sense. But secular analysis alone could not provide the refinements needed for the next step, which was deciding whether to make the offer of a hospital to Father Cyril or to Mother Catherine. It was important, you know. Keep in mind that the strategy was aimed at stimulating conversation about something we did not know and wished to know."

She saw by his expression that Harwell still did not grasp her inference. "We will, of course, have access to their conversation. Everything said there is being monitored through the Wide Field Monitoring System, just as it was done at the Brussels seminar. The computer receives it in a lump, separates individual voices and prints it out.

"Alexei obtained the zodiacal data on Father Cyril and Mother Catherine yesterday and discovered that for our purposes her response to our offer would be far less favorable than his. In all probability she wouldn't have mentioned the offer to Cyril at all. The degree of an individual's dependence on a primary, culturally designated principle can be measured by examination of the zodiacal patterns. Primary scruples will be defended by an individual according to the way he adheres to them. But the matter is complicated because for each of them the chief scruple, their religiosity, has been attained by a difficult choice— the taking of vows—and is therefore bound up with personal possessiveness, what psychiatry terms 'ego involvement.'

"One might suppose that they are roughly equal in the degree of this religiosity, but there are zodiacal reasons why this cannot be. The telling delineations for Mother Catherine imply a strong degree of ethical fusion. This is a common enough alignment and is often independent of factors implying imagination or intelligence. The result is a single conglomerate of ideals which are interdependent and tend to be inseparable; as a result, there is an incapacity for isolating any one of them. A challenge to one is usually a betrayal of the whole; hence the defense is necessarily obsessive. In her case, protecting the identities and confidences of adopting parents would be fully as important as any other aspect of her faith. Therefore her response to our offer might very well be to ignore it, or else to deflect it by involuntary subterfuge. She might feel that even discussion be tantamount to betrayal of everything she believes in—as severe an affront to her religiosity as questioning the existence of God.

"All this is in contrast to Father Cyril. He would make a better theologian than he would a saint. With him, there is no problem of ethical fusion. He is serene, and he is open about judgments and distinctions. If we succeed, it will be through him."

As they drove back to Washington, Harwell asked her if she would listen to the WFMS when she arrived at Interzod.

"No," Rhav said. "I have the feeling that I won't be invited to. Anyway, I would prefer not to know anything more. Besides, I think Alexei is sorry he let the cat out of the bag."

"Did he say so?"

"No. That's not the kind of thing he says."

23

⊙

When Alexei awoke, Kate still slept, one leg entangled with his, her face turned to the pillow, leaving only an ear, a line of forehead and cheek for his inspection. He didn't stir, feeling intimidated by the quietness of her sleep, her nearly invisible breathing and the unfamiliarity of her room. It was early; through the open window the light was still gray, the trees still a dark green. The room was just as they left it, but he remembered only indistinctly their entering it. The rest of it—the loving, the long and earnest loving, the absence of talk, and the library floor where it had begun—he remembered very well, but he tried to put off thinking about it.

That would come later. It was still too close to him and was too much of the luxury of the moment. There was no point in trying to recall a meal one could still taste. Part of the luxury was the strong sensation that he had survived an ordeal, had emerged safely and now stood on the other side as someone quite different than he had been formerly.

He found himself examining a small marble fireplace on the far side of the bed as though he'd never seen it before. Why had he never noticed the frieze of laurel leaves and the sightless cupid at each corner? It was elaborate and preposterous in such a simple room—probably a refinement that suited the wife of the previous owner—yet every detail must be excruciatingly familiar to Kate, since it was what she saw when she opened her eyes every morning. It seemed a poignant symbol of their odd estrangement that he had hardly been aware of its existence.

Two bottles of wine stood on the hearthstone, one unopened, one nearly empty. He remembered going down to the cellar and smashing the lock of his own wine closet while Kate watched and giggled, and then carrying an armful of bottles up to the library. Just before she'd arrived he'd ordered everyone—servants, security guards, everyone—out of the house, including whoever kept the keys to the wine closet.

Why had they settled in the library? It had been more impulse than choice, he supposed, but a fire had been laid there and the enormously heavy blue draperies were closed, since nobody had been in the room for days. Besides, it was fitting because of all the evenings in the past they'd spent there, she crouched in front of him on the low leather bench, the firelight doing soft and maddening things to her hair and skin. All those little affectionate rituals of coffee, cognac and chatter had always been amiable; how had she managed that? Even so, there had always been an unspoken wrongness to them. They had always silently shared the knowledge that by rights such occasions should be a prelude to a culmination of love that would in fact not take place.

But now all that was changed and she *had* come back. That was the only important thing. The three days she was missing after the FBI picked up Eliot in Philadelphia had been agony. Eliot's story was that when they were on their way back from the encampment, Kate had asked him to stop at a drugstore, saying it would only take a few moments. He'd been waiting for half an hour before the police found him. Eliot thought it likely that she had seen him being arrested and had quietly left.

When she called three days later, she had told Alexei that she'd been afraid he wouldn't forgive her so she'd gone to a Philadelphia hotel and remained in her room, crying and trying to think of what to do. Alexei believed the story without reservation. Her voice on the phone had been unnerving. She didn't want him to come pick her up; she wanted to return on her own. Though she didn't say so, he supposed that to her it amounted to some kind of honorable necessity, a way of partly mitigating what she had done.

There had been the possibility of mutual uneasiness, constraint or worse, an attempt to balance the books through explanations that ordinarily would take place when a wife returned to her husband. But this and everything else that might have been tedious had been obliterated by her return. She had chartered a taxi in Philadelphia, and when she stepped out of it, disheveled and protesting her extravagance, her special, artlessly sensual and magical poise took over so completely that he was overwhelmed. As they had exchanged little more than helpless monosyllables, he had mindlessly poured two drinks and lit the fire. Before it had fully kindled, they were in each other's arms.

They had been rather frenzied, he supposed. But the rest of the evening was different. They were a long time at it, the wordless, generous loving, and not entirely sober through much of it. He remembered their search for food in the kitchen. She was partly wrapped in the tartan robe from the library sofa and he had been stark naked while he broke through the pantry locks. They'd faced the same predicament as with the wine closet, and the absurdity of being helpless in one's own household struck them as funny at the time. Now it seemed simply ludicrous. Now that their marriage was truly a marriage, there was no point in living that kind of life. He felt euphoric at the thought that it could be anything they wanted. They could live anywhere and with as much simplicity as they wished. He could even turn his back on Interzod for a year or two and hand over the controls to Varnov, Pen Li and Granby. There might be complaints, but to hell with complaints.

He longed to wake Kate and talk to her about everything. But when he touched her shoulder, she moved closer to him in her sleep and he felt overwhelmed by tenderness and he decided to wait. Once during the night he had woken up to find her shaking him gently. "Now that things have changed, they're going to stay changed, aren't they Alexei?"

"Yes."

Then she rose up on her elbow and caressed his chest with her lips. "Does it have anything to do with my going away, love?" There was an unaccustomed lilt in her slightly tipsy voice.

"No, it didn't have anything to do with it. Or rather, in a way I suppose it did. But not directly."

"If I had known that, I could have gone away sooner. Months ago."

"It might not have worked out this way," he said.

She was silent for several moments, and in the darkness he could feel her eyes on him. "You always said you couldn't talk about it. Is that changed too? Do you want to talk about it now?" she asked.

"No."

She kissed him lightly and put her head down on the pillow.

"Do you mind very much?" he asked her.

"Not talking about it? I don't mind because now it doesn't make any difference."

He closed his eyes. They must have fallen asleep almost immediately.

When he woke again, she was gone. It was late; the room reeked of noon, and it was several seconds before he realized that she was standing quietly by the far window. She turned at a sound they both knew well, the intermittent low-pitched klaxon of the special telephone whose forebodings, priorities and urgency had always been able to rouse Alexei from the deepest sleep. Now he didn't move; to hell with them, he thought. She looked at him expectantly, but instead of bounding from the bed, he deliberately yawned. He knew that there was a surveillance crisis in Dakar and that someone would have to fly to South Africa, where Interzod efforts to sabotage the activities of a man named Vierek had been interpreted as politically motivated by the South African government. It would take skillful liaison to show that it was not Vierek's shabby political views but his zodiacal predispositions to unreasoned mayhem that were the issue.

There was also the alarming natality figure for a spectacularly malignant configuration in Buenos Aires, an event which would eventually mean tripling the staff there. It had already been dubbed the Buenos Aires Blitz. Headquarters was also preparing to deal with a configuration nearly as malignant which would effect a sparsely populated area of southern Florida eighteen days hence.

Each of these was a crisis, and the next day would produce ones of its own as other varieties of human malignancy cropped up in the world, always striving to prosper from whatever it fed on, always seeking the strength to deprive and degrade, to enslave and murder. The warning klaxon meant that someone needed counseling, something needed interpreting or analyzing, but for the first time he decided not to answer. Douglas Gordon and Pen Li Ko would decide that it could wait, or they would come to the decision he would have made.

Abruptly, the sound did stop, and in the silence Kate brought coffee over to him and sat on the edge of the bed. Looking thoughtful, she leaned down and pressed her face against his chest, then sat up again, still pensive.

"Alexei, I'm sorry I never told you about my baby," she said in a very straightforward way. "I know I ought to have, and several times I was on the verge, but somehow I never did. It's something I've never liked to talk about. Keeping it to myself was a habit, and I suppose it was hard to break.

"Besides," she added with a small smile, "I really didn't know how important it would be to you. I remember once hearing a girl say that it wasn't fair for a husband or wife to burden each other with things that had happened before they were married. She used to say that nobody expects a girl to be innocent any more. All they ask is a clean slate in the future. I wasn't sure, but I thought that perhaps you wouldn't want to hear." She paused and looked at him. "Does it make any difference to you?"

"No," he said. It was a lie so necessary that its enormity wouldn't register until later. "But why are you telling me about it now?"

"Because I know you know about it. Maybe it *doesn't* make any difference to you, or maybe you're saying that for my sake—I can't tell. But it does seem important, and the fact that somebody else told you about it makes it worse."

She looked at him inquiringly, but Alexei was silent, hoping that she would continue. "After I talked to you on the phone yesterday, I called my mother. I realized that you'd probably called her and that she'd be worried. That's how I knew you'd found out about the baby. She said you'd asked her about it and that the next day two men had visited her with a lot of questions about it. She didn't tell them anything. You know how she is; she couldn't get it out of her head that the baby had something to do with why you didn't know where I was.

"I've been thinking about it ever since I spoke to her. After I had the baby, I couldn't think about anything else for months. Even while I was acting in that play I'd sometimes find myself wide awake, wondering if I'd done the right thing in letting it be adopted instead of keeping it. You must know about that too."

Alexei nodded. There was no physical contact between them now. She was facing him directly; when she had begun to speak, she had deliberately shifted to the edge of the bed so that he couldn't feel her weight or warmth. "Somewhere in the back of my mind I must have been afraid that you'd criticize me for letting them take the child away from me. I was never sure whether I'd done the right thing. It's the hardest decision I've ever faced. I wasn't even sixteen yet. I didn't even know there *was* such a thing as a hard decision. I thought that all you had to do was make the right choice instead of the wrong one, and that it would always be clear which was which.

"I really didn't make up my mind about what to do until a few days before the baby came. Every time I thought about keeping it and bringing it up by myself I had to admit that I couldn't do a very good job of it. It would be terrible for the child to grow up not knowing who the father was, and someday learning that even *I* didn't know. Besides, where would I get the money to live on? I wasn't old enough to earn much. Less than a year later I was earning more money than anybody in Gumby's Landing, but of course I didn't know that then.

"All that money. And it turned out that in New York it wouldn't have been hard for him—I mean not having a father. I discovered there were two girls in the cast with illegitimate children. The word wasn't even used; it was just that everybody knew they'd never been married. But it was too late by then.

"I was told that once I'd let him be adopted, there was no way to reclaim him. I guess that's only fair. They emphasized that the child would go to a very good home. Not necessarily to a well-to-do couple, but to people who really wanted him. They didn't do it to try to influence me one way or the other, and they were very kind."

"You didn't see your baby, did you?" Alexei asked. "I understand that in these cases it isn't allowed."

"No. When I woke up after the ether, I was already in the recovery room and a sister was sitting by my bed holding my hand. That was the hardest, darling. She wouldn't let me talk about him at all. She only said that it was a normal birth. I remember asking her if he was beautiful, but she only smiled and changed the subject. She didn't want to say anything that would give me something to think about, something I would carry away and which would make it harder."

"But she did say it was a boy?"

"No, it's just that I've always been positive that it was. Whenever I thought about it I always thought of him as a boy. I felt sure about it even before he was born."

"But you can't know for certain if no one told you, Kate."

She looked surprised. "But I *do* know. As soon as I knew I was going to have a baby, I knew it would be a boy."

He didn't pursue this; but there was something else that interested him. He rolled over on his elbow. "Why did you go *there* to have your baby? I mean, to the Catholic home?"

"It just seemed the best thing to do. I didn't have much of a choice, you know. There was the county hospital, but it wouldn't have been very nice, and"—she paused as though trying to remember—"and I couldn't have gone there until just before the baby was due. The sisters took me in when I was in my fifth or sixth month. That made all the difference

—but I guess you'd have to know Gumby's Landing to understand that. It's no place for a pregnant, unmarried high-school girl. It would have been very hard to stay there longer than I did. And if I'd gone to the county hospital I would have had to answer a lot of questions from social workers, things I didn't really want to talk about. The sisters were very tactful. They didn't even ask me who the father was; they only asked if I'd care to tell them. There's a difference, you see."

"Did you tell them?"

"I told them I didn't know. I could have answered simply yes or no, but since they were so nice about it I wanted to be honest with them. That's really the reason I never told you any of this, darling. Nobody likes to learn he's married the high-school tramp. I'm afraid the truth is that I *don't* know who the father was." She smiled wanly at him.

"The people in Gumby's Landing weren't actually mean. They found out I was pregnant as soon as I did, I guess. They avoided me and went out of their way not to talk to me, but it was more from embarrassment than anything else, I think. They simply didn't know what to think or say and so they stayed clear. I can't say I blame them.

"I know how awful it sounds to say you don't know the father, but I discovered a lot of the girls at the home were in the same boat—or at least they said they were. There were twelve of them when I arrived. Some of them were gone by the time I delivered, but others had come to take their place. Most of them had decided to let their babies go for adoption, and most of them told the sisters they didn't have any idea who the father was. It wasn't always true, though. One of them admitted to me that it was her brother, but she couldn't very well tell them that. Some of them just didn't want to be stuck married to their boyfriends. Many of them were very young—one was only fourteen. Another, the prettiest girl there, told me she had been with fifteen boys the month she became pregnant."

She smiled at him again, but Alexei saw that now it was tinged with nervousness, a self-conscious apprehension about his reactions. When their eyes met she stood up, brushing the hair from her eyes, her face set in an expression he failed to understand. "I'll bring you more coffee," she said.

"Forget the coffee," Alexei told her, and he leaned out of bed to grab her by the wrist. But she was already out of reach and walking to the table by the window, where she plugged in the pot.

"Kate, that's not the way it was. You haven't told me everything, have you?"

"I didn't say I'd tell you everything."

"No, you didn't, but the way you told it wasn't *really* how it happened, was it? It wasn't a question of having so many boyfriends that you couldn't possibly know who the father was."

She turned and gave him a long careful look; he could even have called it a shrewd look. "No," she said flatly. "That isn't how it happened."

There were gurgling noises from the coffeepot and she pulled out the plug. "The truth is very simple, Alexei. There were no boyfriends —none at all. Just one: a boy who was too shy to even dare kiss me. I'm going to tell you this because for a long time you've asked me to trust you, and you never explained why, and even asked me not to look for an explanation. It was hard, but I did exactly as you asked—as well as I could. I guess this is your turn to trust me. All I ask is that you don't laugh at me the way everyone else did, or look superior, or tell me I'm crazy. I even want you to try to believe me. No one else believed me, but nobody tried, and I can't blame them.

"I couldn't blame them even then. But Alexei, I honestly didn't do anything with a boy which could possibly have gotten me pregnant. It was awful. I wouldn't have gone to the doctor at all, except that Mrs. Atkins, the assistant high-school principal, called me in and began asking me a lot of personal questions. She was very nice about it, but I was shocked when I found out that she hadn't believed anything I told her. When I came home after school, she had already been to see my mother and told her she thought I was pregnant.

"I agreed to go to a doctor because I was sure he would tell them that I wasn't. I knew I was getting fat, but I thought they were being unfair. Even after the doctor said it was true, I could hardly believe it. But then I saw right away that it was easiest to simply tell everyone that I didn't know who the father was—that *was* something they were willing to believe. Even the boy I had been friendly with couldn't understand it, since he had thought I was a 'nice girl.' I don't know what happened to him; he went to Texas, I think, and his family made it a point not to talk to me any more."

She brought the coffee and sat down on the edge of the bed. "That's about all there is to tell you, darling." She paused, and then asked flatly, "Do you believe me?"

"I believe you, Kate," Alexei said.

Her face softened. He reached for her hand but she moved it away. "Do you really mean that, or do you mean that you'll *try* to believe it?"

"No, I *really* believe you."

"Are you telling me that now because you want to be kind and need time to think it over?"

"I've thought it over," he said firmly. She let him take her hand then; he spread her fingers flat and kissed her on the palm.

"Do you remember when you gave birth?"

"I remember almost nothing. The sedation was very strong. Afterward I realized they probably did that on purpose. The less I remembered the easier it would be for me to forget about it."

"You're probably right. But I meant, do you remember the date you gave birth, the month, the day . . ."

"The month was September, I think, but I tried not to remember, you see. Later I sometimes wondered if it wasn't all a hallucination. I never wanted to be able to look at the calendar and wonder where he'd be on his birthday. All the time I was pregnant, I never had a due date firmly fixed. The doctors could never agree how long I had carried. I couldn't help them; I couldn't even remember when I'd first missed my period. I simply wasn't thinking about being pregnant. Nothing had happened—nothing at all."

24

⊙

The late summer sun held the Monte Vaticano and all of Rome in a full unhesitating light, heightening the gaudy patinas of Roman masonry, enlarging the black furrows of the intricate façade of St. Peter's with rich, stilleto-sharp shadows, and defining Bernini's colonnade, which holds the Piazza San Pietro in an enormous embrace. Everywhere, the unimpeded light rendered Rome chiaroscuro: it was a light with no gray or silver, no glitter, no dazzle; its shadows distorted and disturbed all that architects had devised.

When Harwell had passed by earlier, the piazza had been quiet and nearly deserted. Many of the visiting privileges to the Vatican palace and the museums had been curtailed for the day. He had seen an occasional priest hurrying in the direction of the sacristy, but except for himself and the two young men in sport coats who spoke to each other in Russian, there was no one in lay costume. The two Russians were members of the secret police, according to Partridge, which meant that their delegation had arrived.

Partridge, who had been sent ahead to make arrangements for the presidential party, was the only person Harwell had talked to that day. "I understand you know why the President is coming," the White House special secretary had told him. "That's more than I know. This concerns something beyond the range of my clearance."

Partridge might not know what business the President had with the Holy Father, but he must have seen enough of the procession of prime ministers, foreign ministers, dictators and kings to convince him that the Chief Executive was in august company. In fact, the problem of masking the identity of world leaders known by sight to journalists and tourists was judged to be so insurmountable that it had been decided to ferry such political celebrities from an Italian Air Force base one hundred miles from Rome. Standing by the wall of the papal gardens that morning, Harwell had watched the helicopters descend at the tiny Vatican landing strip, swaying in the wind in ungainly rocking chair motions and rattling the eucalyptus trees. It was the American delegation. Others had been arriving throughout the morning, and there were still more to come.

Harwell, who had come directly from Brussels three days before, was not, strictly speaking, a member of his country's delegation. Several times during the past three days, he tried to imagine what this conference would be like. He'd tried to frame the questions that would be asked, but the result was far from satisfactory, since he couldn't rid himself of his impressions of the final hours of the Brussels seminar.

He and the two other members of the fact-finding committee had returned to deliver their report, which had been hammered out in a night session in the library of Harwell's Washington home. The preparation hadn't been difficult, since the main weight fell on a simple record of their conversation with Mother Catherine. At Harwell's suggestion, they had appended a copy of the Maryland statute dealing with child adoption to show that the convent's practices as enunciated by Mother Catherine were lawful. He doubted whether many of the seminar members had bothered to read it; their response had indicated little interest in minor legalities.

Delayed by an important House roll-call, Harwell arrived a day later than the other committee members and found himself in a maelstrom of questions, suspicions and conjectures. To a vast majority of members, the report was a smashing failure. Harwell had to admit they were right. When the committee had been chosen, the seminar was still in an uproar over the news that the imperative destiny they'd been called to discuss had already been fulfilled. Suddenly all of their flimsy speculations were beside the point; the child *had* been born. When the committee left for the United States, the mood of the seminar had been one of buoyancy, and its members were anxious to be given all the facts about the child. The report had given them none. The facts concerning where and when weren't nearly as important as that of identity, and the committee's investigation had not only failed on that score, but had dwelt lengthily on the impossibliity of ever succeeding.

Still, the report had not been totally ineffectual, because it did focus attention on the tiny Convent of St. Agnes. It made clear that it was there that the main drama had been enacted—not only the drama of birth and adoption, but that of the convent's refusal to cooperate. There was a strong feeling that the committee had not heard all that Mother Catherine knew.

Harwell understood the disappointment that greeted the committee's findings, and the seminar's feeling of frustration and helplessness, as well as its recognition that it could not solve the remaining questions. It was at this juncture that the first informal approaches to the papacy had been made—by committee members acting on their own, working through personal contacts within the Vatican. According to Granby, they were told that the Pope could do nothing for them. He had no information beyond that which had been given out by the staff at the convent.

Some of the delegates were openly skeptical of this reply, and most of them seemed to have quit talking to one another and to have begun cabling the heads of their governments, thus stepping out of their seminar roles and behaving like diplomats and government employees —which, in fact, most of them were. In effect, they had passed the responsibility up the ladder, trusting to the wisdom of the world's political leadership.

Harwell did not know of any advance aggreement on an agenda, as happens in formal international conferences; yet he was sure there must have been some exchange between governments concerning aims and purposes. All he knew for certain was that the day after his arrival at Brussels, the seminar had become virtually defunct; most of its members had drifted away, and the notion of making a plea to the Pope was only one of a thousand rumors. Yet by the following day it was the *only* rumor, and that evening Granby had told him that eighteen of the participating governments had agreed to make a concerted direct appeal to the Pope. They had been the nucleus; by the next day fourteen more had joined them, and the list had grown continuously since then.

As confusion became more pronounced, Alexei and his role as Kate's protector were all but forgotten. Harwell saw that the emphasis had shifted to the Church. There was even speculation on whether the Pope, the Church and the convent were in a conspiracy to conceal the child or to camouflage its own knowledge of the birth's significance, but he did not hear anyone suggest that Alexei be asked for further information.

Predictably, Alexei refused to take part in the present proceedings, but he couldn't very well ignore them. He had asked Harwell to represent him, because of the respect he enjoyed at the White House and his special relationship with Interzod, he would be the person the American delegation would be most likely to turn to for advice and judgment, whatever Rome's decision.

Harwell did not particularly relish the intricacies of this position. For two days he had sat in a small garden at the rear of an anonymous house in the Travertine whose dominant view was the dome of St. Peter's where together he and Granby awaited the arrival of the President and his party. Security arrangements were strict; they would not receive any advance notice. Within a few hours Wembley had arrived on his way to a month's vacation in a Sardinian village. To Harwell he seemed abstracted and rather ill-tempered. He seemed indifferent to the conference about to occur. "There's not much point in it," he said at breakfast. "It doesn't matter how many questions they put to the Pope or how many illustrious people attend—all the presidents, foreign ministers, dictators and what have you. After all, what can the fellow tell them? They already know everything there is to know. From an astrological point of view there's nothing more to be said at this point, is there?"

"There *is* the question of identification," Granby said gently.

"The child?"

"Well, yes, the child."

"Even if the Pope *did* know that, would he know for sure? After all, those people at the convent *do* take pains that a child can't be traced to its natural mother. Why shouldn't everyone be content to leave things as they are? If they care as much as they say they do, I should think they would see it as a time for rejoicing—but also as a time for patience. It certainly isn't the time for inquisitiveness and general mistrust."

"Pen Li feels much as you do," Granby said.

"I'm glad to hear that," Wembley said. "He's got an answer for you—just a theory, really. He says that all these people really want to believe there will be some kind of messianic message twenty years from now, say. It's understandable enough; as far as we know, a message *is* at the core of messianic activity. Buddha and Jesus offered leadership, but it was not the kind that's necessarily easily recognized. They used their lives as examples of what they had to say, and they were pretty low-keyed in their delivery. After all, except for a period of a few months, Jesus was known to only a very few people. That's what makes this business of identification so important to these men."

"Are you saying that they won't know who to believe if the child is not identified?" Harwell asked.

"Pen Li suggests that they won't," Granby said. "I agree with him, but I'm not at all sure that this is all they're worrying about. I keep remembering things I heard at the close of the seminar. Pen Li should have heard it. They're worried about what the Mother Superior told you . . ." He turned to Harwell.

"I know."

"I remember one of the delegates saying he didn't believe there was anything to be gained by approaching the Vatican to learn who the child was," Granby continued. "He felt sure about the messianic potential, he wouldn't cooperate in finding out who the child is or who adopted him because he would want to make sure he was brought up in the bosom of the Church. The assumption was, you see, that the Pope believed the child had been placed in a Catholic home."

Wembley nodded, and then remembered something else. "On the first day of the seminar, a fellow asked me if it was true that Alexei had wanted to make sure that the child would be a Jewish Messiah. I took great pains to explain to him that it didn't much matter who raised the child—Jew, Catholic or Mennonite—that the child's guardian wouldn't be of much influence. Obviously the child is going to be his own man. I pointed out that Jesus was born a Jew and was brought up in contact with members of the priesthood, but that he had always been a disappointment to his people. After all, they were looking for a national deliverance from invading armies; they wanted a Messiah who could be a Washington or a Napoleon. Jesus talked about personal salvation, rather than national salvation, and naturally they didn't listen very carefully. No, I'm afraid that being the guardian of a Messiah isn't an important role; no human is going to have any influence in altering the messianic message."

Rhav arrived the following day but had only a few hours stopover on her way to Rangoon. She and Harwell walked to a restaurant near the Capitoline Hill where she was warmly embraced by the proprietor and his wife. She'd studied music in Rome when she was a girl, she explained, and later she pointed out the *pensione* where she'd lived.

There had been news about Kasjerte, she said. "The government shelved plans to try him. For a while they held him in an insane asylum, but when we protested that the security facilities weren't good enough, they transferred him to a military prison. There was difficulty of some kind, and as punishment the commandant put him in solitary confinement. Kasjerte couldn't stand it. For two weeks he screamed and raved, and then he piled his clothes in a heap and set them on fire. By the time they got to him, he had been suffocated by the smoke.

"Shoun was luckier. Once he was removed from Kasjerte's influence, he shriveled into insignificance. At his trial, he didn't say a word in his own defense. They've put him on an island penal colony in the Bay of Bengal, where he's been made some kind of an accountant. He's still there as of yesterday; Porter checks on him three times a week."

When Harwell brought up the subject of the WFMS, Rhav smiled as though it were something she'd been thinking about. "I don't *know*," she said. "I did ask Alexei about it. I thought I had the right to ask since he'd taken me into his confidence about it and sent me to the convent to set it up. But"—she paused—"I didn't get much of an answer. All Alexei would say was that it had been very inconclusive. I had the impression he was being evasive, and that it was something he didn't care to talk about any more. After all, what could be inconclusive about it? Either Father Cyril and Mother Catherine did or did not discuss the possibility of locating the child."

She paused again. "Just before I left I screwed up my nerve to ask him about it a second time. 'That's all over with now' was all he said. I had the feeling that he doesn't want to hear anything more. Not just now, at least. All his thoughts seem to be about Kate—about his responsibility to her, really. 'I owe her a life,' he told me."

Rhav smiled and looked up as the waiter brought coffee. "He may not be around when we return to the States—at least for a while," she continued. "I saw her only briefly. Alexei and I had our conversation in their garden, and she came out briefly. He's restless when she's not with him. I know they're working out some kind of plan. Travel, maybe. They're giving up that big house. Not only has he shrugged off this conference, but Interzod is going to be less important in his life. He won't give it up entirely, of course—it's too much a part of him—but their life is going to be very different."

Later in the afternoon, Harwell met Partridge again, this time in a bar set in St. Peter's southwest wall. The place had the usual Italian hissing espresso machine and a well-stocked bar. There were several priests there; Partridge was the only other layman. "Are they down yet?" Harwell asked again.

Partridge shook his head and sat down with him. He was worried about security leaks, which would make his job more difficult. "Today my only duties are to explain that the President is sick in bed with a cold and has canceled all appointments, and to say it cheerfully," he said wearily. Harwell understood that this was part of the catechism covering the President's strenuously underpublicized trip. "Italian newsmen are really troublesome," Partridge went on. "The Roman press feeds on sensation."

Harwell was not to be deterred. "But what's happening?" he asked.

Obviously security and the press were all that Partridge was prepared to discuss. He shook his head. "I don't know. I've told you before that I don't have security clearance for what's going on. I can't even ask you questions about it, let alone answer yours. All I know is that the President is sick in bed with a cold and has canceled all appointments for the day. Actually, he'll miss appointments for nearly two days, but if we admit to more than one, the stock market gets nervous." Clearly he wasn't happy. "But since you *do* have clearance," he added, "I can tell you that I overheard it said that it wasn't expected that anything would come out of all this. The actual phrase was 'going all out for the improbable.' Evidently it's an exercise in futility. I'll let you know when he gets out of there."

After Partridge left, a priest took his place at the bar, which was becoming more crowded. Glancing at Harwell's English-language guide-book, he asked, "Are you American?" His speech made it plain that he was.

"Yes. I'm Joseph Harwell." This automatic response contravened Granby's urgings that he remain as anonymous as possible, but at least he had not identified himself as a congressman.

"*Congressman* Harwell?" the priest inquired.

"Yes," Harwell admitted lamely.

"We've met, you know. Possibly you don't remember. I'm Father Cyril Blackman. It was very brief. You were with a Mrs. Abarnel—no, with someone acting in Mrs. Abarnel's behalf."

"I remember."

THE ASTROLOGER

"You were asking about a child."

"I remember."

"I don't believe I would have recalled our meeting except that I was reminded of it just a short time ago, and it struck me as very odd. Is that why you are here?"

"No," Harwell lied.

The answer appeared to relieve Father Cyril of some of his perplexity, but not all of it. "It's extraordinary." He said extraordinary like a man who doesn't say it very often, and then only when he meant it. "I'd like you to have a drink with me," he said. "Do you like Strega?"

"I'd prefer whiskey," Harwell said.

"So would I. Strega really isn't much, but in Italy I get to thinking it is.

"This place has very distinct memories for me," Father Cyril went on in apparent irrelevance after they had ordered drinks. He didn't mean Italy, the Vatican or Rome; he meant this particular bar. "The public doesn't use it very much. It's intended for the convenience of the clergy. At the age of twenty-three I was surprised to discover it. I was an American seminarian and was used to the American Church's conviction that alcohol and bars are profane. Every young priest dreams of the chance of celebrating Mass at an altar here at St. Peter's. Are you a Catholic? No? But you can understand what it means. As a beginning congressman you looked forward to your first speech, didn't you? It might be something like that."

"In my first speech I learned never to memorize a speech before the House," Harwell said. "I sounded like a high-school Hamlet."

"But for a priest there is nothing to be apprehensive about," Father Cyril said. "He thinks he will be elated by it. Anyway, the traditional way of doing it is to have coffee here before saying the Mass, and a stiff drink when you're finished. It's a part of the ritual that isn't religious. But in my case I did the unheard-of thing. You have to understand that all the important altars at St. Peter's are booked well in advance. I waited in Rome for two weeks in order to say Mass at the altar of Pious X. When the moment finally came, I lost track of the time. I arrived forty-five minutes late, too late to say the Mass. I was appalled at myself. It was to have been the highlight of my four years in Rome; my entire stay had been geared to it. I've never felt such a great personal shame before or since. I couldn't afford to stay on for another chance; I had very limited funds and I'd already made arrangements to leave the next day. The only part that I fulfilled was to come here and have a drink before I left." His glance took in the bar, which now was beginning to fill with men in civilian dress. "You know, I kept a very definite impression of this place over the years, or at least I thought I had, but it seems different now. It isn't as large as I remembered it. I think we should have another whiskey."

"I think so too."

"Are you by chance here for an audience?" Father Cyril asked.

Harwell understood that he meant a papal audience. "No, I'm waiting for a friend," he said, a suspect banality, he realized when Father Cyril gave him a sharp look.

They drank with little conversation. When Partridge returned to the bar, Harwell raised one eyebrow, but by a cautious shake of his head, Partridge indicated that the conference was still in session.

"I think I'd like to walk around a little," Father Cyril said. "Will you join me?"

Harwell agreed. Outside, where the light astonished their unaccustomed eyes, Father Cyril started off across the Piazza di Sagrestia with long strides, chattering and gesturing amiably at the sun struck buildings, but Harwell heard little of what he said because he was maintaining a consistent two-stride lead. Then abruptly Father Cyril turned to Harwell coming to a stop. "It's really a remarkable coincidence meeting you just when I did," he said. He remained standing there for several seconds, absorbed in his renewed astonishment, then turned and resumed the walk at a slower, preoccupied rate. "What really intrigues me is why Monsignor Toretti should have mentioned it at all. I'm speaking of Mr. and Mrs. Abarnel's request to help us locate her child. 'We have taken an interest in the work of the convent in your parish,' he said. He sat at this big desk with his hands folded. The Italian clergy can be very high-handed at times. There's a good deal of old-fashioned snobbery in the European clergy—a definite class structure. He asked me to explain exactly how we work, our daily routines and so forth. There's something condescending about a request like that, don't you think? I couldn't answer him without feeling childish."

He stopped again. "Everything about the whole business strikes me as extraordinarily odd. My bishop told me I was to go to Rome to discuss my work with the Monsignor Papal Secretary of State. I was very excited; I understood it to be an honor. But it also struck me as highly unusual. My bishop explained that the Holy Father had expressed a desire to learn more about parish work from direct conversation with clergy from all over the world. It sounded like a wonderful innovation, very democratic and modern. But it doesn't sound like the Church, does it? The Church is neither modern nor democratic. It's hierarchical and dislikes change. When the Holy Father wants to know something, he asks a cardinal or an archbishop, and they in turn ask a bishop. The parish priest is the last to be consulted. The intervening dignitaries are all very important. The more I think about it, the more improbable it seems. Popes aren't flashy; they aren't going to start doing the kinds of things an enlightened corporation president might do at the company picnic.

"But here's the second half. I don't get to talk to the Pope after all, it turns out. I will have a very brief audience on Friday, and other people will be present. When it is my turn, someone will whisper my name from the list, and he will bless my rosary. What I had to say about our work at the convent was said to Monsignor Toretti this morning. He listened and asked a few polite questions. I talked for about an hour before he brought up the subject of Mrs. Abarnel's request. 'We have heard that she asked your assistance in locating her child,' he told me. I can't say I was surprised at this; after all, we had been talking in generalities until then and it seemed natural to turn to a specific case. Besides, if the Abarnels are as well connected as they seem to be, they would naturally take their request as high as they could. But your name came up in the course of the discussion, you see. Probably the Monsignor felt that mentioning the interest of an American congressman would ensure that I understood the seriousness of the request. He also mentioned the President in this connection."

They had come to the great colonnade by the staircase leading to the main portico of St. Peter's. At the far side of the piazza Harwell could make out the two Russians standing with their hands behind their backs.

"If I hadn't bumped into you so soon after this conversation, it wouldn't have occurred to me that I was called to Rome to discuss Mrs. Abarnel rather than parish problems." Father Cyril looked at Harwell carefully. "You can't really blame me for thinking that is the reason for your being here, can you?"

It was an uncomfortable question. "Now, I can see how you might believe that," Harwell told him, "but I'm only here as a tourist. Will you have an opportunity to say a Mass before you return?"

"Yes. Tomorrow or the next day. Toretti arranged it." This time Father Cyril pronounced the name with less severity. "It can't be earlier because the church is closed today. They're working on the dome again; they've always had trouble with it, I'm told. I would have enjoyed showing you the interior; to me it's more impressive than the outside. But the Belvedere is worth seeing."

"I'm afraid there isn't time for me to go with you, after all," Harwell said. "I was waiting for a friend back in the bar when you found me." He glanced at his watch, which he had forgotten to wind. "He'll be there now."

Father Cyril looked disappointed. "Another time, then. It would have given me the opportunity to try to learn why you *are* here. Coincidence isn't ever a very satisfactory answer, but I can see that you would prefer I accepted it." Waving cheerfully, he turned and started across the piazza.

Harwell walked a few yards toward a line of Swiss guards that had been drawn up in front of the sacristy, then stopped and turned back to look at the figure of Father Cyril receding in the distance. The very fact that the priest had been summoned to Rome seemed to be proof that there were things the Holy Father did not know. It would have been simple for Harwell to have owned up to why he was here, and it might have led to an exchange of confidences. But he realized now that he didn't want to know any more than he already did. He believed he understood how Alexei felt. Possibly it was the way the Pope himself felt.

By now the little cafe-bar was packed, and Harwell recognized several faces from the Brussels seminar who, like himself, were now reduced in rank from participants to knowledgeable attendants. One tall man with long reddish mustaches had been at the country house with the Irish prime minister. They were standing two and three deep along the bar, but the place was remarkably quiet. No voice rose above the others, and at moments all conversation seemed to stop, and a kind of muted expectancy reigned.

A middle-aged man addressed him in German, his voice just above a whisper. "Do you understand there is to be a Mass?" he asked.

"A Mass? I hadn't heard," Harwell answered.

The German turned and whispered the same question to someone else. "Like so much else, everything is rumor. Nothing is confirmed," he said to Harwell.

Partridge was wedged at the far end of the bar, his face pink and perspiring. "Have they come down yet?" Harwell asked.

"That's what's being said, Joe. It turns out that everything was over three quarters of an hour ago, and that they're all being given lunch up there. We seem to have been forgotten, and I'm starving."

"Have you heard anything about how it went?"

"May I remind you once again that I don't have clearance for any of this? I'm not supposed to hear any of the things I'm listening to. It's not likely I'll repeat it, however, because I can't make head or tail of it. Everyone seems to be using code. I can't imagine who I'd sell it to, in any case, since all the customers seem to know more than I do." He glanced at the new arrivals, two Chinese, one in the uniform of an officer in the army of the People's Republic of China, the other the civilian in the Mao suit who had been at Brussels.

"Ordinarily I'd feel neglected in not being told what's going on, except that even our ambassador here isn't in on it. They had to maneuver him to Paris on a pretext for a couple of days. Some day I hope you'll tell me why I'm always stumbling on you in such exalted circles."

"I'm not really exalted in comparison with this bunch."

"You can tell me that it's just a case of having to trust the guy who empties the ashtrays," Partridge said petulantly, "but in this case *I'm* that person, not you, and they haven't told me a thing." His glance went to the clock on the wall. "I must go. In three minutes I have to call Signor Malfeo, who will tell me what they have all decided to do with themselves. I imagine he'll tell me that everything is settled, but he won't know what he's talking about because he's not allowed to know, either."

Partridge pushed his way toward the door, the back of his jacket dark with perspiration. Feeling claustrophobic because of the crowd, Harwell followed him until he was slowed to a stop by a series of collisions, ending with a kind of embrace with the young Chinese, whose ornate English Harwell remembered from Brussels. "I am delighted to meet you again," he said. "In my mind I did not think you would feel it worthwhile to come here."

"It wasn't exactly my idea," Harwell answered.

A convulsive movement of bodies propelled the two of them even closer. "My name is Po Lin," the Chinese said.

"Yes, I remember you."

"I devoured your report with great pleasure. You do not believe, do you, that they will behave any differently here than in your own country?"

Harwell was momentarily puzzled.

"They will find it necessary to be consistent, will they not? Especially in their own interests?"

"You're probably right, but of course the Church has many faces," Harwell said.

There was no indication that Po Lin had heard him. "It is true to say that the Church has lost its hold on the people," he said. "They will do anything to regain their vigor, will they not?"

"Anything at all," Harwell said amiably.

"They will fail," Po Lin said quietly. "We will teach the people patience. Two thousand years is not so long to us."

"As but a grain of sand," Harwell said with a straight face. Feeling a lessening of the press against his back, he took two steps in retreat and turned to see a movement at the door. In spite of the crush, the place was silent. A man in clerical garb with a flat wide-brimmed hat stood just inside the door, speaking quietly to a group of men. "The luncheon is over?" someone asked the priest, but Harwell couldn't hear the answer.

The German turned away from the group and came over to Harwell. "There will be a Mass," he said. He seemed plagued by uncertainty. "It will be a special Pontifical Mass. Private. Tell me, do you think you will go?"

"Why not?"

He hadn't thought about it, but this answer seemed to satisfy the German.

"You are right. Most of us will go, I imagine. I read your report. What they told you seems quite reasonable, does it not? It isn't really important that all our leaders here today were unsuccessful."

"Did the priest at the door tell you that the conference with the Pope had been unsuccessful?" Harwell asked.

"Not exactly. I asked precisely that question, and he told me, 'The Holy Father would not think of it that way.' "

The bar was emptying, and most of the crowd was walking across the marble flagstone piazza in the direction of the south portico of St. Peter's, though a few seemed reluctant or undecided. Up ahead was Partridge's moist back, the two Chinese just behind him. Harwell hurried along to catch up with all of them, sharing their intentions.

Now another group appeared, moving in the same direction— older, eminent and famous men who had questioned and listened— coming from the papal chambers. Looking at them, Harwell knew with certainty that the audience had achieved nothing. He spotted the third-ranking member of the American group, an undersecretary of state with a Class A Interzod clearance. Harwell had observed his face many times, when it was puzzled, irritated or contemplative. Now it revealed nothing. None of those well-known faces had changed; they looked exactly as they had when they entered. Nothing had happened to them.

Harwell felt that he was a part of them, part of the general kinship of those who have failed and failed blamelessly. It was what he should have expected. Alexei had known it. These men were not concealing anything. The Pope had invited them to his chambers, had told them what they must have known he would say, and then they had come away.

Harwell was aware that some of these leaders must have entered the chambers believing that the Pope knew nothing more than they themselves did. Others probably believed that he was being evasive, or even false, and that he *did* know or could find out what no one else could. No matter; they had all known what they would hear and had journeyed here anyway. It had been a ritual coming together, then, something the occasion demanded of them. Suddenly Harwell felt that he understood. The intricacies of what had been discussed were unimportant, but the act of assembling to share what they *did* know, to honor it, to give it observance, to celebrate, had been as compelling as though it were part of an ancient liturgy. He realized now that he, for one, had never wanted to know the answers to the questions he had asked Mother Superior Catherine and Father Cyril. And these men surrounding him today doubtless felt as he did, finding the mystery somehow more appropriate, and perhaps as much as anything dreading the ultimate discovery.

As they all crowded together at the entrance to the basilica, Harwell saw a very old, very tall man with a face that had been caricatured thousands of times. As he came closer, he saw that tears were streaming down his cheeks and that he was making no effort to stop them. Then someone took the old man by the arm and led him through the entrance, to be swallowed up with the others by St. Peter's dark golden magnificence.

About the Author

JOHN CAMERON was born in 1927 in Lansing, Michigan, and was educated at St. John's College in Annapolis and at Olivet College in Michigan. He has been an editor, journalist and free-lance writer, and now lives in New York City with his wife and three children.